"*Sawbones* is a thoroughly original, sma[...] perhaps a new subgenre: the feminist V[...]

—*Lone Star Literary Life*

"Melissa Lenhardt has given us an amazing heroine and sent her on a thrilling journey from the teeming streets of New York City to the vast wilderness of the Texas frontier. Dr. Catherine Bennett's adventure will keep you turning pages long into the night!"

—Victoria Thompson, bestselling author of *Murder on St. Nicholas Avenue*

"It was damn brilliant and I absolutely loved it!...It was [the] mix of loveliness with the book's vicious, ruthless side that made *Sawbones* so compelling....I was ecstatic to find out that there will be a follow-up called *Blood Oath* coming out later this year. You can be sure I'll be devouring it as soon as I can get my hands on it." —*Bibliosanctum* (4.5 stars)

"If you are looking for a book that is well-written, has a gripping story-line seasoned with mystery, suspense, [and] a little romance, then you have come to the right place, my friend!...From the first to the last page, *Sawbones* is a raw, gritty tale that takes us back to a time when rules didn't apply, when heartbreak was a way of life and tomorrow was a gift. Weaving facts and fiction Melissa Lenhardt gives us a story so rich in detail and horrific truths, you finish the book with so many questions, so many emotions and ready for more." —*Margie's Must Reads* (4 stars)

"The adventure was nonstop, never giving way to a slow moment....My heart was repeatedly ripped to shreds and mended...a thrilling, unpredictable roller coaster that held my heart from the start." —*My Book Fix*

By Melissa Lenhardt

THE SAWBONES SERIES
Sawbones
Blood Oath
Badlands

JACK MCBRIDE MYSTERIES
Stillwater
The Fisher King

SAWBONES

BOOK 1 OF THE
SAWBONES SERIES

MELISSA LENHARDT

REDHOOK

www.redhookbooks.com

Copyright © 2016 by Melissa Lenhardt
Excerpt from *Blood Oath* copyright © 2017 by Melissa Lenhardt
Reading group guide copyright © 2016 by Melissa Lenhardt and Hachette Book Group, Inc.
Cover design by Crystal Ben
Cover images © Arcangel Images, Shutterstock
Cover copyright © 2017 by Hachette Book Group, Inc.

Redhook Books/Orbit
Hachette Book Group
1290 Avenue of the Americas
New York, NY 10104
hachettebookgroup.com

Originally published as a Redhook Digital Original March 2016

First Print Edition: April 2017

Redhook is an imprint of Orbit, a division of Hachette Book Group.
The Redhook name and logo are trademarks of Hachette Book Group, Inc.

The publisher is not responsible for websites (or their content) that are not owned by the publisher.

The Hachette Speakers Bureau provides a wide range of authors for speaking events. To find out more, go to www.hachettespeakersbureau.com or call (866) 376-6591.

ISBNs: 978-0-316-50539-0 (trade paperback), 978-0-316-38672-2 (ebook)

Printed in the United States of America

LSC-C

10 9 8 7 6 5 4 3 2 1

For Dad

PART ONE

TEXAS

CHAPTER

1

I'll have some fresh ones on the morrow."

I pulled on my gloves and donned a slouch hat. "I do not know when I will be back."

"No, no. O' course. Part of the job, idin't? Not knowin' where you'll be, what you'll be doin'. Hard on a woman."

"No harder than on a man, I assure you."

"O' course." He paused. "It's jus', my costs don't change if you don't show, you see."

I stared at him beneath the brim of my hat. "I'm quite sure I'm not the only one who pays for your services."

"No." He drawled the word out into three syllables while his small, calculating eyes appraised me. "But you pay the best."

Not willingly.

The resurrection man was short, with a broad chest and dirty muscular arms no amount of scrubbing could clean. If his other clients knew he allowed me, a woman, use of his services, they would find another man to do their dirty work. It would be easy enough. Resurrection men were thick on the ground in 1871. If you knew where to look. But, Jonasz Golik was the only one with a dissection room for my use, a female doctor who overpaid for the privilege.

I buttoned my cloak at the neck. "How much?"

"Double."

"That is absurd."

"Is it? What'ud your fancy patients in Washington Square think o' your activities, Dr. Bennett?"

They should be thankful I was constantly learning, staying abreast of new discoveries in anatomy and medical science, practicing difficult surgeries on corpses instead of taking risks with their own lives. The voices of the few that might take this generous view of my nocturnal activities would be drowned out by the outrage of my crime, by the disgust at a woman carving up naked bodies—*of men*—in the dark. It was unnatural, an affront to everything feminine and fine. My male colleagues, though participating in the same activities, would be the loudest critics. They would ruin my reputation and practice with unalloyed glee. Every respectable door would close to me.

I shoved all the money I had into Golik's hand. "How did you learn my name?"

His grin widened as he counted the money, which was more than double his fee.

"I keep my ears open. There ain't many of you, are there?"

"No. There are not."

Despite the thick layer of snow on the ground, I walked home, as I did every night, hoping this might be the day I could banish death's smell from my senses completely. Death followed me like a determined enemy, dogging my steps, clutching at the hem of my cloak, pushing me forward, away from memories best left on the charred, desolate battlefields of my past.

I lengthened my stride, straightened my shoulders, and walked with the masculine purpose I learned masquerading as a young male orderly in the war. Walking alone in nighttime New York City was risky for a man, but lethal for a woman, and my disguise relied as much on attitude as it did darkness. The gun I grasped in my pocket helped.

In the early hours of this February morning, the streets were bare of the libertines who nightly stumbled from the whore-houses on Twenty-Seventh Street back to their mansions on Fifth Avenue and the robbers out to accost them. On a clear night, in my beaten Union slouch hat, worn oilcloth cloak, and scuffed boots, I was no thief's idea of a good mark. That night, though, the snow was too deep and the air too cold for busi-ness to be lucrative. Occasionally, the tip of a cigar or cigarette would burn in the shadows of an alley or a darkened doorway. I kept my eyes forward and my step determined. I had turned my mind to how to disentangle myself from Jonasz Golik when I heard the humming.

The sound was muffled by the snow, but the crunch of foot-steps was not. I paused, turned my head, and listened. The unhurried tread and humming stopped. I walked on, straining to hear over my heartbeat pounding in my ears. When the hum-ming resumed, louder, I turned the corner and ran into an alley.

I leaned against the wall and, with a shaking hand, pulled the gun from my pocket. I was three blocks from home, on a deserted side street whose gaslights had been extinguished by the lamplighter in anticipation of dawn.

I closed my eyes and told myself my imagination was run-ning away with me. The night was quiet, save the distant sound of a carriage. I inhaled, gripped my gun tighter, and edged to the end of the alley to peek around the corner. The street was silent and empty. I collapsed against the wall with relief, chas-tised my overactive mind, and pocketed my gun. I stepped out of the alley and hurried toward the light on the bisecting street.

By the time I registered the sound and movement behind me, the man was upon me, driving me into the wall. My face slammed against the rough brick. A blinding pain shot through my right temple, and I cried out as he pressed his body against my back. The cold blade of a knife rested beneath my jaw.

His free hand forced its way between my body and the wall, searching for the wallet he expected in the inner pocket. When he felt the mound of my breast, his hand stopped and he went completely still. "Well, well. What do we have here?" His voice was pleasant, as if we were meeting in a drawing room instead of a dark alley.

"Please. I have money," I lied. My voice sounded far away, lost amid the roaring in my ears and my jagged breath.

He laughed. My shirt ripped as if made of paper. His calloused hand worked beneath the top of my corset and found my bare breast. I shut my eyes and whimpered with a combination of mortification, disgust, and terror.

His breathing quickened as he fondled my breast. When I sobbed, he shushed me, as if quieting a recalcitrant child. My knees gave way. My gun, heavy in my pocket, knocked against my thigh. I opened my eyes.

I blinked away the blood that dripped in my right eye while my left eye tried in vain to see my assailant. The darkness of the street helped camouflage his features, though nothing could mask his purr of desire or the erection he rubbed against my bottom. I squeezed away my tears and swallowed the bile that rose in my throat at the thought of what this man intended to do to me. My hand slid into my pocket and grasped the smooth wooden handle of my gun. Using every ounce of strength, I pulled the hammer back, sobbing again to mask the sound.

The knife under my jaw bit into my skin. "We're goin' ta the alley. Scream 'n' I'll slit your throat."

6

When he pulled me from the wall, I pointed the gun at the ground between us, closed my eyes, and pulled the trigger. The shot cracked through the snow-muffled silence and echoed, along with the man's screams, between the houses. He released me and I ran toward a carriage passing out of sight on the avenue ahead.

As I rounded the corner I glanced over my shoulder to see if my assailant followed and ran straight into a man. I screamed and tried to pull out of the strong grip that held me.

"Catherine!"

I looked up into the face of my oldest friend. "James?" I threw myself into his arms, heedless of the blood running down my face and neck.

He held me at arm's length and gaped at the blood on his coat. "What happened? Whose blood is this?"

I held tightly to James. "He...I...tried to r—" I pointed a shaking finger down the darkened street.

James steered me toward the carriage and helped me through the open door. "Wait here."

"Don't. He has a knife."

He patted my knee, glancing at my chest and away. "I'll be fine."

I pulled my cloak over my bare bosom and when I looked up, James was gone.

He seemed to be gone forever, but it was probably no more than a few minutes. He climbed in and the carriage started moving before he sat down.

He placed my forgotten medical bag and slouch hat on the seat next to me. "He was gone. There was blood on the snow. Too much to be yours."

"I think I shot him in the foot."

I trembled, pulled my cloak tighter, and avoided James's

eyes. I was afraid I would see judgment and accusation there. He didn't disappoint me.

"Catherine, you are a stupid woman, walking the streets alone at night. Do you honestly think your disguise works?"

My terror turned to anger. "It did work. He didn't know I was a woman until he searched my coat and—"

"And, what? Felt your breast?"

I clenched my jaw, looked out the carriage window, and forced myself not to cry.

"Christ, Catherine! What are you doing walking alone at this hour? Where have you been?"

"It's none of your business, James."

"None of my business," he echoed. "I suppose it won't be my business until I'm called on to identify your dead body one morning."

Against my will, I shuddered. I hugged myself tighter in an effort to stave off the shaking.

James pulled his handkerchief from his pocket and handed it to me. "Did you see him?" His voice had lost some of its gruffness, though not all.

I pressed the snowy white linen to my eyebrow and winced. It would need to be sutured. The cut on my neck was merely a scratch.

I shook my head. "No."

My assailant's laugh echoed through my head.

"Catherine, are you listening to me?"

My eyes focused on my friend. "What?"

The carriage turned the corner onto my street. James tensed and swore under his breath. "Keep your eyes forward and your head down."

Two men stood on the stoop of my house. One man knocked on the door while the other watched up and down the street.

Before he could catch my eye through the carriage window or see my face, I gazed down.

"Are those policemen?" I asked in an undertone.

"Yes."

My maid, Maureen, greeted the policemen with as much warmth as I expected. "Yes? What da ya want?" I could hear her loud, Irish brogue from the carriage. The rest of the conversation was lost as we drove away.

"Where have you been?" James asked again.

"Were you searching for me?"

"Yes."

"Why? James, what is going on?"

"You don't know?"

"Of course I don't know."

"George Langton is dead."

For a moment, I forgot about my brush with death. "What happened? He was healthy as an ox last time I saw him."

"Did you know him well?"

I shook my head. "Only professionally. We spoke briefly, last night, in fact. What does—" I stopped. James's jaw tensed, a mannerism I well knew was his attempt to hold in anger. "Please, tell me what is going on."

"Were you having an affair with George Langton?" The words came out through gritted teeth.

"What? No! Good God, James. Why would you ask me such a thing?"

He stared out the carriage window.

It was answer enough. Indignation straightened my shoulders. "I can't believe you would say such a thing after—" I swallowed. I didn't want to think about what had happened to me, let alone mention it, but that James was so obtuse to my feelings infuriated me and pushed my lingering terror aside.

9

"Beatrice Langton has accused you of murdering her husband."

The hand pressing the handkerchief to my brow fell to my lap. "What?"

"She said you were having an affair and when George ended it, you killed him."

I laughed. "Don't be absurd."

James did not answer, nor did he laugh.

"How did he die?"

"He was beaten with a fireplace poker."

"Heavens. Poor George."

"George? You knew him well enough to call him by his Christian name?"

"A man is murdered, and I am attacked on the street, and this is what upsets you?"

When James remained silent I said, "He was a nice man. Intelligent. He wanted to be a doctor but his father had other plans. He and I would speak, sometimes, about medicine. Theories, new discoveries. He thought it brilliant, all I had achieved. He treated me and my profession with respect, unlike most men I know." I hoped James understood the veiled barb, but he was too obsessed up with the idea I had been fornicating with George Langton to catch it.

"Beatrice Langton has numerous servants who confirm your affair."

"They are lying. I am the family doctor—her doctor—nothing more."

James stared at me with eyes as familiar to me as my own. I could see the scar above his left eyebrow, courtesy of a rock I threw at him during a rather fiery argument we had when we were six years old.

When he remained silent, I understood. James believed the

accusation of the affair because I'd had one before, with him. My voice rose. "My God. You *believe* her, don't you?"

The realization pierced my soul. For how many years had he been gazing at me through untrusting eyes? Was he angry at my supposed loss of morals or with the idea I had chosen to share myself with someone besides him?

"Do you *truly* believe I would be so angry and distraught over a man that I would bludgeon him to death? I am a doctor, James. I could never intentionally kill someone. I would hope, after what we have been to each other, you would at least trust that."

"You shot that man."

"To scare him off, nothing more. He wanted to rape me!"

The word shocked him. Civilized society preferred their euphemisms for such things: *violate, depredate, insult*. But, the word had the effect I wanted; it jolted him, briefly, out of his selfish musings. With genuine contrition he said, "Of course you didn't kill Langton. That's why I came to find you. The police have been searching for you all night."

"It doesn't make any sense."

James moved next to me and took my hand. My doctor's bag was wedged between us. "You were the last person to see him alive. Did anyone see you leave?"

"No. I let myself out through the front door. There was a dinner party going on. Surely he returned to the party."

"I was there. He did not."

"There must be other suspects. Everyone at the dinner party, the servants."

"Everyone at the dinner party was a prominent New York citizen. You are the focus."

"I am the scapegoat, you mean."

"You know how corrupt the police are. It will cost Beatrice

a pittance to get you arrested and thrown into jail. With her father's judicial connections, a conviction is almost assured."

"I did not kill Langton." I turned to the window and we rode in silence for a few minutes. James released my hand.

"You know if you had married me like any right-thinking woman would have done, neither of us would be in this situation."

"You know if you had not asked—no, expected—me to give up medicine, I would have."

We stared out our respective windows, nursing past disappointments and present resentments. I wanted someone to love me because of my mind and accomplishments, not despite them.

I had long since resigned myself to being alone.

But being alone had a price. I was unprotected. My father was dead and I had no family in America, save my maid, Maureen, and James, who worked for Langton's lawyers. My English relations would distance themselves as far from me as possible. James's father, Ezra Kline, was in Saint Louis. He would do what he could to help, but a former professor at Syracuse Medical College had no influence with the police or courts. I tried to imagine what advice he, my mentor, would give in this situation and couldn't. The predicament was so absurd as to be unreal. James and Ezra would do what they could, but it would not be much. I could not fight Beatrice Langton and her family alone.

"What should I do?"

"You must leave town."

"Absolutely not."

"Catherine—"

"No, James. This whole situation is absurd. I did not kill Langton and I will not leave town as if I'm guilty."

"You would rather go to the gallows?"

"I have patients who need me. Who rely on me. And, there's Maureen. I cannot leave her."

"I am trying to help you, Catherine."

"By encouraging me to act guilty for a crime I did not commit? How is that helping me, James?"

"Do you have an alibi? Can you attest to where you've been?"

I thought of Jonasz Golik's beady little eyes and outstretched hand and knew it for a devastating alibi.

"No."

James exhaled sharply. "Stay or leave, you will be accused. What will your patients think? How many of them will stand by you?"

I closed my eyes and shook my head. The only patients who would support me would be the whores I tended on Twenty-Seventh Street. Their support would ruin my practice as much as the accusations against me.

"Will you leave?"

"No."

James lifted his fist and brought it down on his thigh. "Your stubbornness will be your downfall, Catherine."

"Do you want to help me, James?"

"However I can."

"Then talk to Beatrice Langton. Convince her I didn't kill her husband."

"She knows we are lifelong friends. I don't know she'll listen to me."

"You must try. Please. I've worked too hard to lose my life and career over something I did not do."

James nodded. "I will try. What will you do? You cannot return home."

"I will stay with a friend."

"They'll be checking with your friends."

I smiled and, despite having my life upended in the last ten minutes, almost laughed. "Tell the driver to take me to Twenty-Seventh Street."

James balked. "Catherine, you cannot be serious."

"No one knows of my clients there. Not even Maureen. Who would suspect the doctor of choice for New York's society women of hiding in a brothel?"

He shook his head. "No one."

"I will wait there until tomorrow night. If I don't hear from you, I will return to my home." I grasped James's hand. "I know you haven't always agreed with my choice of profession, but I have worked so very hard to be where I am. I do not want to lose it. I am counting on you to save me."

A flicker of guilt darkened his expression and was gone. He patted my hand. "Rest assured, I will do whatever I can."

CHAPTER
2

"Joe Fisher's boardinghouse at one-oh-five West Twenty-Seventh Street is a second-class establishment. It is asserted that the landlady and her servants are as sour as the wine."

Camille King looked up from the small black book that detailed the best and worst places in New York City for gentlemen's entertainment. "It is nothing less than slander. I am seriously thinking of taking legal action."

With the specter of a murder charge hanging over my head, it was difficult for me to join in Camille's distress for her business. Since she was providing my place of refuge, though, I tried. "Against whom?"

"I know exactly who wrote this, the sniveling little twit. To a one my girls hate entertaining him. His pec—Well, I refuse to stoop to his level and denigrate what God cursed him with."

"Very wise."

She drummed her fingers on her desk. "The wine wasn't my fault, by the way. I've since changed suppliers, at great cost, I might add. A cost I won't be able to afford if business drops because of this odious little book." She threw it on the desk.

"I am sure your regulars will stay loyal."

"Yes, yes. But, it is the travelers who make my profit."

"Hmm." I rose from the Queen Anne chair in front of Camille's desk and walked around the well-appointed room. The clock on the mantel said ten after six. "Where is Maureen?"

"She probably stopped off at Saint Patrick's to protect herself with a few Hail Marys before coming to this part of town."

Camille King had been the hostess of Joe Fisher's boarding-house for nine years, ever since the eponymous owner died on the stoop with a knife in his chest. The girls not busy entertaining clients, Camille among them, watched the blood pulse out of Joe's fleshy neck, his slick hands alternately trying to staunch the flow of blood and reaching out to his whores for help. None came. Camille, the most beautiful of the entertainers and the only one who could read and write, took over. She was a benevolent dictator, a much better option for the women who worked for her because she did not expect favors in return for protection.

My five-year association with Joe Fisher's was a fortunate accident. Fortunately for me, a female doctor struggling to survive without patients, a client fell down Camille's stoop, dead from a heart attack, as I walked by. Camille did not need my help—men dying in flagrante was a common occurrence, I would soon learn—and was well prepared for the eventuality. "At least he has his clothes on," was all she said before two burly men bore him off to a more appropriate address to die.

She eyed me suspiciously. "Who are you and what do you want?"

"I am looking for business."

She raised her impeccably shaped eyebrows and looked me up and down. "You're pretty but don't seem the type. You will be a raging success. Come on in."

"You misunderstood me," I said when we were alone in her

parlor. It smelled of fresh paint and new upholstery. "I am not applying to be one of your..."

"Whores?"

"Entertainers. My father did business here."

"Most men do."

"Not in that way. Though I guess he probably did partake in the entertainment."

"He most assuredly did."

I cleared my throat. I did not want to think of my father being serviced by a prostitute. "My father was a doctor. He took care of women on this street. I cannot remember the address, though. I followed him here as a child."

Camille's laugh was as beautiful as her face and figure. "I can imagine that was a shock for you."

"It was. But it also set me on my path."

"To be a missionary? Are you here to save our immortal souls?"

"God, no. I am a doctor, like my father. I want to help."

So began my medical career. Treating whores on Twenty-Seventh kept food on the table until I finally, through James's introductions, broke into the closed society of the New York wealthy. It had only taken treating one woman successfully for the calls from other society women to start flooding in. The irony was not lost on me; my first patient in Washington Square was Beatrice Langton.

Camille's voice broke through my reverie.

"Catherine? Are you listening to a word I am saying?"

I turned from the clock. "Sorry. What did you say?"

Camille rose from her clean desk. She opened the center drawer, dropped the small black book in it, and slid it closed. "I said staring at the clock won't make it move."

"That is not what you said."

"No, but it's true nonetheless."

She stood in front of me, a vision of pale green silk and creamy white skin. Her strawberry blonde hair cascaded down her right shoulder to settle on the curve of her pale bosom. My normal visits to Joe Fisher's were timed during the slowest part of the day, so, thankfully, I rarely saw Camille dressed for the evening. There was nothing worse for my own flagging vanity than to stand next to her in my serviceable cotton dress.

"Don't take this the wrong way, Catherine, but you look ghastly."

"Compared to you, who does not?"

Camille was stunning, much too beautiful to be a whore. Everything about her spoke of good breeding: her carriage, her language, her intelligence, her shrewdness, and her ruthlessness. I had never had the courage to ask her how she ended up at Joe Fisher's, but hoped one day I would.

She shrugged. Camille was not vain, though she knew the worth of her beauty. "It's my job to be beautiful." She took my chin between her thumb and forefinger and turned my face to the side. "I have powder that will cover your black eye, if you'd like."

I thought of what Maureen's reaction would be to the large purple bruise on my face. "Thank you."

"Come, sit." She motioned for me to sit down while she retrieved the powder. She sat on the edge of the divan next to me, turned my face to the side again, and gently patted the soft puff on my cheek.

"You should eat."

"I am not hungry."

"You're pale and have dark circles under your eyes. Or eye, I should say."

"Funny."

"Not to mention frown lines from thinking so hard all day."

I balled my hands into fists. "I wish I understood why. Why would Beatrice Langton accuse me? What have I ever done to make her hate me so much?"

Camille sighed and held the puff away from my face. "Oh, Catherine. For someone so intelligent you are very naive. Beatrice Langton doesn't hate you. She feels nothing for you at all. To her, you are little more than a servant."

I pulled away. "What?"

"Surely you didn't think because they accepted you as their doctor they thought of you as their equal?"

"No, but—"

Camille returned her attention to my cheek. "She is protecting her own."

"What do you mean?"

"She knows you didn't kill her husband, and most likely knows who did. Hell, she may have done it herself. She needs someone to blame, and you're the logical choice. It's easier to find another doctor than train a new footman or maid."

I stood abruptly, appalled by what she'd said, but knowing she was correct.

"You said George admired what you'd accomplished? Women like her resent women like you and me. Strong and independent, things they will never be."

I stared into the fire and tried to square this version of Beatrice with the woman I knew. I never would have said we were friends, but I also never would have imagined a festering resentment for me beneath her starched, uptight exterior. However, my life had been one battle after another with the women Camille described. Why should I be surprised if it was one of these women who might lead to my downfall?

"Please relax. Maureen will be here soon with a note from your friend that all is well."

I turned to Camille. "If it is not?"

"Then you start over. Pretend to be someone else. You have experience with that."

"Yes, well, that was a temporary arrangement, as you very well know. The idea of pretending to be a man for the rest of my life is hardly appealing."

"Why? The opportunities you have to fight for as a woman would fall into your lap as a man."

I shook my head. "I could not carry it off in everyday life. The reason I was able to do it so easily during the war was because everyone was too distracted by all of the death and destruction around us to pay too close attention to Dr. Bennett's baby-faced orderly."

Camille shrugged. "You can still start over. A new place. A new name. A new life."

I laughed. "You make it sound so easy."

"It is. Ten of my girls have done exactly that."

"Unfortunately for me, there are far fewer women doctors than whores. I will stand out no matter where I go."

"Say you are a midwife."

"I cannot imagine only delivering babies for the rest of my life." I looked out the window for the hundredth time. "It is snowing again."

"There are worse things, you know."

"Than snow?"

"Than being a midwife," Camille said, disapproval and anger written on her face.

My stomach clenched with shame. "Of course there are. I apologize, Camille. What a thoughtless thing to say."

Though there were many madams who treated their girls well, Camille was the only one who was determined her girls would have a future outside of prostitution. Each learned to read and write, and depending on their interest, were taught a trade: cooking, sewing, teaching, accounting. Joe Fisher's seemed to be a finishing school as much as a house of prostitution. When a girl saved enough money to leave, Camille gave her a letter of recommendation, claiming to be a rich widow living on Washington Square, and sent the girl on her way. Most girls went west, found a job, and soon after found a husband. Some answered ads for wives, which were becoming increasingly common in the Eastern papers. The West was overflowing with single men out to make their fortunes and in desperate need of women to make their homes. Camille did more to save women from prostitution than any missionary I ever knew, and for that she earned my respect. As a result, as my society practice increased and I whittled down my patients on Twenty-Seventh, only Joe Fisher's remained.

"Please don't suggest I answer some ad to be a frontier farmer's wife."

"I was going to suggest a miner, actually."

I saw the humor in her eyes and knew I was forgiven. I managed a laugh.

"There are an increasing number of ads in the paper for doctors in the West. Towns are desperate for them."

"Are you suggesting I pretend to be a male doctor on the frontier?"

"Not a bad idea, Catherine. I wish I had thought of it. Be a midwife for a few years, until Catherine Bennett is a distant memory. Move to a larger city and put up your shingle. I have contacts who could help you."

"Let's hope I don't need them."

I twisted my hands together and paced, deciding to finally voice an idea that had been nagging me all day. "Camille, do you think my attack last night had anything to do with George Langton's death?"

The madam lounged back on the divan and studied me for a full minute. Finally, I continued. "I know it sounds ridiculous, but how coincidental I am attacked for the first time on the street the same night I'm accused of murder."

She lifted one eyebrow. "You're right. It does sound ridiculous." Camille stood and walked to me. She stroked my hair and turned my face to inspect her handiwork. "Catherine, you knew the risk you took walking alone at night. The streets are full of toughs. You just so happened to cross paths with one."

There was a knock on the door, and Maureen entered looking scandalized and very cold. She held her shopping basket close to her chest.

"Maureen, give me that and come by the fire," I said.

I took the heavy basket from her hands. "What do you have in here?" I lifted the towel covering the basket and found apples, nuts, and potatoes. "What are you carrying this around for?" I placed the basket on the hearth.

"Katie," Maureen whispered, "what is this place?" She eyed Camille with a good deal of suspicion.

Camille smiled. "I'll leave you alone to talk."

She glided across the room and left, closing the door softly behind her.

"Is this a house of assignation?"

"Yes, Maureen. It is."

Maureen crossed herself. "Katie, how could you come to a place like this?"

"Can we talk about that later, please? What did you find out?"

"No, we will talk about it now. How do you even know these people?"

"They are patients of mine."

"Patients!"

"Yes, patients. If it were not for these women and others like them, you and I would have starved a few years ago. Now, please tell me what James said."

I could tell from her expression that we would revisit this conversation at a later date. She pulled a note from her coat pocket and handed it to me. There was no greeting or salutation.

You must leave town at once. A $500 reward for your capture will be in the evening paper.

Camille entered the room, holding the offending paper.

"Master James told me to go to the house and get whatever valuables I could carry and to get to you at once. He also said I was probably being followed. Which I was."

"Were you followed here?" Camille asked.

"'Course not. I went to five-o'clock mass, then asked to see the priest after. Slipped out the side door."

Camille gave me a significant look and a coy smile. "Clever woman." She handed me a broadsheet, wet from snow. "You have made the evening paper."

FEMALE DOCTOR MURDERS PATIENT'S HUSBAND
******

BLUDGEONED TO DEATH WHEN HE ENDED AFFAIR
******

DOC IN HIDING
REWARD
$500

My portrait was underneath the headline. In it I stood stoically next to a table of medical instruments. I threw the paper on the sofa. "I always hated that photograph. Next time I am determined to smile." I sighed. "Well, what now?"

"We get you out of town," Camille said.

"With what? I have no money."

"Yes, you do." Maureen rummaged in the basket and pulled out a purple velvet bag.

"Oh!" I took the bag from her, opened it, and looked down at my mother's jewelry, the last connection I had to a woman I didn't remember. I'd done everything possible to keep from parting with the jewelry five years earlier when I had struggled to start my practice. Sentimentality was a luxury I couldn't afford now. "I hoped to never be desperate enough to part with these."

"It don't get much more desperate than this," Maureen said. She reached back into the bottom of the basket and pulled out a glass jar. "I also got the housekeeping money."

"No, Maureen. You will need that."

"If you think you're going off without me, you've got another think coming."

My eyes burned. "You would do that?"

"Now don't you go to getting all sappy on me, Katie Girl. You know as well as I do that you wouldn't survive one day without me there to do all those things you never think of." Maureen looked at Camille. "If her head hasn't been in a book, then her mind has been wandering off to I don't know where for as long as I can remember. Thinking about veins and organs and wasting diseases, most like. Though why any woman would want to think of those things is beyond my comprehension."

"Mine as well," Camille said as seriously as her subdued amusement would let her. "So, it is up to us to take charge, don't you think?"

Maureen eyed Camille. Despite her best efforts, Camille's easy demeanor and beauty won my devout Irish Catholic maid over.

Clutching the velvet bag to my chest, I turned to the window while the newfound friends made plans for my escape. Leaving New York. Starting a brand-new life out West. It was incomprehensible.

I thought of Beatrice Langton's daughter, Elizabeth, on her sickbed, of Mrs. Watson bedridden for the last three months of her pregnancy, of the drawer full of drawings from sick children I'd doctored, of little Edward Beechum, whose cast I would have removed next week, of the women who thanked me profusely for merely listening and taking their problems seriously. How could I leave them? Who would take care of them?

"I cannot leave."

"What? Why?" Camille replied.

"I have patients who need me."

Camille picked up the discarded paper and held it up. The $500 reward jumped from the page. "Do you really think you will be able to help your patients from jail? The judge will make sure you rot in there," she said with a great deal of bitterness. "Even if, by some miracle, you aren't thrown in jail, do you honestly think any of your other patients will stand by you? That the male doctors you've displaced won't crucify you in the press as well as the drawing rooms of Washington Square?"

All the energy left me. She was right. My career in New York City was over. My pang of remorse at abandoning my patients was pushed aside by Camille's next question.

"Catherine, how does Texas sound?"

Daunting. Terrifying. Remote.

"Perfect."

CHAPTER
3

We will be on solid land soon."

Maureen nodded and inhaled deeply in an effort to tamp down the nausea that had been constant since we sailed out of New York Harbor three weeks before. Her already thin frame had become frightfully gaunt; her face had been green for so long I had almost forgotten her normal rosy complexion. I put my hand over hers and squeezed.

Her eyes were glassy and distant, as if seeing events from the past instead of the thin strip of land sliding into view. The ever-present guilt that her misery was due to me blazed in my chest. I should have argued with more force against her coming, but her presence was so comforting I did not. Nor did I consider how traveling by sea would bring back memories of her journey from Ireland twenty-five years before, and the loss of her family on the voyage.

"We will stay in Galveston for a few days and let you recuperate. I will go to the apothecary when we land."

"You won't. I'll be fine."

Before I could reply, a sailor walked by, his pointed disinterest in us serving to magnify my suspicion. I bowed my head and hoped the thin veil covering my face was sufficient. Maureen's sickness, which had tied us to our cabin for the entire voyage, had been a blessing, though I was sure Maureen did not think so after vomiting for three days. I made sure the cabin boy who brought our food never got a clear view of my face.

Maureen lowered her voice and continued. "You stay away from the apothecary. Last thing you need is to bring attention to yourself."

"I hardly think—"

"You agreed," she said, with more force than I would have expected from her weakened state. "You're a midwife now, not a doctor. I know it's gonna chafe you something fierce, but you have to listen to me this one time. If not me, then Camille."

They were correct. A midwife was commonplace. A female physician would turn heads, pique curiosity, and remind someone of the scandal that had rocked New York City weeks before. I feared the story had made the papers across the country, especially with the bounty on my head. Even if the story had not made the Galveston papers, from the number of ships in harbor, it had certainly traveled to this port and many others by sea.

I grasped Maureen's arm as we wobbled on sea legs down the pier, two sailors from our ship hauling our trunks a few steps behind. The aroma of grilled meats and roasting nuts made my mouth water and my stomach rumble in anticipation of a meal that did not subsist of thin soup and hard, coarse bread. The wharf was full of sailors, stevedores, businessmen, and street urchins selling peanuts and newspapers with one hand and stealing pocketbooks with the other. Even the foul smells of body odor, dead fish, and bird droppings could not diminish my hunger or the thrill of being around civilization once again.

We stopped in front of the wharf office. "Here is fine," I said to the sailors. They loitered, waiting for a coin. I had paid the captain handsomely for the voyage, much more than I should have; by rights, he should pay the men. I could not risk their ire. I pulled two precious coins from my reticule and handed one to each. They tipped their hats and walked away.

"Wait here." I leaned down, checked her forehead for fever, and whispered, "Hopefully James has sent good news."

Inside, I asked the clerk, "Do you have a telegram for me? Maureen O'Reilly?"

"I'll check."

I wandered over to a bulletin board covered with a thick layer of handbills for wanted men. Horse thieves, bank robbers, gunfighters, and outlaw gangs left little room for an adulterous murderer. If my poster had been on this wall, it had long since been covered. I was lifting up the corner of a bill to examine what was beneath when the clerk called me back. He handed me the telegram with a sad smile.

"You are so kind." I walked to a quiet corner of the room, took a deep breath, and opened the telegram from James with a shaking hand.

Regret to inform you cousin Catherine has passed away STOP Body found by river three days after you left STOP Buried in family plot next to uncle STOP Safe journey STOP

I read the telegram three times before my knees gave way and I collapsed into the nearest chair.

Dead? I am dead? Who on earth did they find in the river? I visualized what the waterlogged, decomposed body must have looked like and shuddered. Did James identify an unknown woman as me so I would not always be glancing over my shoulder? I could never return to the East, or use my real name again, but it was a small price to pay for staying alive.

I was dead. They'd had my funeral. I wonder who had showed up, if anyone. Camille and her girls would have attended, as well as my other clients from Twenty-Seventh Street who would not believe me capable of murder or, if so, they would not think the less of me. I smiled as I envisioned my funeral attended only by whores. James had probably been appalled.

I returned to the clerk. "Could you point me in the direction of the customs house?"

The clerk's brows furrowed and his expression morphed from one of sympathy to suspicion. "What business do you have there?"

Not only had Camille arranged our last-minute voyage on a packet ship captained by a discreet regular of hers, but she had also given me the name of another client who would help me arrange the next leg of our journey. "No business. Just calling on an old friend."

"Who?"

"Major Eric Gardner?"

The clerk's weak chin melted into his fleshy neck. "Your old friend sailed under guard for New York City yesterday morning."

"Oh." I dipped my head so the clerk could not get a good view of my face. "How unfortunate. What was the charge?"

"Corruption. Embezzlement. Typical Yankee carpetbagger, coming here and stealing from the Rebels."

I smiled weakly. "Yes, well, thank you for your assistance," I said, and left the office hurriedly.

The door closed behind me and I stared unseeingly at the wharf. There hadn't been time for Camille to plan our escape past "Take this ship to Galveston and call on Eric Gardner." I turned toward the door again, thinking to cable Camille for advice, but stopped myself. I did not want to raise the clerk's suspicions any more than necessary. I was more than capable of taking control of my circumstances. How difficult could planning a journey be? First, we needed to decide where to go.

I glanced down the platform to where Maureen waited. Maureen stood as I walked toward her. "Well?"

I handed her the telegram and saw in her expression my shock from minutes before.

"Does this mean?"

"I'm dead? It would appear so."

Maureen handed the telegram back, crossed herself, and remained silent.

"Come. Let's get some solid food in you and plan our future."

Maureen and I made our way to the Lafitte Hotel, where we sat down to enjoy our first civilized meal in a month and to talk about what to do next.

"I've always wanted to see California," Maureen said.

"California it is." I didn't care where we went, and if Maureen wanted to see California, the least I could do was repay her loyalty with the privilege.

"We will stay here a few days to rest. I am not sure how to get to California from here." I sipped my tea. "We may need to sail—"

"No. I'll not step on a boat again."

"Of course." I reached across and grasped Maureen's knobby hand. "Are you dizzy?"

She sighed. "Tha ground is still rocking."

"Give it time. I will settle you in upstairs before I go find a jeweler. First, try to eat a bit more."

Maureen nibbled on her toast. I leaned forward and whispered, "I need a new name."

I grinned, excited with the prospect of taking on a new identity. It reminded me of the many personas my cousin Charlotte and I put on during my time living in England, each character more absurd than the last. "I was thinking Laura. Dr. Laura Elliston."

Maureen knit her brows and lowered her eyes to her plate of barely touched food.

"What? You don't like it?"

Maureen placed her hand in her lap and sat silent.

"Maureen?"

"You said you'd be a midwife."

"There's no worry now. Everyone thinks I'm dead."

"And how many women doctors are there in the world? Not enough that you won't stand out."

I waved my hand in dismissal. "I'll say I studied with a doctor in England who has since died. There is enough British in my accent to pass. I can accentuate it as well," I demonstrated. "Or, I can say I'm from Ireland." I mimicked her Irish brogue. "I could use your last name." When she didn't appear convinced, I leaned forward over the table and spoke in my normal voice. "You've read in the papers how desperate towns in the West are for doctors. I doubt many will check my credentials."

Maureen shook her head. "It ain't worth the risk, Katie Girl."

"Laura."

"If you're found out, they'll send you back to New York. You'll hang. I canna bear it."

"I'm not going to get found out and I am *not* going to hang." On the voyage from New York I decided I would never hang; I would do whatever necessary to end my life before it happened. I could not tell that to my devout Irish Catholic maid, though.

"Why take the chance when you can be a midwife just as well?"

I sat back in my chair. "I am a doctor, Maureen. A surgeon, and a damn fine one." Maureen frowned, as I knew she would. "I worked hard to get where I am. I am *not* going to throw it away out of fear."

Maureen shook her head and placed her napkin on the table

beside her plate. The disappointment on her face fanned my anger. "What?" I said.

She leveled her eyes at me and laid on the guilt as only she could. "You dinna once mention helpin' people. It's only about you and your pride. I thought I taught you better, but I see I didn't."

We stared at each other across the table, a familiar battle of wills for going on twenty-five years, ever since my mother died of a fever when I was five years old. Our young Irish maid had stepped in and raised me while my surgeon father filled the void his wife's death created by increasing his practice and creating a new medical school. Maureen had called me strong-willed and insolent more than once, and though she didn't understand my desire to be a doctor, she was proud of my accomplishments. At least, that is what I had always thought.

"Of course I want to help people, Maureen. Why do you think I work as hard as I do?"

Her lips were white from the effort to keep quiet. I almost laughed. "Go on. Say what you want."

"I've said it before to no use. Wasting my breath." She stood. "I'm going to rest on a stationary bed." She stepped away from the table, and turned back. *"Laura."*

I rose as well, ignoring the sarcasm. Let her have her little fit. She would come around. "I am going to walk around the town and investigate passage to California. Overland passage."

Ten minutes later, I walked down Galveston's main street with two pieces of my mother's jewelry to sell in my reticule. The sun shone and the salt-tinged air was crisp but not cold, a welcome relief from the blustery weather we left in New York. The smell of roasting nuts pulled me down to the corner of Twentieth and Strand. There, a fat man sold roasted pecans, which I was determined to buy until I saw the unkempt state of his apron and the dirt embedded in his nails. I politely refused and moved on.

A little farther on, an elderly Negro played a violin. A tattered bowler hat lay upside down in front of him, two dull coins struggling to contrast with the faded brown felt. I dropped a shiny penny in the hat with a smile. He nodded and thanked me without missing a beat.

I help people, I thought as I strolled along. Of course I want to help people, to heal. It was the definition of my job. What Maureen did not understand, or could not understand, was I was the sole arbiter of my success. I had no one to champion my abilities, to put me forward professionally. The few doctors who tolerated me thought it was promotion enough if they did not disparage me publicly for having the intelligence to excel in their profession and the temerity to try. My vanity and pride were seen as character flaws, whereas the same attitude in my male colleagues was praised as confidence. Maureen, though she was proud of me, would have preferred I be more circumspect in my self-promotion and present a more ladylike attitude of modesty and submissiveness. Those particular attitudes had never taken with me, though I had tried.

A clump of people gathered on the wharf caught my eye. A portly, nattily dressed man stood on a barrel in the middle of the group delivering an oration that, from the impression of his audience, was at once appealing and suspicious. He was too well dressed to be a minister. A young woman stood next to the barrel, handing out waybills to whoever showed interest. I stepped closer to hear.

"It is, by far, the most picturesque spot for a town in all of the Colorado Territory! In the foothills of the Rocky Mountains, the water is plentiful. Game is abundant. The soil is perfect for farming."

"Yeah, but what 'bout gold? There any gold in that there plentiful water?" The men gathered around laughed.

The orator smiled as if placating a child. No doubt, he'd heard the question before. "None has been discovered as of yet. But, you may be the first! A wagon train is leaving Austin next week, traveling north through Texas to the Colorado Territory. Lots will be sold on May fifteenth and June thirtieth."

Most of the men shook their heads and walked off, murmuring about Indians. The speaker raised his voice and said, "We're traveling under the protection of the US Army, up the line of Western forts."

An old man standing next to me said with a huff of disbelief, "Land promoters. Ain't no one gonna travel up through the Comancheria these days." He spat on the ground and left.

The man climbed down from the barrel with the girl's help. I was turning to leave when he caught my eye and moved in. "Interested in immigrating to Colorado, madam?"

I'd heard a little about the land promoters who haunted the ports of the South, trying to convince people down on their luck to move west. More often than not, when the poor souls arrived, after sinking all of their money into the trip, the Garden of Eden was a barren wasteland with nary a building in sight.

"No, sir. I'm traveling to California." The man grabbed a flyer from the girl and shoved it toward me. I took it out of politeness.

"California, pah. Don't believe all the land of milk and honey you hear about California. Colorado, the Rockies, *that's* where the future is."

"What of the Indian threat?"

"As I said, we will be traveling under the protection of the Army. The Indians will be no threat."

34

"I was talking of the threat to the new town."

"Safe as walking down the street in New York City."

I thought of my last walk in New York City and shuddered. He stuck out his hand. "Cornelius Warren. This is my daughter, Anna."

I hesitated before offering my own. I would humor Maureen's request to pose as a midwife for a bit longer. No need to draw attention to myself in a port city such as Galveston. "Laura Elliston." The name was strange on my tongue. "Thank you for the flyer, sir. Good luck with your endeavor."

I folded the flyer and placed it in my bag next to the jewelry and walked off before he could take a new tack.

As I walked away I wondered if immigrating to a small Western town might be a better option than California. Surely no one in such a venture would bother to investigate my past. Being in on the ground floor, building something from scratch, might be exhilarating. However, if it failed, it would drain what little money I would receive from the six pieces of jewelry we had brought to fund our new life and would leave Maureen and me destitute. No. Better to move to a more populated area where I would be able to support us.

My business with the apothecary was completed in short order, though I lingered over a trunk full of medicine designed specifically for shipment to remote towns in the West and for use on ships. The proud pharmacist could not resist bragging about how lucrative his mail-order business had become since the war ended and more and more people were moving to the territories. I barely resisted buying it. Common sense told me these items—ether, carbolic acid, morphia, quinine, bandages, sutures, saws, scalpels, and clamps—would be readily available in California and not cost me a precious cent to ship there.

I was requesting a quote from the jeweler in the shop next

35

door when the door opened and the bell jingled. I turned, more from habit than curiosity, and was shocked to find one of my patients from New York waddling into the store.

"I thought it was you," Molly Ebling exclaimed. "My very own doctor, in Galveston of all places."

My heart leapt into my throat. "Mrs. Ebling!"

"When I saw you through the window, I thought, 'No, it can't be,'" she said. "Thought it was my eyes playing tricks on me, showing me what I wanted to see instead of what's there. You know Mr. Ebling has long accused me of that. Well, I've always told him I'm not imagining things and here I am, correct once again."

"What are you doing in Galveston?" My voice was faint, hardly discernible from panic, but Molly Ebling needed little prompting to tell her story.

"Mr. Ebling had business here in Texas and I decided to come. Worst decision I ever made. The South is a backwater, full of ignorant, dirty rebels and the Negroes! Never seen so many in my life. We stopped in New Orleans first, that's where I contracted malaria, and I was sick as a dog on the voyage over. Worst experience of my life. Well, I thought so until I spent a month housebound in a hotel. The man treating me is drunk half the time and shaking like a leaf when he's sober. The nurse is about as bad. Maybe worse. Heavens, I think everyone in this town is a tippler. I've always thought those temperance women were a little strident, but I see the inspiration now."

"I'm sure Mr. Ebling—"

"Mr. Ebling nothing. He left me alone in this godforsaken place and went inland to conduct his business. I'm sure I'll never forgive him. He returns tomorrow and we leave next week. Though his business might delay him again. I wonder if he's not purposely prolonging his trip inland. He positively loves this horrid place. I can't imagine why anyone would want to visit unless compelled to by family or business." She stopped and her eyes turned shrewd. "What are you doing in Galveston?"

I knew the question was coming but had been so flustered by her arrival and her rapid recitation of her problems I had not formulated a good lie. I was as surprised as she, probably more so, at what came out of my mouth.

"I am married."

Her astonishment turned to happiness more quickly than I expected. "Oh, I'm so happy for you, Dr. Bennett! I always told Mr. Ebling, I said, 'That Catherine Bennett is a beautiful woman and *smart*. She would make some man the finest wife,' and here you've gone and done it. Another instance where I was correct and he was not. I must keep track of these moments. Well, tell me. Who's the lucky man?"

I tried to remember how to smile shyly. "A man I have known since childhood."

"Oh, you two have always been in love, then." Mrs. Ebling clasped her hands over her heart.

"Yes, we finally admitted we were best suited for each other."

"Well, that's splendid. Of course, it means you will give up your practice. I can't say I'm sorry. I always thought you were an exceptional doctor but it's not a natural profession for a woman. Better you spend your time supporting your husband and taking care of your family. What does your fiancé do?"

"He's a lawyer," I said through gritted teeth.

"I'll have Mr. Ebling contact him. Maybe he could send some business your husband's way."

"How kind."

"How long are you in town?"

"I leave tomorrow."

"You and your husband must drop by the hotel before you leave."

"I'm not sure, Mrs. Ebling. I have many errands to run in preparation."

"Oh, please. I'm anxious to meet the man who won your heart."

I smiled. "I will try."

"Wonderful."

The little jeweler returned. "I can give you one hundred dollars, ma'am."

While lies were coming easily, my luck was not. If the jeweler had come back thirty seconds later, Mrs. Ebling would have been gone. "What are you talking about, man?" I snapped. "I asked how much it would cost to tighten the loose stone."

He considered me to Mrs. Ebling and seemed to grasp the situation. "I apologize, ma'am. I will fix the loose stone at no cost. If you would like to wait?"

I nodded and he walked to the back of the store.

"Stupid little Jew," Mrs. Ebling said. She turned to me and smiled. "I will be waiting for you. Grand Hotel." She took my hands and squeezed. "I am so, so happy for you."

Tears of frustration stung my eyes. "Thank you," I said in an emotion-choked whisper. She tilted her head and with an understanding smile, patted my hand, and left.

I wanted to scream or throw something, but closed my eyes and dropped my head in my hands instead. I gave a silent prayer for Molly Ebling's malaria. It was obvious she was ignorant of my alleged crime and my subsequent death. But, would her husband be? I imagined the scene when he returned from the interior, her bragging about seeing me and complimenting my marriage and his shock at her conversation with a dead woman. At worst, I had a day to get out of Galveston. At best,

Mr. Ebling would not believe his wife, and they would travel to New York in a state of angry silence. But, the silence would not last forever. In as little as three weeks, New York could know I'm alive.

I lifted my head. How long would it take for Beatrice Langton to send the Pinkertons after me?

The jeweler returned from the back room. "Seventy-five dollars."

"You said one hundred."

He shrugged and placed the necklace and cash on the counter. I narrowed my eyes at him, took the cash, and left.

Without question, I needed to leave Galveston. If I lived in a large port city I would run the risk of seeing someone from my past. It might be years before I was forgotten enough to chance living in San Francisco.

I stopped a street urchin and asked for directions to the train station. I hoped the last train off the island had not departed.

I was in luck; the last train left in an hour. I bought the tickets and was putting the change back in my reticule when I saw it. I pulled out the advertisement for Timberline, Colorado, and knew I had found the means of my salvation.

CHAPTER

4

I've never looked so forward to a bed in my life," Maureen said.

The stage rolled to a stop in Austin after 150 miles of bad road, three nights of flea-infested mattresses, and seventy-two hours of Cornelius Warren's constant chatter about Timberline, Colorado.

"Down-filled ticking, I assure you. Ester runs a fine boardinghouse," Cornelius said for the tenth time before jumping out of the stage to assist us.

"Cotton-filled, at least," his daughter, Anna, said.

"As long as it isn't straw." I gave Cornelius my hand and stepped out of the coach to a muffled scream emanating from the two-story house in front of us.

Maureen poked her head from the coach. "Someone's either bein' murdered or giving birth," she said, and stepped out.

The teamster unloaded our trunks and placed them on the porch. He cackled. "Sounds about the same, I grant you. No, mayhap Ester's daughter is having her baby." He placed his hands at the small of his back and stretched. Another scream pierced the night. "Might want to go on in. Doubt she'll hear ya knock."

My mind started working through the scenarios I might see

on the other side of the door. My fingers itched to move, to help, to heal. "Maureen, make sure there's plenty of water on boil. And coffee," I said. Maureen nodded and went into the house with purpose. "Anna, ever seen a child brought into the world?"

"No."

"Would you like to?"

Anna nodded.

"Come along."

"I'll see to the trunks," Cornelius said.

I pulled my father's watch from my medical bag and opened the face. "I may need to get into the black one." Another scream pierced the night. I clicked the watch shut. "Rather soon, I think."

With my medical bag in my hand I entered the house and followed the screams up the stairs.

A tall, weedy-looking young man stood on the landing, running his hands through his hair and pacing the width of the hall. He stopped and talked to a closed door. "Want me to go for the doc?"

"Joe, stop pacing outside that door," said a voice from inside. "Doctor's no use. It'll be over before you find him."

I placed a hand on the young man's arm. He jumped.

"Joe, I'm Laura. I'm here to help."

His relief washed away any questions he might have had about who I was or where I had come from. "Thank you. Ma said the baby ain't turned right, but she won't tell me what that means."

I patted Joe's arm again. "Go on downstairs, Joe. Maureen will fix you a cup of coffee."

"Yes, ma'am."

"Fix us up some, too. I'll help your ma."

He nodded and stumbled downstairs. When he was gone, I contemplated Anna, who stared at the door with apprehension. "Do whatever I ask immediately and without question."

Anna paled a little but nodded. I opened the door.

The light of four lanterns bathed the bed in the center of the bedroom with a warm glow but was not strong enough to banish the sense of panic that hovered over the scene. Sweat-soaked tendrils of hair framed Joe's mother's pale, worried face. Dark half-moon circles sagged beneath her eyes. She pressed on the pregnant woman's stomach with as much strength as her small, exhausted body could muster. The pregnant woman moaned and whimpered like a wounded animal, delirious from pain and the heat emanating from the lanterns. "Open the window." Anna did as ordered.

The midwife looked up. "Who're you? What are you doing?"

"I am Dr. Laura Elliston." Anna eased next to me. From the corner of my eye I saw her surprise at my title, but she remained silent. "This is Anna. Are you Ester?"

At the word *doctor*, the woman's shoulders drooped. Her tension and worry shifted to my own. "The baby's breeched and coming fast. Nothing I've done is working."

A quick visual sweep of the room showed me Ester Mebane knew how to birth a child: a pan full of water, plenty of sheets, string to tie the cord, a knife, a blanket for the baby. She'd probably brought dozens of babies into the world without incident or with only the normal problems attending childbirth. Tonight, this birth was different.

I placed my bag on the dresser and regarded the pregnant woman's face for the first time. She was Anna's age or a little older. "What is her name?"

"Ida."

"She your daughter?" I lifted the sheet from the girl's legs.

"Yes."

Ida was almost completely dilated. I could see the child's behind at the edge of the birth canal. I pulled the sheet back over the girl's knees.

"Anna, go to my trunk, the black one. Bring back the bottles labeled chloroform and carbolic acid. Ester, go with Anna and bring two pans and as much hot water as you can carry. Get Joe to help. Also, a spool of your strongest thread, and a bottle of whisky. Go. Now."

I removed my traveling cloak and rolled up my sleeves. I placed a straight-backed chair at the end of the bed and set my surgery kit on top of it. Ida shifted, moaned, grasped the sheets, and sat up with a bloodcurdling scream. I moved forward and grasped her shoulders. "Try not to push, Ida."

Beneath the sweat, tears, and flush of pain from childbirth I could clearly see the young girl only a few years past playing with dolls. "It hurts," she sobbed.

"I know it does. It will be over soon."

She collapsed back onto the mattress, insensible again. I checked my father's watch and calculated. Her contractions were only five minutes or so apart.

Anna and Ester returned. The two women followed my preparation instructions to the letter and without complaint while I dosed Ida with morphine-laced whisky. I rested my hand on the girl's forehead. "There now, that will help ease the pain."

I moved to the end of the bed and placed most of my surgery tools into the waiting pan of hot water with a few drops of carbolic acid. "Ester, put the thread in there as well."

In the other pan, I washed my hands with lye soap and rinsed them. "Wash your hands," I said to the women.

I doused a clean cloth from my medical bag with chloroform.

"Ester, I want you to be ready to receive the baby. Anna, hold this lightly over Ida's nose and mouth."

With an assurance that belied her youth Anna went to the top of the bed and waited for my direction. Ester stood at the foot of the bed next to me. I nodded to Anna, who placed the cloth over Ida's nose. Ida's body relaxed.

I pushed my right hand up the birth canal until I touched the baby. "Good."

"What?" Ester said.

I pushed against the baby's bottom to move it back into the womb and with my left hand pushed against Ida's abdomen. I closed my eyes and visualized the baby's situation in the womb as I maneuvered it into the correct birth position. Ida's cervix contracted around my wrist. I stopped and pushed back against the baby's desire to see the world. A trickle of sweat ran down between my breasts and my arm trembled with the effort. Finally, Ida's contraction passed.

It was almost time for the next contraction by the time I maneuvered the baby into the correct position. I removed my hand slowly. "Let her breathe." Anna held the cloth aloft.

"She's overdue by about two weeks," I said. I picked up the scalpel.

"Yeah. What are you doing?" Ester said.

"The baby is big, and your daughter is small. She will tear." I took the scalpel and made a one-inch incision below her vagina. "This will help."

The baby crowned, and with the next contraction a beautiful little head emerged. I rotated the baby to release the shoulder, and the baby slid out into my hands. I held him upside down and slapped his back. He gave a lusty, life-affirming cry as I placed him in Ester's waiting arms.

"Congratulations, Grandma."

Tears flowed down Ester's cheeks. "And a fine boy he is." I
tied the cord off and cut it with the scalpel while Ester cooed to
her grandson. "Take him downstairs and clean him. Give him
a sugar teat until Ida is ready to nurse."

I took the pan of soapy water to the window, glanced below,
and when I saw the street was clear, tossed it. I cleared the
chair, sat, and waited for the afterbirth. I glanced up at Anna,
who was staring at me, eyes wide.

"You are a doctor."

"I am."

"Why did you say you were a midwife?"

In truth, the word *doctor* had slipped from my mouth before
I considered the ramifications. I could have easily delivered the
baby as a midwife and kept my identity a secret for a while longer. The horse was out of the barn now.

"People accept women as midwives easier than as physicians."

"Oh, but this is wonderful. Father will be so pleased. Having
a doctor as a founding member of our community. They are
tremendously hard to recruit to the frontier."

"Can we keep my profession between us for a while longer?"

"But, Father—"

"I will tell Cornelius in due time."

Anna nodded but still looked a bit peaked.

"Are you going to faint?"

"I've never seen the like."

"Neither have I."

"You've never—?"

I shook my head. "She would have died giving birth breech.
She's too small."

I caught the flush of blood and afterbirth in the empty pan
and massaged Ida's abdomen to staunch the bleeding. "Take
this," I said, holding the pan of afterbirth out to Anna.

"Do you want me to throw it out?"

"The window? Heavens, no. Place it on the dresser and put a towel over it for now. Bring me that pitcher of water."

"What are you doing?" She handed the pitcher over.

I poured a small amount of water between Ida's legs. "Have you heard of germ theory?"

"No."

"I did not imagine you would have." I rubbed the bar of carbolic soap between my hands, and gently cleaned the blood from between Ida's legs. "About eight years ago, Louis Pasteur theorized disease is not transported through the air, but by direct contamination; physicians and nurses with soiled hands touching other patients is what spreads disease. Pasteur wasn't the first to postulate the idea, only the most recent and well regarded."

I threaded the needle that had been soaking in the carbolic acid solution and tied off the end. I held the threaded needle up. "Purple thread. I would have never guessed, Ester." I leaned forward. "Could you bring a lantern over, please?" With Anna holding the lantern, I sewed the incision I made.

"The Rebels, during the war, ran out of everything. They resorted to using horsehair for sutures. Can you imagine the desperation you must be in to use horsehair? But it was coarse and not easy to work with, so they boiled it to make it more supple." Ida twitched and moaned. I rose and held her by the shoulders while she drank the rest of the morphine-laced whisky. Soon, she was asleep again.

I returned to my task. "Turned out, the wounds that were stitched with the horsehair were less likely to get infected."

"Because they were clean," Anna said.

"Yes."

"Four years ago, Joseph Lister championed the idea of using

46

carbolic acid as an antiseptic during and after surgery. Like any new idea, it has been slow to take hold. It is difficult to change people's minds."

"But, you listened."

I tied off the suture and stood. "The benefit of being shunned by the medical establishment is I can do what I want. I will tell you this: I have never lost a patient to infection, and I never will."

⌒◈⌒

"Ten minutes," Ester said. "Ten minutes from the time she walked in the door 'til I was holding my grandson. I've never seen anything like it."

Maureen and I sat across Ester's scrubbed wooden table from Cornelius and Anna. Anna held a pencil over a small bound journal, waiting to write the next item on our list of supplies to buy and things to do before our wagon train pulled out of Austin in a week's time. Maureen licked the tip of her pencil and made a note on her own list, or appeared to. In truth, she doodled boxes in the margins, having completed our list the night before.

It was three weeks past the night of our arrival and Ester had told the story of Ida's delivery daily, sometimes multiple times, ever since. Her gratitude and enthusiasm for my skills in saving her daughter and grandson were gratifying, a little too gratifying in Maureen's opinion. She believed one compliment was enough, constant compliments were the Devil's playground, and warned me more than once not to let Ester's praise go to my head. When Ester wanted to spread the story beyond the boardinghouse, I pulled her aside and asked her to keep my heroics quiet, as well as my profession. Her face fell, slightly, until comprehension dawned. She nodded once and

47

with a firm expression kept her word, though she couldn't resist talking about it among our group in private.

"She just reached up in there," Ester said, miming my actions with her arm, "and—"

"Yes, yes. That's quite enough. No details are needed." Cornelius fidgeted with the knot of his tie and glanced everywhere but at the women who surrounded him. Anna and I exchanged subdued smiles. Poor Cornelius was outnumbered and it made him extremely uncomfortable. "We were talking teamsters, not—the other. You'll need to hire one to drive your schooner," Cornelius said to Maureen.

"No, we won't."

"Have you decided to take me and Anna up on our offer to travel with us?"

"No need to be so crowded when we can afford our own." Though paying for our outfit had depleted our money to an alarming degree. Only two pieces of my mother's jewelry remained and Maureen and I decided we must not sell them until we were settled in Timberline.

"I agree," I said. As nice as Cornelius and Anna were, Maureen and I wanted our own space. "We purchased one this afternoon, and two rather docile oxen. We shall be fine."

Ester stood at the stove chopping vegetables for a winter stew. "Throwing good money after bad."

"And, why is that?" Maureen asked.

"Won't be doing much riding in the schooner. Most uncomfortable way to travel you can imagine."

"It can't be much worse than the trip from Galveston," Anna said.

"Oh, you'll be surprised. 'Course, you'll walk most of the time."

"I'll be driving the wagon," Maureen said.

Ester stopped chopping and studied Maureen. "Will you, now? I suppose you could at that."

"I agree," Anna said, with an encouraging smile at Maureen.

"I have no doubt you will do a fine job," Cornelius said. "You said your oxen are docile?" The concern in Cornelius's voice and in his expression was plain to all.

I had not been so long without male attention I could not read Cornelius's interest in Maureen. It would have been subtler of him to take an advertisement out in the *Democratic Statesman* declaring his love for my maid. What I could not read, though, was Maureen. She vacillated between anger and embarrassment. Anger appeared to be winning at the moment, though that could be lingering irritation at the compliments being bandied around.

"Yes, they are docile. We have named them Piper and Púca."

"I suppose I'm outnumbered," Cornelius said. "My only concern is your safety." There was a long pause in the conversation, until Cornelius coughed and said, "Meaning the safety of the entire group, of course."

"Of course," I said.

Maureen blushed, but tried to mask it with a scowl. "It's awfully hot in here."

Ester shrugged and went back to her chopping. "Y'all wanted to meet in the kitchen."

I studied Maureen while Cornelius rambled on about the journey. She had fully recovered from her bout of seasickness. Color had returned to her cheeks and her eyes sparkled. I thought back over our past and tried to remember her ever being so happy. As I watched Cornelius try to draw her out and her determined refusal to be, I wondered how much of her color was due to renewed health and how much was due to the attentions of Cornelius Warren.

"Amos Pike'll be our trail boss," Warren said.

"Amos Pike is a good man," Ester interjected. "Rode with my Hiram. If anyone can get you to Colorado, it's Amos Pike." She accentuated her opinion by pointing her knife at us.

"Rode with your husband?" Anna asked.

"With Jack Hayes back in forty-eight."

"Who is Jack Hayes?" I asked.

Ester scooped the vegetables into the cast-iron pot, wiped her hands on a towel, and faced us. "The best Indian fighter Texas has ever seen, and we've had our fair share of good 'uns. Amos was a good 'un in the end, but he didn't start out that way. Not many do, come to think of it."

"What happened?" Anna asked.

"Same thing always does. Comanche raid homesteads; we chase them. Only Amos was the only one who lived to tell. Walked back into Austin ten days after they left, half-dead from exhaustion and full of shame."

"Shame for what?" I asked.

"Living. Buffalo Hump killed his whole outfit. Including my Hiram. Those savages scalped Hiram while he was still alive, gutted him like a fish."

The bloom on Maureen's cheeks faded. I grasped her hand and squeezed.

"Ester, please," Cornelius said. "There are women in the room."

Ester scoffed. "And what'm I? This ain't London or New York, or even New Awlens." Her voice softened a bit and she spoke as if only to Maureen. "It's harder out here, best you know it now." She patted Maureen's shoulder. "You've got mettle, though. I can tell."

Maureen forced a smile, but gripped my hand.

"How did Mr. Pike survive?" Anna's voice was strong,

though it pitched up at the end, as if it was a great effort for her to disguise her fear.

"He hid behind a rock. Worst moment of his life, he said, walking back into Austin to tell the tale and admit his cowardice." Ester returned to the stove.

"I'm surprised you think so highly of a man whom you call a coward," I said.

"I called him a coward at the time, I'll admit. I was torn up about Hiram and not thinking straight." She paused again. "When Amos told the story, well, I can't say as I blame him for what he did. A few held a grudge, but he was young, inexperienced." She brought a cleaver down onto the hindquarter of a rabbit. Bits of fat and gristle flew through the air. She dropped the leg into the stew. "He made up for it by becomin' one of the fiercest Indian fighters Texas's ever seen." She nodded. "I learned a long time ago to don't ever judge a person ifin you ain't been in their shoes." She cleaved the rabbit again. "You got the Army with you. They ain't as good as Rangers, but they'll do."

"Precisely," Warren said. "We will drive up the Western Trail, stop at Fort Richardson before we reach Fort Sill."

Maureen, who had been watching Ester's dissection of the rabbit with fascination, turned her attention to Cornelius. Her eyes narrowed. "The Army's traveling *with* us, right?"

Anna shifted in her chair and stared at the scrubbed wooden table. "Not technically," Warren conceded. "As I said, though, we will be visiting forts along the way and will be well east of the line of civilization." He patted Maureen's hand with a protective affection. She pulled her hand away and cut her eyes at me.

Cornelius was a healthy, handsome man, if somewhat portly and talkative. He tended to run to vanity about his full, silky beard, stroking it for effect more often than he should. But those were hardly characteristics to stand in the way of Maureen's happiness. What could stand in the way, though, was Maureen's concern about me. It suddenly occurred to me she might be trying a little too hard to hide her pleasure at being courted to reassure me she would not leave me.

"You'll be fine. Amos knows what he's doing. You got guns, too, dontcha?" Ester asked.

"Of course," Warren said.

"Doctor? You got a gun?" Ester asked.

I pulled my eyes from Maureen's face. "I'm sorry. What?"

"You have a gun, don't you?"

I opened my mouth to say yes when I realized I had not seen my gun since that final, horrible night in New York City. I must have dropped it after I shot my attacker. Did James pick it up and forget to give it to me?

"I lost it," I replied.

Ester wiped her hands on a towel. "I can take care of that." She walked out of the room.

I narrowed my eyes at Warren. "How safe is this journey, Cornelius?"

"I wouldn't take my daughter on such a journey if I thought there was the least amount of danger involved." He patted Anna's hand.

"I am not frightened in the least," Anna offered. I wondered if her confidence was genuine or based on loyalty to her father.

Ester returned holding a man's shirt between her hands with a reverence usually reserved for the Good Book. She placed it on the table in front of me and unfolded the blue material. The gun and holster were old but well cared for.

"A Colt," I said.

Ester nodded. "A Paterson, given to Hiram by Hayes himself."

"It's the same as the gun I lost."

"You know how to keep it."

"It was your husband's, Ester. I couldn't possibly accept it."

"'Course you can. It's sittin' in a drawer, gettin' cleaned once a month. Consider it payment for saving my daughter and grandson's lives."

I placed my hand over my heart. "Thank you, Ester. I will take good care of it."

"Better yet," she said, eyes glittering, "kill an Indian with it."

CHAPTER

5

I stood atop a lone steep hill. Before me the flowering grasses of the prairie rolled in the wind like the Atlantic before a storm, and the enormous sky surrounded me like a pale blue shawl. I closed my eyes and enjoyed the warmth of the setting sun on my face and the cool breeze tickling my skin. I inhaled and basked in the unique scent of the prairie: flowers, dust, and very faintly, rain.

I turned and watched our wagon train make its way up the Western Trail. Far to the north and just in sight, the trail boss and the chuck wagon were setting up camp for the night. Roughly a half mile away from the night's campsite three schooners and five supply wagons bumped and rattled over the uneven ground. After a small gap, Amos Pike's unhappy herd of cattle stretched out for over a mile. The plaintive mooing of 750 cattle and the whistles and whoops of the cowboys driving them floated on the wind and to my ears. Try as I might, I could not escape the sound.

As far as I could see to the east were herds of cattle destined for the railheads in Kansas. We were a little apart and farther to the west by necessity. Our herd was not bound for the Kansas market but for Fort Sill in Indian Territory, for distribution to more remote forts as well as the Indians who had reluctantly given up their roving way of life for one reliant on the generosity of the government.

I pushed my wind-whipped hair from my face and saw a small retinue of two wagons and ten riders moving up our western flank.

"Well, well. It looks as if our Army escort has arrived," I said. Maureen would be relieved.

I thrilled at the thought of new people to talk to. My fellow travelers were pleasant enough, but ten days into the journey our nighttime conversation had lagged. Our sole fiddle player knew only two songs, and those not very well.

I turned back to the setting sun and marveled at how, in a few minutes, the scenery had changed. The dusty green of the swaying prairie grasses gave way to a sky ablaze with colors I had not seen since the sun set on the battlefield at Antietam. At the time, I credited the bloodied sky with God's anger at man's idiocy and hubris, at the wanton waste of life He witnessed that day. Here on the prairie I saw again the intense red color of an angry God, now tempered with beautiful purples, golds, and deep blues. I longed for the tools needed to sketch what I saw, to put these colors on paper so in years to come I could remember beauty and destruction are inexorably linked in nature and in the heart of man.

⌁

"Where have you been?" Maureen demanded when I entered the camp.

"On top of the world," I replied. I held out a spray of wildflowers. Maureen took them with disgust.

"One of these days you're going to wander off and be snatched up by them savages, mark my word." She shook the flowers in my face.

"Thank you for the flowers, Laura. They're beautiful." I intoned in an imitation of her Irish brogue. "I thought you'd like them."

Maureen would not be swayed from her point, so I let her make it. "They'll do all sorts of unspeakable things to you and I'll have to live with the vision of it my entire life."

"Don't be ridiculous, Maureen," I chided. I removed my old slouch hat and tossed it in the back of our wagon. "They wouldn't dare attack so close to the fort, nor this large of a train."

She lowered her voice. "They don't think like us, Katie. Mind you listen to me for once and stay close."

There was real fear in her eyes. Unlike me, she had taken Ester's stories about the Comanche and Kiowa as the gospel truth. It did not help that when we passed the many abandoned homesteads along the trail, Amos Pike became a raconteur, terrifying everyone with stories of his time as a Texas Ranger before the war. No storyteller worth their salt would shy away from making a tale larger and more colorful than the actual event, and savage Indian tales were ripe for elaboration. The more I heard about the atrocities of the Indians the more I had to believe at least some of it was true. However, Amos, his teamsters, and his cowboys made me feel safe. Maureen, on the other hand, was certain of our impending doom. With the Army arrived and with the knowledge we were less than a day's ride from Fort Richardson, I saw no need to argue with her. I put my arm around her shoulder. "If it will make you easy, I will stay nearer the wagon train."

"Thank you."

"I will shove cotton in my ears to muffle the sound of the cattle and pinch my nose against the smell."

"I don' even hear them anymore. You can amputate a limb without flinching, but the sound of mooing cattle gets on your nerves."

"You are not the first to think I am full of strange contradictions, and you will not be the last."

Maureen reached under the buckboard and handed my holster and gun to me. "Wear this."

"It does not fit."

"I had Herr Schlek punch a new notch for you." She shook the holster at me.

"Do you not trust when I say I won't wander off?"

"You've never listened to me before, why would you now?"

I took the holster and cinched it around my waist. It fit perfectly. Maureen stepped forward and tucked the extra leather beneath the belt. "There. Now I feel better."

Her goal accomplished, Maureen turned her attention to unhitching Piper and Púca from the wagon while I struggled to remove the gun from its holster. "I'm doing something wrong."

"Twist it around to the other side, so the handle faces front," Maureen said. She patted the oxen on the neck. "That's how Cornelius wears his."

"Cornelius doesn't strike me as an experienced gunfighter," I said. I twisted the belt around and drew the gun across my body. "Well, I'll be damned. It is easier."

"Katie!"

Everyone was too busy setting up camp to notice Maureen's slip. I glared at her in admonition.

"Now don't you go turning into a heathen because you're living on the frontier. I won't have it."

"Don't call me Katie," I said in an undertone. We stared at

each other, waiting for the other to crack. I did not want to fight with Maureen. I wanted to regain the tranquility from the hill. I holstered my gun. "I see the cavalry has arrived."

Maureen relaxed, sure of her victory. "None other than Uncle Billy himself."

"General Sherman?"

"In the flesh."

Maureen led the animals toward the creek while I unpacked the wagon. I could not help craning my neck in hopes of catching a glimpse of the general, though I did not expect to see him among the soldiers setting up camp for the night.

I set to my tasks by rote, thinking of General Sherman and his brazen march through Georgia to the sea. Southerners reviled him for leaving a swath of destruction behind him and for the audacity of gifting the city of Savannah to President Lincoln for Christmas in '64. His men loved him for his boldness in the field, his unwavering loyalty to the Union, and his firm belief the Southerners deserved what they got for the temerity of seceding from the Union. I admired him for doing what was necessary, no matter how repugnant, to break the will of the enemy and win the war. The campfire conversation between ex-Confederate Pike and General Sherman promised to be interesting.

By the time Maureen returned from watering Piper and Púca and gathering wood, our Dutch oven full of beans was hanging on the tripod, waiting for the fire. The ingredients for biscuits and a grinder full of coffee beans were on a crate, which served as our makeshift worktable. As Maureen worked on the fire, I took the kettle and a bucket to the creek for water.

I walked a little ahead of the campsite for water unspoiled by the animals and gently picked my way down the creek bank, using the trees as handholds and the exposed roots as stair steps, paying little attention to the creek itself. When I reached the edge, I discovered Sherman sitting in the middle of the creek, bare chested and smoking a cigar. I stumbled the remainder of the way down the bank and almost fell into the creek myself. My face flamed with embarrassment, more from my clumsiness than his nakedness.

Knowing it was what was expected of me, I averted my eyes. "Pardon me, sir. I did not know anyone was around."

"No. I expect you did not." Sherman's clothes hung haphazardly on the low-lying limb of a cottonwood tree, his red long johns standing out from the dark blue and gray of his uniform like a bloody gash. "Please, retrieve your water."

I smiled my thanks and filled my containers.

"I am William Sherman."

"Laura Elliston."

"Where are you from, Mrs. Elliston?"

"Boston, by way of London." Like Ester, my fellow travelers accepted my false history without comment or concern. In fact, I seemed to care more about telling my background than they did about hearing it. No questions were asked of me, nor did I ask questions of them. I suspected we all had our secrets.

"What brings you to Texas?"

"Opportunity and adventure."

He took a long drag of his cigar and appraised me, his eyes lingering on my gun.

"Have we met before?"

I straightened, immediately on my guard. Had Sherman seen my Wanted poster, or a newspaper article about me? It was a question I asked myself nearly every time I met someone new. I forced a smile. "I have not had the honor."

Of course a man like Sherman was unaffected by the compliment. He expected people to be honored to meet him, especially women. "You have met so many people, I suppose everyone you meet seems familiar."

It was a pathetic justification, but he appeared to be satisfied by it. He removed his cigar and used it to point to his clothes. "There is a bar of soap in my pants pocket. Would you be so kind as to throw it to me? Mind you do not throw it over my head. I would hate to have to make explanations to your husband."

I tossed the bar of soap to him perfectly, making a neat splash of water into his face. "I am not married, and have been quite capable of guarding my own virtue these many years."

He shoved the cigar in his mouth and nodded to my gun. "I imagine you are."

I executed a low curtsy, too pleased by half with the image the gun gave me. I doubted Maureen considered this particular protection when she forced the gun on me but would be satisfied with the benefit, nonetheless. I picked up the kettle and bucket to leave.

"Miss Elliston, please allow me to carry the bucket to your wagon. It is the least I can do for your service to me." He held the soap aloft.

I inclined my head, set the bucket on the ground, and scrambled up the side of the creek bank with as much grace as I could muster while holding a kettle full of water. A young soldier carrying a clean uniform for the general met me at the top of the bank.

"Ma'am."

I inclined my head and walked toward our wagon, where Maureen stirred an impressive fire. "Where's the rest?"

I decided to wait to tell her of Sherman. It would be worth it to see her face if Sherman delivered the bucket of water himself.

"It is being carried for me. The bank next to the creek is quite steep."

I ground the coffee, spooned it into the kettle, and set it over the fire to brew. I helped Maureen finish the biscuits. When the young soldier arrived with the water, our hands were covered in flour.

"With the general's compliments."

"Thank you, Private. Please, place it on the end of the wagon and thank the general as well."

The young man scurried off in the direction of a military ambulance. Maureen raised her eyebrows. "The general?"

"You should have fetched the water. You would have gotten the thrill of your life."

Maureen's eyes widened. "You don't mean!"

"He was covered, but only just."

"How did he look?"

I leaned close and scanned our surroundings as if I was about to impart important, private information. Maureen moved closer.

"Like a bare-chested man."

"Oh, you!"

"Hurry down to the creek, Maureen. Maybe you can catch him getting dressed."

"I'll do no such thing!"

"I know how well you like redheaded men. He might be the only one around for hundreds of miles."

"He's married!"

"Excellent point. Which is why I'm sure he'd welcome a little harmless flirting." I motioned at the countryside. "We women are in the minority out here, in case you haven't noticed."

"I've noticed." She looked in the direction of Cornelius

Warren's wagon. Cornelius lifted his bowler from his head with a flourish. Maureen scowled and turned to poke the fire. "Coffee'll be ready in a minute."

I waved to Cornelius. "I know I am out of practice, but I *do* believe Cornelius is wooing you, in his blustering way."

"Humph. If this is what the West is going to be like, men always looking out for a woman to make their life easier, well, I'm not gonna like it overmuch."

"Do you need my gun for protection?"

"I can handle myself, thank you."

"I am sure once we get settled the offers for your hand will slow from a flood to a steady trickle."

Maureen brandished the spoon she was holding. "You aren't so old I won't use this on you."

I moved out of the way, laughing. "You never did when I was a child and deserved it. Why would you now?"

She waved her hand at me as if swatting away a pesky fly and stirred the beans. "It's good to see you laugh again. Even if it is at my expense."

"It has been too long, hasn't it?" We sat on upturned crates with two mugs of coffee, waited for our biscuits to cook, and watched our fellow travelers set up camp.

The wagon train consisted of ten wagons: six loaded with supplies for the Army forts; a chuck wagon for Amos and his cowboys; ours; Cornelius and Anna's; and the Schleks', a German family of six and owners of a trailing menagerie of animals including goats, mules, pigs, and a bitch ready to whelp. Frau Schlek was eight months pregnant. She was so hearty and hale I suspected she could stop, have her baby, and continue without missing a beat. The cowboys had a pool going for which would give birth first, her or her dog; I picked the dog.

When the wagon train had pulled out of Austin ten days

earlier, I told Cornelius we were a sad excuse for a vanguard for a new town. He laughed and assured me the success of Timberline, Colorado, did not rest on our little group entirely. A business partner of his was heading out from Saint Louis with over one hundred families any day now. I was skeptical of his claims, but held my peace. I needed to get as far from civilization as possible and Cornelius Warren and his overeager optimism was my only option.

Maureen watched the Warrens through narrowed eyes. Anna Warren tried to work while her father buzzed around her like a hummingbird trying to decide what flower to settle on. I knew Maureen well enough to see she was itching to go over there and take them in hand.

"You and I make a good team," I said.

"Huh?"

"Beans and biscuits cooking, animals taken care of. We work well together."

"That we do."

"The farther we get from civilization, the safer I feel."

Maureen nodded. "No one in Texas cares about a rich man dying in New York City. They'd probably give you a medal if they found out."

"Plenty would turn me in for the reward."

"Lucky there's no mention of yer troubles out here."

Maureen would know. She had taken it upon herself to check every Wanted poster in Austin and did not find mine. She suggested more than once that the discovery of the dead woman had killed the scandal before it had the chance to spread too far west. She may have been right, but like today with Sherman, I still saw suspicion in everyone's eyes. Not for the first time, I wondered if this fear would lurk in the back of my mind for the rest of my life.

Maureen sipped her coffee, her eyes darting frequently to the Warrens' camp. I was not sure how much of Maureen's interest in Cornelius was due to the man he was or to the man Maureen wanted to mold him into, but I knew she would never leave me if I did not give her a gentle push. I was an adult; I could survive on my own. Though she would always try to change me, she had molded me as much as she could. She needed to move on to her next project and hopefully find some happiness along the way. It was time to give my blessing.

"Maureen."

"Hmm?"

"I believe the biscuits are ready."

She lifted the lid to the skillet and nodded appreciatively. "So they are. You might make a cook yet, Laura."

"I just might. Cornelius and Anna, on the other hand, could use some help."

"Anna's a bright girl. She'll learn."

"Not with Cornelius teaching her. You should take them under your wing."

Maureen's brow furrowed, but her face reddened. "What are you on about, Katie Girl?"

"Don't play coy with me. You know very well what I'm on about." Maureen pressed her lips together and stared into her coffee. I put my mug down and knelt in front of her. "Don't be embarrassed. I'm so very happy for you. You deserve to find love."

"Harumph. Love. More like he needs a woman to take care of him."

"So what if he does? Taking care of people is what you're best at. You took care of my father after my mother died. Raised me. Kept me well in hand for the past ten years."

"And a more difficult job I've never had."

"Think how much more compliant Anna will be. It will practically be a vacation for you."

Maureen laughed, but tears leaked out of her eyes. "Do you not need me anymore, Katie Girl?"

"I'll always need your love and support. But, it is time you and I both step out on our own a bit." I squeezed Maureen's hand. "We will be in the same town, we could even arrange to be next door to each other, if you want. I daresay nothing much about our relationship will change. It's just you'll be sharing a bed with Cornelius."

Now Maureen's face reddened so deeply I was afraid she would spontaneously combust. "We'll not talk about that."

I patted her hand and stood. "I've read books on the act and picked up some rather interesting tips treating Camille's girls."

Maureen gasped and stood. "Katie!"

"You really need to stop calling me that."

"You need to remember you're a lady and ladies do not talk about those things. I'm going to check that Cornelius and Anna haven't burned their beans."

I suppressed a smile. I knew raising Maureen's pique would push her into action.

"Eat those biscuits before they get cold," she said, and stalked off to take Cornelius and Anna under her wing.

CHAPTER 6

After supper, everyone gravitated together to talk, listen to the fiddler play his two songs, and if we were lucky, eat a bit of the dessert Frau Schlek always had left over. On most nights dessert was apple crumb, due to the barrel of apples in their wagon, though I contributed wild berries whenever I came across them in my ramblings.

With shawls wrapped around our shoulders Maureen and I moved to the Schleks' fire, always the largest blaze thanks to the exuberance their youngest showed in gathering firewood. Frau Schlek was telling Maureen the recipe for her fruit crumble when General Sherman and a young officer approached.

"May I join you?" the General asked.

"Of course," Amos Pike said, with more generosity than I expected. Herr Schlek stood and offered the general his chair.

"Thank you."

Sherman talked to the Schleks about their journey. His young lieutenant stood near me, taking in the entire group. A wispy dark mustache struggled to banish the boyishness of his baby-smooth skin. His clear, callow eyes lingered on Anna Warren, obviously pleased at the sight of a beautiful young girl near his own age. Anna's face was flushed, whether from the fire or the lieutenant's gaze I did not know. Since she studiously avoided looking in his direction, I had my suspicions.

"What is your name, Lieutenant?" I asked.

He was well bred enough to shift his focus from Anna to me with a polite smile. No doubt he considered his duty as an officer and a gentleman to humor the middle-aged spinster. I suppressed a smile. "Lieutenant Beau Kindle, ma'am."

"Lieutenant Kindle is readying to see his uncle for the first time," Sherman interjected. "How long has it been, Lieutenant?"

"Eight years, sir."

"Long time," Sherman said. "Most like he won't be as you remember him, Kindle."

"Where is your uncle, Lieutenant Kindle?" I asked.

"He is stationed at Fort Richardson, ma'am. Captain William Kindle," he said, as if I would recognize the name.

"Fought with him at Antietam. He got a bad wound there, if I remember correctly."

"Yes, sir, he did."

I pulled my shawl closer against the chill the name gave me. Antietam. The worst—and best—day of my life. It was the day my father received the wound that would eventually kill him, the last day of my masquerade as a male orderly, and the day I realized my true calling as a doctor. As Sherman took control of the campfire conversation, I wondered if I had helped treat Lieutenant Kindle's uncle.

Sherman spent the next hour talking to us, asking where we came from, where we were going, and sharing more than a few stories of his time in California. He was an amiable fire-side companion while he was on the subject of the joys of the West and the bright future for the emigrants. When conversation turned to his journey in Texas and what he saw of the Indian problem, the aspect of his personality that expected to be deferred to on every subject and had been polished to a bright shine by years of Army command emerged. I watched Amos while Sherman railed against politicians so concerned with ridding their state of "lying, cheating Yankees" that they would fabricate stories of massacres and raids to divert soldiers from the important task of Reconstruction. Pike, at last, could take no more.

"Fabricate stories? Are you blind, man?"

"Blind? I have seen nothing to indicate Indians are raiding up and down the line of settlements."

"What do you make of the abandoned homesteads you've passed since San Antone? You think those people just up and left? These same salt-of-the-earth immigrants you think are going to make the West great? Somehow the lily-livered ones just happened to settle in a line out here? Those that weren't killed in their homes and in their fields were scared east. And why? Because your precious Army don't know how to fight them and because Yankee politicians are more concerned with taking their pound of flesh from us than helping us!"

Sherman's face resembled so many New York granite statues. "My army knows how to fight. Have you forgotten the lesson the Army taught you rebels six years ago?"

"I haven't forgotten the swath of wasteland you left through Georgia, nor has any other right-minded Southerner. Maybe the reason you don't see anything alarming out here is because it coincides with your idea of warfare."

"From what I hear, it's as likely to be white men as Indians." When Pike didn't immediately answer, Sherman pressed his point. "White men paid by ex-Confederates to murder innocent people to draw us away from Reconstruction."

"Reconstruction ended here a year ago," Cornelius said.

"Indeed. So why are Rebel gangs still raiding?" Sherman

asked. "Because the settlers are easy pickings? Or because there is money in it?"

"They could be carpetbaggers as easy as Rebels," Amos said. "And don't you worry. Those white men will swing for what they're doing. What we don't like is the government taking care of Indians, and then the savages turning around and massacrin' our people."

"The peace policy—" Sherman said.

"The peace policy." Amos sneered. "That might be the worst-conceived idea the government has ever had, and that's saying something. Even your Quaker up in Fort Sill thinks it's a failure. And he's the one administering it!"

"These Indian stories are all blown out of proportion."

Pike shook his head in wonderment. "You aren't going to believe it until you see it for yourself. It's a terrible thing more innocent people are going to have to die brutal deaths to get their government to believe there's a problem. I only hope the Comanche has the politeness to murder a bunch of farmers when you're in the neighborhood."

"It's only a matter of time before our men beat them."

"How do you propose to do that? Line them up behind a fence and fire on them until time to charge? That ain't how Indians fight. Never have, never will. You ain't fighting one army with a bunch of commanders of the same mind. You're fighting different nations and tribes within the nations. You don't know where or when they will attack because they don't think like we do. There is only one way to stop them."

"Please, Mr. Pike, tell us."

"Kill or hang 'em all."

"Even the women and children?"

"They don't care about killing our women and children, why should we care about killing theirs?" Amos said.

"That's barbaric," Anna said.

"It is. Nothing else will stop them."

"I know our soldiers, the quality and resilience of the American man, will win in the end," Sherman said.

Though I agreed with the sentiment, it was said with such dismissive arrogance even I was offended.

Amos stood. "I'm glad you have such confidence. I ain't seen no one since Jack Hayes who could outsmart an Indian." He walked off.

Maureen was pale and her hand shook as she lifted her cup to drink. Damn these men for scaring her with their stories. I changed the subject by addressing a nearby cowboy with his arm in a sling. "Walter, how is your arm?"

"Fine, Doc. Though it itches a bit."

"That's normal. I'll remove the cast in a week or two."

"Doc?" Sherman interjected.

My back straightened. My midwife ruse had abruptly ended when I set Walter's compound fracture. Everyone in the wagon train took it in stride. Sherman didn't strike me as the type of man who would approve of a female physician. "Yes, General. I am a doctor."

"I have heard rumors of female doctors in New York, but I never put much stock in such an outlandish idea. All the more reason to get away from that cesspool, I say."

"I trained in London," I said. Sherman shrugged, as if it was the same to him.

"She did a fine job on my arm," Walter said.

"Hell, son, I can set a broken bone. There's not much skill in it."

"When the bone is sticking up out of the skin, I guess there is," Frau Schlek said. "I don't know a man who could have fixed it."

"Thank you, Frau Schlek. Do not bother trying to convince General Sherman of my skills. Men rarely believe a woman could be better than a man at a profession such as medicine. Their doubt only makes me more determined to prove them wrong."

"Let's hope you never get the chance," Sherman laughed.

"If there are more reckless cowboys out here like Walter, unfortunately I will."

"Now, ma'am, I told you my horse got spooked by a snake."

"Yeah, the mysterious, disappearin' snake," another cowboy said.

"Did you hear of the female doctor in New York who killed a man?" Beau Kindle said.

I forced myself to stay relaxed and turned my attention to Lieutenant Kindle. "No."

"She killed him out of jealousy," Beau Kindle said with enthusiasm. At Sherman's expression of disgust, Beau turned red and clarified without the eagerness in his voice. "My sister wrote to me about it."

"I don't know the details," I said, "but it is difficult for me to believe a doctor would kill another person willingly and knowingly."

"Come, now," Sherman said. "People will do anything to survive."

"A romantic disappointment is hardly life or death."

"It's hard to believe a woman would be able to kill a man in cold blood," Cornelius said.

"How would she be able to overpower him?" Herr Schlek asked.

"She poisoned him," Beau said.

Poison?

"Then she bludgeoned him with a candlestick to make sure."

I didn't need to look at Maureen to know she was panicking. I had to hope she would stay quiet and no one would notice her fear, or if they did, assume it was from talk of Indians. Her fear of the Comanche was well known to our group.

"I refuse to believe it," I said.

"Why, did you know her?" Sherman asked.

"No. As I said, I trained in London. I do not believe it because she was a doctor. Our oath is 'Do no harm.'"

"You've obviously never been crossed in love," Sherman said with a laugh.

"I have known plenty of women who have, and none of them have murdered their lovers."

"What happened to the woman?" Anna asked.

"She was found murdered a few days later," Beau said.

"Just deserts if you ask me," Sherman said.

I stood. He was reprehensible. "If you will excuse me, I need to check on the animals." Maureen rose to follow but I stopped her. "Stay and rest," I said. We did not need the group to see us walk off and huddle together like criminals. Plus, I needed to be alone.

Maureen sat back down. Lieutenant Kindle took my spot next to Anna and tried to start a conversation. Cornelius sat next to Maureen. Though she blushed, Maureen stayed put and didn't look vexed with his presence for the first time.

I found Púca and Piper asleep on their feet. I put my hand on Púca's neck to steady myself and took a deep breath. I thought back over the conversation and believed I had handled myself well, given no indication of my connection to the story. And what a story it was. James had not mentioned poison or a candlestick, only a fireplace poker. Which was correct? It didn't matter. The murderess was dead and it was merely a campfire story for men to tell about the idiocy and weakness of women.

I bristled at the idea that jealousy and murder would be Catherine Bennett's legacy instead of the strength and determination of an intelligent woman succeeding at a man's profession.

"Dr. Elliston."

Amos Pike walked up, a large wad of tobacco bulging in his cheek and a flask of whisky in his hand.

"Mr. Pike."

"Would you like some?" He leaned against Piper and held the flask out over her neck.

"Thank you." I sipped the whisky. I held the back of my hand against my mouth to stifle a cough before handing it back.

Amos grinned. "Wish I had bourbon to offer you." He leaned his arms on Piper's neck.

I cleared my throat, but my voice still sounded like a croak. "Why?"

"You give bourbon to people you're trying to impress. Whisky is for Mexicans, Indians, and old Rangers."

"You were one of the best, I hear."

"Believe none of what you hear and half of what you see."

"Are you saying Ester elaborated?"

He took a long pull from his flask. "I doubt it. Ester's a fine woman. There ain't no lie in her." Amos patted Piper on the neck and stared at the ox without seeing her. "It leaves a mark, witnessing something like that." He offered the flask to me. I took another sip. "Ain't goin' to apologize for what I done to avenge it, either."

"No one is asking you to."

Amos drank again and eyed me. "You're quite a woman"—he paused—"Laura."

There was too much emphasis on my Christian name to be coincidental. His smile was sly, but nonthreatening and with a fair amount of admiration. He knew. He knew who I was.

"Did you hear our conversation?" I nodded in the direction of the group.

"Some."

"You think I am her."

He turned his head and spit a stream of tobacco juice onto the ground. He wiped his hand down his long, full, gray mustache. "I saw the poster, what, two months ago? Never forget a face. Not a good likeness, is it?" Amos's gaze traveled over my face and down, lingered appreciatively, before returning. His eyes were alive beneath the brim of his hat. "You're softer in person."

"I did not kill him."

I held his gaze while he studied me. His expression of amused respect slipped to something like disappointment. "No, I don't suppose you did. But you've got it in you."

"What?"

"Killing."

"I do not."

He spit another stream of tobacco, wiped his mustache. "Laura, most everyone comes out here's got it in them. Only they ain't been pushed to the point yet."

"Are you going to turn me in?"

"Well, I'll be honest. I haven't decided yet."

I tried to swallow the rock forming in my throat. Amos was an amiable man. I'd liked him—up until this point. I half-expected him to deny the urge to betray me, to be offended at the idea.

"Five hundred dollars is a lot of money."

And there it was. I kicked myself for my naiveté. If I thought every man in New York would turn me in for $500, why wouldn't every man in the West do the same?

"Then again, I have no cause to be judging others for killing. And one less Yankee in the world ain't a bad thing."

I opened my mouth to defend George Langton, but clasped it shut. Amos Pike didn't care about the individual man, but at the death of an abstract idea like a Yankee, he cheered.

He looked me over again. "I could be persuaded."

It took a moment for his meaning to sink in. To Amos, his proposition was benevolent; he would keep quiet if I would be his nighttime companion on the drive. But there would be no guarantee he wouldn't use me before turning me in. Worse, I had nothing against him to make him follow through on his promise. I had little choice, and he knew it.

I suddenly hated him, this middle-aged man who looked old, with bowed legs and large hands, scarred and calloused from years of hard work, who wore a sweat-stained hat to cover thinning, gray hair. I would not acquiesce easily.

"Why aren't you still rangering? Fighting the Indians?" I asked.

"It's a young man's job."

My laughter was harsh. "Maybe Ester was right when she called you a coward."

He drank from his flask and punched the cork into its mouth with the palm of his hand. "I've no doubt you're a sharp woman, Laura, but mark my words, if your mind don't control your tongue, you won't be long for this world." The threat was more frightening because Amos's expression and voice still held the benevolence from before. "You know why I don't ranger anymore?"

I remained silent.

"There ain't no money in it." He toasted me with his flask and walked away.

CHAPTER

7

Sherman and his retinue left before dawn, with a promise of sending a detachment to escort us to Fort Richardson. Pike declined, assuring General Sherman that his teamsters and cowboys were well able to protect us. Sherman was adamant, not only because it was the Army's task to protect settlers and wagon trains, but also to show his authority over Amos.

To calm Maureen's fears about my wandering, I walked beside the wagon while she walked with Frau Schlek. I was anxious to ramble away from the train, to get some distance so I could think. The decision I made during a sleepless night did not stand up in the light of day. If I acquiesced to Amos Pike, I would be no better than a whore. If I refused, he might turn me in when we reached Fort Richardson.

It was this question that was vexing me when Anna joined me. I forced a smile. "Hello, Anna."

"May I walk with you, Dr. Elliston?"

I couldn't very well refuse without alienating the girl. I agreed, reasoning her company would distract me from my looming downfall.

"Please, call me Laura. I only insist on Dr. Elliston with those it makes uncomfortable."

"Laura. Isn't this a glorious day?"

I noticed the bright blue sky spotted with fluffy clouds for the first time. "It is. It makes one believe in endless possibilities."

"You sound like my father."

"You don't share his optimism?"

"It can be quite annoying."

"Do you like to temper his optimism with gloom?"

"No, just realism."

"What an outlook for such a young girl."

"I am seventeen. I prefer to think of it as balance. Imagine if both my father and I were always looking for a better angle, for a better life over the horizon? Nothing useful would get done. My father is thinking of lunch before he arrives at the breakfast table."

"A dreamer."

"Yes."

"You put his dreams into action?"

"I do as much as a seventeen-year-old girl with little education can do."

"Were you not tutored at home?" Anna had the carriage and speech of a well-born girl.

"Until I was eleven, yes. When the war ended we moved to New Orleans. Engaging a tutor was always something he meant to do, but he never got around to it. What I have learned since has been through my own studies."

We walked in silence. Something kept me from asking directly about her mother. Instead, I searched for a viable excuse for Cornelius's neglect of his daughter's education. Sensing my struggle, she provided one for me.

"He never said, but I suspect he couldn't find a woman willing to teach the daughter of a carpetbagger. Putting me in boarding school was out of the question. He did not want me away from him."

"My father had no such qualms."

"You went to boarding school?"

"Not precisely. I went to live with my aunt in England. I was tutored at home with her daughter."

"How exciting."

"It would have been if I hadn't been under the chaperonage of my aunt. I had my cousin Charlotte to keep me company. She made England bearable."

"How long were you there?"

"Seven years."

"What brought you back to the States?"

"My father. The threat of war. A *scandal*."

"Would it be impolite to ask about the scandal?"

"Yes, it would." I laughed. "My aunt's design in taking me back to England with her was to make a respectable woman of me, and if I made an eligible match, so much the better. My time in England confirmed I did not want a conventional life or marriage."

"You don't wish to be married?"

I considered her question for some time. I finally replied. "If I could find a man to accept me as a doctor, woman, lover, and wife, in that order, I might well consider it."

Anna blushed. She was so young and innocent. I wondered how long her innocence would last in a rough frontier town.

"What do you want out of this move to Timberline?"

"I want my father to be happy."

"What about yourself?"

Anna shrugged. "I'm not sure I'm fit for anything other than being a wife. I have little formal education and no skills."

"You would make an excellent midwife. Or nurse."

"But not a doctor?"

"I'm not sure you have the personality to be a doctor."

"Meaning what?"

"You have to not care what people think of you. You have to be able to ignore what people say to you. You have to love medicine above all else. Most important, you will have to be twice as good as every man to get a fraction of the credit."

"You make it sound so appealing, how could I refuse?" Anna chided. After a few steps, she said, "In seriousness, what made you choose this path?"

I gently prodded Piper and thought how best to answer. The safest course would be to tell her nothing. Catherine Bennett was dead, found floating in the Hudson, and so were her reasons for becoming a doctor. Why take the risk by telling her story, even if I didn't use her name? Had I inadvertently been leaving little clues across Texas for Beatrice Langton's Pinkertons to find if they were indeed following me? I did not think so. Anna's face was full of frank openness, curiosity, and admiration. I wanted to believe I could trust her. I also needed to touch the bravery of a woman I felt less and less connected to the farther into the frontier I traveled.

"My father was a doctor. A surgeon. As a child, I watched and admired what he did. He encouraged my curiosity. When in England, I heard many lectures on science and medicine and was inspired by the great medical discoveries. However, I was young and easily distracted in those days."

I paused before I went on. "The idea was always there, lingering. But, it was during the war when I realized I had talent."

"The war? Were you a nurse?"

"Of sorts. I was rejected as a nurse at the onset of the war because I was too young and too handsome. My father would not intercede on my behalf because he did not want me anywhere near the battlefield. I have always despised being told what I could or could not do, another necessary character trait for female physicians. I went to a rag shop and bought ratty clothes, cut my hair, and presented myself to my father as a male orderly."

Anna's eyes were round. "You didn't."

"Indeed, I did. He was furious."

"I can imagine."

"Because I cut my hair."

"Not because of the danger?" I shook my head in response. "Your hair is beautiful," Anna said, dutifully.

"It is like my mother's," I said, touching the long blond braid that fell from my slouch hat. "He ranted and raved about my 'damnable independence' and my complete lack of respect for his authority or society's mores. When he realized I was going ahead with my ruse with or without his help, he went along to help protect me. I became his orderly, his right-hand man, so to speak."

I swallowed. I had never before told this part of the story. "We were at Antietam. The battle was over but the wounded kept pouring in. I thought they would never stop. The carnage was staggering. I was throwing a leg onto the pile of amputated limbs when I saw an officer sitting by a tree, drunk. My apron was covered with blood and the sounds of the dying soldiers on the battlefield filled my ears. The smell of charred flesh and blood was there, too, but by that time I had gotten used to it. I still smell it, even today. Not always. It assaults me at the strangest times. It's as if it lives deep within me, festers there, rotting."

Anna gasped. Her expression was horrified. "I apologize." I tried to lighten my voice, to regain a storytelling timbre. "The officer. The sight of this unscathed officer getting drunk infuriated me, as you can imagine. I marched over, intent to find out his regiment and report him when he turned his head. The left side of his face had been sliced open by a saber." I ran my finger from my hairline at my temple down to my jaw. "Not only was he drunk, but he was in shock from his wound and from a blow he had taken to the back of his head."

I took a deep breath and continued.

"He was like every other man haunted by war except for his eyes. When he looked up at me, drunk and barely sensible, I somehow knew there was more to this man's melancholy than simply war. It wasn't my job to worry about that, however. I managed to get him up off the ground and into a camp chair. My father was away in the field to attend more wounded and the other doctors were busy with other men. The officer wasn't in danger of dying, but I wanted to help him. I decided to do what I could for him myself.

"I knew I did not have much time. When a doctor saw I was treating a brevet colonel they would pull me away. That was the least of what they would do to a lowly orderly treating an officer. I used whisky to clean his wound, the needle and thread, and my hands. I gave the rest to the officer, told him to drink up, and sewed up his face."

Anna's expression of astonishment made me laugh. "Do you know how to sew?" I asked her.

"Yes."

"You could have done it, too," I said.

"No, I could not."

"Oh, Anna, yes, you could have. You have no idea the depth of your strength until you are truly tested."

I thought back to Amos's comment from the night before, that most of us have the ability to kill and how I was saying much the same thing to Anna; we could rise above our weakness and do the unthinkable. I adjusted my holster. Maybe I did have the ability to take a man's life. The thought unnerved me.

"I hope to never be tested like that," Anna said.

I returned my focus to Anna and my story. "His injury was far from the worst I had seen. While I was sewing, the man stared at me with his bleary but intelligent eyes. They were beautiful, despite being so melancholy.

" 'Why are you smiling?' he asked.

" 'Was I? Do not nod,' I said. 'I suppose I was thinking of my aunt. She would be appalled at the application of my needle-point skills.'

" 'She would not think it admirable you are helping a fallen officer?'

"I laughed at the thought of the expression on Aunt Emily's face if she saw me amid the carnage of a battlefield. 'She would think I could use my talents in a much more acceptable way.' I told him to be quiet so I could stitch his cheek.

"While I was working on him the rest of the world evaporated. The agony and death surrounding me. The sounds of dying men. The smell. What mattered most was fixing his face. When I was finished I knew I had done as good or better job than any doctor I worked with. I knew I could do any of it. It was euphoric."

"Did the officer live?"

"He came to find me a few days later. He wanted to thank the nurse who had sewn him up."

"Nurse?"

"Yes. It seems in his alcoholic haze he saw straight through my disguise. I don't suppose it helped when I talked of needle-point to him. I didn't remember telling him about Aunt Emily until months later." I shook my head, still wondering why I had let my guard down and shared the story with the man.

I smiled at Anna and continued my story. "The doctors and surgeons I worked with were livid, not only because I was a woman but also because I had fooled them so completely. That was the end of my war experience. It mattered little. My father was injured while out in the field and I needed to take care of him. Look." I pointed. "The river."

Ahead of us Amos Pike was organizing the crossing of the Trinity River, the last major crossing until the Red and the last before Fort Richardson. Maureen was walking back from the Warrens' wagon. Her face was flushed. *When did she move to walk with Cornelius?* I wondered.

"Do you not trust me to get Piper and Púca across?" I winked at Anna.

"No."

"I am deeply wounded. Here," I said, placing my hat on Maureen's head. "Your face is red from the sun."

Maureen took the stick from my hand without comment and gently prodded the oxen. Anna and I stopped and watched her.

"You do know your father is courting Maureen?"

Anna nodded.

"Do you mind?"

"No. Do you?"

"Not if it makes her happy." I sighed. "I suppose we should give them our blessing."

"Tonight at dinner."

I nodded and asked the question I had pondered for a few days. "Would you be interested in helping me with my practice?"

"Nursing?"

"At first. You can study the one medical book I have. If you are good enough, and interested, we can write off for more books, and you can apprentice with me."

"You would do that for me?"

"It will be as much for me as you."

"When can we start?"

I grinned. "Let's get across the river first."

"I should go help Father," Anna said. She trotted off a few steps before turning back. "Thank you. *Thank you*, Laura."

I smiled and waved and watched her run back to her father, a youthful spring in her step.

PART TWO

FORT RICHARDSON

CHAPTER

8

I watched the Comanche massacre my wagon train from the safety of a buffalo wallow.

They came with the setting sun at their backs and in the wagon train's eyes. At first I thought it was a mirage until the trembling ground beneath my feet, the war whoops carrying across the plains, and the skittishness of the animals told me it was all too real.

The trembling terror of war paralyzed me, a terror I had worked diligently to forget. I lay facedown on the ground and covered my head with my arms. The sweet aroma of the wildflowers I'd been picking became cloying, sickly sweet, but did nothing to mask the smell of death that blew across the prairie, down into the buffalo wallow, and wrapped its arms around me like an old friend. I closed my eyes and prayed this was a dream, that I wasn't hearing the gruesome noises of death I had struggled so hard to forget. I mumbled long-forgotten prayers as my bladder released.

The screams of the victims and the whoops of the Indians intermingled in a hellish cacophony. Gunshots rang out. Harnesses jingled. Oxen brayed. Men yelled. A dog barked, yelped, fell silent. Far above the din, someone screamed my name.

I sat up on my knees and peered above the tall grass surrounding me in my natural fortress. The chaotic scene that greeted me burned into my memory like a brand. Our ten wagons were strewn over a quarter of a mile, some toppled over and attached to the dead or dying oxen, some flying across the prairie trying to escape. Indians chased those, and within a few feet, the teamsters were dragged from their perches and to the ground. If the fall from the moving schooner didn't kill them, the Indian did. Blood flew through the air, and after a soul-tearing scream, the Indian held aloft the scalp of their victim.

"Laura!"

Through the carnage, I saw four Indians riding away to the east. Anna lay across the lap of a retreating Indian who wore my slouch hat. Anna reached out toward me and screamed my name again. I took a step forward, but was stopped by another bloodcurdling cry.

Rifle aloft, Amos Pike rode into the center of the massacre, shooting repeatedly as he charged. Two Indians dropped before the big Indian with the fresh scalp wielded his gun like a club and knocked Amos from his horse. Semiconscious, he was dragged by one arm to a broken wagon wheel. The large Indian tied Amos's body to the wheel, his arms and legs forming a large "X" while another Indian built a fire amid the surrounding rubble. As the fire caught, the Indians roamed the wreckage, searching for survivors.

I couldn't move, nor could I look away. Fear did not paralyze me, cowardice did. I did not want to die and I knew if I moved, I would. I covered my ears in a vain attempt to block out the sounds of the charnel house a hundred yards away but it grew louder and louder, vibrating the ground until the sound surrounded me.

I heard something that had been haunting every waking

hour of my life for two weeks: the braying of cattle. This time, the sound had a desperate note to it. I sat up again and saw 750 head of cattle stampeding in my direction, driven by Amos Pike's cowboys, their faces sweat streaked and enraged.

A few cattle veered off from the group and threatened to overrun me, but the main mass of cattle put their heads down and charged straight through the destroyed wagon train, overrunning whatever was in their way and stampeding any victim unlucky enough to be alive. The Indians, while surprised, were not defeated, merely momentarily distracted. A few ran with the herd, others mounted their horses and let the stampede run its course. Their horses were eager to give chase, but the Indians held them in check. The Indians turned against the charging cowboys who had been shooting their pistols into the air. They were now trying to shoot stationary Indians while they galloped forward. The Indians leveled their bows and let their arrows fly. Every cowboy, save one, fell from his horse. The last cowboy was chased by the nearest Indian, tackled bodily from his horse, and killed with a few swift blows of his hatchet.

The cattle were gone, leaving in their wake deathly silence and a haze of dust lit by the blazing wagon fires. Through the swirling dust, I saw the Indians lift Amos into the air. He was conscious now, blood running down his forehead from the gash where his scalp used to be. He knew before I did what the Indians intended. With brave defiance, he screamed, "I'll see you in hell!" The Indians laughed and threw him into the fire.

The sounds of Amos's screams reverberated in my head. I wondered, later, if it was Amos's screams I heard or my own, because at that moment, the Indians turned in my direction. In one fluid movement, the largest Indian was on his horse and riding toward me, Amos's scalp flapping against his leg. I could not move. The gun holstered on my hip was forgotten.

I watched Death approach. Everything I had accomplished, every bit of new ground I had broken was rendered moot, was to be destroyed at the hands of an Indian. There was no one left to mourn me, to miss me, to wonder what could have been. I thought of the mother I never knew and the father I missed so dearly and of Maureen, most assuredly dead and waiting for me on the other side, a chastisement on her lips for wandering away from the wagon train. I closed my eyes as the gunshot rang out.

The familiar jingle of cavalry, the pounding of horses' hooves, and the welcome notes of a bugle sounding charge disoriented me. For a moment, I was back at Antietam. When I opened my eyes I saw the Indians mounted and riding off. A small regiment of black soldiers, led by two white officers, ran past me and after the savages, leaving me alone staring at the wreckage of my future, the sole survivor.

⤬∞⤬

It was not a conscious decision on my part to move toward the carnage, but something—a hidden hand, the thought there might be someone I could help—propelled me forward. I stumbled and fell heavily to the ground, the churned earth pillowing my fall. I lay there, resting my cheek on the dark, loamy soil and considered never moving again, of welcoming the death I had embraced only moments before. Feeble moaning cut through the unnatural silence. With dread, I picked myself up and moved forward.

I hobbled over the uneven ground. The smell of blood, burning flesh, and cow manure surrounded me. Amos had long since stopped screaming. All that remained was the crackle and pop of his burning flesh. I turned my back on the pyre. He was beyond my help.

I swallowed a sob and moved forward to find Maureen.

She lay in the middle of the wreckage, Cornelius a few feet away. A savage had taken a hatchet to Cornelius and left his torso a pulpy mess. He had not been scalped, unlike Maureen. Flies were swarming around the bloody mess that was once Maureen's face. The face, which had over the years offered love and support, judgment and condemnation in equal measure was now missing the bottom half, so turning her death mask into a grotesque half grin. Somehow I knew she had been alive when they had taken her scalp, that they had chopped away the bottom of her face to stifle her screams to me.

I clamped my hand over my mouth to keep from vomiting. The feeble moans of the living stiffened my resolve.

I found a coarse blanket nearby and laid it over Maureen and Cornelius. I stared at the flowers I still clutched in my hand, wondered where they had come from, before remembering. I'd planned on tying a ribbon around them and presenting them to Maureen at dinner, with my blessing. I placed them on the blanket and moved on.

I found Frau Schlek staring vacantly into the sky, her hands futilely holding organs spilling out of the gash where her unborn baby should have been. The baby lay next to the blood-smeared wagon, his tiny head crushed, his cord still attached to his mother. Herr Schlek's body was a few feet away, his head farther away still. Their four children were nowhere to be found.

Frau Schlek looked at me. Her mouth opened and closed, and with a Herculean effort, she choked out two words. "My baby."

I knelt down beside her and cradled her head in my lap. "It's a boy." My voice broke on the last word. "A strong baby boy."

She smiled the beatific smile of a new mother and closed her eyes. I stayed with her until she died, stroking her hair and talking in a soothing voice of nothing in particular. I placed the broken body of her baby in her arms and covered them with a quilt from their wagon.

My circuit of the wreckage confirmed what I'd already known: everyone was dead. Four arrows poked out of Walter's chest like pins in a pincushion. The cook's tongue was cut out, his scalp taken as well. The anger and brutality of the Indians was plain on every corpse I found. There was no one to help.

I returned to Maureen and Cornelius. Blood had seeped through the blanket where Maureen's face had been. I stared insensibly at their bodies, barely registering the rumble of thunder in the distance. A light breeze ruffled the flowers. A gust followed, blowing the flowers from the bodies.

My gaze traveled to my wagon, somehow still upright. Piper and Púca lay motionless in the braces, their legs tangled with each other's. I walked to the back of the wagon and removed the bucket of water. How it had survived without toppling, I did not know. I walked over to Amos and threw the water on his funeral pyre. It did little good. I returned to my wagon, replaced the bucket, and stood there.

There was no one to help. No one to save.

My wagon shuddered and lurched forward. I jumped back, looked around frantically, expecting the Indians to have returned. The scent of roasting meat and silence greeted me. The wagon lurched again, followed by a long, plaintive bellow. I walked cautiously to the front of the wagon where Púca struggled to stand on a broken leg. Blood coated her neck, from Piper or another wound, I didn't know. It didn't matter. Finally, a creature I could help.

I pulled my gun from its holster, aimed, and shot Púca in the head.

CHAPTER
9

The smoke from the barrel of my gun left a jagged path as I lowered my trembling arm.

"Ma'am?"

A young cavalry officer sat on a blown horse right outside the line of wreckage. His wispy mustache hung limp with sweat. Dirt coated his baby face, though it did not camouflage his concern.

"Lieutenant Kindle."

"Are there any survivors?"

"No. Only me. Ten dead. The four children have been taken, as was Anna." I choked on her name. I turned away to regain my composure. I picked up the bucket and walked toward the river.

"Where are you going?"

"To get water."

The river was farther away than I remembered. I trailed my hand over the tops of the tall prairie grass, trying to forget the scene behind me, but finding no solace in the beauty around me.

The jingle of bit and creak of saddle signaled the man's arrival. "Ma'am." The voice was deep, confident in the way men in command are, but with an underlying gentleness I didn't expect. Gentleness and pity would break my composure. I kept walking.

"I need to get water."

I heard the soldier dismount his horse and limp through the grass toward me. "My men will do that." He grasped the handle of my bucket and tugged so I would stop. I could smell the mud of the riverbank, see the tufts of cottonwood chaff floating in the air, hear the frogs croaking as if the world had not just ended, as if this were any other day.

He pulled the bucket from my hand. "You've done enough."

I rounded on him. "Done enough? I didn't do anything. Save anyone. They're dead, while I am still here, as useless as I've always been accused of being."

He studied me out of one eye, half in profile, as if trying to place me, or understand me. I was familiar enough with the puzzled expression of doubting men to predict where this conversation was heading. I did not have the energy or the brazenness to argue with the men who had saved my life.

"I apologize."

"I wish we'd arrived sooner."

I looked down at my bloodstained hands and noticed a broken stick protruding from the man's thigh.

"Is that—?"

"An arrow? Yes. I hoped you could help me with it."

"Right. I'm—"

My introduction died on my lips when he looked at me full on for the first time. The long red scar running down the left side of his clean-shaven face was too distinctive to be denied. When my eyes met his, I knew beyond a doubt the officer I helped at Antietam stood before me.

"I—"

"I've also been shot in the shoulder."

"Let me see." I stepped forward and raised my trembling hands. I grasped them into fists to still them.

"You aren't well."

"I'm fine." I lifted my hands in surrender. Thank God they did not shake. "Would you like to unbutton your coat?"

He unbuttoned with his right hand and winced when he tried to take it off with his left. I pushed his hand away as I pulled the coat open at the shoulder. I slipped my forefingers through the bloodstained hole in his shirt and pulled, exposing the wound.

I slipped my right hand beneath his coat to his back and probed around the wound with my left. The man stiffened. "It didn't quite make it through," I said. Blood seeped from the wound, but would be easily staunched with a tight bandage.

I stared at the arrow in his leg and wondered how in the hell I was going to remove it.

"Can you walk?"

"Yes."

"Come with me."

I focused on my wagon and blotted out the activity around me, the officer's orders to bury the dead. I climbed into my wagon. Clothes spilled out of Maureen's trunk, and our box of kitchen wares had been ransacked, but my medical trunk and bag were untouched at the front of the wagon. I picked my way through the clothes on the floor and retrieved my medical bag. "Do you need my help removing your coat?"

He unbuckled his holster and handed it to me. Together, we removed his navy wool coat. His scrutiny was unnerving. I hoped he did not recognize me. If he did, would he have known my name?

I doused a square of cloth with whisky and cleaned around

the wound. "A pressure bandage should suffice until I can take the bullet out." I mumbled to myself as I worked.

"General Sherman mentioned you."

I pulled the bandage tight around his back and across his chest. "Does that hurt?" I asked.

"No."

I smiled and continued to wrap. "You are a poor liar—" I paused and looked at him questioningly. I did not know his name.

"Kindle. Captain William Kindle."

"Lieutenant Kindle's uncle." I tied off his bandage. "That will do for the moment." I was trying to avoid the wreckage of the wagon train and to avoid Kindle's penetrating gaze, which left me few places to focus. I dropped my head to assess the arrow protruding from his thigh. "Now for your leg. There isn't much blood, which concerns me."

"You're afraid the arrow is plugging its own hole."

"Yes." I eyed his suspenders. "I need a tourniquet."

"By all means."

I looped the suspenders loosely around his knee, moved them up above the arrow, and tied them off. "Sit here."

He sat on the back of the wagon while I climbed inside. Images flashed through my mind: Frau Schlek's gaping stomach, her husband's head caked with blood and dirt, Maureen's mutilated face. My back to Kindle, I covered my mouth and fought against nausea. Could I do this? I had to, needed to. He was grievously injured. If I didn't help him, I was sure he would die. I dropped my hand from my mouth. I couldn't live with myself if another person died today due to my cowardice. I pulled a bottle of whisky from my medical trunk and handed it to him.

"Thank you." He removed the cork and took a swig. His sun-weathered face was noticeably paler than it had been moments before, setting off the redness of the scar. He finished taking a drink and caught me staring. He wiped his mouth with the back of his hand and said nothing.

"Are you light-headed?"

"A little."

So am I, I thought. "Maybe you should lie back."

"No."

"As you wish." I cut his pants around the wound to clear the field. I cleaned the leg around the arrow with the whisky-soaked cloth.

"Have you ever done this before?"

"Not much call to remove arrows in . . . London. Have you?"

"Once or twice."

"What would you recommend?"

"You have to cut the arrow out."

"Oh." I bit my lip.

"Do you have the tools necessary? I have a knife in my boot, if not."

"No, I have the tools."

"Is there a problem?"

I looked up from his leg. I didn't want to admit to him my idea had been to yank the arrow out, check the bleeding, and assess my options. "No."

Lieutenant Beau Kindle came around the wagon.

"There are no other survivors," Beau said. He looked at me. "Are you sure they took Anna?"

I nodded.

Ester's and Amos's voices echoed in my head. The sights, sounds, and smells around me validated their stories of the Comanche, but about what happened to abducted women they had always remained silent. A shake of the head and, "Better to be dead" was all anyone ever said.

"Should I form a party to go after them?" Beau asked.

"We cannot," Captain Kindle said.

"Sir, we must."

"We don't have the men. We must bury the dead. There is a storm on the way, and it will be dark soon."

"Sir, allow me to take some men and follow the war party."

"Did West Point teach you how to track Indians, Lieutenant?"

"No, but one of your men..."

"No one in this group can track a band of running Indians. You need a scout, which we do not have."

"Uncle..."

"In the Army, you are a lieutenant under my command, not my nephew. You will address me as Captain or I will have you reassigned to a clerking position in Saint Louis. If you argue with my orders again, I will have you court-martialed. Do you understand, Lieutenant Kindle?"

The young man's face was red, his lips pressed into a thin line. "Yes, sir."

"Sergeant Washington."

"Yes, suh." A large Negro soldier stood a few feet away.

"What's the situation?"

"There's two animals fit to pull a wagon. This is the only wagon standing, though we can probably salvage another. The rest are busted."

"Do we have any horses that aren't blown?"

"Yours and mine, suh."

"Lieutenant Kindle, take Corporal Oakes to the fort immediately and relay our predicament to the commander. Inform him of the abductions. Tell him we will wait here for reinforcements."

"Yes, sir." The young man saluted, turned on his heel a bit too precisely, and left.

The shaking in my hands had moved to my legs. Try as I

might, I could not keep them from trembling beneath me. I climbed into the wagon and sat down in the guise of readying my instruments to perform surgery on Captain Kindle's leg. Sitting did not help. My entire body shook as if overcome by chills. Already Maureen's pleasant countenance was being replaced in my memory by her death mask. I heard my name being screamed through the din of battle and saw myself cowering in the buffalo wallow while, one hundred yards away, an Indian chopped Maureen's face apart to silence her.

Far away I heard the discussion of burying the dead. Sergeant Washington and his men had placed the bodies in a broken wagon bed they would lower into a large grave en masse.

"Doctor?" Captain Kindle's voice was full of concern.

I took a deep breath and stood. I grasped the metal rib of the wagon cover and placed a protective hand over my roiling stomach, swallowing the urge to vomit. I needed to concentrate, to push my personal tragedy and guilt to the back of my mind and focus on Captain Kindle's wound. I turned around and faced my patient. "How are you feeling, Captain?"

"Fine." His color was worse.

I tossed a crate onto the ground and climbed out of the wagon. I set the crate upright and asked Kindle to sit. "I need to determine if a vein was nicked."

Kindle sat. It would be so easy to yank the arrow out and deal with the clear wound.

As if reading my mind, he explained. "The arrowhead is attached to the shaft with animal sinew. It softens in the body and loosens the arrowhead. You'll yank the shaft out and will have to search for the head."

"How far are we from Fort Richardson?"

"Ten miles." He looked at the darkening sky. "With a storm coming."

Over my shoulder I noticed the clouds gathering in the west for the first time. Thanks to the many hours spent in Jonasz Golik's basement, I knew I could complete the operation without incident. However, performing the surgery in our current circumstances, in the middle of the prairie, with a storm gathering on the horizon, was not ideal.

Captain Kindle watched me without a word. I called for the nearest soldier.

"Please find two barrels and place the side of a wagon across them. It will have to do for an operating table. I also need someone to make a fire and boil water. Quickly, now. I do not want to attempt this in the rain."

The soldier looked toward Captain Kindle, eyes wide, waiting for direction.

"Do as she orders."

When the soldier was gone I said to Kindle, "You're in luck. I have chloroform."

"I don't want chloroform."

"I didn't ask you what you wanted."

"Nevertheless, I do not want to be unconscious."

He was still studying me when Lieutenant Kindle and Corporal Oakes rode up to take their leave. Beau Kindle took in the soldiers preparing the table with confusion. "What are you doing?"

"Preparing to operate on your uncle's leg."

"You can't do that."

"Would you rather do it in my stead?"

"Don't be absurd."

"Lieutenant," Captain Kindle barked. "Keep a civil tongue in your head."

Beau Kindle dismounted and spoke in a low, controlled voice. "Captain, forgetting the fact we don't know what her skills as a surgeon are, do you think it wise to put your life in the hands of a woman who has been through this?" He gestured at the wreckage.

"No. But, I see no other choice."

Despite the captain's rousing endorsement, I endeavored to put Lieutenant Kindle's mind at ease. "I understand your concerns, Lieutenant. You have no reason to believe I am up to the task. Rest assured, your uncle's well-being is as important to me as it is to you."

I willed my hand not to shake and placed it on Lieutenant Kindle's arm. "Please, go quickly to Fort Richardson. Bring the post doctor back if you must. I will do what I can to make Captain Kindle comfortable until you arrive." I gave Lieutenant Kindle the most modest, feminine smile I could muster.

"You're wasting daylight, Lieutenant. You have your orders," Captain Kindle said.

Somewhat placated, Beau Kindle saluted, remounted his horse, and kicked it into a gallop. Corporal Oakes saluted, turned his horse, and followed.

The smile dropped from my face. "What would you have me do, Captain?"

Captain Kindle was slumped against the side of the wagon, visibly in pain. "Sorry?"

"Would you have me operate on you or make you comfortable until you arrive at Fort Richardson, where your leg will inevitably be amputated?"

He did not reply. I moved in front of him. "Captain?" His eyes met mine. They were full of pain, as I remembered them. "Trust me."

After a long, unsettling pause, he nodded.

I motioned for the soldiers to place the makeshift litter near the wagon.

"My leg is numb."

"It is because we have stopped the blood flow." I blotted his perspiring face with a clean, soft cloth. "I will take good care of you."

I threaded two needles, my shaking hands making the task more difficult than usual. I turned slightly away from Kindle, enough to hide my tremors but not so far as to ignite his suspicion. Trembling hands would do little to burnish Kindle's nascent trust in me. I knew my mind and hands would settle when the time came. Until then, I needed a distraction.

"How long have you been in the Army?"

"Twenty years."

"Indeed?" I poured carbolic acid into an iron skillet full of water and dropped my instruments in it along with the two threaded needles. "You aren't old enough to be a twenty-year veteran."

"West Point when I was eighteen. How long have you been a doctor?" he asked with great difficulty.

"Officially? Four years. I assisted my father for many years prior." I glanced at him. "Don't think you will get me to tell you my age, Captain."

"I wouldn't dream of asking."

"Sergeant Washington, can you help him?"

Washington and a private tried to move Kindle to the table. He held up his hand to stay them. "I do not need help."

The wind increased, bringing with it the metallic scent of the oncoming thunderstorm. Thin tendrils of lightning flashed across the distant sky. A rumble of thunder followed.

Sergeant Washington and the private looked at each other with concern on their faces. Washington glanced at me and quickly looked away. I pulled him aside.

"How much time do we have, Sergeant?"

"Ten minutes before the storm. Maybe fifteen, ma'am."

"Would you please have a couple of your men clear a space on the floor of my wagon for the captain to lie on? They can take everything but the trunks outside."

"Yes, ma'am."

While Washington directed the men, I turned my attention back to Kindle. He sat on the edge of the table, light-headed and woozy.

"Time to lie down, Captain."

"Cut around the wound, follow the shaft down with your finger to find the arrowhead." I folded his coat and put it under his head.

"Anything else?"

"Pray it's not in the bone."

"Private," I said to the nearest soldier, "would you please bring me a pan of warm water? Sergeant Washington, get another soldier and go wash your hands in the remaining warm water with this." I handed him a bar of carbolic soap. "Do not touch anything to dry your hands. I will give you a clean cloth when you return."

I washed my hands and when the three men returned, I handed the skillet of acid-soaked instruments to a small soldier standing nearby. I positioned him and Washington at the head of the table and foot of the table, respectively. "Captain, do you have any orders you would like to give your men before you go under?"

"Sergeant Washington, will the bodies be buried before the storm comes?" Captain Kindle asked.

"Yes, suh."

"You know what to do?"

"Yes, suh."

Kindle nodded. "I leave the regiment in your hands."

"No need to be so dramatic, Captain," I said. "You'll be with us again in no time."

I was laying a cloth soaked with chloroform over his nose and mouth when Kindle stayed my hand. "I don't know your name," he said.

"Call me Laura." His brows furrowed in puzzlement and concentration. "Is something wrong?"

"No."

"Trust me, Captain. I want you to live as much as you do."

"Precisely what I want to hear from my doctor."

"Are you ready?"

"Yes."

"I'll be here when you wake," I said, and placed the chloroform-soaked cloth over his nose.

CHAPTER

10

The reverberations of a thousand cannons shook the ground. I covered my head as the earth swayed underneath me. The barn creaked and groaned, instruments rattled on their trays, bottles of medicine clinked against one another as the rumbling sunk into the blood-soaked Maryland mud. Rain pinged on the metal roof, slowly at first, then increasing until the individual notes transformed into a long symphonic chord.

Where was my father? It was long past time for him to have returned from the field. I should have never let him go. I should have gone in his stead.

I groped in the darkness, touching trunks, crates, canvas, a blanket, and finally, the bandaged chest of a man. A flash of lightning illuminated my surroundings and I jerked back.

I sat up, shaking. I was not in Smith's Barn near Antietam Creek but in a covered wagon on the plains of Texas. The wind rocked the schooner, threatening to topple us. Across from me, the wagon's smooth canvas cover was pushing against the thin ribs supporting it. I worried the cover was not secure enough and tried to remember if we had untied it for any reason during our journey. With a snap, the canvas blew out like a sail, just holding together with the sudden change of wind direction. Wet canvas slapped me on the back.

Lightning illuminated the scene again and I caught a glimpse of Captain Kindle, unconscious on the floor of the wagon. His bandages were still secure and his face was devoid of color, save the long red scar across the left side of his face.

I groped for his hand and pressed my fingers against his wrist. His pulse was weak but steady. I couldn't remember where I had placed my stethoscope nor could I see around me to search. Through touch, I placed my ear on Kindle's chest and listened to him take deep, clear breaths. I sat back, as content as I could hope to be in the current situation, and waited for the next flash of lightning.

Where were the other soldiers? Were they in the abandoned wagons or sitting on the plains, under oilcloth, their backs to the storm? Had they been through so many storms there was no fear in their hearts? Or was the fear of a storm inconsequential compared to the fear of being captured and killed by the Indians?

I thought of Anna and the children. What were they enduring this violent night? Were the Indians abusing Anna at this moment? Had they used her and killed her like some broken doll? What about the children? Surely they wouldn't...I shook the image from my mind. I could not allow my thoughts to wander there. No. It would not happen. Even savages wouldn't do that.

I covered my head with my arms. What did I know? Look at what they had done to Maureen. To Cornelius. They cut a baby from a mother's stomach and burned Amos alive. How could I dare give these Indians the benefit of the doubt? They had proven correct every horrible assertion about their nature with the brutality of their attack.

Maureen. I tried to get the image of her wasted face from my mind. I rubbed my eyes with the palms of my hands until they burned, but the image of her jawless face still did not leave. Grotesque and bloody, it morphed into a gaping grin, mocking me, mocking the idea I would ever be free of this day and my complicity in the outcome. My actions, traced from an impetuous decision in childhood to my cowering in a buffalo wallow, irrevocably led her to the most heinous of deaths, to the death she most feared.

~∞~

It was dawn and I was alone. The air in the schooner was heavy and gray with diffused light. I rose to call out to Maureen when the sight of a small bloodstain on the bed of the wagon stopped me. Kindle. He was gone.

Dizziness washed over me as I stood and forced me to sit back down. Every part of my body ached and I wanted nothing more than to wrap myself in a blanket and lose myself in a long forgetful sleep. Sounds from outside the schooner prompted me to move again, but more slowly. I needed to find Kindle. He was my patient, his well-being my responsibility.

Rain poured from the sky like water from a pitcher. Thunder rumbled across the flat featureless landscape. Gray flashes of lightning punctured the waterlogged sky. Overnight, the loamy soil had transformed into a quagmire of deep red mud. A few soldiers roamed around the wreckage. I searched the scene for Kindle from the cover of my wagon and realized the soldiers were not aimlessly roaming, waiting for help to arrive.

"You!" I yelled. A young soldier looked up at me, his eyes wide with surprise. He looked around him, wondering if I was addressing him or someone else. I jumped out of the wagon and struggled through the sludge to confront him. "You put that back!" I jerked a box of Cornelius's cigars from his hand and held them to my chest. "These aren't yours, young man!"

"Ma'am?"

"I said these aren't yours!"

"Are dey yours, ma'am?"

"They most certainly are not! They are Cornelius's. Everything in this wagon is his and you are not to touch it!" I looked around at the soldiers looting the wagons of the dead. A few of the soldiers put back what they had in their hands; others shook their heads and resumed their search. Sergeant Washington appeared in front of me.

"Is there something I can do for you, ma'am?"

"You can tell these men to stop stealing!"

Sergeant Washington's gaze was steady, but he didn't respond.

"Well? Are you going to tell them to stop?"

A voice from behind me replied, "No."

I wheeled around to see Kindle walking toward me using a stick as a cane with one arm, the other arm in the hasty sling of torn cloth I had made the night before. His complexion was still pale but some of his natural color had returned. His eyes were shadowed by the cavalry hat he wore and disguised further by the rain pouring from its brim.

"What are you doing walking around on your leg? You're bleeding again."

"Yes, I know." He addressed Sergeant Washington. "Find a hat for the doctor."

Still clutching the cigars to my chest I futilely ran my hand across my hair, which was plastered to my head. I was too angry to care.

Kindle stepped in front of me and lowered his voice. "Believe me, I don't want to be walking on this leg any more than you want me to. But I must show a brave face in front of my men, so keep your admonishments to a low growl, please."

I lowered my voice. "Speaking of your men, they are stealing the possessions of the dead."

"Looting is a military tradition."

"Looting your vanquished enemies, yes. I didn't know white settlers were the enemies of the Army. Or are all whites the enemies of your Negroes?"

The shadow of his hat made the anger in Kindle's eyes terrifying. But the anger of men always brought out my defiance. I raised my chin and met his narrowed gaze.

"Suh."

Sergeant Washington was a few feet away, holding out a wide-brimmed hat toward Captain Kindle. I recognized it immediately as the hat of one of the abducted boys. Kindle took the hat and thanked Washington, who with a quick glance at me, walked away.

Kindle lowered his voice to a terrifying level. "I will be forever in your debt for saving my life but do not ever speak of my men in that way again. Your people are past caring what happens to their possessions. If my men can find an item or two they may use to barter for something else, or maybe something they will keep to make their lives better, they will do so, and with my blessing."

He grimaced and touched his bandaged shoulder.

"Is your shoulder bothering you?"

"No." He dropped his hand. "When soldiers from the fort arrive it will make what my men are doing seem quaint. If there is anything you want for yourself from your fellow travelers, I recommend you put it in your wagon immediately."

"I suppose I should stand guard over my own possessions."

"Nonsense. They would not dare touch your possessions." Kindle looked away and nodded his head. The soldiers around me resumed their search. He held the hat out to me. "You will need this for the journey to the fort."

"No, thank you, I will not."

I tried to stomp off dramatically but the deep mud and rain hindered my progress. I climbed into my wagon and sat on a crate. Water dripped into my eyes and off the tip of my nose and streamed off the hem of my skirt onto the wagon floor. I was furious at the looting, furious at myself for implying such a wretched thing about his men, and furious with Kindle for being so maddeningly logical.

I was soaked through, freezing, and my dress smelled of vomit and urine. I closed the canvas flaps of the wagon to give myself a modicum of privacy and shed my wet clothes. I wrapped myself in a quilt and indulged in a bout of self-pity and silent crying.

I wiped my eyes with the corner of the blanket and took a deep breath. The soldiers from the fort would be arriving any minute. It would not do for them to find me a blubbering, naked mess.

My fingers were clumsy with cold, making everything more difficult than it should have been: the latches on my traveling trunk and the small buttons down the front of my dress. I decided to switch to a different dress with fewer, larger buttons when someone knocked on the outside of the wagon.

"How are you feeling?" Kindle said.

Horrid. What a stupid question.

I gave up the idea of changing into a different dress and continued on with the small, pearl buttons. When finished, I smoothed the navy cotton and took a deep breath. I peeked through the back of the schooner and tried to smile.

"Fine, thank you."

Guilt overcame me at the sight of Kindle. Standing in the rain, water pouring off his hat and onto his shoulders, his scar a vivid red gash down his pale face, he looked as bad as I felt.

I opened the flap. "You need to get out of the rain. Can you climb in?"

I helped as much as possible as he struggled in. He stood, hunched under the cover of my wagon, dripping water, trying not to shiver. I removed his hat and threw it aside before removing his cloak. I grabbed my quilt, still warm, and wrapped it around his shoulders. He leaned heavily on his stick, shaking. "Can you stand for a moment more?" He nodded. I quickly arranged blankets to cover a crate and helped him sit down.

"I would suggest you lie on the floor but doubt you would do it." I made sure the quilt was tight around his shoulders and sat across from him.

"Thank you, this is fine."

I put my hand on his forehead and discovered he was burning up. "You shouldn't have gotten out in this weather, Captain." I removed my hand to retrieve laudanum to at least make him more comfortable and to dull his pain.

"No. The coolness of your hand is comforting."

I placed one hand on his forehead, the other on his cheek. He closed his eyes and murmured his thanks. I sat there for a while, moving my hands to cool different part of his face and watched as he relaxed and his shivering abated. Leaning his head back against the wet canvas of the wagon, he slept.

I removed my now-warmed hands and reached for the laudanum, pouring out a small amount in a tin cup and topping it with whisky. I set the cup beside Kindle and stood, gently walking around him to peer out the back of the wagon.

Would the rain ever stop? The soldiers' eagerness for loot appeared to have been dampened by the relentless downpour, and they had disappeared, to where I didn't know. The overturned wagons were righted but still harnessed to their dead oxen, whose staring eyes, lolling tongues, and terrified expressions told the tale as well as the arrows sticking out of their flanks could. Through the wreckage and rain I could see the mass grave. Maureen's grave. To mark the grave the soldiers had fashioned a crude cross from the spokes of the burned wheel and a piece of rope. Using the charred wood was macabre, offensive, and brought back images and smells from the day before I would sooner forget, but I understood why the soldiers had chosen them.

The grave was necessarily shallow, the storm coming upon us the night before in such haste as to preclude anything deeper than a few feet. I wasn't sure there was enough earth covering the bodies to stand the rain for too many days.

I grasped the rope lashing the canvas to the schooner and let the tears come. The sound of the storm, the thunder, and the constant patter of rain on the roof of the schooner masked the sounds of my sobs. I was exhausted, spent emotionally and physically. I wished I had died with Maureen; Death's eternal sleep was more inviting at that moment than at any other. What lay before me I knew not. I knew only I did not have the will to move forward and find out. I couldn't imagine a time in my future when I would be happy again.

So absorbed in my own misery and bleak future was I that I did not hear Kindle rise and move to stand behind me. Sound around me shifted and I understood for the first time what it was to sense someone's presence without seeing them.

I gathered my emotions as best I could but did not bother to hide the tears pooling in my eyes nor the stains that marked my cheeks. When I faced him I found such empathy and understanding in his expression I almost lost myself to crying again. I fought valiantly, and successfully, against the urge to throw myself in his arms. At that moment, I wanted to be comforted, for another's strength to course through me and give me courage. The last time I had been comforted in that way was at the death of my father. Maureen, so slight of build and full of devastating grief of her own, showed the depths of her natural tenderness and empathy.

Empathy I never repaid.

"Did they say words over the grave?"

"Yes. Sergeant Washington did. If you would like to pay your respects..."

I nodded. "I should have gone before." Instead of berating your soldiers for looting, I thought. I sniffed and wiped the tears from my cheeks with the sleeve of my dress and apologized. "I fear my emotional state is confirming your nephew's opinion of my fitness as your physician."

"On the contrary, Doctor. I would question the character of anyone unaffected by the events you've been through."

Unlike most men of the age, he did not look away from my discomfort, but rather took my hand and said in a weak voice, "I am truly sorry for your loss."

His hand was too warm. I stepped forward and touched his forehead. "You should stay sitting down, Captain. You have a fever and look ready to collapse." I moved my hand to his cheek as I said this. "I have portioned a dose of laudanum for you."

"No, thank you. Not yet."

I stared at the gray-flecked stubble on his chin. He studied me in his silent, steady, unnerving way. The schooner, never large, shrunk until the urge to escape from Kindle's presence overpowered me. I dropped my hand and turned my face away.

"You should stay off your leg as much as possible."

I helped settle him again. He stretched his injured leg in front of him and leaned his head back against the canvas.

To take my mind off my lingering nausea and the beginnings of what promised to be a raging headache, and to distract Kindle from his pain, I turned the conversation to him.

"Why do you carry a knife in your boot?"

"You don't want your opponent to know every tool you have."

"Do you get into a lot of fights?"

"Not anymore. Old habit."

I nodded. "How long have you been at Fort Richardson?"

"A little over a year. My regiment was sent here to help build the fort."

"Is that common? For the Negroes to be given menial tasks?"

"You'll see soon enough everyone at a fort is given menial tasks, regardless of race." Kindle winced as he adjusted his leg. "I confess I volunteer my men for fort-bound duties more than other regimental officers."

"Why?"

He closed his eyes and did not answer for a while. "I'm not eager to lead more men to their deaths," he finally said.

"Why do you remain in the Army?"

He smiled slightly. "I have asked myself that question many times." He paused. "I thought of retiring back in sixty-eight but the thought of returning to my family's plantation did not appeal to me."

"Plantation?"

"Yes. In Maryland. I haven't been there since right after the war. I'm sure it's gone to ruin. I always hated farming. It's why I went into the Army."

"Did your family have slaves?"

Kindle nodded. "We did. I tried to help a slave escape once, when I was twelve."

"What happened?"

Kindle's smile was thin. "My brother caught wind of what I was doing. Instead of stopping me, he let me go on so the punishment would be severe. The slave was caught five miles away."

"And were you punished?"

"We both were."

When he did not seem eager to elaborate, I changed the subject and quizzed him about the fort.

"In Texas, there is a line of forts on the Western frontier." With his forefinger he drew a slight arc in the air. "From the Rio Grande in the south to the Red River in the north. Fort Richardson is the northernmost fort."

"Whom is it named for?"

"Fighting Dick Richardson. A war hero. Union, naturally. Our primary purpose is to protect the settlers and cattle drives from Indian aggression."

"Are you always as successful as you were yesterday?" I could not keep the anger out of my voice.

"Forgive me if I don't have the strength to detail why our task is nigh impossible to complete."

"Forgive me for my rudeness. Rest."

He shook his head. "Tell me how you happened to be here."

"Oh!" I said, taken aback. "It isn't an interesting story. I saw an advertisement in the paper about a new town in Colorado and decided to see the West."

"What town?"

"Timberline."

Kindle's eyes lost their faraway aspect and narrowed. "Timberline?"

"Yes. It was a new venture. I have the flyer here somewhere," I said, and halfheartedly looked for it.

Kindle waved his hand. "Interesting you traveled through Texas with the railroad available."

"I have always been more of an adventurer than was good for me. Obviously."

Kindle might have been in pain but I could tell he was an intuitive person and bought none of my story.

"What will happen to the captives?"

Of course he noticed my abrupt change in subject but he moved on without comment. After hearing what he said, I would have rather he not.

"The children will be adopted into the tribe and treated well."

I could barely get the words out. "What about Anna?"

"How old was she again?"

"Seventeen."

Kindle grimaced and said nothing.

"Don't think you will offend my sensibilities. Tell me plainly."

"They will abuse her. Savagely. Repeatedly. Every one. If she survives, the squaws will beat her before one of them takes her as a slave. If one of the raiders takes a liking to her she will become his wife. Chances are she will be sold to another tribe where the abuse will start again. She could be eventually ransomed to the Quakers."

I swallowed the bitter taste in my throat. "She will live?"

"If you call that living."

Anger welled inside me, anger at the folly of traveling through such dangerous country. For what? Would any of our lives have been better amid the hardships on the frontier? I wondered for the first time why I hadn't sailed for England. Or San Francisco. Why had I so quickly agreed to Camille's suggestion of finding refuge in Texas? If I had stopped for a moment and considered, weighed every option, I was confident a better solution would have come to me, one that would not have led to Maureen's brutal death.

"You should pray for her death. If she survives and is rescued or ransomed to the Quakers, she will be shunned, by men and women alike."

"I would never shun her."

"No. I don't suppose you would." He studied me for a long while. He took a deep breath, shifted in his seat, and said, "I should prepare you for fort life."

"Please." I grasped at this conversational life raft, although I had little intention of staying at Fort Richardson long enough to adjust to its hardships. I forced down my latest wave of nausea, an ailment I had never suffered from but hadn't been able to rid myself of since the night before, and ignored the throbbing in my head. I longed to drink Kindle's dose of laudanum.

"It isn't glamorous. It's dirty, remote, shabby—the buildings not erected by my men, naturally—and we're chronically short on supplies."

"You're quite the salesman, Captain Kindle. I can hardly wait to arrive."

"Fort Richardson does have one redeeming feature you'll find intriguing, and quite possibly, difficult to leave."

"Forgive me if I am skeptical, Captain. Any romanticism this adventure could boast has been completely erased over the last twenty-four hours. I cannot imagine a primitive Western fort is going to have anything to entice me to stay a moment longer than absolutely necessary."

"Not even the most modern building between Fort Worth and El Paso?"

"I have never been to Fort Worth or El Paso, but if they resemble the Texas towns I have seen, then they are dirty, remote, and full of drunken cowboys. Boasting you have the most modern building on the Texas frontier is, I fear, faint praise."

"What if I told you this building was a hospital?"

I smiled. "I've worked in many types of hospitals: a barn, a tent, a field in the middle of a battle, a church, a modern structure in New York City, a dirty room in a Lambeth workhouse, even a ship. I look forward to adding meanly constructed Western forts to the list."

Curtains of rain fell from the sky, closing the schooner from the barren plains outside. The gray light of the storm diffused the air around us, softening edges, muffling the rest of the world. Kindle's pain was apparent by his clenched jaw and hooded eyes, which were too focused on me for my comfort.

"Please take a sip of the laudanum."

"No."

"Are you hungry?"

"No."

I stared outside, trying to avoid his probing gaze.

"Have we met before?" he asked.

"Captain! They're coming!"

The voice outside the tent saved me from answering with a lie.

"You need a better sling." I found a shawl of Maureen's, tied two corners together, and placed it around Kindle's neck, keeping as much distance between us as the small space allowed. I adjusted the sling and gently nestled his arm in the soft folds of the well-worn cloth, trying to hide the border of embroidered flowers and leaves as best as I could. "Your cloak will cover the rest." I put his hat on his head and fastened his cloak around his neck. "Wait. I'll help you down."

I retrieved my father's cloak from my trunk, turned it inside out, and fastened it around my shoulders.

"Clever," Kindle said, admiring the brown oilcloth that now covered my shoulders and dress.

"Yes, isn't it?" I said. "My father struck upon this idea when he was caught in a storm after visiting a patient. Two cloaks in one." I smiled, remembering how excited Father had been when he showed me the cloak Maureen had fashioned from his idea and the look of pride on Maureen's face as he praised her work.

"Didn't he have an umbrella?" Kindle asked.

I laughed. "He hated umbrellas. They always turned inside out on him."

Kindle held out the boy's hat. "You'll need this."

I looked at the juvenile, flat billed hat and could not bring myself to take it. The thought of the little boy who had worn the hat only the day before extinguished the short burst of joy the memory of my father and Maureen had given me. My throat thickened as my loss—the loss of those children and what could be happening to Anna at the moment—reasserted its place at the forefront of my mind. Kindle, as if understanding my every thought and emotion, placed the hat on my head. "Until you can buy another."

I stepped out of the schooner and with Sergeant Washington's assistance helped the captain disembark. Kindle stood at attention and awaited the arrival of his commander, the model of the battle-hardened soldier ignoring his pain and suffering to perform his duty.

A regiment of cavalry rode up at an impressive clip, throwing mud onto the chests and legs of the horses and men behind. At the front of the column was an erect young man with a bushy mustache that barely concealed the scowl underneath. Kindle's men miraculously appeared from nowhere and were lined up in perfect formation, staring ahead into the near distance at nothing. Not one eye of Kindle's regiment flickered to the column. Kindle limped forward a few steps and waited, leaning heavily on the stick in his right hand.

The cavalry slowed to a trot and stopped in front of Kindle with a precision borne of long days of drills and the unbending leadership of their commander. Kindle saluted. "Colonel Mackenzie."

Mackenzie returned the salute. "Captain Kindle. What are you doing on your feet? According to Lieutenant Kindle, I expected to find you dead."

"Not quite, sir."

Niceties over, Mackenzie looked around the destroyed wagon train. "What is the situation here?"

"The dead have been buried. My regiment and their horses are rested and ready for orders."

"You are to return to the fort. I am following the savages. Any idea what band did this?"

"Based on the arrows retrieved, Kiowa, sir."

"They fled north?"

"Yes, sir."

"Returning to the loving bosom of the Quakers. The cattle?"

"Gone, sir. We didn't have time to search before the storm and darkness fell."

"What the Indians didn't steal will have been incorporated into other herds east of here. If we're lucky, there are some stragglers. Lieutenant Kindle!"

The young man disengaged himself from the clump of officers behind Mackenzie and rode to the front. "Yes, sir!"

"Take your uncle's regiment and retrieve as many cattle as possible."

Disappointment and anger flickered over the young man's face. "Yes, sir!" he said with more enthusiasm than his features showed.

Kindle stepped forward. "Colonel Mackenzie..."

Mackenzie interrupted him. "We will rest for five minutes."

The order to dismount rang down the line. Mackenzie dismounted his horse, which was led away by a corporal, and walked toward Kindle. Their conversation was almost lost amid the rain and the sounds of the regiment dismounting and moving en masse to the wagons. I watched as the men rifled through the belongings of my fellow travelers and with great force of will stayed rooted by my wagon and kept my black thoughts to myself.

"You look like hell, William. You aren't coming, so don't ask. Sherman is apoplectic. If I am not mistaken, this 'war' with the Indians is about to come to a head. Good officers are hard to find. I will need you."

"Yes, sir."

"Sherman's ambulance is on its way to take you and the survivor back to the fort." Mackenzie looked at me for the first time, though I was sure he had been aware of my presence from the moment he arrived.

Kindle made the introductions. "Colonel Ranald Mackenzie, Dr. Laura..." Kindle realized with embarrassment he didn't know my last name.

"Elliston."

Mackenzie studied me like a scientist would a newly discovered species of fly. He stepped forward, and despite the continued rain, removed his hat. "Ma'am. Thank you for assisting my officer."

"I did what any doctor would have done."

"Dr. Elliston has taken great care of me amid less than ideal circumstances," Kindle said.

Mackenzie nodded and replaced his hat. "What can you tell me of the raid?"

I was nonplussed. I motioned to the wreckage. "They were massacred. What more do you need to know?"

"What direction did they come from?"

"West."

"How did you survive?"

I did not want to admit to hiding in a buffalo wallow to this man. "Captain Kindle's regiment arrived and chased the Indians off before they could kill me."

"Were there any defining features to the Indians you saw? Their dress? Scars?"

I shook my head. "I do not remember. It happened so fast. The cattle were stampeding, throwing up dust."

Mackenzie nodded, and with no further information to be gleaned, lost interest in me. "Mount up!"

The corporal handed Mackenzie the reins to his horse. "Captain, do as the doctor instructs. I need you back on your feet. Lieutenant Colonel Foster will be in charge while I'm gone." He mounted his horse. "I leave it to you to give direction to Lieutenant Kindle and your regiment." Mackenzie waved his arm forward and kicked his horse into a canter. His regiment followed. Soon, they were lost in the rain.

"Lieutenant Kindle!"

"Yes, sir."

"Round up as many cattle as you can find in three days and return with them to the fort. You'll probably find most of them near water."

"Yes, sir."

Lieutenant Kindle saluted, which Kindle returned, and mounted his horse. "Regiment! Mount up!"

Sergeant Washington materialized. "Suh? I've put two guns in the wagon for you and some ammunition. Is there anything I can do for you before we leave?"

"No, thank you, Sergeant."

Washington saluted Kindle and tipped his hat to me before mounting his horse and riding off with the rest. As their column rode out of sight, uneasiness settled over me. We were at the mercy of any band of Indians that might stumble upon us. Two rifles, my pistol, Kindle's pistol, and a secreted knife would hardly be enough to protect us from savages such as I saw yesterday.

When Kindle's regiment rode over the horizon and out of sight, they took his energy with them. He sagged, and for a terrifying moment, I thought he was going to collapse.

"Please, don't swoon!" I rushed over and grasped his arm. "I'll never get you up from the ground by myself."

"Men don't *swoon*. We fall." Despite the irritation in his voice, he allowed me to help him to the schooner.

"Lean against the back, here." I hurried into the wagon and tossed out the two crates Maureen and I had used for makeshift tables at night. I jumped out, splashing mud on us. "Sorry." I used the crates to make crude steps for Kindle to use.

"I'm not sure I can." His breathing was shallow, his face frightfully pale.

"You must try." I climbed back into the schooner and offered my hand. Holding on to my hand, he stepped onto the lower crate with his good leg and pulled the injured leg up. He stood for a moment, breathing deeply, the strength in his hand crushing my knuckles. He repeated the actions onto the next step and was standing, triumphant and pale, on the bed of the schooner when his good leg buckled, tumbling him forward and taking me down with him. There was a sharp pain in my shoulder as it connected with the edge of a trunk and I knew no more.

CHAPTER

11

I woke, gasping for air, the weight of Kindle's body crushing my chest. Panic-stricken, I tried to push him off. Excruciating pain shot through my shoulder and I realized my left arm was numb and useless. I tried to push Kindle off with my right arm to no avail.

"Captain Kindle!"

His head was on my injured left shoulder and turned away. "Captain!" I reached my right hand across and tried to slap his face. "William!" He didn't move.

"Forgive me." I grabbed a handful of his hair and pulled his head off my shoulder and shook his head. "William! Wake up!"

His face had taken on the gray tinge that so often preceded death. I dropped his head back on my shoulder and searched his neck for a pulse. Relief shot through me when I found it, but it was faint. "Damn you, Captain. You are *not* going to die on me!"

It was futile to attempt to push him off; he was too heavy and I was weak from lack of food. My useful arm was heavy, as if filled with lead. The other was deadened. There was hardly enough room on the floor of the schooner for one person, let alone enough to wiggle myself from under Kindle, but I tried anyway. I had made little progress for what seemed like an eternity of trying when I heard an unknown voice.

"God almighty! Excuse me, Captain!"

"Wait! Who's there?" I peeked over Kindle's shoulder and saw a soldier standing at the end of the wagon, his mouth gaping open and his face flaming red.

"I didn't mean to disturb," he said, moving off.

"NO! Come back here and help me!"

"I doubt Captain Kindle..."

"Good God, man! This isn't what you think. Captain Kindle is unconscious. Get in here and get him off of me. He is injured and I need to help him!"

The man was hopeless. He stared at the floor of the wagon. "How?"

"Go through the front and pull me out from under him." Comprehension dawned and soon the man was in the wagon and had grasped me under the arms and was pulling. My scream scared the man half to death and he dropped me when I was mostly free from Kindle.

"God almighty, ma'am. You're bleeding!"

The front of my dress was soaked with blood. A large stain was centered over my heart, precisely where Kindle's shoulder had lain. "It is Captain Kindle's blood, not mine," I said. "Turn him over. Quickly. Careful of his shoulder and leg."

"What's going on here, Sullivan?"

Four soldiers were crowded around the end of the wagon. "Captain Kindle is hurt," Sullivan replied.

"We know that. Did'ja already forget the ten miles of mud we just rode through to bring him back?"

"How long will it take us to get to the fort?" With my one good arm, I folded clean linen into a thick bandage and pressed it to Kindle's shoulder.

"It took us three hours to get here. The horses need to rest."

"We need to leave now."

"What's wrong with your arm?" Sullivan asked.

"Helping Captain Kindle is of the utmost importance at the moment. My shoulder can wait. I will need all of your help."

One look at Kindle and the men understood what I left unsaid. They performed each of my directives without question.

Sherman's ambulance had been modified from a wagon used to transfer wounded soldiers in the war to part office, part bedroom. A wooden bench along one side of the wagon covered with a thin mattress served as his bed. On the other side a small desk and bench were attached to the floor and side of the wagon. Before that was an open space, presumably for his trunks. Behind the driver's bench were two built-in chairs original to the ambulance that would have been the seats for the steward and nurse or doctor.

With great care, the men moved Kindle to the bed, and with haste, moved my trunks full of medicine and clothes. I had a pang at the thought of leaving the rest of my possessions on the plains for looting by others but quickly chastised myself for my greediness. I could buy whatever I needed again. My thoughts from then on, and for days to come, turned solely to saving William Kindle's life.

I sat next to Kindle on one of the trunks. I held his hand, dabbed his face with a wet cloth, and spoke to him in a soothing voice about nothing as the ambulance struggled through the mud across the plains. I cleaned his wounds and changed the bandages. When he regained a semblance of consciousness, I forced him to drink water, followed by a dose of laudanum. He murmured, incoherently for a while, then opened his eyes and looked straight at me. Confusion followed by recognition and a smile. "You," he said in a voice barely above a whisper.

"Yes, Captain. I'm here. We will be at the fort soon."

It was not soon enough for me. By the time we arrived at Fort Richardson, the sun had set behind the dark storm clouds, creating a night darker than any I had seen before. The fort looked forlorn and abandoned in the rain-shrouded darkness, the only proof of life being windows of faint candlelight struggling to break through the inky morass.

I readied Kindle and myself for arrival as well as I could with one arm. My left arm was still numb and the pain in my shoulder was excruciating. I determined it was dislocated, a much better prognosis than the break I initially feared. I could not reset it alone, nor did I trust any of the soldiers accompanying us to help me. I hoped there would be a nurse at the post hospital competent enough to help.

Flashes of lightning and booms of thunder heralded our arrival. Men waiting under the protective awning of the hospital porch ducked their heads and raced into the pouring rain to remove Kindle from the ambulance. Soon, my feeble attempts at helping were shunted aside and I stood and stared as the hospital appeared and disappeared with each blink of lightning. The flashing lightning and rumble of thunder gave the long, stone building a sinister air.

A bull of a man with a bushy mustache and round spectacles stood at the top of the steps and yelled at me through the rain. "Ma'am?"

I shook off my shock at the looming hospital and followed him inside.

"This way," he said, and led us to the right and into the north wing of the hospital.

"Do you have a surgery table?"

"Yes."

"Put him there and bring as many lights as possible. I need

boiling water as well. Sullivan, take a man and bring my medical trunk, please."

The wing was a large open space partitioned off by crude walls made of wire, wooden posts, and standard-issue Army blankets. The soldiers placed Kindle on the area serving as the operating theater and went in search of lamps. I stopped the steward with my good arm. "I need your assistance."

"Of course."

We retreated into another curtained area. "Have you ever set a shoulder?" I rubbed my left shoulder.

"Yes."

I lay down on the cot and bent my elbow at a ninety-degree angle. "Go on."

He gently held my arm, moved it across my chest and back. He extended it past my body and perpendicular to the floor, and with a jolt of pain more excruciating than anything I ever felt before, it popped back into place. Relief was immediate, though it took a minute for me to catch my breath. "Thank you." I rolled my shoulder and flexed my tingling fingers. Full feeling would take time but at least I would be able to use my arm. I sat up. The steward's eyes were wide.

"What? Did I scream?"

"Yes, ma'am."

"Sorry."

Four men were standing back from the table, holding oil lanterns, eyes as wide as the steward's. "What is the matter? Surely you've heard a woman scream before."

"Yes, ma'am," one man said. "Ain't ever heard one cuss."

"Did I? I am sure God will forgive me." I looked to the steward. "Will you check on the boiling water? I also need as many clean bandages as you can find."

The steward nodded and left. I directed the soldiers with

the lanterns to the other side of the table and asked one to hold his light up to Kindle's face. The yellow glow from the lantern made Kindle's complexion look somewhat better. I lifted the bandage covering Kindle's shoulder wound and found it slowly seeping blood.

I appraised the men standing around me. "I don't suppose any of you are a nurse."

A chorus of "No, ma'am"s was faint under the sound of rain pounding on the roof. "I didn't think so. Is there a nurse here tonight?"

Blank, uneasy stares greeted my question.

"I can help."

A Negro woman stood in the doorway of the makeshift room. She was taller than I and had a regal bearing more common in the upper echelons of New York society than former slaves. A white apron, stained brown, protected her dress, which, even in the semidarkness surrounding her, I could tell was well made and rich in color, if a little threadbare. A multicolored cloth was wound around her head in an impressive turban. Though her eyes never left my face I knew she had taken my measure from top to bottom. How I fared in this measurement I could not tell, nor did I care.

"You have nursing experience?"

"I have helped in the hospital for months, ma'am."

Sullivan spoke up. "I don't think sitting by the bedside of dying niggers qualifies you to help operate on the captain."

"Would you like to help instead?" He was angry at my rebuke but said nothing. "What is your name?" I asked the woman.

"Caro."

"Take off your apron and follow me."

She followed me to the basin where we washed our hands.

"You will hand me instruments when I ask for them and clean blood from the wound with a clean cloth when I ask."

She nodded and I handed her a towel to dry her hands. "Do not touch any part of your clothes now that your hands are clean."

We returned to the table and I explained to her briefly what each instrument was called and when I might need it. She listened silently, never taking her eyes from the instruments. When I was finished she only nodded.

"Miss Elliston!"

A dripping wet General Sherman stood in the doorway of the curtained area, a look of astonishment and anger on his face.

"General Sherman, a pleasure to see you again."

"What do you think you're doing?"

"Preparing to remove a bullet from Captain Kindle's shoulder."

"Where is Dr. Welch?"

"I don't know who that is."

"I wasn't asking you."

The steward returned with the water and bandages. "Dr. Welch stepped out."

"Stepped out where?" Sherman roared.

"He didn't say, sir."

"It matters not," I said. "Captain Kindle is *my* patient and the surgery cannot wait. You are welcome to either leave the room or grab a lantern."

The soldiers in the room went still and silent, almost as if they were holding their breath. In two strides Sherman had wrested the lantern from the soldier at Kindle's head and stood erect, holding it and glaring at me with his blazing blue eyes.

I smiled up at Sherman. "Let us begin."

I remember Kindle's surgery in great detail, from the incision to removing the bullet to cleaning the field and to stitching the wound. When I tied off the final stitch, the rush of energy required each time I performed surgery evaporated as suddenly as it occurred. I struggled for mental coherence lest I lose the trust of the men who surrounded me. I directed everyone without mercy and with what I suspect was much more fire than necessary. With fresh bandages soaked in carbolic acid on his shoulder and thigh, Kindle was soon settled on a cot topped by a straw-filled mattress and I in a straight-back wooden chair next to it.

A touch on my shoulder woke me. I looked around, disoriented. A small beam of light from a lantern shone on a man who was sleeping peacefully in front of me. I stood and leaned over him. I lifted his wrist and took his pulse while my own racing heart slowed and my senses returned.

Kindle. Fort Richardson.

Maureen.

Anna.

I swallowed my nausea and stood upright.

The steward stood next to my chair, holding out a tin mug of coffee.

I took it gratefully. "Thank you."

"Don't thank me until you've had a taste."

It was horrid and my face showed it.

"I've never learned to make a good cup, and the dregs we have here don't help."

"Thank you anyway." I forced myself to take another drink. It was still vile.

"How is he?"

"His color has improved and his breathing is steady. Good signs."

"How's your shoulder?"

My arm was resting across my abdomen in Kindle's sling. "Stiff."

"Let me sit with the captain while you get some rest."

"No, thank you. I am fine."

"It is General Sherman's orders."

"Is it?"

"He thought with what you've been through..."

I wanted to accept his offer, find a bed, pull a blanket over my head, and mourn Maureen, Cornelius, and Anna. God, how I hoped Anna was dead and not being violated. I closed my eyes as images of what might be happening to my young friend flickered in my mind, alternating between the phantasmagorias of Anna's abuse, Maureen's face, Cornelius's gaping chest, Herr Schlek's severed head, the baby.

I inhaled to stave off my threatening tears. No, I did not want to be alone to think. Not yet.

"What time is it?"

"Midnight."

I placed my cup on the small wooden table next to Kindle's bed and with one hand freshened the damp cloth I used to mop his fevered brow. "With all due respect to General Sherman's orders, I thank you, but I will stay with him through the night. This is a critical time. I should be here. And your coffee will keep me up for hours, I fear."

"Do you need anything?"

"No, thank you."

As the man left the curtained area I stopped him. "What is your name?"

"Waterman. Corporal Waterman."

132

"It is a pleasure to meet you."

He ducked his head and bid me good night.

My shoulder was not only stiff but also painful and swollen. I had waited too long to set it. The agony when I removed it from the sling would, forever after, make me more sympathetic to my patients' pain. I lifted my arm as high as I could and lowered it a few times. I needed full mobility as soon as possible. A one-armed doctor might be serviceable; a one-armed female doctor would be useless. Soon, I was short of breath and perspiring freely. With a groan, I returned my arm to its sling.

With Kindle sleeping soundly and sleep impossible, I explored the hospital. Our wing was divided in half, with the side closest to the administration block used as an operating theater and what appeared to be two officer's rooms. A walkway spanned the length of the wing and on the other side of the makeshift curtain walls was an open ward consisting of six beds, close together. A wood-burning stove sat in the middle of the walkway, its chimney snaking up, over two of the beds and out through the roof. A fine layer of soot on the floor and beds outlined the path of the chimney. One bed was unmade, as if the patient had just left.

The stove was cold and only a few embers could be found when I stirred the ashes inside. I was relighting the fire when Caro, supporting a frail soldier, emerged from the far end of the ward.

"Go on, now, Jethro. Jus' a li'l farther. Lean on me, son." Her voice was soothing, as smooth and light as fresh honey poured from a pot. The man was shivering uncontrollably, making it difficult for her to hold on to him. She was, in essence, carrying him across the floor. I closed the door to the stove, placed the poker aside, and moved to help.

"You will be no help with one arm, but thank you."

I stepped out of the way. She settled the man into his bed with great tenderness and care. "Go on and rest now, Jethro," she said. She smoothed the blankets over her patient, straightened, and turned to face me.

"What is wrong with him?" I asked.

"Diarrhea syndrome. So Welch says."

"Oh." I stared at the poor man and wondered how long he had to live. Diarrhea was an ailment medical advances had not been able to solve. Some recovered, some did not. Keeping the patient comfortable was the only course of treatment. "What is being done for him?"

"Nothing. Welch refuses to treat him because he's a lost cause and a Negro."

"I'll examine him in the morning. We can at least make him comfortable. Will you be here or are there other Negress nurses to attend him?"

"There are others, but I'll be here."

"I will see you in the morning."

I checked the fire was fully caught and was leaving when Caro asked, "How is the captain?"

"Much better. Thank you for your help earlier. You did a wonderful job."

She tilted her head to the side and examined me as if I were a curiosity. "Thank you."

"You have experience in nursing, don't you?"

"Only with sitting by bedsides and assisting in births."

"Were you a slave?" Her enigmatic smile made me realize the foolishness of my question. "What I mean is were you an inside slave? What did they call them? House slaves?"

"Yes, that's what they were called. My mother was. We were sold when I was eight years old."

"Where did you go?"

"I don't know where my mother went. I was sold to a brothel in New Orleans."

I bowed my head and stared at the embers in the stove. Caro did not need to elaborate. I could imagine what her life would have been like. Though my imaginings did not compute with her demeanor, and I now realized, her speech, which fluctuated depending on whom she was addressing.

I was on the verge of asking more details when I saw in her countenance the same reserve I struggled to maintain since I had left New York. "Is there anything you or Jethro need?"

"No, thank you."

I nodded and left.

Finding Kindle still asleep, I moved through the administration block and into the white soldiers' ward. All ten beds were occupied. I left quickly. The smell of dirty, gaseous men was overpowering and rekindled my queasiness.

The back of the administration block was a mess hall with a kitchen attached. At the front of the block, looking out over the porch that wrapped around the building, were the doctor's office and the dispensary. Waterman was asleep on a cot in the latter office. There were stairs off the hallway but I had little energy and no desire to climb them and look at what were most likely storage rooms.

I returned to Kindle, mopped his brow with a freshened cloth, and sat down. Within minutes, my chin drooped to my chest and I was asleep.

CHAPTER

12

The sun had barely risen behind heavy gray clouds when General Sherman marched into the hospital.

"How is he?" he demanded.

I patted the dying man's chest before rising to face Sherman. "There isn't much hope. All we can do now is make him comfortable."

Sherman was shocked. "I looked in on Kindle. I thought his color was good."

I walked into the operating theater and washed my hands in the basin. "Oh, Captain Kindle will be fine, in time. I was talking of the Negro soldier, Jethro."

"How long until *Kindle* is back on his feet?"

"It depends entirely on Captain Kindle. Some men can withstand incredible amounts of pain and function as if completely healthy. Others are laid low by the smallest of ailments for an indeterminate amount of time. From what little I have seen of Captain Kindle, I would assume he is the former. If I had to hazard a guess, I would predict he will be fit for administrative duty in a week, patrols in four."

We stood in the doorway of Captain Kindle's "room," staring at the subject of our conversation. A small snore emanated from his slightly gaping mouth. His countenance was relaxed, devoid of pain.

"When he woke a few hours ago, I gave him a significant dose of laudanum. The more rest he gets the quicker he will heal."

"Four weeks is too long. I need him completely healthy. I trust you to get him there."

"I am sure the fort doctor—"

"Fort Richardson is without a doctor for a few weeks. You will fill in until the new doctor arrives."

"I will do what I can, but—"

"I was impressed with the job you did, Miss Elliston. I doubt you will have another patient as critical as Kindle. A new doctor is on the way from Sill. In the meantime, you will have no trouble treating the normal ailments found on a fort. Richardson seems to have a fair few playing Old Soldier. Take care of it. We need our men in the field hunting Indians."

"You are appointing me fort doctor?"

"Temporarily, yes."

Flabbergasted, I could not find the words to accept Sherman's offer.

"Waterman told me you were insistent on staying by Kindle's side last night. Very noble, with what you've been through. Most women would have collapsed. You proved to me you have the mettle to withstand whatever's thrown at you. Am I wrong?"

"No," I finally managed. "Thank you for your belief in me. I will not disappoint you."

"I expect not. I've left a letter of recommendation with Lieutenant Colonel Foster. If you perform your duties to his satisfaction, you will receive it when you leave. It should open a door or two for you wherever you decide to go."

"Yes, it will," I said, almost overcome with gratitude. "Thank you, General."

Sherman's steely eyes softened. "I am sorry for your loss," he said. He slapped his leather gauntlets in his left hand and his granitelike expression returned. "I am off for Fort Sill. Get these men back on duty," he demanded, and marched out of the hospital. He climbed into his waiting ambulance and the retinue I watched approach my wagon train three days prior commenced its journey to Fort Sill.

Had it only been three days?

Reveille sounded and soldiers went about their early-morning tasks amid a leaden gray mist that clung to the ground. The fog shifted around the soldiers, giving the scene a dreamlike quality.

General William Tecumseh Sherman had appointed me, a woman, fort doctor. Temporarily, but even so, leading a hospital, no matter how remote or underprovisioned, was an opportunity I would have never expected to come my way in my lifetime. If I performed to Lieutenant Colonel Foster's standards, I would leave Fort Richardson with an invaluable reference. With the name Laura Elliston on a letter signed by Sherman, I could contradict any accusation against my identity. In a few weeks I would truly be free of my past.

I was familiar enough with the Army to know "a few weeks" could mean one week to untold months. My knowledge was gathered during the war when resources had been stretched to the limit, and I didn't imagine it would be too different at a remote outpost like Fort Richardson.

Where would I go? The idea of living on the frontier was despicable. I needed civilization, despite the potential danger of chance meetings with people I might know. I supposed I might make it to San Francisco after all.

I sighed with relief and smiled.

Waterman was waiting for me at the office door. "I suppose you heard," I said.

"Yes, ma'am."

"What time does Dr. Welch usually arrive?"

"Midmorning. The log is on the desk."

"I would prefer examining the patients with no preconceived notions. The general believes we have a fair few malingerers. What do you think?"

"I'm not a doctor, ma'am. I perform whatever task the doctor sets me."

"Will you have a problem working for a female physician?"

"No, ma'am."

"Excellent."

The smell of baking bread and bacon was pronounced, and though my stomach was still unsettled, I knew I needed to eat. "Could we eat?"

"This way," Waterman said. He motioned for me to precede him into the mess hall.

"What is up there?" I asked as we passed the stairs.

"Storage and the death room."

I noted the narrow, steep stairs. "Seems an inconvenient place for preparing the dead," I said.

"A stone death house is being built behind the hospital. If it ever stops raining, we'll finish it."

The kitchen was a small room with a wood-burning stove and a worktable piled high with dirty bowls and cooking implements. Along the walls and in the corners, stacked crates and barrels doubled as shelves for canned goods and spices. Ladles of various sizes and states of cleanliness were hooked over a thin-gauge wire strung up along one wall. A wooden wall that separated the kitchen from the storeroom held pots, pans, and skillets on nails hammered into the wall. On the longest wall in the room, unbroken by windows, hung a single clipboard.

A thin man with stooped shoulders and a wooden leg was at the worktable using a rusty, opened tin can to cut biscuits. He turned and gestured to the vacant wall. "I hope you came here to tell me I'm getting shelves."

Waterman replied in a weary voice, as if this was a recurring conversation. "I've told you, Martin, I've put the request in."

Martin made his plea to me. "Shelves aren't too much to ask, are they? I've got a whole wall waiting for them."

Waterman answered for me. "No, Martin, they're not. Each time I write to the medical department, I request supplies to build them. Every time, I'm turned down."

"Sutler has the supplies."

"What would you like me to pay him with?"

The cook looked surly but didn't answer.

"That's what I thought," Waterman said. "Martin, this is Dr. Elliston. She will be in charge until the new doctor arrives."

"Can you get me some shelves?"

"I will do my best."

The old man grunted and returned to his biscuits.

Waterman made the two of us plates of beans, bacon, and warm biscuits from an earlier batch. We were leaving when the cook stopped me. "Can't eat biscuits without a bit of sorghum." He poured a heaping spoonful of dark syrup over my biscuit.

"Thank you," I said, with as much gratitude as I could muster. The flaky biscuit was lost underneath a pool of viscous syrup.

When we were out of earshot, Waterman whispered, "He is trying to bribe you. He doesn't share his sorghum with anyone."

"I've never eaten it."

We spent the next few minutes eating in companionable silence. After taking a tentative bite of a syrup-covered biscuit I delivered my verdict. "It is very good." After a few bites of food I would have considered bland under any other circumstances, my hunger increased and it took every ounce of my willpower to eat with dignity. Strength and energy from this plain but hearty sustenance flowed through my limbs. Even the coffee tasted better.

I heard a distant bugle and within a minute the mobile patients shuffled in for breakfast. A couple of the men were laughing, talking, and looked anything but ill. When they saw us their levity was replaced with a fearful suspicion, and a stooped-shoulder shuffle replaced their healthy steps. I ate the last of my biscuit and wiped my mouth with a coarse napkin. "I will be with Captain Kindle. Would you steal a biscuit for the captain to eat when he wakes?"

"Yes, ma'am."

I smiled my thanks, gave the men in line a quick disapproving glance, and left to check on Kindle.

I smelled Welch before I saw him. It was the sour smell of stale whisky and a body odor I would come to associate with many men in the West, just as the smell of filth and sewage was characteristic of the seedier parts of New York City. Welch stood over Kindle, holding the captain's wrist in one hand and his pocket watch in the other. Welch dropped Kindle's hand, pushed his watch into his vest, and with a slap on Kindle's face, tried to wake him up.

"Captain! Captain!"

"Stop that this instant."

Welch ignored me and continued his attempt to rouse Kindle. Patches of red tarnished Kindle's pale complexion.

"Mr. Welch, stop hitting my patient this instant!"

He stopped and turned his bloodshot, glassy eyes to me. His

hair was dirty and stringy, reminding me of the wet mop Maureen used on the flagstones in our New York kitchen. His face was not bearded but was unshaven, a look that would be disreputable even if his teeth were not brown and rotten. I knew instinctively this man was not a doctor.

"Who the hell do you think you are?"

"Dr. Laura Elliston, Captain Kindle's physician, and as of an hour ago, the acting post surgeon. You are Mr. Welch, I presume."

"Dr. Welch."

"I highly doubt that."

Waterman stood behind me, much to my relief. A quick glance over my shoulder revealed Caro standing a few feet behind Welch.

"A woman is questioning my credentials as a doctor?"

"If you have any credentials at all, yes, I question them."

Waterman stepped forward. "Your services are no longer needed here, Silas. General Sherman made it clear before he left that Dr. Elliston is to take charge. If you would like to see the letter he left for Colonel Mackenzie, you are welcome to. You will receive your back pay when the payroll comes from Fort Sill."

"You just do what you're told, don't you, Waterman?" Welch smirked. "Path of least resistance."

"My job is to follow orders, not pass judgment on what the orders are, or who is giving them."

"Keep tellin' yourself that."

Waterman grabbed Welch and pulled him out of the room. Welch turned his eyes full of watery hatred on me. "You won't last long here, bitch," he growled, fists clenched.

"That's enough," Kindle said.

Welch's pugilistic approach to waking Kindle had worked, much to everyone's surprise. "Captain." I put my hand on his good shoulder as Kindle tried to prop himself up. "Don't bother yourself. Corporal Waterman and I have this under control. Rest."

Welch wrenched his elbow from Waterman's grasp and with an air of pride, pulled at the lapels of his coat. "Yeah, better rest up and enjoy the last few days with two arms and legs. You know as well as I do you're as like to walk out of here half a man as you are to walk out of here at all. Especially with a woman 'doctor.'"

"Get him out of here," I said.

Welch shrugged away from Waterman and gave me a final, withering look. "You have no idea what you've gotten yourself into, missy." Welch backed out of the doorway and into Caro. He pushed her away. "Don't touch me, nigger."

Caro towered over Welch by five or six inches. Instead of being intimidated by the epithet Welch had hurled she stood her ground. Welch ran his hand through his greasy hair and left. Waterman followed. I nodded to Caro and turned my attention to Kindle.

"Look who's awake," I said.

"Am I?" Kindle asked.

"Unfortunately, yes. I did not plan on slapping you awake for at least two or three more hours."

Kindle's smile was weak, his eyes half-open. He offered his good hand to me and I took it. His fingers were long, lean, and surprisingly unscarred, the hand of an artist, not a cavalry officer. He squeezed my hand and slurred his thanks to me. What he was thanking me for I had no idea, nor did I care. With my foot, I pulled my chair closer and sat, still holding Kindle's hand. He went in and out of consciousness, trying valiantly to stay focused and engage me in conversation. I chided him to be quiet and get some sleep. With the gentle admonishment, he relaxed and let the laudanum take him under yet again.

CHAPTER

13

It is almost time for rounds, Doctor."

I lifted my head from my chest and realized with chagrin I had fallen asleep holding Kindle's hand. The light through the window had cleared from the gray of morning to the brightness of midday. Finally, it had stopped raining.

Caro watched me from a chair across from Kindle's bed, her hands folded in her lap. Waterman stood in the doorway. I didn't know who had spoken.

"Rounds. Yes." I placed Kindle's hand on his chest, stood, and gasped as a knife edge of pain slashed through my shoulder. Waterman was beside me at once, supporting me.

Caro rose and portioned out a dose from the laudanum bottle on the table next to Kindle's bed. "You must take something for the pain," she said.

"No. It will subside in time. I must have my faculties for rounds."

I still wore the navy dress from the day before, with its large bloodstain on the chest. Thankfully, the material was dark enough it didn't show, but it was stiff and uncomfortable. "I would like to freshen up. Change." It dawned on me that only my medical trunk was here. "Where are my things?"

"They were taken to Captain Kindle's quarters," Waterman said. "I didn't know what else to do with them."

"Where are his quarters?"

"Across the parade ground."

I had no frame of reference for what that meant since the darkness, rain, and urgency of the night before had obliterated any opportunity for viewing the fort, and in the time since, I had scarcely looked out the window of the hospital. It sounded like a journey of a thousand miles. "Is there an apron I can wear?"

"Yes." Waterman retrieved an apron from the office and handed it to me. I looped it over my head, and with a grimace at the pain in my shoulder, tied it around my waist. It would have to do for now.

"Lead on," I said. Fighting against the pain, I rolled my shoulder to loosen it up.

We walked through the administration block and into the south wing of the hospital. In the light of day, the lack of funds and supplies frontier Army forts suffered from was plain. Metal cots with straw-stuffed mattresses served as beds. Small, four-legged, rickety tables stood next to each. Army blankets hung crookedly over a few windows, all closed against the fresh air, which, according to reigning medical theory was one of the causes of infection and disease. A few beds were draped with fine-mesh nets to combat bugs. Others were bare of anything save a pillow and a moth-eaten blanket. Every bed was taken.

The infirm soldiers stood at the feet of their beds, some easier than others. One man, under the chimney of the wood-burning stove, was bedridden due to an amputated leg. Soot dusted the blanket covering him. A few soldiers, untethered by beds, stood in a group at the end of the hall, here to be examined for a small complaint, chronic illness (most likely of a sexual nature), or hoping to fake a believable case of Old Soldier for a day or two of respite from monotonous daily tasks.

When the men realized I was taking Welch's place and would be examining them, many left rather than have to explain their complaint to me. It was just as well; I did not have the energy to feign politeness and concern for maladies that were a direct result of carnal weakness or drunkenness. I knew they would return for treatment eventually—or seek out Welch in town on their own time—when I would be rested and free of pain, my Hippocratic nature restored.

I examined the man with the amputated leg first. A sheen of perspiration covered his pale face. His eyes were bloodshot and rimmed with bruises. His lips were pale and cracked like a dry riverbed. His breathing was labored, not from an obstruction in his lungs, but from the effort to ignore the pain in his right leg. I enlisted the aid of the soldier assigned to hospital duty to remove the bandages.

"What is your name, soldier?"

"Jonah Howerton, ma'am."

"When was his last dose of laudanum?" I asked Waterman.

When Waterman didn't answer, I asked again, with less politeness.

"He hasn't had one in a couple of days."

"Did you say a couple of *days*?"

Waterman looked down at the log he held in his hand and didn't answer.

With difficulty, Howerton answered for him. "Dr. Welch said...we were running low of laudanum and...could only give it...to cases that need it...Was time I got used to the pain...without the help."

I glared at Waterman. "We are low on supplies," Waterman confirmed.

"Give him thirty drops. I assume we have that much."

"Yes." Waterman noted it down in his log.

Two facts struck me when I turned my attention to the soldier's exposed stump. First, whatever Welch's credentials were or were not, he had extensive experience in amputation. If I was honest, it was a better job than I would have done. Second, the leg was ripe with infection. The soldier would die from it, and soon. I motioned for the orderly to rewrap the wound.

"We are going to move you out from under this chimney and get your dose of laudanum. Which bed would you like?"

"One where I can see the creek."

"Will do," I said. I patted him on the shoulder and moved on.

I moved through the remainder of the patients quickly, diagnosing scurvy for three, malingering for two, and a possible case of syphilis, until there were only five of the twelve beds occupied.

Howerton was settled into his new bed with a laudanum-induced expression of idiotic pleasure over his face. I was removing the blanket from the window opposite his bed when a jolly, booming voice rang out.

"Well! If this isn't a sight for sore eyes!"

A fat man with gray hair and a bushy mustache stood in the doorway at the opposite end of the hall, resplendent in the cleanest garments I had seen on a man since Galveston. His uniform positively shone with color—the dark blue coat, the butter yellow stripes on his pants, the red sash tied at his waist, his polished brass buttons—throwing the muted colors of his surroundings into shadow. Immediately, I became conscious of my own disheveled and dirty state.

For such a fat man he was surprisingly light of foot, gliding over the floor toward me, his paunch cutting through the air like the prow of a ship. He extended his hand. "You must be the doctor everyone is talking about! Lieutenant Colonel Charles Foster," he said, pumping my hand.

"Laura Elliston."

"If you aren't the prettiest thing I've seen since San Antonio," he said with a laugh. "Though don't repeat that around any of the other officers' wives. They may get offended."

I had no doubt he gave the same compliment to every woman he met, but I agreed to keep his secret with a smile.

"I don't think I've ever seen a fort hospital so empty. Mackenzie will be thrilled. We need all the healthy men we can get."

"You can trust I will not encourage malingering," I replied. "Which is what the majority of the men were guilty of."

"Good, good!"

"I am surprised at the number of obvious cases. I only met Mr. Welch briefly and was not impressed, I'll grant you. But, even someone with minimal medical knowledge could see these men were not sick."

"Well, there are always men that will try to get something for nothing and nothing for something, if you know what I mean. What is important is you've rooted the bad ones out and put them back to work. Sherman wanted it. Mackenzie will be thrilled. As am I! Tell me, how is Captain Kindle? Fine man and officer."

"I was on my way to check on him."

Foster stepped aside to allow me to pass. Instead of leading him straight through to Kindle, I led Foster into the dispensary where Waterman was mixing the laudanum. I abated their puzzlement quickly. "Welch said something earlier that at the time I thought was vindictiveness, but after examining Private Howerton, I wonder."

"Who is Private Howerton?" Foster said.

"The soldier with the amputated leg," I replied.

"Right, right. What did Welch say?"

I rubbed my throbbing head, trying to remember through the haze of the last few days. "Something to the effect of Kindle not leaving here a whole man."

Waterman furnished the quote, word for word.

"Yes, thank you, Waterman. I wondered, Lieutenant Colonel Foster, is there a history of infection and amputations at the hospital here?"

"I would hardly know," he replied. "Mackenzie and I have been here barely two months."

"Did the former post surgeon relate any concerns?"

Foster's lip curled in disgust. "He was a repulsive man. High on opium half the time. Wouldn't take what he said with a grain of salt."

I turned to Waterman, who answered, "There have been a fair number of amputations."

"Warranted or not?"

"Warranted."

"Infection is a problem."

"Infection is a problem in every hospital," Foster said. "It's a fact of life, hardly unique to the Army or Fort Richardson."

"Yes, I know, but..."

"Best you can do is treat them and hope their constitution is strong enough to see them through. I have no doubt Kindle is one of those men."

"I am sure he..."

"Sherman came by to see you this morning, I hear. He said the men would rather work than be treated by a woman and he was right." Foster laughed. "I admit I had reservations about his decision to make you fort surgeon temporarily, but after seeing you clean out the ward and receiving a letter from Sill stating our surgeon is on his way, my reservations vanished. There's no harm in you acting the part until a real doctor comes."

"Act the part?"

"We have a fair few women and children here. You can treat them. I'm sure they will find it quite a lark to be seen to by a woman doctor."

I pressed my lips together, the urge to flay Foster with a piece of my mind almost too much to resist. I thought of Kindle's health and continued to state my case, my voice as steady as I could make it. "Sir, if you will let me finish. My concerns..."

"No need to do more today. Why don't you go get some rest and refresh yourself? You've been through quite an ordeal and I do believe I see a bit of dried blood." He waved his finger in the general direction of my chest.

"Yes, it is Captain Kindle's blood, which at this moment is inconsequential. I am trying to tell you I believe infection is endemic in this hospital, and unless we want Captain Kindle to lose his arm and leg and possibly his *life*, we should move him out of the hospital immediately."

In the silence following my outburst all that could be heard was the distant *clank* of Corporal Martin cooking lunch. Foster's good-natured smile wavered for a moment before settling in again underneath the protection of his mustache. "There is no need to raise your voice, Miss Elliston."

I thought of the letter from Sherman this man had in his possession and put on a conciliatory smile on my face. "I am sorry, sir. With everything that has happened..." I trailed off with a sigh to let Foster think my female emotions were coming through instead of professional anger.

"Do you believe it truly necessary to move him?"

"I do not see the harm in it."

"Don't you?" Foster said. "Moving him would make him more likely to pick up some germ or another. No, it's probably best he stay right where he is. Though we do need to move the Negroes out of there."

"Sir, the theory that germs do not move through the air is becoming more widely accepted. Many believe once infection gets into a certain area—building, hospital, ship, even a room—it is likely to always be there. There were some hospitals during the war that had few losses due to infection, almost none in fact, and there were others where it was rampant. If we even slightly suspected this hospital was the latter, would not it behoove us to move the captain, if not out of certainty, at least out of overprotectiveness of a man that, from all accounts, is a fine officer?"

Foster pursed his lips in thought. "I don't see it as necessary, but I suppose there's no harm in it. If you deem it necessary, Kindle shall be removed. Would his quarters be an acceptable location?"

"I am sure they will be fine," I replied.

"Waterman will see to it," Foster said.

"Thank you, Lieutenant Colonel."

"Whatever you need, Miss Elliston, you come to me." With a small wave of his hand, he left.

CHAPTER
14

I stood on the front porch of Kindle's quarters, taking in the sights and sounds of the fort. Richardson was an enormous square stamped in the middle of the plains, bordered on the west by a meandering creek and supported by a town a half mile distant. The Army had taken full advantage of not having natural boundaries limiting the size of the fort, centering Richardson with a large parade ground where soldiers on horseback and foot drilled daily. But the sight of the three hundred men on evening dress parade and the attendant sounds of jingling cavalry tack and unified movements did little to alleviate the fear in my breast at the exposed and sprawling fort. On the short journey from the wagon train to the fort, the idea of the protection the fort and its soldiers would provide had done as much as could be expected to lift my spirits. In the twilight of my first day at Fort Richardson, the reality of the fort sunk them again.

Even with Kindle's truthful description the day before, the fort I had conjured in my mind resembled the bastions of the East: solid in construction, uniform in appearance, and surrounded by fortified walls. Those buildings had a comforting permanence about them, with their wooden or stone facades seemingly a part of nature around them, as if the earth had sensed our human need for protection and offered up its resources. We were comforted in the knowledge it would take great violence to eradicate these edifices of our destiny. In contrast, Fort Richardson looked like the stick models of soldier forts children construct in their gardens, whose sole purpose is to mimic the inevitable grand destruction by the tin soldiers populated in and around it.

Soldiers and cavalry lined up on the muddy expanse of the parade ground. With the experience of weeks on a dusty trail and the sucking quagmire of mud I crossed hours before when transferring Kindle from the hospital to his quarters, I appreciated the effort the men put into making their dress uniforms spotless, though I wondered at the necessity of such a parade in weather like this. Lieutenant Colonel Foster, the most resplendent and spotless of all, walked the length of the parade ground on boards laid down to protect his boots from the mud.

The sun set behind the hospital in a striking display of red, orange, and yellow, with a few clouds deflecting the colors into muted hues of purple and blue around their edges. The soldiers stared straight ahead, and I wondered who among them was appreciating nature's performance and who was oblivious.

"It is beautiful, is it not?"

A woman appeared before me floating at the bottom of the porch steps like an apparition. Her black dress was high necked and fitted through her torso, showing off one of the smallest waists I had ever seen. The cut of the dress was simple and rather regimental and lacked ornamentation save the row of polished gold buttons on her sleeves. I resisted, with difficulty, the urge to salute.

"Quite beautiful," I agreed, returning my gaze to the sunset.

"This is my favorite time of day," she said. "Some think dress parades are pointless out here on the frontier. I think standards should be kept, no matter where you are. The standards are what make the Army what it is. Don't you agree?"

It was easier to agree than to correct her misapprehension that my appreciation was for the various shades of blue lined up before me.

"I am Harriet Mackenzie."

"Laura Elliston. You are the colonel's wife?"

"His sister."

The order for dismissal rang out across the fort. The soldiers dispersed to their next tasks amid a low murmur of talking, the creak of leather, and the occasional burst of laughter. More than a few noted our presence.

"How is Captain Kindle?" Harriet Mackenzie asked, watching the soldiers.

"Resting."

I glanced over my shoulder. A thin muslin curtain floated out of the open window, behind which I could see Kindle lying on a cot. He was in the same position I had left him in an hour earlier when I had taken a much-needed break to change my dress and perform a quick toilet in the room I would be occupying on the second floor.

"You have had a rather eventful few days," Miss Mackenzie said. When I did not reply she continued. "I am sorry for your loss."

"Thank you." *How many times have I offered the same condolences? How hollow they sound.*

"Is moving Captain Kindle into his quarters entirely appropriate?" Harriet asked.

"As his doctor, I believe it is."

"Oh, I am not questioning your reasoning behind the removal." She chuckled as if the idea of her challenging authority

154

was absurd. "I am quite sure you are familiar with the latest medical theories. Though we are removed from civilization, we still must maintain appropriate behavior. It is more critical here, when we are so removed from society, lest we forget the standards and morals that separate us from the savages."

I must have looked incredibly stupid since I did not have any idea what she was talking about. She continued in a patronizing manner.

"As I believe Lieutenant Colonel Foster mentioned to you, we have a fair few young women, officers' wives as well as children, in residence. It would hardly be appropriate for a woman, such as you, to be living under the same roof with a man. They are young and might find the arrangement shocking."

"You do not?"

"I do not approve, to be sure. I am hardly shocked."

It was a bald lie, but she pulled it off well. "You said 'a woman such as me.' Whatever did you mean?"

"An unmarried, somewhat young, handsome woman."

I did not know whether to slap her or laugh at her. Laughter won out, which offended her more than a slap would have. It was a relief to laugh.

"Yes, the situation would be much easier if I were old and ugly." I wiped the tears of laughter from my cheeks. My left shoulder smarted from the sudden movement.

"Really, Miss Elliston! I hardly find this situation cause for laughter."

My mirth died. "It is Dr. Elliston, Miss Mackenzie, and I will beg you remember it. I am sorry I am not older and uglier to spare the gentle feelings of the young wives, but I cannot change my appearance, even if I were so inclined. I have always found it repulsive and ridiculous the idea less attractive women are somehow more qualified to take care of men on their sickbed."

"I never meant to imply you were not qualified…"

"Furthermore, if I wanted to attach a man, which I decidedly do *not*, I would not need the aid of the heightened emotions of a sickbed. I am a doctor and Captain Kindle's health is what I am interested in ministering to. My second objective is perform the duties set upon me by General Sherman, then leave this country, which—the beautiful sunset notwithstanding—resembles nothing more than the seventh circle of hell to me."

"Dr. Elliston, your language is hardly appropriate."

"There is that word again! Oh, how I have always loathed the word *appropriate*! It is a word used most often by women without the courage or imagination to think and do for themselves and by men who routinely engage in inappropriate behavior behind closed doors."

It took a great deal of effort for Harriet to remain civil after my outburst. If she had shown even a bit of emotion or told me plainly what she thought, I would have respected her much more. Instead, she wrapped herself in the cloak of responsibility and civility her position as the commander's sister required. "Lieutenant Colonel Foster requested I organize a time for the women and children to see you for their complaints."

I sighed and rolled my aching shoulder. What I wanted more than anything else was to sleep. "Get with Waterman and select a time. I do not know the post schedule or, indeed, the depth and breadth of my responsibilities. I am sure I can find an hour or two to see the women and children."

"I will tell everyone you are a war widow. It should lend you the respectability you are sorely lacking. Good evening."

She left.

I smiled. Maybe Harriet had more spirit than I gave her credit for. I took one last look at the fort before me, noting excessive activity near the corral, and went to check on Kindle.

I walked softly into the simply furnished parlor. A small fire glowed from the grate and a dimmed oil lamp sat on the table next to Kindle's bed. I did not notice Kindle was awake until I sat down in my chair. "You're awake. And, smiling."

"Have you ever been on the stage, Miss Elliston? Forgive me—*Doctor* Elliston."

"You heard."

"It would have been difficult to miss, even if the window had not been open."

"I suppose I should be chagrined. Alas, I am not. How is your pain? Your voice is strong." I listened to his heart with my stethoscope.

"The pain is tolerable, but not for much longer, I fear."

I draped the stethoscope around my neck. "Can you sit up?"

He nodded and took my offered arm. "Your lungs sound good. Wait while I position a pillow for you."

I placed a flat pillow and a rough blanket folded into a thick square behind his back for support and helped him lie back.

"What is wrong with your arm?" he asked.

"What?"

"Your left arm. You wince every time you move it."

"I didn't realize."

I retreated into the kitchen for the plate of beans and biscuit I had commandeered from the hospital kitchen. "You should eat something. This doesn't look like much but I had it this morning and it was surprisingly good. I'm sorry to say Corporal Martin doesn't like you enough to share his sorghum syrup."

"You're ignoring my question."

"Yes, I am."

"I won't stop asking until you tell me what happened."

"If you must know, you collapsed and I happened to be in the way. Not to worry. It popped right back in and is only a little stiff as a result. Please, don't look so abashed. I am fine. It wasn't bad enough to keep me from taking a bullet out of your shoulder."

"I am sorry, Laura."

"I'm fine. You, on the other hand, need to eat."

"What am I doing in my quarters?"

"I had you moved here."

"Apparently. But, why?"

"To decrease your chance of infection."

I moved my chair closer to his bed and held the plate in my lap. I handed him the biscuit.

"Biscuit and beans," Kindle said with little enthusiasm. He took the biscuit and bit into it. "You know what I miss about the East more than anything?"

"The food?"

"Yes. I have not eaten a memorable meal since Saint Louis in sixty-four." He took another bite. "I should probably amend that. I have had many memorable meals, unique in ways that would not be considered polite conversation." I handed him a glass of whisky. He drank and after a small sigh of pleasure asked, "What was your last memorable meal?"

"Oh," I chuckled. "There are so many to choose from."

"Tell them all."

"Good Lord, no," I laughed. "That would make my dissatisfaction more acute, longing for what I cannot have."

"You haven't been here long enough to be dissatisfied, surely."

"*Dissatisfied* isn't the right word. None of this is what I expected." I smoothed my skirt and picked at an invisible loose thread. What was it about Kindle that made me want to talk, to tell him everything? Would he be shocked? Turn me in for the reward? Or would he proposition me as Amos Pike had? I resisted the almost overwhelming urge to confess, more to retain my good opinion of Kindle than out of fear of the consequences. He was not a man to be put off, however. If I didn't tell him something, he would probe and prod until he discovered my secret. "I thought the stories were exaggerations. Maureen believed. I teased her about it. I should have known."

"Why?"

I smiled and chuckled. Because of Antietam, I thought. I couldn't very well tell him that. I feared that talking to William Kindle would always be a battle between telling him too much and telling him nothing.

"Funny, I believed Sherman's story of white men raiding as Indians quicker than Amos and Ester's stories of Indian attacks."

"Who is Ester?"

"The woman whose boardinghouse we stayed in, in Austin. Her husband was tortured and killed by Comanche. Is it true? About white men?"

Kindle nodded. "Men come west to either get rich or to escape from the law. The ones who come to escape usually get rich by stealing and killing."

"Are they as difficult to catch as the Indians?"

"No. Usually, they leave a pretty clear path when they ride into a town and cause problems. There's one group who's so good at what they do we didn't even know they existed until recently. We still don't know who any of them are, who the leader is. They're the worst bunch we've seen."

"I suppose Harriet was right, in a way. It is important to remind us of our civility lest we become savages." I shook my head. "I shouldn't have come west. If I hadn't, Maureen would still be alive."

"Do you think so?"

"I never saw raiding Indians in Washington Square."

159

"I thought you were from London."

"I lived in London as a child."

"That explains your fluctuating accent." He finished his whisky. I took the glass from him and placed it on the table. "Maureen would have died no matter where she was. It would not have mattered if she was walking through a city or crossing the Trinity River. God determined it was her day."

"It does matter *how* she died, though, and that responsibility lay firmly at my own feet."

He shifted in his bed. "I have seen boys on their deathbeds saying the right things but still unable to mask the fear of the beyond written in their eyes. I've seen men sitting in a tent, eating dinner one minute and joking about their deaf grandfather and blind grandmother, the next minute they are cannon fodder. Which is the good death and which is the bad?"

"The boys died well."

"Is it better to know you are dying? To waste away in front of your own eyes and the eyes of those who love you? The other death is horrible in its suddenness, but its unexpectedness is also a blessing. They died happy. Your friend, Maureen, was she happy before she died?"

I thought of the change in Maureen while we were on the trail, the brightness in her eyes, the bloom on her cheek, the possibility of a home with Cornelius in her future, and my inability to bless it. My head throbbed. My answer was faint. "Yes."

He closed his eyes. "You are responsible for her happiness. Not for her death."

"Are you saying death is predetermined by God but happiness is not? That Maureen would not have found the same happiness in New York, though Death would have found her regardless?"

"Yes."

"That's a novel philosophy."

He opened his eyes and smiled. "I'm under the influence of opium and whisky. I don't know what I'm saying." He swung his legs off the bed and sat up.

"What on earth are you doing?"

"I want to stand."

I caught him before he fell. I helped him sit back down and admonished him. "One biscuit and you think you can conquer the world. You must rest for at least a couple of days."

"That is excessive."

"Do I need to remind you of your two surgeries inside of one day?"

"No."

"I will anyway. You've had two major surgeries in less than a day. Your body needs time to heal itself."

"I've been injured before and returned to duties quickly with no adverse effect."

"I didn't say you wouldn't return to duties quickly. I told General Sherman you would be up and about in a week and in the saddle in four."

"Four weeks?"

"I was being conservative. If you do exactly what I say, you may be back in the saddle in two."

"Try one."

"Try two." I crossed my arms and tried to hide my wince of pain. "Would you rather be in the saddle in one with pain or in two without?"

"I am not in pain now."

"Captain, you are an incredibly bad liar."

"I am normally a good liar. Maybe you are more intuitive than most."

"What I am is impervious to flattery."

"No woman is impervious to flattery."

"The distinction here is I am a doctor first, a woman second. If you continue to lie to me, Captain, and treat me as you would a weak-willed woman who faints at the sight of blood, I will not be able to treat you appropriately, which will only prolong your recovery. Now, if you will listen to me instead of patronizing me I can explain your treatment plan."

"If Miss Mackenzie could hear you she would fully believe you do not have romantic designs on me."

"Do you think I was lying to her?"

"I suppose not, which rather breaks my heart."

"Maybe I should amend my treatment plan since you are well enough to flirt with me, though rather badly."

"I apologize. I am out of practice."

"Your behavior is highly inappropriate and a bit shocking after pontificating on death and happiness not a minute ago. We don't want to give credence to Harriet Mackenzie's ridiculous idea my treating you is inappropriate."

"You're right. Forgive me."

"We'll say no more about it. Now. Your plan."

"Let me guess. Rest."

"Yes. We will gradually decrease your laudanum and increase your activity. For the first two days, bed rest. A few times a day I will help you stand and walk around a little. It will exhaust you, which will encourage rest. On the third day, you will get out of the house and move around the fort. Sit on the porch and hold court if you like."

"Thankfully, holding court is not my job."

"We can sit on the porch and play backgammon. I saw a board in the parlor."

"I cannot be seen sitting on the porch, playing backgammon,

even if I am recuperating. If Mackenzie is right, Fort Richardson is going to be the main staging ground for whatever retaliation Sherman has in mind."

"Is that how it works out here, an eye for an eye? It's no wonder it's so dangerous."

"Sherman's pride has been wounded. Whoever attacked your group probably just rang the death knell for the plains Indians." He shifted. "Thank God Mackenzie is in charge."

"As opposed to whom?"

Kindle laughed. "Almost anyone else. Especially Custer."

"I thought he was one of the best Indian fighters."

"Don't believe everything you read in the Northern newspapers. Let's just say the difference between the two is studied calculation versus vainglorious impetuousness."

"And I suppose Custer is the latter?"

"In my experience, yes."

"Colonel Mackenzie went after the Indians who attacked us?"

Kindle nodded. "They'll evaporate into the Territory. Maybe they'll try to sell the cattle they stole back to Sill. They do that, you know." He laughed. "If they weren't so savage, you'd have to admire them."

"Forgive me if I don't admire them. Now"—I stood—"let me check your wounds."

"Speaking of wounds, what is that awful smell coming from my shoulder?"

I washed my hands in the basin on the table. "Carbolic acid, if applied correctly to wounds, has been shown to significantly decrease infection. It should keep it at bay altogether, especially now that you are out of the hospital."

As I went about my task, Kindle's scrutiny weighed on me. I kept up a commentary on the state of his wounds to keep my focus on my task and away from him. I did not want him

163

to suspect that my irritation with his banter had to do with anything other than my desire for professional respect. He said not a word during the exam, but waited until he was dosed with laudanum and settled back on the bed.

"May I ask you a question?"

"Of course."

"How do you feel?"

From my toilet earlier, I knew my appearance showed plainly my inner torment. I liked Kindle too well to lie to him. "Terrible." The admission of which made the headache and nausea, my constant companions since the massacre, more prominent. "Though good enough to take care of you."

"Will a nurse come soon to relieve you so you can rest?"

"There's no need."

"I insist," he replied. His eyes were drooping and his words were slurring together. "Promise me you will send for one and take care of yourself."

"I promise," I lied, as he drifted off to sleep.

CHAPTER

15

As it turned out, Caro came of her own accord, around midnight, giving me the opportunity to have a few hours of uninterrupted sleep. The next morning, as the sun broke through the thin curtains fluttering in the open window, I took full stock of myself for the first time.

The mirror over the dresser was small with a long diagonal crack down the center, but not small enough to hide how gaunt and haggard I looked. Dark circles ringed my eyes, making my naturally fair complexion look more faded than usual.

My headache was abating but still present, throbbing steadily in time with my heartbeat. The nausea was absent, thankfully, replaced by ravishing hunger, due in no small part to the smell of bacon floating up the stairs.

I splashed cold water from the porcelain basin on my face and rinsed my mouth out. I removed my shift and bathed myself with a coarse, damp washcloth. I dressed in a clean dress and almost gagged at the smell of wildflowers. I rummaged through my trunk and found a sachet of dried wildflowers Maureen had made from the ones I picked for her the first day of our journey across Texas. I stared at the small pouch and tentatively lifted it to my nose. As I sniffed the musky scent of the prairie—grass, dirt, a hint of sage, and the muted sweetness of the pervasive bluebonnets—the sounds of the massacre ricocheted in my head.

I dropped the bag, covered my ears with my hands, and squeezed my eyes against the images. My breaths came in short bursts, and I rocked on my heels, trying to get control of myself. With great effort I forced myself to think of a happy memory, of my childhood in England with my cousin Charlotte. The pasties we would steal from the kitchens, the small dollhouse we played with, reading *Jane Eyre* to each other and falling in love with Rochester, fighting over which of us would win him if we had the chance. My smile slipped when I wondered if I would ever see Charlotte again. I steadied my breathing. When I opened my eyes, they were drawn to the open bottle of laudanum on my bedside table.

The wooden platform bed creaked under my weight as I sat down. The room smelled of freshly lumbered wood and I wondered how long Kindle had lived in these quarters. Had he and his men built this small house? It would have been a cozy place to live if it weren't marooned in the middle of the prairie and surrounded by heathens.

I picked up the cork stopper and remembered with chagrin the night before. Sleep was kept at bay by visions of the attack and morbid fantasies of the exposed fort being overrun by an army of thousands of Indians. My mind also drifted to Anna. The thought of her being raped repeatedly and mercilessly finally drove me to my medical bag and the bottle of laudanum now sitting innocently, and half-empty, on my bedside table.

My racing heart beat with every throb of my head. The temptation to banish my vivid visions with more laudanum so I could get through the day was seductive. I lifted the bottle to drink deeply when the image of my dear father, lying in a crude wooden coffin, coins covering his eyes, stayed my hand. My wonderful, honorable father had spent the last few months of his life behind the same haze I yearned for. The bottle reminded me of my humiliation at the man he became, and how I, in my youthful hubris, scorned his justifications and excuses.

Slowly, I replaced the cork stopper and dropped the bottle into my medical bag. As appealing as the idea was, I couldn't afford to be pulled into insensibility. Sherman had given me the opportunity to turn this tragedy into a positive and I was determined to succeed.

Resolved, I pinched my cheeks, patted my hair into place, and left the room.

Kindle was propped up in bed and looking much better than I had expected, due in no small part to the half-eaten plate of bacon and eggs he balanced on his lap. In the kitchen, Caro hummed an unfamiliar tune and periodically had brief conversations with herself about her tasks. The scene was an unpleasant reminder of the happy days of my childhood when my father would read the paper at the kitchen table, eating the breakfast Maureen served, while she puttered around the kitchen, singing Irish tunes and admonishing me to mind my manners. Another memory to file away for later.

"You look well enough to, dare I say, ride a horse?"

"I believe I am," Kindle replied. "Though I am under strict instructions to play the invalid for at least another day."

"Two days."

"We shall see."

"You're dressed," I said, noting his blue breeches, shirt, and unbuttoned waistcoat.

"Yes, Caro helped me this morning while you were having a lie-in."

I bristled. "A lie-in?"

"A much-needed rest."

"Please, Captain, don't mind my vanity. Abuse my outward appearance as much as you like."

"I doubt you have a vain bone in your body. I, on the other hand, am quite a dandy. I must be presentable for the hordes of well-wishers who are sure to visit me."

"I understand, though your garments will make it inconvenient to check your wounds."

Caro walked in from the kitchen, holding a metal coffeepot. "I checked the bandages before getting him dressed, ma'am. No infection."

I resisted a sharp retort with difficulty and forced myself to relax and smile. My recent testiness was not a typical characteristic of mine and was even grating on *my* nerves. "Wonderful. Thank you, Caro."

"You're welcome. I made coffee. I'll bring your breakfast."

"Thank you."

With no professional tasks to distract me I stood in the middle of the drawing room floor—though to call it a drawing room was generous in the extreme—acutely embarrassed, as if I was standing in the bedroom of a man and not a patient. Turning my back on Kindle, I took in the view of the wide-open prairie out the back window of the room. "Why does this fort not have walls?"

"It's believed walls offer a false sense of security. Without them, we are always vigilant." He paused before continuing. "It's not in the Indian's nature to assault a fixed position, such as a fort. They prefer to raid homesteads and small groups where they have the advantage of numbers and surprise."

"Like wagon trains."

He was saved the necessity of answering by the brief return

of Caro with two cups of coffee. I thanked her, forced it down, and marveled at the lack of disgust on Kindle's face after taking a large gulp. "I've had worse," he said.

I walked across the room to the front window. Every soldier had a task and was performing it, if not exactly with enthusiasm, at least with a languid purpose. Kindle's quarters, along with the other officers' quarters, made up the southern boundary of the fort, affording me a view of half the buildings on the eastern "border," the hospital to the west, and straight ahead, a row of picket-style buildings.

"Those are quarters for the enlisted men," Kindle said.

I pushed away the uneasiness his clairvoyance gave me and asked him about the buildings to the right.

"Adjutant's office, reading room, quartermaster's office, bank quarters. Just out of sight, near the corral, is the sutler's store."

"Reading room?"

"It was the pet project of the first commander's wife. Harriet—Miss Mackenzie—teaches the children there in the mornings. You're welcome to borrow any book that interests you."

"Is it used by the men?"

"Not as much as I would like, but some. Behind the barracks are mess halls for the men and on the far side of the fort are the stables and corral."

"North of the hospital?"

"Bakery, ordnance store, magazine, guardhouse."

Caro entered the room again and placed the plate on the table. Kindle thanked her and complimented her cooking. "The eggs were perfect, Caro. Thank you."

Kindle, finished with his breakfast, watched me eat. "Shouldn't you be sleeping?" I asked.

"I'm waiting on you to take me on a turn around the room.

You promised me one or two today. I have been looking forward to it for hours."

I shook my head and hid a smile. What an inveterate flirt. "How did you sleep, Captain?"

"A dreamless sleep of a baby. You?"

"The same."

For a moment, I thought he was going to call me on my lie, as I had him the night before. Instead, he said, "You may call me William, you know. Or Kindle, if my Christian name is too familiar."

"I'm not sure it's appropriate, especially in light of my conversation with Harriet Mackenzie."

"We're alone and I won't tell," he whispered.

The bacon was so crisp and perfectly cooked it crumbled in my mouth, a hazard when I laughed and almost choked.

He moved to help me but I held out my hand for him to stop and coughed a few times. Caro came to my rescue, slapping me forcefully on the back, which didn't help much.

"Thank you," I croaked, and waved my hand at her. She retrieved a glass of water, which settled the matter. When she was back in the kitchen and humming, I chastised Kindle.

"You need to stop flirting with me."

"Am I?"

He looked so shocked at the notion it made me wonder. "Aren't you?"

His laugh was musical, as dissonant to his appearance and chosen career as his unblemished hands and flirtatious manner. I tried to be offended but his laugh was infectious.

I laughed as well. "You are incorrigible."

"Precisely what my mother always said."

I folded my hands together and stayed as far away from him as possible. "I know what you're doing."

"Flirting?"

"Yes, as a way to distract me from my grief. I appreciate it, more than you know." My throat closed with emotion. I coughed and continued. "I can tell it is taking a great effort for you to keep my spirits up."

"I am trying to keep your spirits up?"

"Most assuredly."

"It cannot be because I find you lovely and want to get to know you better?"

My stomach gave a pleasant little flutter. How my body could betray my mind at this moment, I didn't know. I kept my voice light, though part of me wanted to cry. "I've seen my reflection in your rather small, broken mirror. Lovely is not the adjective that comes to mind."

"Maybe it's your conversation."

"Do you remember them?"

"I would remember more but my doctor insists on dosing me with laudanum." He put his plate aside. "It's heartening to know you think my motives are so noble. However, I must confess I am flirting with you for two selfish reasons. One, it keeps my mind off my pain."

"Oh. Yes, of course," I said, slightly disappointed.

"Two, you become charmingly flushed when I flirt with you. I am not in so much pain I don't receive satisfaction from making a beautiful woman blush."

It would have been easy to bask in his attention. He was charming, handsome, and easy to talk to. It would have been nothing to let Kindle harmlessly flirt with me while he recovered and shake his hand with an affectionate good-bye when I continued on my journey. But I knew to let him have too much control would be dangerous.

I dropped my eyes to the floor and said in a small voice, "If you are not careful, Captain, you will have me falling in love with you."

I let the silence stretch before looking up at him with a mischievous smile. The expression on his face in the moment before he realized I was teasing him was a disturbing mixture of astonishment, expectation, and desire, the latter of which confirmed my suspicion that Captain Kindle was, indeed, a quick healer.

"I must warn you, Captain. I spent my youth among some of the most shameless flirts in England. I escaped with my heart intact and, dare I say, impervious to cheeky men who wish to toy with my emotions."

"I would never dream of toying with your...emotions."

I stood and walked to the window. I held my hand to my fluttering stomach. I shouldn't be this happy. Why shouldn't I be this happy?

Maureen. Anna. Cornelius. The children.

My hand massaged my thickening throat and tears burned my eyes. How could I feel so much pleasure so soon after Maureen's death? After witnessing Amos burned alive? What kind of horrible, selfish person was I?

"I'm sorry, Laura," Kindle said. "It is insensitive of me to act as if we are not where we are, and you haven't been through what you have."

I turned abruptly to him to rebuke him for using my Christian name without permission and to agree with him on his insensitivity, to portion out to him some of the guilt I had for enjoying his company so much. Instead, the sound of light footsteps on the front porch stopped me. After a perfunctory knock, Harriet Mackenzie walked in. She ignored me and went straight to Kindle's bedside.

"Captain Kindle, I'm thrilled to see you in such great spirits."

"Thank you, Miss Mackenzie. You have Dr. Elliston to thank for it."

"Indeed?" Harriet replied. Still, she refused to acknowledge I was in the room.

I stepped forward. "Hello, Miss Mackenzie." She acknowledged me with a thin smile. "Don't let him give me too much credit. I am sure his robust constitution is to thank for his appearance and good mood."

"I come from hearty stock," Kindle agreed.

"Hearty stock or not, you need your rest," I said. "Would you like another dose of laudanum?"

"I think I will try whisky instead. I don't like the way laudanum makes me feel."

"I will leave some for Caro in case you change your mind." I took in Harriet's hat, gloves, and reticule and asked, "Where are you off to, Miss Mackenzie?"

"To town and I thought I would see if there is anything the captain needed."

"No, I am right as a trivet. But thank you for thinking of me."

She nodded at Kindle, then posed the same question to me.

"I'm not sure, to be honest. I want to get settled a bit more, in the hospital and here, before I go on a shopping spree."

Harriet laughed. "Jacksboro's offerings will hardly support a spree. I will be happy to take you on a tour of the town in a couple of days."

The offer surprised me. "How kind of you."

"If you need anything before, the sutler's store might have it," she said. A moment of silence ensued. "Well, I must be going. Can I walk you to the hospital?"

"Yes, thank you. I am not even sure what time my rounds are."

"Eleven fifteen," Harriet and Kindle said in unison. They laughed. "Fort life is the same everywhere," Harriet said.

"What time is it?" I asked.

"Ten o'clock," Kindle answered.

"Do you not have a watch?" Harriet asked.

I thought of my father's watch. "No. Most of my possessions..." I cleared my throat as the vision of the devastated wagon train came to mind. "I do not suppose there is any chance of recovery?" I asked Kindle.

He looked down at his injured arm. "No, it's most likely been looted by now."

"Then a watch will be at the top of my list for our shopping spree," I said with false enthusiasm. I grasped my medical bag, gave Kindle instructions to rest, and promised to check on him at dinnertime.

While struggling to sleep the night before, my behavior toward Harriet had weighed on my mind. Though always pushing against the role society wanted me to play, I always understood how to play the role within the bounds of propriety. With Harriet, I had failed spectacularly and risked alienating her unless I was contrite. I also didn't know what kind of influence she exerted over Lieutenant Colonel Foster. The thought of the letter of recommendation waiting for me spurred me on.

"Miss Mackenzie, I'd like to apologize if my behavior yesterday was offensive." Harriet raised her eyebrows. "There is no *if*," I amended. "It was offensive. I do not apologize for the sentiments, but I do apologize for the way in which I delivered them."

"I was not in the least offended by your delivery. I have ample experience in dealing with personalities affected by... events. Short tempers do not discompose me. Your attitude about your living arrangements does concern me and will continue to do so. Our differences do not have to preclude a civil acquaintance, do they?"

"They do not."

I stopped at the foot of the hospital porch steps. Harriet walked a few feet away and turned. "I thought you would agree. You strike me as a pragmatic woman."

"I like to think so."

"May I ask, what made you want to become a doctor?"

"My father was a surgeon."

"He supported your endeavor?"

"He wanted me to marry and have children. When he died, I had no one left to object."

"Your mother?"

"Died when I was five years old."

"Where exactly did you study, again?"

"In London."

"What college?"

"I studied with a surgeon. An apprentice, I suppose you could say."

She nodded, as if I'd confirmed her suspicion I wasn't a real doctor.

"I suppose Sherman didn't care. That you don't have a degree."

"I suppose my performance saving Captain Kindle's life was enough qualification."

"Not for my brother, however. Before he left, he asked me to investigate your background."

I swallowed my panic, and for the first time, thanked God for the remoteness of Fort Richardson. "I will happily give you my mentor's name. If you will wait an hour, I will walk to the telegraph office with you. To ensure it is directed to the correct person."

Harriet pursed her lips. "The telegraph does not reach Jacksboro. Only Fort Worth and Fort Sill."

I tried to hide my relief behind calm disinterest and confidence. "Wait here and I will write the name and address down for you."

I went into the hospital office, wrote down a name and address, and returned. I handed it to Harriet, secure in the knowledge that by the time a message got to England and back, I would be well free of Fort Richardson.

Harriet folded the paper and put it in her reticule without reading it. She wore a black dress for the second day in a row. While the color was flattering with her olive complexion and dark hair, I suspected she chose her attire for a different reason. "Did you lose someone in the war?"

Her lips tightened very slightly before she answered. "My fiancé. He died at Gettysburg."

"My condolences. The cost of war never ends."

Harriet dropped her eyes to her hands. "No." She sniffed and glanced up at the hospital. "Good luck today. I know how much is riding on your success." She nodded to me and turned toward town, but not before I saw grief shadow her face.

CHAPTER

16

I watched Harriet walk away with pity, which I suspect she would have loathed. She was a woman with no place, save by her brother's side. Unmarried and without a profession, she most likely relied on the charity of her brother or surviving parents. Reliance meant subordination. She could not be her own person and would naturally resent a woman like me who could.

I spent the hour before rounds reading the hospital logs, discovering that drunkenness, venereal disease, and dysentery were the most common ailments. Most of the few fighting wounds that were treated resulted in gangrene and amputation, solidifying my theory the hospital was a breeding ground for the infection. I was pondering ways to combat this when the bugle sounded, signaling hospital rounds. I added brief comments about Kindle's surgery and the previous day's examinations, noted my theory about the infection and steps to alleviate it, and rose to attend my patients.

The south ward was empty, save the five patients from the day before.

"My, my. Quite a different scene from yesterday."

Waterman did not reply but stood at the foot of Private Howerton's bed with clipboard in hand for instructions.

"Private Howerton, how do you like your view?"

"It's nice, ma'am. Thank you."

"How do you feel?"

His smile was lazy, his eyes hooded. "Much better since you've been here."

Ignoring the soreness in my own shoulder, I removed Howerton's bandages. "Why are bedridden men such determined flirts, Waterman?"

"I have never had a bedridden man flirt with me, Doctor."

I raised my eyebrows at Howerton. "I can't understand why, Waterman."

"Neither can I, ma'am."

Jonah Howerton smiled. He stared out the window opposite as I examined his leg. "When I got here the creek was covered with trees."

"Was it?" The smell of the infection spreading up his thigh was overpowering.

"I helped cut 'em all down. To build the enlisted quarters. We had to move farther upstream to find wood."

"Is it dangerous being so far away from the fort?"

"Nah," Howerton said. "Never saw an Indian. More like to hurt yourself with an ax than from an arrow."

"Is that what happened to your leg?"

He nodded. "My Pa's gonna be mad it was a damn tree took my leg and not an Indian arrow."

"I am sure he'll be glad to have you home no matter how your injury occurred."

Howerton shook his head. "You don't know my Pa. It's bad, ain't it?"

I nodded.

Howerton swallowed and stared at the ceiling. Tears pooled in his eyes and his mouth twitched in his effort to keep from crying. "Lumberjackin's my family trade. That's why I was on the detail. Angered my pa somethin' fierce when I joined the army. I didn' wanna be a lumberjack, see? I can't go home a half a man from a lumberjackin' injury."

I hesitated. Private Howerton would never leave the hospital. Amputating his stump at the hip was pointless. The infection had spread and I suspected it was in his blood. His time on earth could be counted in hours, not days.

"I can't face my father. I'd rather die."

A soft voice spoke up from behind me. "What's this I hear, Private Howerton?"

A young woman not more than twenty years old stood next to Corporal Waterman, holding a small Bible in her hands. Unlike the romantic heroines populating literature whose nondescript features added up to a beautiful countenance, the young woman's face was a cacophony of striking features resulting in a homely, unattractive appearance. Her long thick eyelashes almost touched the perfectly arched eyebrows that framed wide-set hazel eyes. Her Roman nose beaked toward her small, bow-shaped mouth. A pale, round face was supported by a defined jaw and small chin, all of which rested precariously on a long, swanlike neck.

"Hello, Mrs. Strong," Howerton said, his face showing more animation than I had seen. "Wondered if you'd given up on me."

"Nonsense." It was plain to me from the girl's pallid complexion and bright eyes she was ill. "I apologize for being late." She turned to me. "I am Alice Strong. My husband is Private Howerton's commanding officer. Since he is on patrol and unable to check on Jonah, I have undertaken the privilege of sitting with the private each day. Do you object?"

"Not at all. I am Laura Elliston."

"Yes, I know." The girl took my proffered hand and squeezed it with more strength than her demeanor suggested.

I pulled her a little away from the private's bed and said in a low voice, "Private Howerton does not have long to live."

"I suspected as much."

"You are ill."

She shook her head. "I am fine." I had said the same lie too many times in the past few days to believe her. I admired the girl. She came to sit by the bed of a dying man despite her own infirmity. "Letters to loved ones might be a good idea," I said, glancing at Howerton.

She nodded. "I'm glad I came to sit with him."

When she moved away I put my hand on her arm. "Please come see me later."

She did not reply, but sat down next to Howerton's bed. "What would you like for me to read today?"

"You know, ma'am."

"Jonah it is."

Waterman stood next to me. "Give him as much laudanum as we can spare," I said. "It won't be long, I'm sure."

The examinations of the other men were achieved in short order and we moved onto the north ward to check on the black soldier, Jethro.

A different Negro woman sat next to the dying man's bed, sewing scraps of material together. Jethro's face was drawn and ashy, his eyes vacant.

I checked his pulse, which was faint and thready. "You must drink something, soldier," I said. I looked at the woman sitting by the bed. She stood and poured some water into a tin cup.

He shook his head. "No, ma'am. It goes right through me."

"Yes, I know, but if you do not..."

"I'm know I'm gonna die, ma'am."

"You think so?"

"Yes, ma'am. I'm ready."

I put his hand down and patted it. I nodded at the nurse. "I will check in on you later today." I heard her entreat Jethro to drink as I left.

I walked past the office and into the dispensary. I noted the gaping holes in the rows of the various powders and medicines lined on the shelves of a wooden cabinet. A large, scrupulously clean worktable sat in the middle of the room and took up most of the space. A scale and weights sat atop it, waiting to be used. "You do an excellent job of organization, Corporal Waterman."

"Thank you, ma'am."

"Where are the rest of the medicines?"

"This is all we have."

"I find that difficult to believe."

"We're chronically short on supplies out here, not only with medicine, but with everything. You saw we're using blankets to cover the windows."

"Yes."

"We had nothing to use in the winter."

"Why do you think that is?"

"Ma'am?"

"Why do you think you are short supplied? Chronically?"

"Dr. Elliston, I have no idea," Waterman replied, a bit of exasperation showing through. "I follow the orders I'm given. I requisition what we need and organize what the Army gives us, whether it's sufficient to our needs or not. I do the best with what I'm given."

"Just like a good soldier does."

"Yes, ma'am."

"Hmm." I stared at the shelves. "Do you happen to have a cane or a crutch? I need one for Captain Kindle."

"Yes, ma'am. In the storeroom upstairs. I'll get it for you."

"No, I can get it. Thank you." I turned at the door. "Give Jethro thirty drops of laudanum."

"So much?"

"I thought you followed orders. Or does that only apply when men are giving the orders and they relate to a white man?"

Waterman's face reddened. "No, ma'am. I was thinking, respectfully, that much might not be prudent given his dehydrated state."

"You are right. But he will die in a day, maybe two. I want to make him as comfortable as possible."

"Yes, ma'am."

I sighed. "It seems to be my primary function here, helping people die comfortably."

⚭

The second floor of the administration block was a mirror of the four rooms downstairs. Three were used for storage and one was the death room, though not for much longer. The stairs leading up were narrow; I could imagine how inconvenient it was to maneuver a body upstairs on the canvas stretcher and downstairs in a coffin.

Three storage rooms were being used but one would have been sufficient for all items, with room left over. Waterman had obviously organized the three rooms in anticipation of them one day being fully stocked. I found a cane easily, though it was too short even for me; it would be useless for Kindle.

With only five patients and Waterman's levelheaded organization and leadership taking care of the menial tasks of ordering supplies and managing the soldier orderlies and laundresses, there was little for me to do. I decided to take the long way back to Kindle's quarters and give myself a tour of the fort.

I exited through the rear of the hospital and walked past the under-construction death house to Lost Creek, the fort's natural western boundary. All that remained on the banks of the creek were outcroppings of rocks and saplings, which gave a clear view of the prairie beyond and the town a half mile distant. Behind the hospital, the creek widened into a still pool, fed from the north by a rushing, graduated waterfall surrounded by a natural wall of rocks. I passed a soldier hauling two buckets of water as I walked down the creek bank to the edge of the pool. I felt a pure solitude, and despite everything I had been through, a surprising measure of contentment. I closed my eyes and inhaled, letting the sound of the water and birdsong fill my senses.

The soft nickering of a horse broke my reverie. Across the creek, partially hidden by the rock outcropping, a tall man stood next to a gray horse. His hat was pulled low, obscuring the part of his face not covered by a full, unkempt beard. Though I couldn't see his eyes, I knew his hard gaze was directed at me. My previously comforting solitude turned oppressive, threatening. The man before me became the specter of the savage on the plains, rooting me to the ground as if I'd been planted there millennia before. We stared at each other across the expanse of the creek, each unmoving, until he tipped his hat and it dawned on me he knew me and wanted to frighten me.

A chorus of laughter floated down from the creek bank behind me. Three women, with woven baskets overflowing with uniforms, descended the bank. Their laughter died when they saw me.

"Sorry, ma'am," one said. "Were you taking a dip?"

"A what?"

"Bathing, ma'am."

"No, I..." I motioned to the man across the creek. When

my gaze followed my hand it rested on nothing. "Where did he go?"

"Who?"

"There was a man, standing there with a horse."

"I didn't see no man," the woman said.

"A gray horse. He had a full beard," I added, as if giving details would make him appear again.

"Maybe it's Cotter Black," a redheaded woman said in mocking tones, and playfully shoved the youngest of the three women. The young girl's eyes widened.

"Shut it, Adella. Don't go putting notions in her shallow brain," the oldest woman said.

"Who's Cotter Black?"

"Only the worst killer in Texas," the young woman said.

"Don't listen to Ruth," the oldest-looking woman said. "She believes every story these men tell her. The more outrageous the better."

"Everyone says he rides a big gray horse. Was the horse big?" Ruth asked.

"It was gray."

"He paralyzed you with his eyes, didn't he? They say he can do that."

"Good God. See what you've done, Adella?"

The redheaded woman grinned. "Sorry, Mary. It's just too easy."

Mary shook her head and changed the subject. "Are you the new doctor, then?"

"I am."

"A woman doctor. I've seen it all."

"'T'aint no different from a midwife, I suspect," said Ruth.

"No, it is rather different," I said.

"She's arrogant like a doctor," said Adella, "I'll give her that."

"I heard you saved Captain Kindle's life," Mary said.

184

I shrugged. "He has not died yet, at least."

"So you think he's gonna?"

"Not if I can help it."

"Have you seen him naked?" Adella asked. "I've always wanted to see him as the Lord made him. He's a fine-looking man, and that's a fact."

"You ain't ever gonna see him, neither," Mary said. "You ain't his type and even if you was, he wouldn't be interested in your dirty snatch."

I coughed, not hiding my shock at their language very well. "You are laundresses, I presume."

"Aye, we're laundresses," Mary said.

"With lots of boyfriends," Ruth added.

"If one of our *boyfriends* happens to drop a coin or two on the floor." Adella shrugged.

"There ain't been much lost coin lately," Mary said. "Payroll hain't come in a long while."

"Do you get examined? For diseases?" I asked.

"By who? Welch? He'd be as like to molest us and call it 'examinin'' and be on his way, but not afore tellin' us he'll have to come back next week to make sure, then demandin' payment."

"I'll examine you," I said.

Adella narrowed her eyes and said, "What do you want in return?"

"Nothing. At least, there's nothing I need at the moment."

"But we'll owe you."

"Not necessarily. If you aren't comfortable with me examining you gratis, think of an affordable way to pay me. It doesn't have to be money. You do not have to pay me. It is entirely up to you."

"Why would you do something for nothing?"

"Don't bother, Adella. She don't have no intention of seeing us," Mary said.

"Certainly I do. Why wouldn't I? Is now a good time?"

"Sure," Mary said. "This laundry can wait."

"You do the laundry in this pool?"

"No, we carry laundry around for the fun of it," Mary said. "What's your name?"

"Laura Elliston. Come with me."

I led the three of them into the hospital. A soldier carrying a bucket covered with a towel walked past us to the creek. "One minute," I said to the women, and walked over to the soldier.

"Private?" The soldier stopped and put his bucket down, exhaled, and wiped his brow with his sleeve.

"Ma'am?"

I coughed when I stopped in front of the soldier. "Is that from the hospital latrine?" I asked, pointing to the bucket.

"Yes, ma'am."

"You are dumping it in the creek? Behind the hospital?"

"Yes, ma'am."

"Our drinking water comes from there, as well?"

"Yes, ma'am."

"Please tell me you use a different bucket."

"I clean it out first."

I waved my hands. "No." I placed my fist against my nose and mouth to stave off the queasiness from the stench wafting up from the bucket. "Dump it downstream from the pond, please."

"But, with all this rain, the shit washes away real quick."

I shook my head. "I don't care. Dump it downstream. Get a clean bucket, one that hasn't been used for feces, and haul your water. First, take it to the cook and have him boil it."

He walked off without responding. I doubted he would follow my orders at all.

I motioned to the laundresses and led them around to the

front of the hospital. "Two of you can wait outside on the front porch while I see the other. Who would like to go first?"

"I will!" Ruth said.

"This way," I corrected when she walked toward the enlisted men's ward.

"But that's where the niggers go!"

"This is also where the private rooms are." I led her into the room Kindle had recently occupied and motioned to the cot. "Sit there. I'll be right back."

I found Waterman measuring medicine. "We have a problem."

"Ma'am?"

"The creek. We're dumping our waste into the pool where we get water."

"We don't have a problem with dysentery, no more than other ailments."

"With more soldiers coming daily, we might. Have the cook boil the water we give patients. And find an unsoiled bucket we can use to haul water."

I returned to Ruth. She sat on the cot, knocking her feet together in boredom. I washed my hands in the basin. "When was your last menses?"

Ruth shrugged.

"How old are you?"

"Fourteen."

"Fourteen!" She looked much older. "Have you *started* menses?"

"If you mean am I a woman, yes." Ruth was obviously proud of this.

"Does it come regularly?"

"My curse? No."

Though sure of the answer, I asked anyway. "Do you have relations with men?"

"'Course I do. I'm the most popular girl."

I can imagine, I thought. The coarseness of her demeanor, her uneducated speech, and her brown crooked teeth (which she tried to hide with close-mouthed smiles) did little to diminish her beauty.

"Do the men wear a sheath?"

"Yeah." She didn't look at me when she answered.

I took her pulse, felt her neck, and looked in her mouth and throat.

"Lie back."

With my stethoscope I listened to her lungs and heart. When I pressed her abdomen, it was hard.

"You're pregnant. About four months along, I guess. Did you know?"

She nodded. "I been terrible sick o' the morning. It's been hard keepin' it from my ma."

"Your mother?"

"Mary. Please don't tell her. She's gon' to be some mad. She tells me every time, 'Ruth, use the sheath,' and I do. Honest, I do. But, he didn' wanna and he's so smart and handsome, I couldn' say no!"

"Is this the only time you did not use a sheath?"

"I never do with him. He don' like it."

I sighed and helped her sit up. "Is he a soldier at the fort?"

She nodded and tried to hide a smile. Immaturity and infatuation won out. "He's an officer and he..."

I held up my hand. "I don't want to know." With the mood I had been in the past few days I had no doubt I would confront the man and give him my unvarnished opinion of his actions. I didn't need to alienate the Army, my only option for leaving Fort Richardson safely.

"You won't be able to hide this from your mother forever, you know."

"I been dreadin' tellin' her sumtin' awful. She'll make me get rid of it."

"You don't want to?"

"I seen what they do to get rid of 'em and I don' think I can take it. I don' like pain."

"Childbirth is painful."

"Yeah, but after you got a baby."

The girl was staring off into the distance, lost in the fantasy of having and loving a child. It was no doubt a fantasy devoid of the realities that would face her: raising a bastard on the frontier with little to no money and, if a girl, dooming her to a life of want and prostitution like Ruth's own.

"When Wally finds out, he'll not allow nothin' to happen."

"Ruth..." I wanted to tell her she was being stupid, that no officer would claim the child of a whore as his own.

"His wife ain't woman enough to give him a baby, but I am!"

"His wife? He's *married*?"

"An ugly, plain girl. He married her to get his commission."

"He sure does talk a lot to a child whore," I said under my breath.

"I ain't his whore! He ain't ever paid me."

"That's even worse, Ruth."

"He don' treat me like men treat whores. That's what I'm trying to tell ya. He don' think of me like that. When he finds out, he'll marry me."

"He's already married!"

"He don' love her. He loves me."

I shook my head. It was useless to argue logic with a fourteen-year-old girl.

"You won't tell Mary, will ya?"

"No. When she finds out and tries to force you to take care of it, you insist she find me."

"You would'na let her, would ya?"

"What on earth do you think you are doing?"

Harriet Mackenzie stood in the doorway of the cubicle, her face flaming red.

"Treating a patient."

"This... child cannot be a patient of yours."

"She asked for medical assistance and I am giving it to her. According to the most basic definition, she is my patient."

"She appears healthy enough to me. What's her ailment?"

"It's none of your business!"

"Those women on the porch are with her, I assume."

"You assume correctly."

"You cannot treat those prostitutes," she said, lowering her voice to a harsh whisper for the last word.

"Of all the people on this fort, they are the most important people to treat. Women follow instructions to curb venereal disease much better than the men do."

Harriet's mouth pressed into an even thinner line and her nostrils contracted. "Alice, please take the children to the reading room."

I had not noticed Alice Strong standing behind and to the side of Harriet. She was drawn and pale, staring into the middle distance with red-rimmed eyes as if holding back tears. Alice jumped when addressed. She looked at me as if from far away. "Private Howerton died ten minutes ago." She glanced at Ruth, turned, and left without another word.

"If you will excuse me, Harriet. I need to finish examining my *patients* and attend the dead."

Harriet stepped into the cubicle. "Leave," she said to Ruth. Ruth stood and languidly, with an insolent glare at Harriet, left.

I spoke before Harriet opened her mouth. "Are you worried the officers' children will know what those women are?

If so, you give them too much credit. To them, they are the women who do the men's laundry. Indeed, it's what they were doing when I met them by the creek. I didn't see anything on their figure that said 'prostitute,' but I didn't look too closely, I admit. Was there a sign somewhere? Maybe a scarlet *A* embroidered on their breasts?"

"I might have known you would treat my concerns with so little respect."

My resolve to be polite to Harriet and cultivate her friendship went out the window. "Are you treating *me* with respect? In one day you have questioned my morals, my professionalism, and have tried to dictate what I should and should not do. As far as I am aware, you have no authority over me or my responsibilities as fort doctor."

Harriet gave a bitter, unbecoming laugh. "Fort doctor? Please don't delude yourself. You're nothing more than a tool to get men out of the hospital and into the field. You are no more a doctor than I am."

It took absolutely every ounce of strength I possessed to not slap Harriet Mackenzie across the face. I reminded myself that my loss of temper and composure was precisely what she wanted. My sudden awareness that she truly and utterly hated me was shocking and cooled my temper more than venting my feelings would have done.

"Regardless of what you believe, until I am told differently by Lieutenant Colonel Foster or Colonel Mackenzie, I will act as the fort doctor. Until you can approach me with the civility you expect of me but are unable to yourself extend, I have nothing further to say to you."

I went to the front porch where Alice, still dazed, was ushering the children and women down the steps. "Alice."

She turned but did not lift her head. "After I attend to Private

191

Howerton, I will come to the reading room to examine anyone who still wishes to see me."

Alice looked up at me and was on the verge of saying something when Harriet breezed down the steps. "Come along, Alice." The young woman dutifully followed, as did the others, like ducklings waddling after their mother.

Mary stood next to Adella and Ruth, arms crossed and chin lifted. Adella smirked as if she had expected it all, and Ruth bit her nails and stared at the floor. Through the open front door, I saw Waterman directing two orderlies as they carried Howerton's body upstairs to the death room. I turned to Mary and said, "Who's next?"

CHAPTER
17

The aroma of fresh-baked bread that met me when I left the hospital was a welcome relief after preparing Howerton's body for burial. It was a task I rarely, if ever, was required to perform in New York. Apparently, though, the Army believed its surgeons should perform the duties instead of paying the local barber who served as mortician.

I followed my nose to the bakery north of the hospital, where a fat woman was setting out loaves of warm bread to cool on a long, meticulously scrubbed wooden table. She offered me a thick slice slathered with fresh-churned butter. The bread melted in my mouth and butter dribbled down my chin. I wiped my mouth with the handkerchief I kept tucked in my sleeve and saw Welch walk hurriedly past the guardhouse and behind the stables. I thanked the baker and, my curiosity piqued by Welch's demeanor, followed.

The stables were among the most solid fort buildings. Great care was taken with the horses, the West's most valuable commodity. Horseflesh was considered by many to be worth more than a man's life. A few soldiers saw Welch pass the corral; one called out to him. He continued on as if he did not hear.

I turned to follow when a man called out to me. "Miss Elliston?"

He was short, stocky, and hirsute with bowlegs and muscular arms. His shiny black bowler sat high on a broad, tall forehead. The lower half of his face was covered with a wiry ginger beard of indeterminate style, or possibly every style, as if he was resistant to cutting his beard in order to keep every styling option open. He held a pencil lightly in the meaty fingers of his right hand. His left hand held a notebook. He looked like a fighter and even had the scarred knuckles to testify to a previous life or a source of side income, but his inquisitive expression and the tools in his hand marked him as a newspaperman.

"Yes?"

He smiled and revealed a mouthful of teeth, much to my surprise. "I knew it had to be you. My name is Henry Pope. I'm the editor of the *Jacksboro Union Leader.*"

"Mr. Pope."

He removed his hat and held it over his heart. "First, let me say how sorry I am for the ordeal you've been through."

"Thank you, Mr. Pope."

"I understand how difficult it must be right now, with the memories of the massacre so fresh in your mind. I wouldn't wish to have you relive those horrible events of three days ago for anything."

But you will ask me to anyway.

"Truth is, there are so many stories of the Indian atrocities they have lost much of their impact."

"Have they?"

"It is hard to believe, but it is true. People don't want to hear about it anymore."

"I'm grateful," I said. I tried to see where Welch was but could not. A soldier leaned his back against the side of the nearest barn, hat low over his eyes, one foot propped up on the wall. He was the only soldier nearby not engaged in an activity.

"Our readers are interested in *you*, though."

I returned my attention to Pope. "Me?"

"Yes. A woman operating on the officer who saved her life? In the middle of a thunderstorm? That story sells newspapers."

"The storm had not come."

He continued as if I had not spoken. "Then performing a second surgery, mere hours later, amid lamplight with Uncle Billy himself holding the lamp."

"It sounds as if you know the story. There is nothing I could possibly add."

"It's true?"

"It's truer than most newspaper stories I've read."

He smiled with bitterness. "I know what you're implying. We don't have a good reputation, newspapermen. I assure you, I don't print lies, nor do I go in for hyperbole. I find the truth is usually more unbelievable than anything I could make up." He leaned forward. I could smell the faint aroma of whisky on his breath. "Between you and me, I don't have much of an imagination."

"Again, I don't see what I could possibly add." My eyes were drawn to where the solitary man stood. Two soldiers walked by the man, laughing and talking. They glanced at the man and went silent. He didn't move or acknowledge them but kept his eyes on the ground.

"Background, Miss Elliston." I turned my attention back to Henry Pope with exasperation. "Where are you from? What got you interested in medicine? Where did you get your degree? Information such as that."

"Mr. Pope, I must confess something to you." He leaned closer. "I don't like talking about myself. I would prefer if you printed your story with the information you have."

He nodded. "I understand." He put his pencil in his hatband and his notebook in his vest pocket. "I am sure it won't be difficult to write to the medical colleges in the East and get the basic information. How many women doctors are there?"

He was sly, our Mr. Pope. It was an open secret the West was full of people running from their past. My evasion fueled his suspicion that I was as well. I could not risk his curiosity. "You could, Mr. Pope. You will not find me on the rolls of any of the colleges taking women students."

"Why is that?"

"Well," I said, before launching into an elaborate lie. "I received my degree in England. It is not technically a degree, though in England I assure you it is as legitimate as any lambskin you receive in the Union. You see, I read under a venerable doctor in England precisely because I couldn't get into a college in my home country. I apprenticed with him for four years, until his death. With no patron in that country, I decided to come west, where specific credentials might not be as important as they are in the East and where I might be able to become successful based on my skills instead of my school. It is so difficult when people assume you do not have the intelligence or skills to succeed because you might not have the right pedigree or gender. Don't you agree?"

I could tell my story hit a nerve with Henry Pope. "Indeed, I do. Miss Mackenzie didn't tell me all of that."

"Miss Mackenzie?"

"Yes, the colonel's sister. I saw her mailing a letter in town. She suggested I talk to you." Pope tilted his head to the side. "She doesn't like you much, does she?"

My smile was thin. "Now, if there's nothing more, I must get to the sutler's store before dark. Captain Kindle needs a cane."

Pope reached into his jacket, pulled out a folded handbill,

and opened it. He glanced between the paper and my face. "I see a resemblance."

I sighed and pretended to be bored, though I well knew what he held in his hand. "And, what is that, Mr. Pope?"

He held up my Wanted poster. In the picture, I stood ramrod straight next to a table arrayed with my medical instruments and a copy of my degree from Syracuse Medical College. My dark dress was plain, my expression severe, my hair pulled tightly back into a bun. Weeks later and thousands of miles away, I hated the picture still.

"I'm offended you see a resemblance, Mr. Pope. Who is she?"

"Catherine Bennett. You haven't heard of her?"

"The woman who killed her lover in New York?"

"Yes."

"They talked of her around the campfire. I don't know her. I thought she was dead."

"That's the report." With one last look at the photo, he folded it and returned it to his pocket.

"And did Harriet Mackenzie see the resemblance, as well?"

"I didn't show it to her."

"You want to keep the reward for yourself."

Pope shrugged.

"I'm sorry to disappoint you, Mr. Pope, but I'm not Catherine Bennett."

"Well, I'm a newspaperman. I won't let facts stand in the way of a good story."

"Very admirable, Mr. Pope. You do know once you print that story Jacksboro will be overrun with bounty hunters. When they discover I am not who you proclaim me to be..." I shrugged and glanced at his scarred knuckles. "It's a good thing you are a fighter. I look forward to reading your article."

I walked away, hoping Henry Pope would rather have the

reward for himself than print the story and have a horde of bounty hunters to compete with. The man leaning against the barn pushed himself to a standing position and sauntered off toward the parade ground. He didn't divert to any task, nor did anyone call to him in recognition. He passed the officers' quarters, turned around, and tipped his hat.

He was no soldier. He was the man from the creek.

Had he overheard our conversation? It was possible. We hadn't kept our voices low. Across the parade ground, the man had disappeared as if I had imagined him. But I had not, nor had I imagined his interest in me.

I clutched my stomach and looked around. A few soldiers watched me, but none approached. I inhaled and smiled, hoping it would settle my racing heart, and went in search of Welch.

Welch was not near the corral where a soldier was breaking a palomino or walking across the parade ground or in front of the eastern buildings. Wondering if he kept to the outside of the buildings, I walked around the sutler's store. Besides an empty wagon driving down the road behind the buildings there was not a soul in sight. I was wondering where Welch went and what business he could possibly have at the fort after being discharged as I walked to the front of the sutler's. The bell jingled and the door opened. A soldier with a handmade quilt under his arm held the door open for me. "Ma'am," he said with a nod.

My breath caught and I grasped my chest.

"Ma'am? Are you sick?"

I inhaled a shaky breath, my eyes riveted to the quilt he held. "That's a nice quilt, sir."

"It is, ain't it? Got it for my wife."

My eyes met the man's. He looked as if he was afraid I was

about to swoon. I tried to smile, but my lips tightened into a grimace. "What a thoughtful present."

"Her quilt's got fleas all in it."

"I'm sure she'll like this one." I stepped into the sutler's store. "With a little scrubbing the bloodstain should come out."

"How did you…?" The door closed on the soldier's confused face.

It looked like any other general merchandise store in Texas. Rough-hewn shelves held all manner of items a soldier might spend their thirteen-dollars-per-month salary on. Whisky, beer, tobacco, canned fruit, and canned meat held places of honor on the shelves. Other items less in demand but more necessary included shoelaces, needles and thread, combs, soap, blankets, quilts, shoes, shirts, underclothes, paper, pencils, and boot polish. Women's clothes, shoes, mirrors, and brushes were available for the laundresses to purchase, or if they were like the soldier I'd met, for the men to get for their wives or girlfriends.

I fought back the impulse to ransack the place, like Jesus in the temple. I remembered the activity I saw in this part of the fort the first night in Kindle's quarters. If I was not mistaken, and I was confident I was not, the sutler had looted the massacre site of the dead's possessions and was now selling what he could for a substantial profit. My blood boiled at the idea of the sale of my abandoned possessions (abandoned not because I did not want or need them but because of circumstances out of my control) going to line the pocket of some stranger.

The shop was empty. A door to a back room stood partially open, through which I could hear the muffled voices of two men. I stood by the counter and feigned interest in the candy jars.

"It's *his* fault I was dismissed."

"He don't think so."

"It's the truth."

"The truth is if you weren't an incompetent doctor and a drunk they would have looked past your absence."

"I'm competent enough to line everyone else's pockets. All I'm asking for is a little help for all I've done."

"You've been paid."

"It ain't enough."

"It was."

"Before I lost my income. Doctorin' in Jacksboro ain't gonna be enough."

"Ain't our problem."

"You tell him he owes me and if he don't pay me in cash he'll pay another way."

A long silence followed. The man replied, "You're drunk."

"I ain't that drunk, and I mean it."

I was focused on listening and not paying attention to what I was doing. I dropped the glass lid I had removed from the jar of peppermints. It clattered onto its base but thankfully didn't break. It did, however, alert the two men to my presence in the shop.

The sutler walked through the partially opened door and looked at me cautiously. "Hello, ma'am. I didn't hear you enter."

"I just walked in. I accidentally dropped the lid to the peppermint jar. I had to smell them. It reminds me of home."

"Are you searching for anything in particular?"

"A cane. For Captain Kindle. I'm Dr. Elliston." I held my hand out.

"Yes. I've heard so much about you. The canes are right here." He motioned to an umbrella stand full of canes: plain hickory canes of various sizes, a walnut cane with an ivory knob handle, a thick stick with a natural handle skillfully carved into a horse's head and rubbed almost smooth with use, and a black ebony cane with an ornate brass handle. The shelves behind the counter were filled with an impressive variety of medicines.

"How is the captain doing?"

"Fine. I'm sorry, I missed your name."

"Forgive me." He bowed. "Franklin is the name. Tom Franklin."

I pulled a plain hickory cane from the stand. "How much for this cane?"

"For the captain, it's free."

"How much for a bag of peppermints?"

"For the doctor who saved the captain's life? No charge." Franklin scooped a large portion of peppermints into a paper bag.

"Thank you. You won't stay in business long if you give away your merchandise," I teased.

He handed me the bag of candy. "It'll be our little secret."

"Thank you." I took the bag, smiled, and walked to the door. In the middle of the store I turned back, shyly.

"Mr. Franklin? I hope...I don't know quite how to ask you this."

"Ask me anything."

"The items on this table"—I motioned to the table to my right—"I believe they are mine. I am sure it is a misunderstanding." I roamed my eyes over the items I suspected came from our wagon train, clothes and small household items. I wondered what had become of the larger items he couldn't sell in the sutler's store, such as tables, chairs, and iron stoves. They were valuable and would not have been left for another looter if he could make a profit.

"Yes," he said. "A grave misunderstanding. I assumed the possessions you wanted to keep were taken with you."

"On the contrary, I left a wagon full of items. It was more important we get Captain Kindle to Fort Richardson quickly."

"Please, take what is yours."

I sighed theatrically. "They have such horrible associations with them now." I picked up a bonnet Maureen had bought in Austin and sniffed. It smelled like smoke and burning flesh.

"I can understand."

"Could I...? No, I couldn't ask it of you." I turned away as if under high emotion and sniffed dramatically.

"What is it, Dr. Elliston?"

"I..." I turned back to him. "Would you be willing to take these things off my hands? For a small price. Maybe a hundred dollars?"

Franklin laughed. "That's no small price. I won't be able to get half as much for your items."

"You sold my blanket for five."

His eyes narrowed. He realized I was playing him. "I will give you fifty."

I picked up a silver pocket watch and opened it. In the front was a picture of my father and mother on their wedding day. It was easily the most valuable item on the table. "Seventy-five and you will supply Corporal Martin with the materials he needs to build shelves in the hospital kitchen."

"Ain't a good deal for me."

"I hoped we would be able to work this out ourselves." I sighed again before smiling at the sutler. "People have been so nice to me here. Like Henry Pope. Do you know him?"

"The newspaperman."

"Yes. He wants to do a big story on me. I demurred, of course. But, now that I think of it, I would greatly enjoy telling of my experience. Every facet of it."

He took the hint. Franklin smirked. "Seventy-five dollars and shelves is a reasonable price."

I shook his hand. "Thank you." I lifted the pocket watch. "I cannot part with this. It is a family heirloom. You understand."

"Perfectly."

I smiled. "I'll take cash."

He moved behind the counter and took seventy-five dollars from his till and handed it to me with a forced smile.

"Nice doing business with you," I said.

"It is the least I can do for the woman who saved Captain Kindle's life."

"Captain Kindle is universally respected?"

"He is highly thought of in many quarters."

"I must do what I can to make sure he regains his health. Good day."

⁓⧈⁓

I went straight to Foster's office. I wondered how the Army could let a man like Franklin openly deal in the goods of the dead, the people the Army was here to protect.

"Ah, Dr. Elliston." Foster stood when I entered his office. "I was coming to find you."

"Were you?"

"Yes. Harriet Mackenzie came to see me. It appears the two of you have gotten off on the wrong foot."

"That is putting it mildly."

"I understand your point of view."

"How do you know my point of view?"

"Harriet told me you were examining the laundresses in the hospital in an effort to stave off"—he coughed—"you know."

"Does the Army have a problem with that?"

"No. It's the second most-common complaint of our soldiers."

"What is the first?"

"Drunkenness, unfortunately. As to the other, it is an admirable idea and a good one. Since women are the cause of it they should be responsible for stopping it..."

"I don't think…"

"But, I do agree with Miss Mackenzie that it's inappropriate for you to examine these women in the post hospital. In the officers' room, no less!"

"Where do you suggest I examine them?"

"In their quarters." He gestured vaguely. "They are on the road to Jacksboro somewhere."

"Where would you like for me to examine the officers' wives and children?"

"In the hospital, naturally."

"I don't see the difference between one civilian and the other."

"Don't be obtuse, Doctor. You know there is a difference."

"I suppose I must treat the enlisted men's wives with medicines from my own stores?"

"You have stores of medicine?"

"Yes. A trunkful that was, thankfully, brought with me to the fort. Otherwise, Tom Franklin's inventory of medicine would be fatter."

"What are you saying?"

"I find it curious the Army is short-supplied but the sutler's shelves are almost overflowing with medicine."

"His is a private business. It has nothing to do with the Army."

"It is on your fort. Why don't you requisition the items you need from Franklin and pay him back when the supply train arrives?"

"He charges exorbitant prices."

"Which you allow?"

"Again, it is a private business."

"Here at the Army's discretion. Threaten to revoke his permission unless he loans you what material you need."

"The arrangement doesn't work that way, Miss Elliston. If it became common practice for the Army to steal goods and services from the people who support the fort we would never be able to contract with another sutler. He may charge too much, but the men rely on his store for items the Army does not supply. Our supply problems should be remedied when the new surgeon arrives from Sill with the supply train and payroll."

"The shortage is severe. As far as I can tell, what items you are receiving, which are always fewer than ordered, are not making it into storage. I believe they are on Franklin's shelves."

"That is a harsh accusation! How do you suppose he is getting our supplies?"

I did not want to accuse Waterman without proof, which I did not have. "I do not know."

"I won't even try to illustrate for you how difficult it is to supply remote forts such as Richardson. Flooding from this rain isn't helping. There are thieves all over Texas, mostly lawless, Godless Confederates who look for any chance to take from the government, and there are more than enough wagon trains and supply trains to choose from. Really, Dr. Elliston, I appreciate your concern but this isn't something you need to worry about. What I need you to do is to take care of the soldiers who come to you with complaints, figure out whose sickness is genuine and whose isn't, and treat them. Leave supplying the fort to me. What's in your hand?"

"My father's watch."

"A nice heirloom to give to your son one day." Foster was shifting papers around on his desk and losing interest in my complaints and me.

"Imagine my surprise when I discovered it on a table in Tom Franklin's store, along with most of my other possessions."

Foster was still focused on his papers, distracted. "Hmm."

He stacked the papers, straightened them, and looked up with a smile. "Is there anything else?"

"Did you even hear what I said?"

"Yes, Miss Elliston, I did. It is a lovely watch and will make a wonderful heirloom."

"Franklin was selling this watch—my father's watch that was given to him by his father—in his store. I have already gotten a lesson on soldiers looting from Captain Kindle in the aftermath of the massacre. As reprehensible as it was, I overlooked it because these soldiers have little of their own. Am I to understand it's normal for merchants to loot the abandoned possessions of unfortunate victims and sell them for a profit?"

"The key word there is *abandoned*, Miss Elliston."

"It is *Doctor* Elliston. They were abandoned because their owners were brutally murdered. For someone to take their possessions and sell them without regard to respect for the dead beggars belief."

"What would you have the alternative be, Dr. Elliston? Leave these perfectly good items in the middle of the plains for the next set of settlers, or cowboys on a drive to loot? Because make no mistake, there will be little left before long. Anything useful will be taken. Those poor dead people have no need for candles or coffeepots six feet under the ground."

"It is reprehensible he is selling these items."

"You think he should give them away?" Foster laughed.

"Or leave them for other settlers, yes."

"It is nice to see a woman such as you—"

"A woman such as me?"

"—have such charitable feminine instincts but what you propose has no place in the hardscrabble environment on the frontier. Living here is hard and people try to make their way any way they can. Now, I don't mean to be rude but—"

"You will be anyway."

"In case you haven't noticed, which would be ironic considering what you've been through, we are in the middle of a war. I receive reports daily about Indian attacks on innocent settlers. They are raiding up and down the Texas frontier, even into Mexico. We have patrols leaving and returning daily and new regiments arriving from across Texas. The fort commander is off hunting the Kiowas who massacared your wagon train. One of my best officers is incapacitated. I have too many other more important matters to deal with and don't have the time, patience, or inclination to listen to soft-hearted pleading from a woman about a subject she is wholly ignorant of."

"Tell me, Colonel, what is *your* cut of the sutler's business?"

Foster's complexion, already flushed, turned a mottled red. He pulled an envelope from beneath a stack of papers and tapped it in his hand. My name was clearly distinguishable on the front. I swallowed the bile in my throat and wished I could take my accusation back.

Foster's voice dropped to a whisper. "I should kick you off this fort this instant and throw this letter in the fire. I told Sherman you wouldn't be up to the task. Fortunately, the new surgeon should be here within the week. Until then, you are restricted to treating the patients you currently have and any women and children who don't question your credentials or abilities. Waterman will take care of the administration of the hospital. As soon as the surgeon steps foot on Richardson, you will be required to leave, finding your own way to wherever you were bound before fate thrust you on the Army's charity. I do not want to see or hear from you again, do you understand?"

"Yes, sir."

Nauseated and shaking with anger, I left.

Though my anger—at Pope, Franklin, Foster, but mostly myself—had diminished to a glowing ember by the time I entered Kindle's quarters that evening, seeing Harriet Mackenzie sitting at his bedside fanned the flames of my temper.

"What are you doing here?"

"Watching over Captain Kindle."

I envied Kindle's peaceful, drug-induced sleep. "Where is Caro?"

"I sent her away."

God, the woman was insufferable. "You had *no right* to do that."

"As a friend of the captain's I want to help in his recovery however I can. Surely you will not let your animosity toward me cloud your judgment in regards to the captain's health?"

The physical pains the day's events had pushed from my consciousness surged forward on a wave of exhaustion. A headache lurked behind my eyes, throbbed in my temples, and threatened to travel to the base of my skull. The constant dull pain in my shoulder intensified and my mouth took on the tangy, metallic taste that was a precursor to vomiting. I had no energy to spar with Harriet and the small part of me resistant to doing whatever was expected of me, the pinprick of my essence that would never leave me, wanted to disappoint Harriet's ploy to bait me. Mostly, though, I wanted to be alone.

"No. I will not." I leaned the cane against the table next to Kindle's bed and placed my medical bag, the peppermints, and a book next to the almost empty bottle of laudanum. I took Kindle's pulse, touched his forehead, listened to his breathing, and ignored Harriet Mackenzie.

"*The Tenant of Wildfell Hall*," Harriet said. "Did you get this from the reading room?"

After leaving Foster's, I had gone to the reading room to calm down and to wait for the women and children who wished to be examined. None showed.

"Yes."

"I have never read it. Should I?"

"When I finish it, I will tell you." I buckled my bag. "Caro and I arranged between each other and another nurse for eight-hour shifts. Caro's ends at midnight. Wake me then. Help yourself to the peppermints."

It was a lie but Harriet didn't know it. With the book and my bag, I headed for the stairs.

"Laura."

"Yes." Exhaustion was pulling me further and further into its comforting embrace.

Harriet stood and turned to me. "I want to apologize. For not accepting your apology this morning with more grace."

"Thank you."

"Also, for implying your interaction with Captain Kindle is anything other than professional."

I nodded and climbed the stairs. Harriet's voice stopped me again.

"Is there anything I should know about Captain Kindle's care? Anything I should do?"

"If he wakes and is in pain, give him a dose of laudanum in whisky."

Harriet nodded. "Sleep as long as you need. You look exhausted."

"I am."

I undressed to the sound of a bugler playing taps, signaling the end of my second day at Fort Richardson. By any measure it was horrid. A soldier dead, a child pregnant, a crooked sutler, a curious newspaperman, and an angry fort commander.

I sat on the side of the bed and stared at nothing, listening to the plaintive notes of the bugle, remembering the times I had heard it honor fallen soldiers during the war. The final note wavered and slowly died, leaving sadness in its wake. Tomorrow I would hear it twice.

I removed the bottle of laudanum from my bag, uncorked it, and sipped. The bitterness of the opiate was soon replaced by a spreading warmth and sense of peace. I took another drink, lay down on the bed, and closed my eyes. The day's events lumbered through my mind. Alice and Ruth, Harriet and Foster, Welch and Franklin. The tall man from the creek walked toward me, his face shaded by his hat. As he drew closer, the sun burned away the shadow, revealing a bloody maw where his mouth should have been and a face of rotting, decayed flesh. The flesh burned off in the sun. The bones disintegrated into dust the color of blood. The wind picked it up and threw it up to the open arms of a bright blue sky.

CHAPTER
18

I was surprised to find Harriet here when I woke."

Kindle sat on the edge of the bed, readying to take his first turn around the room. I put the cane next to his left leg and moved to his right side. His right arm was secured in a sling.

"She offered to sit with you so I could rest. Since it will be difficult for me to give you much support with your arm, you will need to put most of your weight on the cane."

He nodded.

"Are you ready?"

In answer, he grasped the cane and stood. I put my injured arm around his waist and hoped he wouldn't need my assistance. I wasn't sure how much help I would be. His left leg was shaking, but his right was strong, his cane firmly planted on the ground.

"Can you take a few steps?"

Fine beads of perspiration speckled his forehead. His breathing was quick and shallow. "Yes."

"You don't have to. Standing is enough for now."

"I cannot impress you if I merely stand."

"You don't need to impress me, Captain."

"Didn't I tell you to call me William? I intended to, if not. The last few days are vague."

"You did. Please, sit back down."

"I want to sit there." He pointed to the chair I had occupied when he woke. It was only a few feet away. He stepped forward with his good leg and followed it with his bad. After three more slow steps, I turned him around and he sat down heavily. "That was exhausting."

"Do you want to revise your prediction of being back in the saddle in a week?"

"No. I have set that as my goal and I will achieve it."

"Do you always achieve what you set out to do?"

"Almost always. Don't you?"

"Almost always." I straightened the blanket on Kindle's bed and sat on the edge.

He took a few deep breaths. Finally, his brow cleared.

"Does it make you nervous?" he asked.

"What?"

"That I always achieve my goals?"

"I suppose it depends on what goal you are speaking of."

"Getting back in the saddle."

"In that case, no. I have no doubt you are going to best my prediction. As your doctor, however, I will continue to preach caution. I know enough of you from our short acquaintance to suspect you are a determined man." He shifted in the chair. "Tell me when you want to move back."

He straightened his injured leg. "It's nice to sit."

"Have you eaten?"

"I'm not hungry. Why do I feel worse today than yesterday?"

"Your body is over the shock of the surgery and is working to heal you. It has a difficult task ahead. Which is why you need to rest as much as possible and eat, even though you don't think you're hungry. When the sun rises, I will go to the bakery and beg a loaf of bread."

"How was your day?"

"One of my five patients died. Private Howerton. Of infection after an amputation."

"Thank you for moving me."

"You're welcome. I met the local newspaperman."

"Pope? Nice man. Saw him fight once before the war."

"He wants to write about your surgeries. He knew everything. I told him there was nothing I could add."

"I'm not surprised. News travels fast in the West."

I flushed. "Does it?" I asked in a weak voice. Even if I had manipulated Pope into not writing about me, how long until the story of my survival and actions with Kindle traveled from campfire to campfire and back East? Or until Pope decided to claim the bounty for himself? One more thing to worry about.

"Pope is not your typical newspaperman. He'll stick to the truth."

I laughed. "Oh, he's typical enough. What do you know about Welch?"

"Not much, other than his disdain for treating Negro soldiers. Luckily, my men are a healthy lot. Why do you ask?"

"I accidentally overheard a conversation between Welch and Franklin yesterday."

"Franklin recommended Welch to the previous post surgeon as a civilian doctor not long before that man died."

"Lucky for Welch he didn't have anyone looking over his shoulder."

"What do you mean?"

"After seeing how many of the men in the hospital were playing Old Soldier—easily seventy-five percent—and hearing Franklin and Welch, I think Welch was being paid by soldiers for treatment. When they aren't sick."

"Unfortunately, many of the men we have are crooks and

thieves. They join under assumed names to escape the law. No surprise they would do whatever they can to get out of work. Welch taking advantage is less surprising."

"It doesn't bother you?"

"Of course it does. It's up to the individual officers to watch out for and discipline his men. And it is up to Foster and Mackenzie to manage the officers."

"Foster thinks I'm a hysterical woman."

"Why would he think that?"

I shrugged. "Would you like to play backgammon? I'll get the board." I rose and went into the parlor to retrieve the game. I held the box against my chest and silently berated myself. I'd determined earlier to not mention my confrontation with Foster to Kindle. He would support his superior officer and I frankly wasn't in the mood to be lectured. Why in the world the comment had slipped out of my mouth, I had no idea.

I returned to Kindle's room, moved a small table between us, and set up the board. Kindle placed his hand over mine. "Why would Foster think you are hysterical?"

I stared at Kindle's hand and tried to remember the last time I'd been touched gently by a man. I pulled my hand away and continued setting up the board.

"I accused Foster of being in on Franklin's crooked dealings."

"You what?"

"I know I was rash and I regret it. But he refused to listen to me. What was I supposed to think?"

"Not that the second in command is grafting from the Army."

"Have you seen the hospital stores? They are shockingly low. Franklin's shelves are stocked to the rim with our medicine."

"Do you know it for a fact?"

"No. But, I suspect it. Franklin is a crook, through and through."

"I don't disagree with you, but there's no proof Foster is crooked. You need to apologize."

"I know I do, William. It's infuriating when I'm dismissed because I'm a woman. If a man went to him with the same concerns, he would listen, I'm sure of it."

"I'll talk to Foster."

"No, you will not. I don't need you to fight my battles, thank you. I'm perfectly capable of groveling for myself."

"I doubt you have ever groveled."

"You'd be surprised." I shook the cup with dice with more force than necessary and threw them on the board. "Oh, did you want to go first?"

He waved his hand slowly across the board. "By all means."

We played in silence for a few minutes. "I apologize," I said.

"For?"

"Sometimes I let my passion get the better of me."

He shook the cup. "You never need to apologize for that with me," he said, and threw the dice. "Why did you become a doctor, Laura?"

"My mother died when I was young, and though Maureen raised me, I had a fierce independent streak. She couldn't control me and my father was too distracted by his profession to give my behavior much thought. He was a doctor and from a young age, his profession fascinated me. My earliest memory is sitting on his knee and looking at the diagrams of skeletons in a medical book. I think there were times he went on calls to get away from me and my questions. One day, I asked to go with him, which he flatly refused."

"How old were you?"

"Twelve. I followed him anyway. I was so small it was easy to hide in the shadows."

"We were both incorrigible twelve-year-olds."

I chuckled. "I suppose so."

"Where did your father go?"

"To a brothel. I knocked on the door, thinking it was the house of a patient. I told the woman who answered the door I was there to assist my father. She thought it was comical. My father didn't."

"I imagine not."

"Luckily, he was there in a professional, not personal, manner. But I timed my little rebellion poorly. Or precipitously. It depends on your perspective. My aunt was in town from London. My father's anger was nothing compared to Aunt Emily's. She convinced my father to let her take me back to England and promised to get me married off to the first fool who would take me."

"Were there no takers?"

"None I would take. I have always hated being told what I should and should not do. The more determined Aunt Emily was to marry me off to a simpleminded third son of an earl, the more determined I became to return to the States."

"Obviously your aunt didn't get her way. How did you manage it?"

"I'm not sure your good opinion of me could survive that tale." I chuckled.

"Now you have to tell me."

"Maybe one day. You look tired. Are you ready to move back to bed?"

"Not yet. I was hoping you could do something for me."

"What do you need?"

He rubbed his bearded chin. "A shave."

I held a bowl of soap in one hand and a brush in the other. "There's one condition."

"Yes?"

"You must tell me more of yourself."

"What would you like to know?"

I placed the only lamp on the table next to his chair and turned up the wick as far as it would go. The glow of the lamp threw the rest of the room into total darkness, marooning the two of us on an island of muted light. I rubbed the brush in the soap. The silence of night amplified the sound of the brush lathering his face. His eyes were closed, allowing me the opportunity to study him unobserved.

His face was weathered, but not leathery, and unblemished save the fine lines at the corner of his eyes and mouth and his scar. His lips were pink and soft, the lower lip slightly fuller than the upper, with a distinctive line in the middle above the faint cleft in his chin. His dark hair was longer than I remembered from Antietam and his eyebrows would grow into impressive heights as he aged unless a diligent barber kept them in check. I smiled at the vision of unruly white eyebrows framing his clear blue eyes as I applied the soap with small circles down his neck, up his face, and across his scar. "How did you get your scar?" My voice sounded unnaturally loud in the surrounding silence.

"In the war."

I put the soap and brush down and picked up the razor. "I'll be shaving your neck with a sharp razor. I can induce you to give me more information."

"You're a doctor and are bound by the Hippocratic oath."

I put the razor down. "I won't shave you."

"I'm your patient. You're supposed to do what I ask."

"I'm your doctor. Shaving patients is normally done by nurses, if at all."

He didn't respond. I took the towel draped over his shoulder to wipe the soap from his face, when he spoke.

"My brother gave me this scar."

"Lieutenant Kindle's father?"

"Yes. He fought for the Confederacy, much to my father's delight."

I picked up the razor and moved behind him. I lifted his chin and was about to run the blade up his neck when I paused. "I warn you: I've never done this before."

His eyes met mine. "I trust you."

Nowhere on his face was safe to look. His eyes probed too deeply, his scar inflated my pride, his lips sent my imagination whirling and my stomach tumbling. I focused on the razor and drew it in a long stroke up his neck. I wiped the blade on the towel and repeated the action. "Your family was divided by the war."

"We were divided long before, but always with the faint hope of reconciliation. You asked me why I stay in the Army. I believe I owe it a debt. It enabled me to escape my father, his legacy of cruelty."

He paused. The sound of the razor scraping away soap and whiskers was the only sound in the room. "I wish I'd had the courage to stand up to him. Joining the Army was a cowardly way to get out from under him."

"Leaving your family took courage."

His smile was wan. "Courage would have been staying and challenging him. And, my brother."

"The man who charged after the Kiowa three days ago is anything but a coward. And, he took a bullet and arrow for his trouble." I wiped the razor clean. "I haven't thanked you."

218

"There is no need."

"There is." My throat thickened. "I will always be in your debt."

He lifted his slinged arm, slightly. "I believe we can call it even."

I smiled and nodded. I took my time shaving Kindle, partly out of inexperience and a desire to do a good job. The longing to expand the intimacy of our conversation frightened me, but not enough to speed my task.

"Were you and your brother close?"

"No. John thought I was weak."

I shook my head in disagreement, but didn't respond. I focused on making long, straight lines through the soap, but knew his eyes studied me. I tried not to blush. "Your scar," I said, prompting him to continue.

"The family farm was near Antietam." The razor paused, almost imperceptibly, at the name. "Reports were John's company would be in the battle. They were the rear guard. I knew he would do whatever he could to go home and see his family. Protect them. I knew he wouldn't like what he found."

"What did he find?"

"His wife and children gone to Boston to be with my wife and her family."

The razor paused again. His wife? My stomach dropped. Of course he was married. I'd been stupid for not assuming as much. I blushed at my teasing and familiarity with him, a married man. My mortification was quickly replaced with irritation with him so blatantly instigating the flirtatious relationship. I could not let it pass. "Your wife?"

"Yes. Victoria's family is in Boston. She lived with them during the war."

I pressed my lips together and focused on shaving him as quickly as possible and promptly nicked his chin.

I swore under my breath and pressed against the cut with a clean portion of the towel. "I told you I've never done this before." My voice was testy.

For the second time that night, Kindle touched my hand. When he spoke, his voice was quiet. "Victoria died in a carriage accident in sixty-four. John's wife, Emma, was with her."

I hated myself for my relief. "I apologize," I said, hoping he understood I apologized for thinking ill of him as well as consoling with him for the loss of his wife. Kindle didn't remove his hand, nor did I release the pressure against his chin. He rubbed his thumb across the top of my hand. For a long moment, I was mesmerized by how his light touch erased every ache and pain I'd felt over the last week until all I felt was a prickle where his skin touched mine.

Finally, I regained myself and removed the towel. "That should suffice."

He dropped his hand and continued with his story as if nothing had passed between us, though his voice was rougher, almost hoarse. "Emma was a Northern sympathizer but she supported John, as any wife would do. As the fighting got closer to the farm, she wrote to Victoria and asked for help to move the kids to safety. My wife's family was happy to take her in."

Kindle cleared his throat and continued in clearer tones. "The day of the battle, I found John at home, as I knew I would, with my bedridden father. The slaves Emma had left to care for Father left to fight for the Union Army as soon as they moved into the neighborhood. Frankly, I'm surprised they stayed as long as they did. My father was the worst kind of slave owner.

"When John saw Father, wasted from disease and starvation, lying in his own urine and feces, he flew into a rage. This is the result."

"He blamed you?"

"Yes."

"What happened to your brother?"

"He died in a prisoner-of-war camp not long after I sent him the letter telling him of Emma's death. After the war, I retrieved his body and buried him on our family plot. He was in a camp for officers, so there was little trouble finding his grave."

I nodded. He was lucky. So many families still didn't know where their fallen sons, husbands, and brothers were buried. Most were buried where they fell—under a tree with a notch marked in it, next to a roadway, or in a mass grave at Andersonville—families had the letters of other soldiers to use to locate their loved ones, with many of those soldiers dead themselves.

"I left for the West the next day," Kindle said.

"Your father?"

"Is buried next to John."

His short, clipped answer said volumes. There was more to the story he did not want to tell. "I'm so sorry."

"It was a long time ago."

I wiped the razor on the towel and moved in front of Kindle. He said no more. I focused on my task, determined to ignore his steady gaze and the tension in the air between us.

"I remember you doing that," he said.

"Doing what?"

"Biting your lip when you concentrate."

I smiled. "Yes, my aunt used to chastise me for it."

"When you did needlepoint?"

"Yes," I laughed. "How did you...?"

The smile fell from my face. He remembered me from Antietam. I wiped the blade again. "When did you recognize me?"

"Immediately."

"Why didn't you say anything?"

"I've been second-guessing my memory—you were dressed as a man, after all—until you mentioned Aunt Emily. Why haven't you said anything?"

I turned and placed the razor next to the basin of water, dampened the edge of the towel, and wiped the excess soap from Kindle's face. He remained silent, waiting.

"Finished." I held a hand mirror in front of his face.

"Thank you. I'm a new man."

"I suppose if doctoring doesn't work out for me, I can always be a barber." I measured out a dose of laudanum. "Take this. It's time to return to bed, Captain."

"I am not drinking that or moving until you answer my question."

"I didn't recognize you."

Kindle scoffed. "You can lie to everyone else, but you cannot lie to me."

I stared into the opiate-laced whisky I held and was tempted to take it for myself. It wouldn't do a bit of good, though. Kindle was determined to have an answer.

I dared to look in his eyes. I almost laughed at the belligerence I saw there. I liked him all the more for it. "Men aren't the only ones who have a past to run from."

"Whom are you running from?"

I hadn't seen the stranger from the creek again and, as a result, his shadow had diminished until I believed I had been seeing threats where none existed.

"My own hubris, it would seem."

He studied me for a moment, nodded, and held out his hand for the whisky. He threw it back in one gulp and handed the tin mug to me.

"That wasn't so hard, was it?"

"It was excruciating." I helped him stand.

He looked down at me. "I'm beginning to think you're keeping me drugged and senseless because you don't enjoy my company."

"You've caught me out. That is precisely my goal."

He grinned. "Excellent."

I shook my head and couldn't help but smile. "How do you know I'm lying?"

"You have a tell."

"I do not."

"Yes, you do. No, I will not reveal it."

"You're incorrigible."

"You've said that."

"And a terrible backgammon player."

"Another reason you are drugging me, no doubt."

"One more day of rest and I will decrease your pain medicine. I promise."

I turned him around and helped him settle onto the edge of the bed.

He tilted his head back and stared at me with the same opiate grin I had seen on Howerton earlier in the day. "I'm glad you were a woman. You were much too beautiful to be a man."

I scoffed.

"What?"

"You are easily the quickest healer I've ever treated."

"I'm motivated."

"To get back in the saddle, yes. I know. Lie down."

With a mischievous smile he complied without arguing. I pulled the blanket over his chest and tucked it under his slinged arm.

"Your lip biting. Very endearing. Like a child concentrating."

"You don't know what you're saying."

"Yes, I do. Your name wasn't Laura."

I gathered the soap, bowl, razor, and mirror to return them to Kindle's room and did not reply.

"When I inquired about you, the name they gave you wasn't Laura."

"Sleep, Kindle. We will talk about this later."

"It doesn't matter."

"What doesn't matter?"

"What you're hiding. Or running from. I don't care."

"You don't know what it is."

"It doesn't matter." He closed his eyes. "Everyone has secrets."

CHAPTER

19

Over the next week, the number of patients under my care dwindled to zero. The day after my accusation against Foster, the four men in the hospital miraculously recovered and returned to duty. Jethro died and was the first soldier buried in the newly created Negro section of the Jacksboro graveyard. Being his commanding officer, Kindle made his first outing to attend the funeral the following day. While he leaned heavily on his cane, he showed no outward evidence of pain. Soon, Kindle would leave on patrol for Kiowa and Comanche, besting my prediction of a four-week recovery by two.

Kindle's regiment returned, with few cattle to show for their efforts, in time to attend Jethro's funeral. Sergeant Washington, as the ranking Negro NCO and close friend of Jethro, conducted the service. After taps and after the first shovelful of dirt thundered down onto the wooden coffin, I turned to leave. When Kindle didn't follow I returned and stood next to him, wondering what else there was to do. The mourners were silent as four soldiers filled the grave. When the mound was smoothed and the cross hammered into the ground, Sergeant Washington laid a baseball glove on the mound. Another soldier placed a bat with a hole bored into the barrel and a baseball next to the glove, which I noticed was without the leather laces required to hold it together. Caro, wearing a black turban in place of her usual colorful one, offered a pipe. One by one, the soldiers placed small trinkets, mostly common household items, on the grave and walked away. When all had been placed, Kindle touched the small of my back and ushered me away from the graveyard.

"What were they doing?"

"It's a slave custom. They give the items to the dead so their spirit won't wander."

"They're for the spirit to use?"

"I suppose it's one way of looking at it."

"He won't get much use from the baseball glove and bat."

"The items are rendered unusable so they won't be stolen."

I held my tongue. My accusation against Foster hung between us like an albatross. I still had not apologized to the lieutenant colonel, much to Kindle's irritation.

"How's your pain?" I asked.

"Tolerable."

"You're determined to make the timeline I gave General Sherman seem conservative, aren't you?"

"Yes. I'm tired of lying in bed, staring at the ceiling and playing backgammon."

"Only because I'm beating you."

"You're only beating me because I'm in pain. And, you distract me."

I ignored the comment. "As your doctor, I have to warn you I believe you are doing too much, too soon."

"I'm needed on a horse, not in bed."

I knew to try to talk him out of his goal would be pointless, not only because I had discovered in the last few days that he was exceedingly stubborn but also because I knew that, though my objections were based on sound medical opinion, my conservative treatment options would seem like concerns of a woman.

"When do you leave?"

"Sometime next week."

"The later the better. The more time you have to recover at the fort the better for your long-term recovery. You don't want to use a cane for your entire life."

"Not this particular cane, no. I wonder why you didn't scam Franklin out of a much more stylish one. What does it say about your opinion of me you that looked at the options and chose plain hickory?"

"You cannot be serious for a moment, can you?"

"When the moment warrants it, I can be serious."

Though we were walking a few feet apart, the change in his demeanor and the timbre of his voice made the expanse of the prairie surrounding us feel as intimate as an embrace.

What passed between us two nights earlier was ever present, making it more and more difficult for me to keep our relationship professional. I found myself anticipating the time I spent with him, looking forward to it as the most enjoyable part of my day. Kindle's personality suited me perfectly. He was honorable and evenhanded, kind to enlisted men as well as officers. He was blessed with a ready wit but not at the expense of others. But, for all of Kindle's honor and kindness, he was still a man, and a traditional one at that. I didn't know what was more terrifying: the idea he would expect me to give up medicine or the idea he wouldn't.

I stopped walking. We were quite alone on the road between the fort and Jacksboro.

"Why are you determined to make this difficult on me?" I demanded.

"Make what difficult?"

"Leaving." Kindle's expression of astonishment caught me

off guard. "I am staying until the new doctor arrives. No longer." Kindle narrowed his eyes. "I assumed you knew."

"No."

Kindle dropped his cane and cradled my face in his hands. My breath caught at the sudden, intense longing for this, the touch of a man. Kindle's touch. I had long since accepted desire as a sensation lost to me, sacrificed on the altar of my professional goals. Now, being held by Kindle, I wondered why I couldn't have both. "You cannot deny this."

I reached up and touched the nick on his chin.

He stroked my cheek and slowly pulled me toward him. Kindle kissed me hesitantly at first, as if he expected me to bolt any moment. My mind screamed to leave, to protect myself from the hurt this would lead to. My body, bombarded by the scratch of his stubble on my chin, the softness of his lips, and the slight scent of horse and leather that lingered on Kindle's clothes, craved more. When Kindle wrapped his arms around me and pulled me nearer, I melted into him and gave myself over to the hunger I'd denied myself for too long.

The distant nicker of a horse and the sound of jingling tack broke through my muddled mind. I tried to pull away, breathless and flushed, but Kindle held me firmly against him. He was correct; I couldn't deny what was between us. Yes, I wanted him. But, I could not have him. I knew I would carry the ache of loss for years, but in time I would forget.

"People are coming," I said. He released me. I patted my hair, and ran my hands down the front of my shirt. I turned and walked toward the fort. Kindle followed.

"We shouldn't have done that."

"It is exactly what we should have done, what I've wanted to do since I saw you standing in the schooner, staring out at the rain."

"You're being incredibly selfish."

"Selfish?"

I stepped off the road and stopped, waited for the two riders to pass, and said in an undertone, "In a week you will be gone, with a real possibility to never return."

"Patrols rarely resul—"

"Where does that leave me? A week of sneaking around to not insult the sensitivities of the officers' wives, mourning the loss of yet another person I care for? No, thank you."

"I'll return."

"You don't know that. It'll be difficult enough to endure your absence as things stand between us now. I don't think I could bear it if things were different."

He reached out to touch my face. "Laura…"

I stepped back. "No. Please don't. You're being cruel."

He dropped his hand. He leaned on his cane, staring at me in shock. After what he had told me previously of his father, I regretted the word choice.

"When the surgeon arrives, nothing will hold me here."

"Stop lying, Laura. Not to me."

I looked away. The two riders were almost out of sight. The man on the gray horse was turned in the saddle, staring at us. His hat was pulled low over his eyes, but his gaze rooted me to the spot all the same. The man grinned, touched his hat to me, turned, and rode on.

I turned to Kindle. "Did you see that man?"

"What man?"

I pointed down the road, though the two men were lost from sight. Instead, Beau Kindle loped toward us. "On the gray horse. I saw him across the creek the first day I was here and later on at the fort."

"What about him?"

My eyes met Kindle's. I could not tell him I worried the man

229

was watching me without divulging my past. "I've seen him multiple times. There is a malevolent air about him."

"The frontier is full of *cruel* men."

Kindle's lips, so recently full of tenderness and longing, hardened in a thin line. His anger didn't quite reach his eyes, though. The eyes that had struck me so at Antietam showed the real Kindle, the man I knew I would ache for long after I'd left Fort Richardson.

"You are nothing like him," I said.

With a disheveled appearance and jaunty grin, Beau reined his horse in a few feet away. "Captain, Dr. Elliston."

"Beau," I said.

"Where were you?" Kindle asked.

"In Jacksboro."

"You missed Jethro's funeral."

"I didn't know him."

"But you're one of the commanding officers of his regiment. You should have been there."

Beau's face turned a mottled red. Before he could answer with the insubordinate retort that was surely on his tongue, I asked, "Were you in Jacksboro on business?"

Beau blushed, giving me a clear indication of what kind of business took him to Jacksboro. "Of a sort," Beau said.

Before Kindle could berate him, Beau said, "Did you hear about Pope?"

"The newspaperman?" I said.

"Yes. Beaten to a pulp last night. His shop ransacked."

"Pope?" Kindle said.

"Yes, the former boxing champion himself was beaten to within an inch of his life. His jaw was broken, as was his press. He won't be communicating in any way, shape, or form for some time to come."

"Poor Mr. Pope." I did not wish Henry Pope harm, but I silently thanked God a threat to my identity had been neutralized. "Is there a doctor in Jacksboro seeing to him?" I asked.

"Welch."

"Do they have any idea who did it?" Kindle said.

"I heard the name Cotter Black."

Kindle tensed. "What did you say?"

"Cotter Black. Apparently that's the leader of the new gang raiding around here."

"The phantom Mr. Black is blamed for every bad thing that happens," I said.

"You've heard of him?" Kindle said. His face was pale.

"The laundresses mentioned him the other day. Why?"

Kindle looked in the direction the malevolent man had ridden. "Nothing."

"Lieutenant, come to my quarters at noon," Kindle said. His voice was strained and terse. "You're dismissed."

Beau executed a jerky salute and rode away.

Kindle walked off. Gone was the slow amble from before. Now, he moved as quickly as possible, almost angrily.

"William," I said, rushing to keep up with him. "Slow down."

He stopped and glared at me. I reeled at the transformation in his face. His eyes. "I know Beau is irresponsible, but—"

Kindle continued. "I am not angry with Beau."

We crossed the bridge spanning Lost Creek and the fort came into sight. Activity had increased significantly with the return of Kindle's regiment as well as a rider carrying a dispatch from Sherman and addendum from Mackenzie. The four children from the wagon train had been ransomed to the Quakers two days after the attack and were safe at Fort Sill. Sherman, while glad the children were unharmed, was incensed federal Indian policy could allow the killers of white settlers to reap benefits from kidnapping the orphans and evade justice. Sherman's own near brush with the same band of Kiowa fueled his anger and the new Army objective of "Kill them all." To that end an increase in military strength in Texas was in motion with regiments from as far away as Saint Louis being routed to Texas forts, such as Richardson and Griffin. Mackenzie was somewhere in Indian Territory, still searching for the perpetrators of the Salt Creek Massacre, as the attack of my wagon train was now being called. Most people thought it futile; Indian Peace Policy didn't allow the pursuit of Indians into Indian Territory, which was why this part of Texas was being bombarded with raids. What would be done with the Indians if they were caught no one could tell.

At the front of the hospital, Kindle turned and said, "If you'll excuse me, I must see Foster."

His coldness was like a dagger. Though I wielded it, too, when turned on myself, the pain of it was shocking. "Of course. Thank you."

I watched him limp off until he was lost amid the activity of the fort.

"Doctor?"

Waterman stood in the hospital doorway.

"Yes?"

"This was delivered for you a little while ago."

He handed me an envelope and returned inside. My name was written in a clear hand on the front. I removed and unfolded the reward poster the newspaperman had threatened me with my second day at Fort Richardson, now crinkled, torn, and covered with Henry Pope's blood.

CHAPTER 20

"Who brought this?" Waterman looked up from his work. I brandished the envelope with a shaking hand. "Who?" My voice cracked. I coughed to cover it.

Waterman shrugged. "A soldier. I'd never seen him before. He must be with one of the new regiments."

"Tall? Bearded?"

"Yes. Why? What is it?"

I should have regained my composure before asking Waterman about the letter. Now, his curiosity was piqued. "Nothing." I folded the envelope and tucked it in the waistband of my skirt. "Are the supplies for the aid kits in the north ward?"

"Yes."

"I'll get under way."

I walked into the empty ward and around the private-room partition. I clutched my stomach and mouth against the nausea that overtook me, again. This Wanted poster would follow me for the rest of my life. Would I ever be free from it?

"Doctor?" A nurse called out.

I straightened and inhaled to compose myself. "Yes. Coming."

For the next few hours the nurse and I created crates of

medical supplies to be included on the supply wagons accompanying each patrol. It was repetitive, mind-numbing work but gave me the perfect opportunity to think.

Who had sent me the letter and why? Beau's report implied Pope wasn't in any condition to mail a letter, let alone address it in such a pristine hand. But, if not Pope, who? The man who had beat him? Cotter Black? Had Welch found the letter when attending Pope and seen the resemblance between the picture and me? I didn't think so. It was a horrid picture and Welch had only met me once, when he was drunk.

I stopped what I was doing, went to the office, and opened the log to one of the last pages of Welch's entries. I fumbled removing the envelope from my waistband. My hands shook as I compared the writing on the envelope to Welch's log entries.

Welch's entries ranged from barely discernible scribbles, made most like when he was drunk, to such precise writing it made me wonder if the same hand had written it at all. Neither clearly resembled the writing on the envelope, but neither were they discernibly different.

"Damn," I muttered.

I stared at the envelope. Was this the only copy of the reward poster in Jacksboro? If so, what proof would Pope or whoever had sent this have of my identity? None. It would be my word against theirs. I stood and walked into the kitchen. Through the back window I saw Corporal Martin smoking and talking to the men detailed to build the death house. I opened the stove, tossed the envelope on the embers, and poked at it with a metal rod until the evidence of my past was nothing more than ashes. I closed the stove, replaced the poker, and dusted my hands off before returning to the office.

I gazed out the window of the office and onto the parade ground full of soldiers on dress parade. Kindle limped down the line with Foster, inspecting the troops. My eyes lingered on his hands. The memory of them cradling my face settled my nerves, until the knowledge they would never do so again shattered them anew.

The front door of the hospital flew open and banged against the wall. Waterman walked out of the dispensary, wiping his hands with a towel.

"Hello, Waterman! Where's Dr. Welch? Had a bit of excitement near Fort Phantom Hill." The officer was young, good-looking, and covered in dirt from the trail. The crude bandage on his right calf was stained with dried blood.

"Welch isn't available, Lieutenant Strong," Waterman said. "Dr. Elliston can see to your wound."

"Well, find the man quick. I want to get this cleaned up before I see my wife. She'll faint dead away at the sight of this bandage."

The man limped into the north ward. I shared a conspiratorial smile with Waterman and followed.

The lieutenant was taking off his gun belt and coat when I entered. "Oh, hello," he said. "Are you a new nurse? I don't think I have seen you before."

"I only arrived a few days ago."

"Welcome to the end of the earth," he said with a smile. "I'm Wallace Strong."

"Dr. Elliston."

His smile wavered a fraction. "Are you really?" He gave me the once-over and his smile returned. "I should have guessed you weren't a nurse."

"Let's see what we have here." I cut the bandage away to reveal a wound that went clear through his calf.

"How did you get this?"

"From an Indian. They had us pinned in a buffalo wallow.

Circling around us," he said, using his hands to illustrate. "I didn't notice it until later."

I turned away from the young man, remembering my own experience in a buffalo wallow, and busied myself with instruments lying on the table. My heart hammered and my breath came in short bursts. "They rode away?" I asked in as steady a voice as I could manage.

"Typical Indian. They got bored, I suppose. We held them off for two days. This morning, we woke and they were gone."

"The good news is there is no bullet to remove. I need to clean the wound thoroughly, apply carbolic acid to the area, and wrap it in a clean bandage. You are not to remove the bandage for a few days, unless the wound bleeds. Then return to me and I will see to it."

Lieutenant Strong looked at me in some confusion. "I only wanted a clean bandage."

I was ready to frighten him with the possibility of gangrene when Beau Kindle bounded into the room.

"Strong, you son of a gun. I heard you were back. Already malingering, I see."

"Kindle! How are you?"

"Better than you, it would appear. What happened?"

"It's nothing," Strong replied. "I didn't know I was hit until one of my soldiers noticed the blood on my trousers. Forget about that. Tell me about traveling with Sherman."

Waterman had discreetly entered the cubicle. I sent him to the kitchen for hot water. I stood in the background and pretended to be busy while I eavesdropped on their conversation.

Lieutenant Kindle pulled up a chair and sat next to the bed. "Obviously, I wasn't in his inner circle, but I heard enough to know he was skeptical of the claims of Indian attacks. We didn't see a bit of it, and he was sure the reports making their way to

Saint Louis were a bunch of ex-Confederate politicians who wanted to switch our focus from Reconstruction to the Indians."

"Surely he doesn't think Mackenzie…"

"Like I said, I was not privy to specifics, but that was the general idea I gleaned from conversations I heard between him and the people he talked to on the trail."

"What about the abandoned farms along the frontier? Did he think people gave up for no reason?"

Beau Kindle shrugged. "You should have seen the angry townsmen here in Jacksboro when Sherman met with them. He barely listened. He was more interested in getting back to the fort and having dinner with the officers and their wives."

"I'm sorry I missed it."

"Your Alice especially charmed him."

Strong laughed. "My Alice?"

"You don't give her enough credit, Strong."

"I give credit where it is due. I've never seen Alice charm any man."

"Doesn't mean she is incapable of it," Beau replied.

"Has she charmed you, Kindle?"

"I'm not so desperate I'll flirt with a married woman."

"Met the laundresses already, have you?"

"Been to Jacksboro."

"Don't tell me you've paid for it!" Strong laughed and slapped Beau on the shoulder. "I'll introduce you to Ruth. A sweet little thing who's great company when she keeps her mouth shut."

I looked up and glared at Strong. So this was the father of Ruth's bastard, and Alice's husband. I could see how someone as ignorant as Ruth would be so easily taken in by the confident young officer. I could see, as well, how plain Alice would suffer the indignities of being married to a libertine rather than not be married at all.

"Enough about whores," Strong said. "Tell me more about Sherman."

"He was anxious to get on his way and would have, if not for the attack on the Warren wagon train."

"The supply train bringing the cattle?"

Beau nodded. "We met them the previous day and camped with them. Five or six families had attached themselves to the train." Beau paused. "The things they did to those people. Burned one alive and butchered this one woman's face until she was almost unrecognizable as a..."

I dropped the instrument I held, recalling my presence to the two men. Lieutenant Kindle, when he saw who I was, stood and turned bright red. "Dr. Elliston, I didn't realize..." He glanced to Lieutenant Strong for help, but Strong merely looked puzzled. "Strong, Dr. Elliston was the only survivor of the mas...attack. Captain Kindle's regiment arrived before... He was injured, my uncle, and Dr. Elliston saved him. Performed surgery out there on the plains with a storm coming. You should have heard Kindle's men sing her praises," Beau said. "I took his men to retrieve the lost cattle, you see. We returned last night."

Waterman returned with a pot of hot water. "Lieutenant Kindle, if you'll excuse us," I said.

He left, but not before telling Strong he would let Alice know where he was. He was out of the ward before Strong could keep him from alerting his wife.

Performing the mundane task of cleaning and binding Strong's wound helped still my racing heart. Visions from the attack weren't so easy to banish, nor was the realization my experience had become another atrocity to detail with a morbid fascination borne of relief—relief you and yours were safe— and the thrill of dread that one day you might not be.

"You lost your family in the attack?"

I nodded.

"I'm sorry." After a moment he continued, his voice hard. "That's why we have to do whatever we can to stop these savages! Eradicate every last one of them off the face of the earth. That's the only way we are going to be safe."

I thought of Maureen's destroyed face for the hundredth time and hoped I would be there when the last Indian was killed; a small part of me hoped I would be the one holding the gun.

"How did you survive?" Strong asked.

I placed two squares of cloth soaked in carbolic acid on both wounds, wrapped a clean bandage around his leg, and tied it off.

"I was a coward and hid in a buffalo wallow. Like you."

CHAPTER
21

My second interview with Lieutenant Colonel Foster went smoother than the first, due to my concerted effort to control my temper. I needed to get back in Foster's good graces, first by groveling, and then by showing my worth as fort doctor.

"Lieutenant Colonel, I would like to apologize for my behavior the other day. I let emotions supersede logic and made an ill-advised accusation."

"That will happen with women, I grant."

If Foster had been the least bit observant, he would have seen me clutching my hands so tightly my knuckles were white. I smiled and said, "I do hope you won't hold it against me."

"Of course not!" His demeanor changed to one of bonhomie. "I admit I was angry at first. Miss Mackenzie helped me see where you were coming from, though I still do not agree with you."

"Harriet?"

"Yes. I saw her while visiting Kindle the next day. You were at the hospital, I believe. Doing an outstanding job!"

I chastised myself for my jolt of jealousy at the idea of Harriet visiting Kindle. He'd shown his preference that morning on the road to Jacksboro.

"I accept your apology. Now, don't take this the wrong way, but no one ever comes to see me but that they want something."

"I've completed the crates of medical supplies for the long patrols."

"Excellent!"

"I also treated the bullet wound Lieutenant Strong received on his patrol."

"How is he?"

"He will be fine."

"Good news. He is an excellent officer. Need him in the field." The compliment was losing its effectiveness; Foster said it of everyone.

"I understand the smaller patrols have no medical officers."

"No."

"The officers and some of the men perform medical attention as needed?"

"Correct."

"With your permission, I would like to train a soldier in each company in the basics of medical attention. The quality of the first aid a soldier receives can be the difference between a healed wound and a chronic one."

Foster leaned back in his chair. "Go on."

"What I would like to teach them, specifically, is the importance of cleanliness. Cleaning their hands before attending to the wound, keeping the wound clean, covering the wound with a clean cloth. I would also train them on using carbolic acid to clean and cover the wound."

"Is that the vile-smelling stuff you put on Kindle?"

"Yes."

"How long would this training take?"

"An hour at most. I have checked the hospital stores and there is not enough carbolic acid to supply the patrols. However,

I will make up the difference from my supply, which can be replaced when the fort's stores are replenished."

"I cannot say when that will be," Foster said. "You may be gone before it happens."

"Yes, I could be," I said, slowly.

"I assume you plan to continue on your journey, or have you decided to make Jacksboro your home?"

"No. Continuing on is my plan." I thought of the bloody Wanted poster. "I would like to leave as soon as possible." My stomach clenched at the thought of Kindle.

"When Major Kline arrives you can accompany the next wagon train destined for Fort Sill. From there, you can travel to the nearest train station or, if you prefer, take a stage to... Where were you going again?"

"California."

"I've wondered, Doctor, whatever in the world motivated you to come west? I can understand a man venturing out alone, but a woman is a different matter."

"Have you forgotten, I was not alone?"

He paused. "No."

"Thank you for the offer of escort to Fort Sill," I said, happy my groveling had at least changed his mind about throwing me off the fort with no assistance. "Until then, I would like to be of some use."

"Yes, the training." Foster took up his pen. "It sounds like a good idea. Can you start tomorrow?"

"I will need to prepare. The day after?"

"I will tell the officers to send a man."

"A bright soldier who will not mind receiving instruction from a woman would be preferable."

"Is there anything else?"

"No. Nothing. Thank you, Colonel Foster. Since there are

so few soldiers who are sick I have felt quite useless these last days. I do hope my gender is not keeping sick men from getting the attention they need."

"More troops are arriving daily. I am sure your ward will fill again in no time. At the least, it will fill with drunkards when payroll arrives."

"Yes, but the new surgeon will arrive as well and I will be no longer needed."

"I imagine Major Kline will find something for you to do."

"Major Kline is the doctor? Major *Ezra* Kline?"

"Yes." Foster stopped writing. "Do you know him?"

The blood drained from my face, but my voice didn't betray my nervousness. "By reputation. He was a professor at Syracuse Medical College and has been at the champion of Pasteur's germ theory of disease."

"Rejoined the Army after his wife died. I'm sure he will be happy with your training the troops. He has been trying to innovate in the medical department for years. If there's nothing else…"

"Thank you, Lieutenant Colonel." I walked to the door and turned. "One more thing." Foster put his pen down and tried to hide his exasperation. "Since Captain Kindle is recovering so well, my nightly presence is unnecessary. My continued residence in his quarters is inappropriate. As such, I am on my way to town to find lodgings."

"An excellent idea."

"Do you know when Major Kline will arrive? So I can estimate the amount of time I will need to procure a room?"

"Any day now."

"Wonderful. Thank you for your time."

I left Foster's office more alone than ever. I suspected, despite his effort at pretending otherwise, Foster was humoring me until he could kick me off his fort, with Sherman's letter in hand or not, I didn't know. Harriet had done an excellent job of keeping herself and the other officers' wives clear of my bad influence. I had rejected the one person I had a connection with, a decision I regretted and admired in equal measure. I would miss Kindle's company but the pain of the later, inevitable parting would be greater than my current regret.

I walked around the back of the officers' quarters, past the detached kitchen, and across the dirt wagon track that circled the fort. In front of me, the plains stretched out to infinity, broken only occasionally by scrubby trees and large clumps of cacti and topped with a clear blue sky. A slight breeze, crisp and refreshing, danced over the tall grasses. I brushed my hands over their tops as I walked and enjoyed the tickling sensation.

I could never live here, I thought. It was too open, exposed, not only to human danger (though where was there not an element of human danger?) but also to nature. The memory of the storm was almost as terrifying as the Indians. The ferocity of both was unbelievable, nightmarish. As days wore on and life returned to normal rhythms, the events took on a dreamlike quality. The further away I moved, the less real they seemed. I could almost believe I had imagined both, that the memories were someone else's, or a story I heard, a fairy tale designed to scare children. Then the nausea and headache would return, or my shoulder would ache. The openness of the land, though beautiful in its own way, reminded me of my vulnerability and kept my constant companion, fear, close to my heart.

I closed my eyes and rubbed my sore shoulder. I endeavored to hide the pain of it from everyone, especially Kindle. Weakness, in any form, would diminish my effectiveness. The stress of keeping up appearances, of pretending to be strong physically, mentally, and emotionally, was unbearable.

My solitary life stretched across the plains before me. The journey from Richardson to Fort Sill and on to the railroad. The gentle swaying of the train as it chugged west toward the Rocky Mountains. My mouth watered with the idea of a good meal. Then, where? Another country? Another town on the frontier? Opening a practice, always being on call, traveling through the frontier in the dead of night to deliver babies and see to the dying.

Or, should I turn east and go home? I thought of the house I left, my family home. A thick layer of dust would now cover my possessions. I thought of my closet full of dresses and hats, ten years out of style but still serviceable for the few social occasions I attended. In New York my focus had been on medicine, on keeping up with the latest discoveries and putting them into practice. Social engagements held little interest. With the prospect of no society a reality, I longed for the camaraderie of women and the attention of men. But, that would not be my life in New York. What waited for me there was a noose.

I sighed and opened my eyes. Introspection was a luxury I couldn't afford. The sun was high in the sky and I had much to do before it set that evening.

Then, I saw him. His dark brown skin and black hair stood out against the blue sky, his white horse contrasting with the green of the prairie grass. I lifted my skirt, turned, and ran as fast as I could, straight into Kindle.

"Laura," he said, grasping my arms. "What's the matter?"

Words would not come. I was gasping, crying. I pointed a shaking arm to the south. Kindle's gaze followed and he instinctively moved in front of me. His body tensed as I stood behind him and watched the Indian ride toward us. A moment passed and Kindle relaxed. He raised his hand in greeting, which the Indian returned with a smile.

"He is a Tonkawa. One of our scouts. Are you okay? You are shaking like a leaf."

"No, I'm not okay," I snapped.

"What are you doing out here?" Kindle asked, an edge to his voice.

"Thinking. Trying to find solitude. Lord knows it's scarce, like everything else in this godforsaken place."

The Indian called a greeting to Kindle. I left when Kindle returned it. He might be able to embrace one Indian while fighting another, but to me they were savages, every one.

"Who is that?" the Indian asked.

"The most frustrating woman I've ever met," Kindle said.

Without turning around, I slammed the back door of his quarters in response.

⟨∞⟩

The sun was setting with a brilliant show of colors when I arrived at the laundresses' quarters. The vibrant hues cast a warm glow on the dull beige canvas tents and gave them a homey appearance they lacked in the harsh light of day.

Women ranged in front of the three tents, relaxing and laughing with a camaraderie borne of personal familiarity and a lack of societal restraint. Most cared little what the world thought of them. Those who did lived apart, did their jobs diligently, and waited for their husbands, brothers, or fathers to visit from the fort or return from patrol.

As with every strata of society, there was a hierarchy among the laundresses, with Mary as the leader. The women deferred to her in everything—most willingly, some grudgingly and suspiciously—always waiting for the first sign of weakness to exploit. They would have a difficult time deposing Mary, as even in mirth, which was how I found her when I arrived that evening; her suspicious eyes were roving across her acolytes.

"Lookie here, ladies," Mary said. "It's our own personal doctor come visiting. To what do we owe this honor?"

"I was in town and thought I would stop by to check on my patients."

"Did'ja now?" she replied, her eyes giving evidence of the calculation in her head.

"Yes, I did. May I?" I nodded to a vacant crate.

Mary motioned her acquiescence with the demeanor of a queen.

"Thank you." I sat and placed my medical bag next to my feet.

"You wanna drink?" Mary offered. "We're celebratin'!" Each woman held a tin cup full of clear liquid.

I thought of my day: the scene with Kindle, the realization Foster wanted me gone, the Indian, and the imminent arrival of Ezra Kline. Another terrible day. I hardly had any other kind at Fort Richardson. "Why not?" Adella poured. "What are you celebrating?"

"Farmer came by to visit and left us a jug of his homemade corn mash. Pretty good, ain't it?"

I sipped from the mug and nearly choked. "Yes," I managed to say amid the women's laughter. "Very good." The mash went down easier on the second sip. By the third, my glass was empty and I was holding out my cup for more.

"Slow down there, Doc," Adella said. "Stuff's strong."

"Whatcha doin' in town?" Ruth was sitting at Mary's feet with her arms crossed over her stomach, trying to cover a pregnancy ready to show. My eyes traveled from her stomach to her face and I smiled encouragingly.

When I examined Mary and Adella I had discovered they

suffered from venereal disease and poor nutrition, but were in good health otherwise. I advocated the use of sheaths during intercourse for the former and an increase in the amount of vegetables they ate for the latter. They laughed and said how many vegetables they were able to eat was up to God, the weather, and how much the quartermaster decided to give them when the fort garden produced.

"Yeah," Mary said, "what were you doin' in town? I'd a though' you'd be snuggled up with the captain tonight."

"I'd much rather be visitin' the captain than a bunch of women," Adella said.

My face burned. "I don't know what you are talking about."

"No need to be shy with us, Doctor," Mary said. "Adella saw you and the captain on the road today."

I hoped the setting sun, the heat from the fire, and the corn mash would account for the embarrassment burning on my face. "I'm sorry you saw that. It was an unfortunate event the captain and I both regret."

Adella laughed. "You sure did'na look like you thought it was unfortunate when it was happenin'. Not as I blame ya. He's a fine-looking man. I wouldn' mind being on the receivin' end of that unfortunate event."

"Leave her alone, Adella," Mary said. "Can't ya see she's shy of it?" The women continued to chuckle and exchange knowing looks but, thankfully, dropped the subject.

"So, what was you doin' in town?" Mary insisted.

"Procuring lodgings," I said.

"Don't trust yourself being alone with the captain, do you?" Mary said.

"No," I replied.

"I wouldn'a trust ya, either," Adella said. "You was clutchin' on to him somethin' fierce."

"No. I did not mean…What I meant was…" I stuttered along, grasping for coherence.

"Maybe ya should lay off the mash, Doctor," Mary said, taking the cup from my hand, spilling a bit on my dress in the exchange. "Sorry." She tossed the rest of the mash on the fire, which flared up in response. "Strong, see?"

Determined to clear up the confusion, I continued on. "What I meant was, no, I am leaving because the captain has recovered sufficiently so he no longer requires someone to watch over him at night. It is only right that I, as a civilian, would find other accommodations."

"You could stay with us!" Ruth offered.

"Don't be stupid, girl," Mary said. "The lady doctor can't stay with a bunch of laundresses. You gonna stay at the hotel?"

"Yes. It will suit my needs sufficiently until I leave."

"Leave?" Ruth said. "Where are you going?"

I smiled. Her disappointment made me strangely happy. "Staying in Jacksboro was never part of my plan."

"But, the Injuns!" Ruth said. "They're all stirred up and killin' white people all around. It ain't safe!"

"Not to mention the gangs of white men ridin' around, raidin', killin', stealin', and makin' it look like Injuns," Adella said.

"They's worse than the redskins, if you ask me," Mary said. "What kinda man would do that to his own?"

"They say Cotter Black's the resurrected corpse of a rebel officer come back to revenge himself on his murderer," Ruth said.

"Don't be stupid," Mary said. "Can't no man rise from the dead."

"Lazarus did," Adella said.

"Well, I don't know about you but I ain't seen Jesus around Jacksboro performing miracles lately," Mary replied.

"You've mentioned this Cotter Black before. What does he look like?" I asked Mary.

"I don't know of no man that's ever met him, let alone seen him."

"That's cuz no one who runs across him lives to tell the tale," Adella said.

"So, he is a phantom? A bogeyman made up to scare people?"

"There's usually always a bit of truth in rumors," Mary said. "Mind you, I don't think he's a ghost, but I suspect he's realer than not."

"When I leave, I'll be traveling with the Army," I said, "which is as safe as it is possible to be, I suppose."

"You hope so. Heard some officer returned today with an arrow in his leg," Adella said.

"Not an arrow. A bullet went clean through his calf."

"What officer?" Ruth said.

"When do you expect to leave?" Mary asked.

I shrugged. "It depends on when the new surgeon arrives and when another patrol is destined for Fort Sill."

"I hope it ain't for a while. I like you, Doctor. You're an interestin' lady," Mary said.

"Thank you, Mary." I looked at the women sitting around the fire with me. "I like you, too," I said to the group. "Even though you tease me mercilessly."

"Everybody needs a good teasin' now and then. Hell, if we can't laugh at ourselves, who can we laugh at?" Adella said. "We ain't paid you for examinin' us. You can't leave until we pay ya."

"I told you not to worry about it."

"What officer was hurt, Doctor?"

I couldn't ignore Ruth's question any longer. "Wallace Strong."

I could tell by the expression on Ruth's face my suspicions had been correct: Alice's husband was the father of her child.

⸎

I walked back to my quarters across a dark, quiet fort, passing a few soldiers along the way. They tipped their hats and I saluted them, giggling to myself after they passed before returning my focus to walking a straight line across the parade ground.

Kindle was sitting on my porch—*his* porch—when I arrived.

There was no moon out tonight, but the sky was full of stars. The shadows on the porch were dark, hiding Kindle's face. Only the glowing end of a cigar held in his hand was visible. "Where have you been?"

"I didn't know you smoked," I said. "No one agrees with me but I don't think it can be good for you to inhale smoke into your lungs."

He raised the cigar to his mouth and took a deep drag. The glowing end lit his face and revealed anger and concern in his eyes. He blew a stream of smoke from his mouth and replied. "I'll keep it in mind. Where have you been, Laura?"

"To town."

"Alone?"

"Yes, and why not?"

Kindle was in front of me in two steps. "You should not have walked back in the dark." He sniffed. "Have you been drinking?" he asked, incredulous.

"Maybe a little," I replied.

"In town?"

"No. I visited my patients and they offered me a glass of corn mash as payment."

"Patients?"

"The laundresses near the creek. One of them is pregnant. Stupid girl."

"You drank corn mash?"

"Unfortunately, their customer didn't pay them in bourbon. Though a little corn mash goes a long way, I can tell you."

"You're drunk," Kindle said.

"No," I replied. I tilted my head to the side and looked up at him. "Maybe a little." I lifted my hand and demonstrated. With the same hand, I touched his scar. "I did a good job."

"You did."

"You should probably thank Aunt Emily. She forced me to do needlepoint."

"When I meet her I will."

"I'm glad you didn't die."

"Which time?"

"Either. Both." I dropped my hand. "You want to kiss me again, don't you?" He didn't reply but his eyes traveled to my lips. I was drunk enough that a part of me wanted him to take me by the hand and lead me into his quarters, but sober enough to know he wouldn't. "You cannot, though I wouldn't mind."

"That's the corn mash talking."

"Yes, it is." I sighed and glanced over my shoulder. "I have no doubt Harriet is peeking out the window behind us. I don't see her but her beady little judgmental eyes are watching, mark my words."

"You and Harriet are more alike than you would care to admit."

"I don't want to talk about Harriet, or Foster, or Cotter Black. My friends say I should be snuggled up with you. That was their word, *snuggled*. It is a funny word, isn't it?"

"Your friends?"

I nodded. "The laundresses. They're the only people who

252

have welcomed me. Besides you, of course. Adella saw us. Today on the road. 'Clutching at each other something fierce' was her description. Too accurate, I'm afraid."

"I'm sorry."

"Don't be." I smiled sadly, and chanced to look in his eyes. "There were two people on the road, don't forget." I tried, but could not hold his gaze. "You understand why we cannot... Why I cannot... Why this is for the best."

"You'll never convince me it's for the best."

"Maybe you're right," I said. "Under these circumstances..."

"If the circumstances were different?"

"What do you want of me? Mistress or wife? Neither would suit my personality."

"Does being alone suit you?"

"Until now it has suited me very well. Would you tell me to give up my profession?"

My heart broke when he didn't answer. I turned my face and stared out onto the empty, dark parade ground. "I would ask you to give yours up, as well. I wouldn't be a good soldier's wife."

He remained silent.

"You see, I'm correct. Neither of us could give the other what they want." After a pause I said, "Now I have lost the warm and tingly sensations from the corn mash, but don't worry. I'm not angry. It's my own fault for asking you the question I didn't want to know the answer to."

Kindle stepped away, leaned against the post, and smoked his cigar. "What were you doing in town?"

"I am moving to the hotel tomorrow. You are well enough. It's inappropriate for me to stay in your quarters."

"You are *not* moving to town."

"I've already talked to Foster about it."

"I won't allow it."

"You won't *allow*?"

"Stay in my quarters. I leave on patrol tomorrow."

"What? You can't."

Kindle inspected the glowing end of his cigar. "Are you speaking as my doctor, or as my..."—he looked up at me—"...friend?"

"You aren't recovered enough. What if you reopen one of your wounds?"

He crushed his cigar out and flicked it over the side of the porch. He crossed his arms and legs and gazed out at the parade ground. "I've survived on the frontier for years before I met you, Laura."

I thought I was going to be sick. I wasn't ready for him to leave but knew I could do nothing to stop him. "I daresay you will survive many more." I held out my hand. "I suppose this is good-bye."

He took my hand. "It doesn't have to be."

"It does."

He nodded but didn't release my hand. "Promise me one thing."

"Yes?"

"Don't leave the fort. Stay in my quarters for the remainder of your time here."

"Why?"

"It's safer."

I grinned. "Are you worried about Cotter Black?"

His eyes bored into my own. "Yes."

My smile slipped. "Why?"

"Cotter Black was the name of a slave we owned. The one I helped escape."

"And, you think he's the one—"

"No. That Cotter Black is dead."

"I don't understand."

"There's only one person who would use that name and he's buried next to my father. It is most like a coincidence." He ran his thumb across my own, bringing back memories of the other moments we'd touched and what had passed between us. "Nevertheless, promise me you'll stay at the fort."

I lifted one shoulder. "If you wish."

He smiled and lifted my hand. His lips lingered for a few moments. "Good-bye, Laura." He released me and turned. I grasped at his hand, wanting to prolong our time together, the feel of his skin on mine, but caught the cuff of his coat instead. "Wait." My voice cracked.

He stopped.

"Your bandages." I cleared my throat to steady it. "I should check them before you leave. Show you how to change them if they get soiled."

He shifted, moved nearer. I forced myself to pull my gaze from the top button of his coat to his face. I smiled and tried to act nonchalant, to pretend it wasn't a ploy to prolong our parting. "Unless you've seen me do it enough you know how." He didn't answer, but moved toward the door of his quarters. "No, the hospital. I am out of carbolic," I lied. Though I didn't want to part yet, I also didn't want to be alone in a house with him. The hospital would give a gloss of professionalism to my unprofessional ruse, though if past was prologue, Kindle saw right through me. Like the gentleman he was, he motioned for me to precede him down the steps and kept any teasing comments he might have said to himself. We walked across the parade ground without speaking.

The hospital was silent save the occasional cough from one of my two patients in the south ward. Waterman met us in the front hall in his shirtsleeves, putting his glasses on. "Dr. Elliston?"

"Sorry to wake you, Waterman. Captain Kindle leaves on patrol tomorrow. I am giving him a lesson on changing his bandages."

Waterman nodded once. "Can I help?"

"No, thank you. We shouldn't be long. Go back to sleep."

Waterman nodded and left us alone in the dark hall. Kindle watched me, silent and grave. "You remember where the surgery is," I said. "I will be there presently."

Kindle's boots echoed on the wooden floor, scraped, and were silent. I inhaled a shaky breath, regretting the corn mash and the impetuous suggestion to change Kindle's bandages. The best I could do would be to brazen it out, remain professional, and shake his hand good-bye. I gathered my supplies and followed him to the surgery. My step faltered at the door; Kindle sat on the table, shirtless, his left shoulder bandaged expertly. I placed my equipment on the table next to him and lit the nearby lamp. I lengthened the wick and held the light up to his shoulder. I shifted the lamp to my left hand and used my right to lift Kindle's arm. When it was perpendicular to the ground he inhaled sharply. "Hurt?"

He nodded.

I put the lamp down and unwound the bandage from his shoulder, rolling it up as I did. I peeled the square of carbolic acid–laced cloth from the wound and was happy to see very little seepage on the cloth. I lifted the lamp and studied the sutured incision. "Very little redness. I can remove the stitches when you return. How long will you be gone?" I put the lamp down.

"Ten days. Maybe more."

My stomach flipped. "So long?" I hoped he hadn't heard the disappointment in my voice.

"It's a short patrol. They can last up to a month."

I swallowed the thickening in my throat and told myself I was nauseated from the corn mash. I held up the brown bottle I brought with me. "This is a carbolic-acid-and-water solution." I dripped a bit of the solution onto a fresh piece of cloth. "When your bandage becomes soiled, dampen a piece of cloth with this solution and place it on the wound." I did so. "Hold it for me, please?" Kindle held it while I wrapped the long strip of cloth around his shoulder and under his arm. I kept up a litany of instructions, trying to distract myself from his steady, penetrating gaze, but unintentionally distracted myself from his hands, which I realized were on my hips when I stopped talking.

"Um, I am sure Sergeant Washington can help you with wrapping your shoulder. He seems a competent young man. Do any soldiers in your regiment have experience as an orderly?" I corked the carbolic acid–solution bottle and tried to move away. He pulled me forward and cupped my cheek with one hand.

"No," he whispered, his breath light on my ear. I closed my eyes and tried to focus.

"Foster is allowing me to teach some men basic first aid. I will teach one of your men when you return. If I'm here still," I said, my voice low and strained. Kindle pressed his lips on my neck just below my ear. I leaned into the hand cupping my face. He pulled me closer and his lips became more insistent, sending shivers down the left side of my body.

"We mustn't," I said, without conviction. "Waterman…"

"Is snoring."

I listened and heard a long, rattling snore. "He should sleep on his side."

"You should stop thinking about Waterman." Kindle took my earlobe between his teeth and gently tugged. I reached out for the lamp, turned the wick down to the barest glow, and gave in.

My hands found their way to his broad back, and pulled him closer, raking my fingernails across the smooth skin. He trembled and said my name, before pulling the collar of my shirt open and kissing my shoulder.

"William," I said, breathless. "We are proving every criticism of female physicians correct."

"Which ones?" The scrape of his stubble contrasting with the softness of his lips—good heavens, his tongue—made my stomach burn with what must have been desire. No one had ever made me feel the way he did.

"Emotions." I couldn't think. "That women cannot separate our emotions…our patients…Inappropriate."

"Have you fallen in love with many of your patients?" He spoke, but his lips never left my neck.

"My patients are mostly women and children." I grasped the hand still cupping my face and turned my lips to it, kissing it frantically.

"Good."

I grasped his head in my hands and pulled his lips away from my neck. "Stop. I cannot think when you do that."

"You think too much." He dipped his head to my neck again, and I didn't stop him.

"One of us has to keep our head about us."

"Why?"

"You are leaving, in six hours, to be gone for two weeks. I may be gone when you return. Foster will put me on the first patrol bound for Sill when the new doctor comes."

Kindle stopped and slowly lifted his head. His eyes were clear and challenging. "You and I both know you will be here."

Leaving was precisely what I'd wanted since the moment

I stepped foot in Fort Richardson. Now, the idea of leaving and never seeing Kindle again was almost as terrifying as the bounty hunters on my trail. The longer I stayed, the more likely I would be discovered.

I tried to pull away. "Aren't you arrogant."

Kindle held me fast. "Stop it."

"Stop what?"

"Pretending I am nothing to you."

I lowered my head and pinched the bridge of my nose against a headache starting behind my eyes.

"Too much corn mash?" Kindle teased.

I looked up at him. "I suppose," I said, though I knew it to be the same persistent headache I'd battled since the massacre.

Kindle pulled me to him. "Take care of yourself, Laura." His strong arms encircled me, and his lips found my neck again. I leaned into him and pushed the fears of my uncertain future out of my mind.

I placed my mouth next to his ear and whispered, "William, it isn't that you mean nothing to me, it's that you mean too much."

Kindle stilled as my lips kissed his scar from temple to jaw, moved to his chin, and finally his mouth. It was as if an entire new world had opened to me, one where colors were brighter, emotions were heightened, pain and suffering and unhappiness were unknown. During those moments alone with Kindle I understood how lust and desire, love and longing, could start wars and ruin lives.

Our kiss changed from passionate to tender and back, until finally playful. "Heavens," Kindle teased, eyes dancing.

"You're mocking me."

"Hardly." His expression turned serious. "You *will* be here when I return."

I stared into the eyes of a man used to getting what he wanted, a man who no doubt believed my objections to being an Army wife had been swept away on a wave of desire. Kindle didn't know this interlude was an ending, not a beginning. Selfishly, I wanted to hold this memory within me, to take it out in some distant future when I needed to remember that for a brief moment I had known and understood passion, and love.

If I allowed myself I could see a future full of possibility, of happiness. But, I could also see the disappointment on his face when I told him about Catherine Bennett, about the lies and accusations that drove me from New York City, about the need to hide, to be someone else. To run for the rest of my life. Sneaking away while he was on patrol would be cowardly, yes, but I could not face his expression of horror when he learned all, nor the rejection sure to follow.

"Laura?"

I held his gaze and lied without blinking. "Yes."

CHAPTER
22

"What do you mean there is no water?"

I stared at the tools necessary to illustrate to these men the concept of sterilization and cleanliness to reduce the chance of infection in the field—clean cloths, carbolic acid, water, lye soap, whisky in a pinch—and thought of the time wasted the day before organizing and readying my presentation. Foster had known the challenges these men would bring up yet had not informed me. Clearly, my impression he was humoring me to keep me busy and out of his way had been correct. I felt foolish and more than a little angry.

The five men tried to hide their amusement. Joseph Murphy spoke first. "Well, he don't mean there ain't no water, necessarily, though there are plenty of times when there ain't. What Sullivan is trying to say, Doc, is if we're pinned down and the choice is between drinking water and washing our hands with it, I suspect our mouths will win that battle every time."

"You crossed so many rivers and cricks between here and Austin it's hard to believe water would be in short supply," Sullivan said. "But, see, out there"—he motioned to the west—"that there is the Llano Estacado. Ain't no water up there, and that's where them Indians are. When they ain't hiding out in Palo Duro Canyon."

"Any water we might chance upon is white as snow but smells like the bottom of a shitter. Excuse my language," Murphy said.

I waved the profanity away.

"You can imagine what it tastes like."

"I think I'd rather not."

"We'd rather not drink it," Sullivan said. "But sometimes you have to."

"Whatever you do, do not use it to clean a wound," I said.

"Truth be told, ma'am, most of the time men get sick from the cooking more than from fighting Indians."

"I can count on one hand the times we've fought Indians on patrol. We spend most of our time chasing their trail and never seeing hide nor hair of them," Murphy said.

I lifted the bottle of whisky. "I suppose suggesting you use whisky to clean—" The men's laughter cut off my comment. "Yes, that's what I thought." I replaced the bottle.

"Don't look so sad, Doc. This hasn't been a total waste of time. You got me outta stable duty, and for that I thank you," Sullivan said, to the general laughter of the others. The men walked toward the door.

"Where are you going? I'm not finished," I said. "I have you for thirty more minutes and I'm going to teach you what you need to know. Whether you use it or not will be up to you, your commanding officer, and the circumstances, but at least you will know what needs to be done."

Almost every point I made was met with skepticism and frontier logic, the latter of which I struggled to contradict. But, their resistance to change was no different from what I encountered from men almost daily back East. The best I could do was to give them the correct information, teach them how to use it, and hope one day they would remember what they'd learned and put it to use.

The bugle sounded for sick call and the men wandered off to their duties. I cleaned up my tools and was wondering what I would find to do for the rest of the day with no patients or projects when four men, stooped over and grasping their stomachs, filed into the south ward. One soldier heaved and shuffled as quickly as he could to the latrine at the end of the ward. We heard him vomit and soon after heard the *splat* of diarrhea. The other men stood at the end of the bed and appeared to be concentrating on holding their bowels together. I examined each man thoroughly, though even with the most cursory examination I would have come to the same conclusion. Waterman and I settled the men in the beds closest to the latrines and made them as comfortable as possible.

"Is the creek the primary source of water for the fort?" I asked Waterman.

"It's the only source."

"We are disposing of the hospital waste downstream, like I requested?"

"Yes, ma'am."

"What about the rest of the fort?"

Waterman shrugged. "Whatever's most convenient."

I chastised myself for not mentioning my concerns about the creek pollution to Foster.

"Get Martin to boil water, and lots of it. I'll round up a couple of laundresses to watch over these men while we inspect the creek."

My inspection of the creek was delayed with the steady arrival of more sick soldiers. The south ward was soon overflowing and white soldiers were forced—most unwillingly—to the Negro ward.

"We have forty men, twenty beds, and eight latrines," I said to Waterman.

"And counting. We need more room. And latrines."

"Go to the quartermaster, get as many tents as you can. I'll speak to Foster."

⌒⊗⌒

When I arrived at Foster's quarters, he and Harriet were sitting in his parlor, drinking tea and planning a dinner party. It was such an incongruous scene from what I'd left it was like walking into a dream.

"Dysentery?" Foster said in horror.

"Yes."

"How many men are ill?" Harriet asked.

"As of ten minutes ago, forty."

"Forty! Are you sure?" Foster said.

I was becoming inured to Foster's slights and doubts. "I saw enough dysentery in the war to know it when I see it. According to the logs, it's been a regular complaint. This spike is most likely due to the increased number of soldiers on fort and the lack of oversight regarding the dumping of waste."

Foster's mustache twitched at the vague reprimand.

I continued. "The hospital cannot hold that number of men under normal circumstances, let alone with this complaint. We need a temporary ward and a latrine dug well away from the fort and water supply. I hope I have not overstepped my bounds, but I sent Waterman to the quartermaster to procure as many tents as possible."

"You'll need men, I suppose."

"Yes. A detail to set up the tents and help stock them and one to dig the latrines."

Foster stood. "You'll have whatever you need. Excuse me,

Miss Mackenzie." Foster called for his orderly and retired to his office.

Harriet gathered her paper and pencil and stood as well. "What can I do to help?"

"Make sure the soldier who cooks for the officers, women, and children is boiling water before using it. The last thing we need is for the women and children to get sick as well. We will be stretched thin enough with the men."

Harriet nodded. "What else?"

"Come find me. I am sure there will be something for you to do."

Within two hours, the detail of soldiers Foster had assigned me erected the open-air tent and dug a latrine forty feet long and three feet deep with a crude bench for the men to sit on while they attempted to relieve their bowels. With a kerchief covering his mouth and nose, the youngest soldier and newest recruit threw lime on the excrement to minimize the miasma.

Harriet arrived shortly afterward and worked alongside me through the night, with occasional help from the nurses, orderlies, and a few officers' wives, trying to make the sick men comfortable and encouraging them to drink the water Corporal Martin was constantly boiling. Dysentery is a debilitating, degrading ailment, with no cure, that has to run its course. All I could do was manage their pain as best as possible and hope it didn't turn chronic, as it had for Jethro, and kill anyone.

I was glad Kindle was on patrol. With his body fighting to heal his two wounds, he would have been more susceptible to illnesses such as dysentery. It was difficult enough watching men I didn't know suffer, but keeping distance and objectivity was part and parcel of the medical profession, and a skill I never had difficulty cultivating. Watching Kindle suffer from the degrading symptoms of dysentery, and being helpless to heal him, might have been more than I could handle.

Since parting from Kindle in the small hours of the morning, my emotions had been in turmoil, battling with my logic and reason, and for the first time in years, they were winning as often as not. Nothing had changed; I would never be an Army wife or mistress, and Kindle would ask me to give up medicine. I knew Kindle was stubborn, but I wasn't sure he knew the depth of my intractability as well. I would never give up medicine. Even for love. Even for Captain William Kindle. Until I thought of the way he touched me, the sound of his low voice in my ear, the scratch of his stubble on my chin as he kissed me, his shudders as my fingers traced the muscles on his back.

As I had dozens of times, I shook the memories free and went back to work, thankful for the distraction, and guilty for it.

At two in the morning, the temperature dropped and the rains came.

I stood at the edge of the tent and looked out at the latrine. Soaked through and miserable, eleven men sat hunched over, most trying and failing to defecate. Harriet walked up beside me. We stood in silence for a few minutes.

"We're going to need more blankets," she said.

I nodded. "We've cleaned Franklin out. I'll go to town in the morning." Another man walked out of the tent and into the rain to the latrine. "Need help, Private Cahill?" I asked.

"No, ma'am. Thank you."

I sighed.

"What is it?" Harriet said.

"I hate being so useless."

"Useless? Look at everything you've done in less than a day."

"Yes, but I cannot help these men. Cure them. They suffer and all I do is watch their misery and offer a blanket."

Lanterns hung from the tent poles but barely broke through the darkness. A rush of rain pounded on the tent, making it almost impossible to talk. Alice Strong walked past me and Harriet, offering each soldier watered-down whisky to drink. Even in the semidarkness, I could tell she was exhausted.

"You and Alice should go rest."

"What about you?"

"I drank a cup of Waterman's coffee. I'll be awake until eighteen seventy-two."

"I'll stay with you."

"No. I'll need you here tomorrow when I go to town."

I knew Harriet studied me but I didn't turn to face her. "You said you'd seen this enough in the war to know it was dysentery. Were you a nurse?"

My shoulders sagged. Did I say that? I couldn't remember. Couldn't this woman let me be, even for a day? Is this what my life was going to be like, constantly trying to decide on the best lie to tell? I was exhausted, mind and body, and did not want to argue or spar with Harriet Mackenzie. As I watched the soldiers suffer in the rain, I'd had enough.

I faced Harriet. "When this is over, I will tell you everything. Until then, will you please leave me be and let me do my job?"

After a moment, she inclined her head and went to Alice. The young woman listened, looked at me, and followed Harriet out of the tent, leaving me alone with forty suffering soldiers who I could not help.

⌗⌗⌗

I was draping a blanket over Private Cahill's shivering shoulders when Dr. Ezra Kline walked into the quarantine tent. I eased Cahill down onto his cot, but kept my eyes on Dr. Kline, who was scanning the tent in search of someone. When his eyes landed on me, his face paled and his eyes widened.

"Rest, Private." I patted Cahill's chest.

"I'll try, Doc."

I walked across the tent to Dr. Kline.

"Dr. Elliston?"

"Yes." I offered my hand. His hand was warm and plump, with short, squared-off fingers, the hands of a researcher, not a surgeon. "Pleasure to meet you, Dr. Kline. I've heard so many good things about you."

"I've heard many things about you as well." There was disapproval in his eyes. I'd expected nothing less.

"Let me brief you."

I ushered him around the tent, telling him all that had been done over the last two days to stop the outbreak before it became unmanageable and introducing him to Harriet and the officers' wives. He listened attentively, his head bent in concentration and hands behind his back like the professor he was, with only the occasional question.

"I finally had the chance to inspect the creek this morning. A little more than a mile upstream we found the carcasses of about fifty dead dogs. Private Murphy told me they purged the fort of stray dogs two weeks ago. Instead of burying or burning the dogs, the soldiers dumped them in the creek. The cattle from the wagon train I was with is also using the creek in the same area. That, in combination with the dumping of fort waste near the hospital, is what I believe has caused this outbreak."

Dr. Kline nodded. "And, what is your recommendation?"

"I sent Privates Murphy and Sullivan to town to procure four barrels and told them to drive up the creek until they find uncontaminated water. They should be back sometime this afternoon with fresh water. I've also ordered all the cooks to boil their water before they use it. I intended to speak with Lieutenant Colonel Foster on the possibility of digging a well. I am not sure the landscape will support it, but it might not hurt to try."

"Excellent work, Dr. Elliston. You did everything I would have, and a few things I wouldn't have thought of. When you are finished here, come to my office so we can speak about the rest of your duties."

I inclined my head in acknowledgment.

"Miss Mackenzie," Dr. Kline said, and left.

I turned and saw Harriet standing nearby, listening.

"Dr. Kline," Harriet said.

I busied myself at the quarantine for as long as my nerves could stand, then walked across the parade ground to the hospital.

He sat at the desk reading the surgeon's log, his half-moon spectacles perched on the end of his nose. The sunlight from the window streamed through the bushy halo of hair around the back of his head, making him look like a portly angel auditing Saint Peter's heavenly list. I couldn't help but smile. He would have hated that description.

"Uncle Ezra."

The old man turned to me with a frown on his brow and lips, but the eyes peering over the top of his glasses were full of mischief.

"Little Katie Bennett," he said. He removed his glasses and sat back. "What in the hell is going on?"

Ezra Kline had met my father, Matthew Bennett, in medical school. They initially did not care for one another, both being competitive and used to being the smartest person in the room. They soon realized their medical interests lay in different fields—Matthew's in surgery, Ezra's in research and teaching—and instead of spending their energy competing, decided to each help the other in their areas of weakness.

Though their paths took them to separate parts of the state

after graduation—Matthew to opening a struggling practice in New York City, Ezra staying on at Syracuse Medical College as a junior professor and researcher—they were in constant contact through letters and regular holiday visits. Each stood up for the other at their weddings, and Ezra offered much-needed solace to his old friend at the death of my mother. Before being sent to England at twelve to live with my father's sister and her family, I spent weeks at a time in Syracuse visiting Ezra, his wife, Dorothy, and their son James. Ezra, though always reserved about my desire to become a doctor, was instrumental in my acceptance to Syracuse Medical College.

The emotions of the past weeks rushed out of me in a torrent of tears. Ezra moved a chair into the corner of the office and gently led me to it. I sat and gave in to my flooding emotions in a way that would have embarrassed the most volatile of Gothic heroines.

"There, there." Ezra handed me a clean, soft bandanna. "Dry your tears." He patted me on the shoulder and returned to his chair to wait.

He did not have to wait long. Now that I had someone to confide in, to explain everything to, the need to get my story out, to justify the decisions I made, was overpowering.

"I don't know where to start."

"At the beginning would be good."

I told him everything, from James's assistance in leaving New York, to Salt Creek, to Sherman giving me command of the hospital.

"You left out the most interesting part," Ezra said.

"What?"

"Operating on Captain Kindle."

"Oh."

"News of your deed has reached Fort Sill. Most like it has made the Eastern papers as well."

I rubbed my forehead. "Which means it's only a matter of time before someone wonders who this female doctor is."

Ezra nodded.

"Well, now you are here I can move on."

"Where will you go?"

I shrugged. "Far from Indians, I can assure you." I paused. "Have you heard from James?"

"He sent me a letter not long after you left New York."

"And? Did he say anything about the dead woman?"

"Yes. He said it was you." When I didn't respond, Ezra continued. "Imagine my shock when I saw you."

"Why would he lie to you?"

Ezra's normally benign demeanor hardened for a moment. A sad smile softened his expression and he said, "James and I haven't had the best relationship since Dorothy died. I am not surprised he kept me in the dark."

"So you don't know who the woman was?"

"No. But, it ended the story. There were a couple of follow-up stories in the Saint Louis paper about you; then it died."

"What were the stories?"

"It's not important, Catherine."

"What were the stories, Ezra?"

He didn't look at me as he talked. "They painted a picture of you as a harlot. Having affairs with multiple married men. Patients' husbands. Other doctors."

I paced the office, twisting my hands and trying not to cry. Why would Beatrice Langton assassinate my character? To what end? "That woman is despicable. You don't believe a word." When he didn't respond, I added, "Do you?"

"No, though running away made it easy for people to come forward and slander you."

I stopped in front of Ezra. My stomach felt weighted with stones. "Who else?"

"Other doctors speaking on your arrogance. Prostitutes defending you. A resurrection man."

I closed my eyes and inhaled. "Jonasz Golik."

"Yes. I heard you were a longtime customer for him and paid well."

I exhaled and opened my eyes. "Only because he threatened me."

Ezra shrugged. "It was the nail in your coffin. The prostitutes didn't help."

I resumed pacing and thought of Molly Ebling. It had been almost six weeks since I had seen her in Galveston. Had it only been weeks? It seemed another lifetime. She was most likely back in New York City with the knowledge I was alive. How long until the brave doctor in Texas would be connected to Catherine Bennett? How long until the man who sent me the bloody poster decided to expose me, or worse yet, abduct me and take me back East?

I stared out the office window at the fort. A wagon full of soldiers sitting atop a stack of pickets rolled past the hospital, bound for the newest enlisted men's quarters under construction on the edge of the parade ground. They looked dirty and exhausted. One man had a crude bandage wrapped around his arm. I thought of Kindle. Was he keeping his bandages clean?

I pressed my hand against my abdomen. There was no question about staying or going now; I needed to leave before Kindle returned. I couldn't bear to see his expression when he heard of this Catherine Bennett, the harlot.

"What are you going to do?" Ezra's voice was quiet.

I sighed. "Leave as soon as possible. I cannot go back to New York. There is no question I must leave Fort Richardson."

"I gleaned Foster doesn't like you from five minutes with the man, though he is impressed with what you've done with the outbreak. I could persuade him to keep you on here as a civilian surgeon as long as I promise to keep you in line."

"As much as I love you, Ezra, not even you could do the latter. It is only a matter of time before bounty hunters realize who I am. And I do not like it here. It is too open, exposed. There are Indians everywhere." As I spoke, my resolve to leave hardened, and I felt better. "I have not felt safe since. As much as I would like to stay with you, I cannot. Foster has promised to let me travel with the first patrol heading to Fort Sill. From there I will take a train west."

Alone.

I pushed away the fear that realization engendered. I was intelligent, resourceful, and with a profession that would keep me from becoming destitute. There were prostitutes and pregnant women everywhere. I would survive.

Ezra stood. "I am sorry about Maureen."

My throat closed, rendering speech impossible. I nodded and tried to smile and waited for the mild chastisement for bringing Maureen west I had expected. I was relieved when it did not come. With Kindle gone, the dysentery outbreak, and Ezra's familiar presence, I knew my emotions would vent at the slightest provocation. I'd cried enough for one day.

He patted me on the shoulder fondly. "Come, give me a tour of my new hospital."

CHAPTER

23

The next week was a whirlwind of activity. Payroll and a full supply train had accompanied Ezra from Fort Sill, replenishing medicines to the hospital stores as well as drunkards to the hospital ward. Every day more tents appeared on the outer edge of the parade ground as regiments gathered at Fort Richardson to disperse to various parts of the plains in search of the Comanche and Kiowa raiders. The dysentery tent slowly emptied as men got past the worst of the disease.

With the fort filling up with soldiers and the number of beds for men and officers dwindling under the demand, Foster requested I move to a hotel in Jacksboro to make space. It was a relief to move out of the house where I thought of Kindle constantly. I gave only a passing thought to the promise I had made the night before he left.

With the worst of the dysentery outbreak over, Foster decided a celebration was in order. He ordered two of the cattle from my wagon train and a pig from the fort's herd to be slaughtered for the soldiers' celebration, and Harriet organized the dinner party for the officers and their wives she and Foster had been planning when the outbreak started.

I was flattered, somewhat humbled, and surprised at being

included among the guests. Since Ezra's arrival, I saw little of anyone outside of the hospital and quarantine tent, restricting myself to solitary walks to and from my lodgings in town and assisting Ezra in whatever way necessary to make his settlement at Fort Richardson smooth. I supposed the distance I kept from Foster and Harriet had the beneficial effect of lessening their perception of my many faults and sins. What else, besides Ezra's intervention on my behalf, could account for the inclusion in their number of someone so likely to disrupt an otherwise jolly dinner party?

As modest as the dinner party would be considering the location, I was giddy with excitement at the idea of forgetting we were so far removed from civilization for a few hours. I also realized this could be the last time for a good while, if not ever, I would have the opportunity to relive scenes from my youth in England. I was quite determined to be on my best behavior, for my enjoyment as well as my dinner companions'.

It would also give me an opportunity to wear the gown Camille had packed for me when leaving New York. As useless as it was on the frontier, I could not bring myself to discard it and the silk gown doggedly traveled with me across Texas, crushed beneath the weight of my more serviceable dresses. I was admiring my reflection in the mirror and how the sky-blue silk brought out my eyes when a knock at my door alerted me Ezra had come to escort me to the fort. I settled my mother's sapphire and pearl necklace—the last and most valuable of her jewelry—around my neck, patted my hair, and preened. I turned serious and chastised myself. "Behave."

My step faltered at the top of the stairs. Kindle, in full dress uniform, stood next to the front desk, staring into the dining room opposite. He fairly took my breath away. My joy at seeing him, at the realization he was returned safely from his patrol, was overcome quickly by irritation. He was scowling, as if escorting me was the last thing he wanted to do. His expression checked my step for only a moment before my back stiffened and I descended the stairs.

"You've returned."

He frowned over my shoulder at someone in the dining room. When he finally deigned to look at me he said, "You moved into town even though I told you not to."

I prickled. Maybe our parting wouldn't be as difficult as I thought. "On Foster's demand. Take it up with him."

He gave me his arm and led me from the hotel to the wagon. When I was settled he leapt into the driver's position and snapped the whip at the horse. The startled horse jumped forward and took off at a brisk trot.

We rode in uncomfortable, formal silence. I had imagined many variations of our possible reunion, but nothing like this. The man next to me seemed like a stranger. Had I dreamed the interlude in the hospital?

The stars were the only light from the clear sky but hardly provided enough light to see the road. I gripped the seat as the horse barreled through the night, hitting every hole in the road on the way.

"Would you mind slowing down, please? It is much too dark to be driving in this way."

"This horse is familiar with the road."

The wagon jumped as we hit a deep hole, almost bouncing me from the seat. I grabbed at his arm. "Really, Kindle. Are you trying to throw me out of the wagon?"

"Don't be absurd," he replied, but he slowed the horse to a slow trot.

I straightened myself and moved as far away from Kindle as possible. "I don't know why you agreed to drive me if you were determined to be as unpleasant as possible. Or was that the point?"

My spirits fell when he didn't answer. I wanted nothing more than to return to the hotel. The prospect of engaging strangers in polite, pointless conversation for hours, so recently an appealing idea, became unbearable. This dinner party would be the last opportunity I had to enjoy Kindle's companionship. Soon, I would leave for Fort Sill and never see him again. If he was going to be hostile toward me the entire night, I would rather return to the hotel and spend it by myself.

He steered the wagon onto the road behind the hospital and slowed the horse to a walk. I heard the rushing water of Lost Creek to my right.

"Being rude to you was not the point," Kindle said. "I apologize."

The grip of pain around my heart lessened a little. "Is something the matter? How do you feel?"

"Fine."

Through the darkness his profile was just visible. I reached out and laid my hand on his arm. "Kindle, what's the matter?"

His jaw muscle clenched and he pulled the wagon to a stop. He shifted in the seat until he faced me. "I saw a man in the hotel who looked like someone I used to know."

"Who?"

He inhaled. "My dead brother."

"Well, that's wonderful, isn't it? Why didn't you talk to him?"

Kindle shook his head. "It isn't wonderful. If it was him, and I'm not entirely sure it was, he's after me."

"Because of his wife?"

Kindle nodded. "Among other things. You have to stay at the fort tonight."

"What? Why?"

"I—" He shook his head, as if rejecting an idea too absurd to be valid.

"If you're worried about my safety, don't be." I leaned forward and whispered dramatically. "There is a lock on my door."

A small smile played on his lips as he studied me. "I've missed you."

I removed my hand from his arm and tried to give my voice lightness my heart didn't share. The armor I'd built up around my soul during Kindle's absence was weakening, and to what purpose? In two days I would be gone. "You've missed my nagging you about your health?"

"Among other things." My mind went straight to the last night we were together, and unless I was much mistaken, so did Kindle's.

I kept my voice light. "At least you are not angry with me. You looked quite frightening in the hotel."

His eyes softened. "I could never be angry with you."

"Give me time. I infuriate everyone, eventually."

He laughed and clicked to the horses. The wagon lurched forward and we drove to the front of a large tent on the edge of the parade ground near the officers' quarters. A private who looked at my chest with appreciation assisted me down. When he saw me watching him, he blushed. I grinned archly at him and walked around the gig to take Kindle's arm, his admiration showing clearly in his expression. I thought of Maureen and how she would disapprove of all of the appreciation being shown me.

It'll give you the big head. Lord knows your ego is large enough.

The pain at her loss was still there, would not leave for years, most like. But, there was happiness at the remembrance as well.

Kindle's gaze traveled from my sapphire and pearl necklace to my face. Unlike the private, he did not blush, but his expression spoke volumes. Before entering, he leaned over and whispered in my ear. "You look ravishing."

My breath caught. I could not have checked my flush of pleasure if I tried.

⁂

It was a few moments before I realized conversation stopped on our arrival. My smile wavered and died under the scrutiny of ten pairs of eyes, all in various degrees of surprise or disapprobation. Harriet turned away from us and resumed her conversation with Lieutenant Strong and Alice. Ezra stood with an older civilian couple, his hands behind his back and his head slightly bent, trying to hide his amusement. The couple looked upon me with more curiosity than condemnation, which, along with Ezra's comforting presence, was all the recommendation the strangers needed. I moved to meet them with a tremulous smile as embarrassment warred with the elation of Kindle's compliment and the dread at my removal from him two days hence.

"Dr. Kline. I was disappointed when you did not turn up to escort me from town." The woman quietly cleared her throat and though I never took my eyes from Ezra, I could sense from the edge of my vision the couple exchanging an amused, knowing glance.

"You know what a poor carriage driver I am. I doubted you wanted to walk the half mile in your gown."

"A doctor afraid of carriages is a singular quirk," the woman said. "How ever do you make calls?"

"A benefit of being in the Army. The patients come to you,

and if they do not, someone else always drives. Dr. Elliston, I would like to introduce you to Jacksboro's Mayor Stephen Carter and his wife, Edna."

"It is a pleasure to meet you," I said.

As I would find out in my short acquaintance with them, Stephen and Edna Carter were unique in many ways, not the least of which being their stature. Edna stood over six feet tall and Stephen barely came up to her shoulder. Everything about them was outsized, from their disproportionate stature to their gregarious personalities to their infectious laughs.

"It is our pleasure, Doctor," Edna Carter said. "Dr. Kline has been singing your praises since we arrived, hasn't he, Stephen?"

"Indeed."

"Says you are one of the best surgeons he has ever seen."

Ezra's head was bent down as if in thought. I could see the lingering ghost of a smile on his lips. "Has he?"

"Yes. He says he could not have done as good a job managing the dysentery outbreak or operating on Captain Kindle as you did, and under the circumstances! In the middle of a thunderstorm!"

"It was before."

"I'm not sure I truck with the notion of a woman doctor, but Dr. Kline assures us you have the appropriate professional frame of mind to treat any patient, man or woman."

"What a long conversation you must have had already. I didn't realize I was so late."

Harriet Mackenzie walked up to our little group and interjected. "I can vouch for her management of the quarantine. No man could have done it better."

"Thank you, Harriet," I said, in genuine astonishment. I hadn't forgotten my promise to tell her everything and wondered when she would force the issue. I hoped it wouldn't be tonight.

"Hello there, Miss Mackenzie," Edna said. "Lovely party you've thrown together."

Harriet bowed her head in modest acceptance of the compliment. "Yes, Harriet," I said. "It is lovely."

It was. The large rectangular tent was supported by two hefty wooden columns, between which a long table was formally set for sixteen with china, silver, and crystal. Standard Army-issue oil lamps, disguised with strategically placed boughs of the native Texas sage that grew in profusion around the fort, alternated down the length of the table with small bottles of fresh wildflowers. My gaze lingered on the wildflowers as memories of the massacre flashed through my mind. Amos's screams as his flesh burned ricocheted in my head. I closed my eyes against Maureen's gaping jaw.

"Laura?"

I opened my eyes. Harriet's hand was on my arm, her expression full of concern.

A private in formal dress uniform walked by holding a tray of wine. I stopped him and took a glass. I lifted my uninjured shoulder slightly and said, "I will never look at wildflowers the same again."

Harriet's brows furrowed.

"It's a shame your brother isn't here, Miss Mackenzie," Edna said.

Harriet turned her attention to the Carters. "Oh, the colonel hates dinners such as these. Why do you think we are having it now?" When the Carters' booming laughter died down, she continued. "It turns out this is a celebration for you, Laura."

"Me?"

"Yes. Lieutenant Colonel Foster received a dispatch an hour ago from Fort Sill. The men who led the Salt Creek attack have been arrested."

"You don't mean it!" Edna Carter said.

"I do, indeed. They made the mistake of bragging about it and some of the Indians loyal to the government informed General Sherman."

"The Peace Policy says the Army, or any law enforcement, can't pursue Indians into the Territories," Ezra explained.

"Lawrie Tatum, he's the Quaker agent at Fort Sill, invited the chiefs to his house. Sherman met them on the porch and confronted them," Harriet said.

"I would have liked to see that," Stephen said.

"They denied it. But too many heard their bragging. When they tried to resist, the doors and windows of the house opened and there stood a regiment of soldiers with guns."

"Heavens," I said. "Will your brother return to the fort soon?"

"No. Poor Ranald is still out in the Territory, searching for them."

"What happens now?" Edna said.

"I do not know. Arresting three chiefs in the Territory is unprecedented," Harriet said.

"Sounds like Sherman is writing new rules," Stephen said.

"So we are celebrating your survival and the coming justice of the savages responsible," Harriet said.

I leaned forward and stage-whispered, "Don't let Lieutenant Colonel Foster hear you. I am the last person he would want to celebrate."

Harriet smiled and shook her head, though she didn't disagree. "What a lovely dress, Laura. How extraordinary it survived."

"Oh, it didn't," I said. "I bought it back from the sutler

yesterday." Edna's, Stephen's, and Harriet's astounded and uncomfortable expressions were worth the warning headshake I received from Ezra. "I am joking, of course. The Indians were less interested in our things than in killing and torturing us. Though, they may have very well looted our possessions more thoroughly if Captain Kindle and his men had not arrived."

"Here he is to save you again," Harriet said. Kindle stopped between us with a small smile on his face.

"I didn't know I needed saving."

"From the Carters," Harriet said with good nature. "They will talk you into staying on in Jacksboro, I am sure of it. They can be persuasive."

"I would like to persuade her as well," Ezra said. "I need a civilian surgeon and Dr. Elliston would require no training, already being familiar with hospital and fort."

"You may try all you like. I don't believe I will ever be truly safe in this wide-open country."

"You miss the closeness of the city?" Edna asked.

"No. I miss the trees," I said, to general laughter.

"What say you, Captain Kindle?" Harriet said.

"I miss trees as well."

"Come now, be serious." Harriet laughed. It was the first time I'd heard her laugh and I was surprised by how infectious and musical it was. "Help us convince Dr. Elliston to stay."

I turned to Kindle and said, "Yes, Captain, persuade me to stay. I daresay you are the only one who can."

He bowed his head to me and with an amused smile said, "As to her skills as a doctor, I am now and will always be her greatest champion. Regarding her feelings about the area, if she doesn't feel safe on a fort full of soldiers I am not sure there is anything I can do or say to change her mind. Though I would be happy to plant trees if it would help."

"It would be in vain," Harriet said. "If the Army did not cut them down for construction, the good businessmen of Jacksboro would."

"Quite right," Stephen Carter said.

"I suppose it's settled," I said. "I do appreciate the effort, Mayor and Mrs. Carter."

Edna Carter laughed. "We don't give up so easy, do we, Stephen?"

"No."

Thankfully, we were called to table.

Harriet pulled me slightly aside. "It is interesting Dr. Kline knows your professional proclivities so well on such a short acquaintance."

"I suppose one good doctor knows another."

She nodded and smiled to someone on the other side of the room before looking back at me. "I have not forgotten your promise."

"No, I don't imagine you have."

"Dr. Elliston?" Ezra offered his arm and I took it.

"Excuse me, Harriet."

I took Ezra's arm and said beneath the low rumble of movement, "Thank you."

"What was that about?"

"She's suspicious and dislikes me on principle."

"What makes you think she dislikes you?"

I laughed. "Don't let her compliment about my management skills fool you. She despises me. Why are you encouraging the Carters? You know I cannot stay."

"They're persistent. But, don't worry. I'll distract them."

"I thought you were to collect me tonight."

"So I was, but Kindle insisted. Now I understand why."

I looked at him sharply. Had my expression on entering the tent betrayed me? "What do you mean?"

"You're the most beautiful woman here. My son was a fool to let you go."

I blushed. "You're biased."

"Yes, but it doesn't mean I am lying."

I looked around. Kindle held out Harriet's chair and took the seat next to her at the head of the table. I sat in the chair Ezra held out for me. "Considering my rivals, the compliment has little weight."

"Pettishness does not become you, Katie," he whispered in my ear. "Why do I suspect you haven't told me everything?" He glanced pointedly in Kindle's direction. "We'll talk later."

I was relieved as well as irritated Harriet had placed me as far from Kindle as possible. My emotions about him fluctuated so wildly, from elation to embarrassment, despair to hope, I could not trust myself to act rationally in his presence for an extended amount of time. The mere fact I could not master my emotions angered me and left me feeling a vulnerability the expanse of nature around me only amplified. While I knew I should, logically, thank Harriet for in essence making this dinner easier for me to enjoy, I was irritated the choice had been taken from me without my consent, that I couldn't prove to myself I possessed the strength of character needed to confront my conflicting feelings for Kindle.

I determined to not betray my crossness by word, look, or action. Indeed, I decided to use my powers of entertainment and attraction, honed in the countless London drawing rooms of my youth, on the two young officers I was sitting between, Beau Kindle and Wallace Strong.

Strong was handsome, gregarious, and shallow and if I had not known the baseness of his character through my association with Ruth, I would have enjoyed conversing with him much more than Beau Kindle. But his easy charm couldn't hide a character that extended to nobility only in whatever way would promote his esteem in the eyes of his equals. His wife, Alice, sat opposite and would glimpse at her husband with an adoring, fearful expression as often as would be considered polite while in conversation with Stephen Carter. Occasionally, Strong would wink at his wife, which caused Alice to blush and lose her train of thought. That they were ill-suited was patently obvious. I had too much experience in the marriage trade to question how the match had come about. No doubt her familial connections had furthered Strong's career and, quite possibly, made him a decent fortune. In return she possessed a handsome, unfaithful husband.

The switch in conversation partners could not come quickly enough. My hope that talking to Kindle's nephew would be like talking to Kindle himself was soon crushed. Beau was a pleasant young man and could talk on a wide range of subjects, but he was impetuous, opinionated, and a trifle thoughtless. In short, he was young, unpolished, and infused with a sense of bravado only found in conjunction with inexperience. He, as well as Strong, looked at the Army in general and the frontier in particular as a great adventure, nay a lark, a place where they could make their names alongside those heroes of the war: Sherman, Grant, Custer, and Sheridan. They could not get on the trail soon enough. They were confident that since now they were in the thick of it, with their energy and fresh ideas, they would make short work of the savages. As fervently as I wished for the Indians to be eradicated and cared little for how the goal was achieved, I doubted Beau Kindle held the secret to solving the Indian problem in his young brain. I determined to steer him to a subject I was more interested in.

"When we first met you mentioned you had not seen your uncle in many years."

"Eight years, ma'am."

"You would have been a child. Was he much changed since you last saw him?"

"It would be difficult for him to not," Beau replied. "Time has told on his countenance. There's sadness about him I don't remember. Visits from Uncle Billy were always anticipated."

I thought of the man in the hotel lobby, possibly William's brother, and wondered how Beau would react if it were. "Your father was Captain Kindle's older brother?"

"Yes."

His reluctance to talk of his father was evident. Perhaps, like Kindle, he didn't have fond memories of his father, so I turned the conversation. "Did you always want to be in the Army?"

"Yes, because of Uncle. The captain was my guardian after my mother died. I spent my youth in boarding school in New England. On the captain's recommendation I was accepted to West Point."

"Your mother died with the captain's wife?"

"Yes, with his wife and child in a carriage accident in sixty-three. Not long after Antietam."

"His wife and child?" I asked. In our conversations, Kindle had not mentioned a child.

"You didn't know?" Beau asked in some surprise.

I smiled and pushed my misgivings aside. "Most of our conversations during his recuperation were necessarily one-sided. The laudanum," I explained.

I glanced down the table at our subject and found him staring at us with a questioning gaze. I knew he would not be pleased to be the focus of our conversation. I turned back to Beau and found him giving Alice Strong an encouraging smile.

When Alice caught my eye, she blushed, which made her much more attractive, and turned her attention back to Stephen Carter, who was slurping up the last of his oxtail soup.

I asked Beau, "Do you have siblings?"

Beau's face lit into a smile. "Yes, a younger sister. She lives with my late aunt's family in Boston. She's a governess."

"What does she think of your Army adventure?"

"She would much prefer me to follow my aunt's brother into banking. A safer occupation, she says."

"As well as dull, I daresay."

"Precisely what I said."

"I have known my share of bankers and you don't strike me as the type."

"What a grand compliment. Thank you."

Our conversation paused as our empty soup bowls were removed. "My sister is worried I will be killed by the savages," Beau said, laughing at the absurdity of it. He still possessed the naive belief he would live forever.

"You should not belittle her concerns," I quietly replied.

Beau was chagrined. "Of course not. I apologize for my thoughtlessness," he said. "Miss Warren reminded me of my sister."

"Anna?" I replied.

Beau smiled. "Yes. Did you know her well?"

"I was coming to know her well. She was an intelligent girl."

"The captain has tried to temper my expectations of finding her, but I will not give up hope."

"Nor will I," I said.

The serving soldiers placed our entrée of beefsteak, potatoes, and greens in front of us. The service might have been formal but the food still suffered under the shortcomings of the area. The plainness of the fare was limited to its outward appearance.

The steak was perfectly cooked, the potatoes soft and creamy inside their thin, red skins, and the greens were seasoned with bacon and salt, which masked their naturally bitter taste.

After a moment enjoying our meal, Beau continued. "I hear you will be leaving us on the next train to Fort Sill."

"Yes. Day after tomorrow."

"We are to accompany the train as far as the Red River before turning west on patrol."

"We?"

"The Tenth."

The morsel of potato I was swallowing lodged in my throat. I wondered why Kindle hadn't bothered to tell me of these plans on our drive from town.

"Where will you go from Fort Sill?" Beau asked, oblivious to my discomfort.

"I'm not sure," I replied. "Colorado, or California."

"Unless we can persuade her to stay in Jacksboro," Edna Carter said across the table. "Excuse me for eavesdropping," she added without the least bit of chagrin.

"What's this?" Lieutenant Colonel Foster said from the end of the table.

"Stephen and I are trying, without much success, to persuade Dr. Elliston to stay in Jacksboro, open a practice."

I will give Foster credit; he managed to hide his appalled expression quickly, but not fast enough for the existence of it to amuse me. I smiled at Edna Carter. "You may convince me yet."

"I thought you were set on Colorado?" Harriet said.

I turned to her. "Yes, the mountains do appeal to me. Though, Jacksboro has its own appeal." I let my eyes flicker to Kindle before settling back on Harriet and noticed, with great amusement, her irritation, thus confirming what I long suspected; her animosity toward me was fueled, in part, by her affection for Kindle.

"Indeed, it does," Stephen Carter said. "With the increased number of soldiers here, as well as the presence of Colonel Mackenzie, Fort Richardson will be an important part of the war on the Indians."

"I wouldn't rely on Richardson for your town's success," Strong said. "We'll make short work of the Indians." Beau raised his glass and interjected a "Hear, hear," then continued. "Once we have them on the reservation, the Army will need fewer forts on the frontier."

"If it comes to pass, Richardson has an excellent chance of being one that survives. The hospital alone would be argument enough to keep this fort over, say, Fort Griffin. Don't you agree, Dr. Kline?" Stephen Carter said.

"It would stand to reason."

"On the cattle drive north, I received quite a Texas history lesson from the head cowboy, Amos Pike," I said. "We passed more than a few Army posts abandoned as the line of settlement moved west. Doesn't it stand to reason this fate may well befall not only Richardson but Griffin and all forts along the line, as well?"

"We're putting the cart before the horse," Edna said. "First, the Army has to beat the redskins. The treaty was supposed to be the end of the attacks, but they're worse than ever."

"What treaty?" I asked.

"The Medicine Lodge Treaty," Kindle replied. "Signed in sixty-seven."

"The Indians are violating it," Foster said. "Going off the reservation to hunt buffalo and raid white settlements."

"Are we sure it's only Indians raiding?" Edna said.

"Don't tell me you believe those stories of that Black fellow," Foster said.

"The stories are becoming harder and harder to disbelieve," Stephen said.

"There may be a problem with ex-Confederate bandits on the border, but what is happening here is the Kiowa and Comanche. Mark my words. The idea it's white men is preposterous," Foster said.

"Ten years ago I would have agreed with you, Lieutenant Colonel," I said. "I've since seen too many atrocities civilized men do to each other, even their own brothers, to so easily dismiss the idea."

"You speak of the war?"

"I do."

Foster's face turned red. "You cannot compare war with criminality borne of greed."

"Some would argue war is borne of greed. Though I would not be one of those people, of course." I smiled sweetly.

"Have any of you heard the newest idea to exterminate the Indians?" Harriet interjected.

"No," Edna said.

"Kill the buffalo," Kindle said.

"Yes," Harriet said. "Sheridan believes if the buffalo are exterminated the Indians will be forced to live on the reservation and will have no incentive to leave."

"How will they get food?" Alice Strong said.

"The government provides food for them now," her husband said. "Which they take but still leave to hunt."

Ezra spoke for the first time. "I spoke to the Indian agent at Sill. He is an old friend of mine, and he told of the gross shortages of food they receive to disburse to the Indians. They are starving and angry the government is not holding to our side of the bargain. That is why they leave. That is why they raid and kill."

"You sound as if you are justifying their actions," Foster said.

"Not at all," Ezra replied. "We should not perpetuate the idea there is no *reason* behind their actions."

"Don't tell me you buy the Eastern idea of the 'noble savage,'" Foster sneered.

"There is nothing noble in what they do. But, I also know the white man has broken every treaty we have ever signed. With every instance of Indian savagery, the Army retaliates with their own."

"What do you mean?" I asked.

"The Army does not always limit its attacks to warriors," Ezra said. "Villages full of women and children have been destroyed."

"Is that true, Lieutenant Colonel?" I asked.

"Dr. Kline makes it sound like we're murdering them. This is war and they are the enemy. I would think you, of all people, would understand, Miss Elliston."

"Women and children didn't attack my wagon train."

"The children you are so protective of will grow up to be warriors," Foster said.

"As much as I want those responsible to pay for what they did, I would not want women and children murdered in retaliation."

"It is up to the officers to control their men," Kindle said. "Too often, they're not up to the task. Too often, they are the ones who need to be controlled."

"You sound as if you speak from experience, Uncle," Beau Kindle said.

Kindle glared at his nephew. Had Beau forgotten Kindle's threat at the massacre site? I wondered if Kindle would follow through on his threat to send Beau to Saint Louis. "You cannot serve in the Army for as long as I and not witness bad decisions as well as good. Attacking the food supply is a good one. By all means, eradicate the buffalo. Kill the Indians' horses. Those are much more humane solutions than human extermination. With the new quicker and cheaper hide-tanning process, there is plenty of money for Eastern businessmen to make on the buffalo hides."

"We have returned to my original point, greed," I said.

"I believe the original point was convincing you to settle in Jacksboro, but the conversation has taken such a crooked course I'm not entirely sure," Edna Carter said, to general laughter.

"I am sure Dr. Welch is capable of handling the ills and births of Jacksboro," Foster said.

"You haven't heard?" Edna said.

"Heard what?"

"Welch is dead." A chorus of exclamations rang out around the table. "Yes, found this morning in the alley behind a saloon."

"Died of drunkenness, no doubt," Harriet said.

"He *was* stinking drunk," Stephen said. "But, drink is not what killed him. He was beat to death with a cane. Killer left the cane buried in his skull."

Except for Edna, Alice, and myself, the women around the table gasped.

"Sir!" Foster said. "Watch your language. There are women present."

Strong, a gleam in his eyes, looked down the table to Kindle. "Captain, I hope your cane isn't missing."

Kindle stared in the middle distance, his face white. Harriet put her hand on Kindle's arm. "Captain, you're pale. Do you feel ill?"

"I am fine, thank you."

"Yes, but where is your cane?" Strong teased.

Kindle reached down to the floor and lifted the cane I had given him.

Edna was not to be distracted from her goal by an indignant lieutenant colonel, a pale captain, or a teasing lieutenant. "So you see, Dr. Elliston, your services are desperately needed."

"I appreciate your efforts. Indeed, your attentions will make me quite vain." I glanced at Kindle, who was again staring off in a distracted manner. "However, it has been arranged for me to accompany a wagon train to Fort Sill in two days. Thank you, though. It is nice to be wanted."

"You'll be missed," Harriet said, inclining her head. I almost believed her.

"How gracious of you to say so."

The remainder of dinner was uneventful, as if everyone hoped polite discourse could alleviate the tension from the disagreement and the news of Welch's death. A dessert of wild blackberry cobbler with a flaky crust, the one course not limited by the inhospitable nature of the plains, mollified Foster. I feigned attentiveness and responded sufficiently well when asked a direct question that my reticence was not unduly noticed. Only Alice Strong and Kindle exceeded my level of taciturnity. As the forced chatter swirled around me, I remembered the conversation I had overheard between Welch and Franklin and wondered who the unnamed "he" they referred to was. Was Welch's death somehow connected to that conversation, and as a result, to the graft going on at the fort? Or was it connected somehow to Henry Pope and the bloody Wanted poster I'd received days earlier? Or both? I wiped the corners of my mouth and idly surveyed the table, studiously avoiding

Harriet and Kindle's vicinity, while wondering what kind of man was capable of cold-blooded murder.

⚜

When we rose to depart, Kindle and Harriet made their way toward me. My breath caught at the hunger in Kindle's eyes. I knew precisely what he wanted and also knew if left alone with him, he would have it with very little effort on his part.

Harriet threaded her arm through mine and said, "Remember, you promised to share a sherry with me after the dinner."

I knew I'd done no such thing, but readily acquiesced. I couldn't imagine a safer refuge from Kindle's desire than Harriet's parlor. I tore my eyes away from Kindle and focused on Harriet. She glanced between us with a knowing expression. I imagined the first thing out of her mouth when we were alone would be, "You are a very poor liar."

"Let me know when you are ready to return to the hotel," Kindle said.

"I'll take care of getting her home safely, don't you worry," Harriet said. I almost hugged her in relief.

Kindle's expression cleared and he bowed his head. "Dinner was superb, Harriet. Good night."

Kindle moved to a clump of officers at the far end of the tent. It was on the tip of my tongue to thank Harriet for rescuing me when I realized what our tête-à-tête meant.

We walked across the parade ground to her brother's quarters. I stood in the middle of the parlor while Harriet lit lanterns. She replaced the glass over the final lantern and said with a wry smile, "You look as if you're about to meet a firing squad."

"An apt description."

Harriet adjusted the lantern's wick higher. The warm light

illuminated her troubled expression. "Please, sit. I will pour the sherry."

Two wooden straight-back chairs sat at an angle before the fireplace. The lantern sat on a small table between them. The windows were open but offered little in the way of a breeze. It was only the first of June and the heat was oppressive. I couldn't fathom what July or August would be like.

Harriet handed me one of the small goblets of sherry and sat in the other chair. "It's like a monk's cell, isn't it? To Ranald, material possessions are merely lodestones to haul across the country as he performs his duties. All of his possessions fit in one chest." Harriet shook her head and sipped her drink.

"You and your brother are close?"

Harriet tilted her head. "He is a bachelor and I am a spinster. My other living brother is a naval officer and at sea most of the time. His family would take me in, but I don't relish the role of spinster aunt stuck taking care of the children."

"You said living brother; did one die in the war?"

"No. He survived the war to die in the Far East. He was a naval officer, as well. The Navy is in our family's blood. Ranald rebelled and went into the Army. We aren't here to talk about my life, though."

"I suppose not." I sipped my drink and stared into the empty fireplace.

Harriet placed her glass on the table between us. "I went to see Henry Pope today."

"How is he?"

"In pain. Angry."

"Understandable."

"At you."

"Me?" My voice broke on the word. I cleared my throat. "I can't imagine why."

"Come now, Catherine."

I stood and went to the window that looked out over the plains. The stars were pinpricks in the coal black sky. "He told you."

"He cannot speak. He showed me a poster. It is not a very good likeness of you."

I closed my eyes and nodded. "So he had more than one."

"I'm sorry?"

I turned to face Harriet. "Mr. Pope showed me the poster the day we met. I thought I'd convinced him that to print the story would bring bounty hunters down on Jacksboro. He wouldn't get his story or the reward. I hoped to be gone before he got either. After Mr. Pope was beaten, someone sent me a poster covered in bloody fingerprints."

"You don't think Henry—"

"No. His attacker."

"But, why?"

"I have no idea. If Pope's attacker is a bounty hunter, why not just claim me and take me back East? There was no cause to beat Henry Pope."

Harriet picked up her sherry and stared into the middle distance, lost in thought. We drank in silence.

"Why haven't you revealed who I am?"

Harriet's focus turned to me. She exhaled a small laugh. "You expected me to rush to the sheriff, no doubt." When I didn't reply she continued. "I know how the press is, how stories take on a life of their own, divorced from anything resembling the truth." I suppose my skepticism showed on my face. "Have you heard of the *Somers* Affair?"

I shook my head. "No."

"It haunted my father until the day he died." Harriet waved it away. "It isn't important. Tell me your account of what happened in New York."

297

"Do you have anything stronger than sherry?"

"I do not." She rose and smiled mischievously. "But, Ranald does."

I threw back the rest of my sherry, picked up Harriet's glass, and took both to the kitchen. When I returned, she was pouring two stiff shots of whisky into tin cups. She handed me one, clinked her cup against mine, and said, "To the truth."

I nodded and drank. "It started in the early-morning hours of February ninth, after I left the resurrection man."

Harriet's eyebrows rose almost to her hairline and she leaned away from me. I chuckled. "You might want to sit down. It gets worse."

I was thankful I'd vented my feelings while telling Ezra. The last person I wanted to show weakness in front of was Harriet Mackenzie. She listened without interruption and was so quiet when I finished I thought she might have fallen asleep.

"You treated William at Antietam?"

Of all the things I told her, the aside about treating Kindle during the war was what stood out? "I did."

"Ranald was there. In the engineering corps." She picked up her empty tin cup and stared into it with remorse. "He never spoke much about the war, but I gathered Antietam was more terrible than most."

"I think that could be said about every battle."

She nodded and looked up at me. "I wanted to nurse, during the war. But I was too young. I stayed home with my mother and two younger brothers and did what I could, which always felt like too little."

I thought of Harriet's efficiency and empathy during the dysentery outbreak. "It was the Union's loss. You would have been a tremendous nurse."

Her face relaxed into a pleased smile. "Thank you." A rare

moment of camaraderie passed between us, until her smile faded and she glanced back into her empty mug. "Are you in love with William?"

"Are you?"

She laughed, and I again noticed how beautiful it was. "No. Though I do esteem him more highly than most of Ranald's officers. As does Ranald. William's gone through much to get where he is. It would be a shame for the Army to lose him."

"I agree." I straightened my shoulders, and despite the terror in the pit of my stomach, asked, "Are you going to turn me in?"

She exhaled and slumped slightly before rising and going to the desk in the corner. She opened the middle drawer, removed a piece of paper, and held it out to me. I didn't need to look at it to know it was Pope's Wanted poster. "I cannot promise Pope will not. I don't know how many of these he had."

I took the poster and stared at Harriet, trying to understand who she was, what motivated her. As if sensing my confusion she took the poster from my hand and put the corner to the lantern's flame. When it was sufficiently caught, she walked to the fireplace and threw it in. In silence, we watched it burn to ash.

Harriet walked to the door. "I will have Foster's orderly take you to the hotel. You are welcome to stay here, though I know you will not."

I stepped forward. "Harriet?"

Her hand on the door latch, she looked over her shoulder at me.

"Thank you."

She smiled and nodded and opened the door. I heard footsteps on the porch and Sergeant Washington appeared, his hat in hand. "Miss Mackenzie, ma'am. Captain Kindle ordered me to get the doc to her hotel."

Harriet stepped back and opened the door wider.

I stopped in front of my hostess. "Thank you for the sherry."

She reached out as if to take my hands, but patted me on the forearm instead. "Thank you for sharing it with me. Sleep well, Laura." Her expression closed off and she looked away.

I followed Sergeant Washington to the wagon and let him help me up onto the seat. Before he alighted, Harriet called him back. She spoke to him briefly in a low voice. He nodded, and returned. The ride into town passed in silence. One not knowing what to say and the other worrying she'd not said enough.

CHAPTER
24

With the loss of Welch as town doctor a constant stream of patients called for me at the hotel desk, no doubt sent by Edna Carter. I arranged with the owner the use of a back room for the day so I could see the patients in a more appropriate setting than a bedroom. Alice Strong was my fifth patient and it was not even ten o'clock in the morning.

"Why is Sergeant Washington sitting outside your door?"

"He is waiting to take me back to the fort tonight."

Alice furrowed her brows, as if the explanation didn't quite make sense, but didn't push further. The explanation didn't make sense, but it was easier to lie than to explain that Kindle felt it necessary to have a guard at my door. I could only imagine his reasoning had something to do with his brother since I hadn't seen or spoken to him since the night before.

Alice avoided my gaze and looked around the tidy room. A wooden rectangular worktable absconded from the kitchen served as my examination table, much to the irritation of the cook. My depleted trunk of medicine stood open in the corner, my medical bag on a small table next to a chair. "Is this all of your things?"

"My medical supplies, yes. My trunk of clothes is upstairs

in a sorry state, I must admit. I was in the middle of packing when my first patient arrived. I was eager to leave the task. Maureen was always the packer."

"I heard the sutler looted your things," Alice said.

"Did you?" I said in some surprise.

Alice gave me a bitter smile. "I hear a great many things people do not intend me to hear."

"Are you an eavesdropper, Alice?"

"On the contrary, I am more like a servant. I hear everything because no one sees me."

I opened my mouth to contradict her but stopped. I thought of the dinner the night before. Alice had sunk into the surroundings, unobtrusively, and been completely overlooked save the one question she asked. The conversation moved on without her and she was forgotten again. Because she was ugly, she was ignored, forgotten, and assumed to be stupid or lacking in enough assertiveness to be interesting. The anonymity of her appearance and docile nature placed her in a unique position to be abreast of information that would not be shared with beautiful women with sharp minds and eyes.

"The sutler was generous enough to allow me to reclaim my things," I said. "Since I'm not traveling by wagon and have no way to transport some of them, I sold them back to him. He robbed me blind, but I did procure the materials for shelves for Corporal Martin in the hospital kitchen. He gave me a bottle of his sorghum syrup in gratitude. I've made a friend for life."

She smiled. "You leave tomorrow morning?"

"Yes. I'm moving back to the fort for the night. It is more convenient since we leave so early."

"Where are you staying?"

"In the hospital. With the completion of the death room behind the hospital, there is a vacant room upstairs." I chuckled at the expression on Alice's face. "Yes, my sentiments as well. What's the matter? Are you ill?"

"I am better, thank you."

"If you aren't ill, what can I do for you?"

Alice cleared her throat and continued to look away. "I—" She stopped, struggling, her face reddening with embarrassment.

I encouraged her to ask me whatever she wanted.

"I would like your advice on marital relations," she blurted. She sighed, relieved of her burden at last.

Good heavens, I thought, with a fair amount of inward panic. "What kind of advice?" I said, in my most professional, calm voice.

"I didn't know what to expect in regards to marital relations and I am afraid my ignorance is why I am unable to get with child."

"Most women are ignorant, Alice," I said. "Ignorance is not a detriment to getting with child, I assure you."

"Yes, of course. My barrenness must be caused by something I'm not doing."

"How long have you been married?"

"A year."

"A year is not so long."

"It's an eternity!"

I motioned to the one chair in the room. "Won't you sit down?" I asked. "Have you regular abdominal pain?"

"Only during my time."

"No other?"

She shook her head.

"What about during... relations?"

"In my abdomen? No."

"It is painful other places?" She nodded. "Did you have any illness in childhood?"

"No. I have always been healthy."

"Have you talked to another doctor about this?"

"Yes, before I came west. My mother forced me to see her doctor. She is concerned at my failure." Her words were laced with bitterness.

"What did the doctor say?" I asked, sure of the answer.

"He told me to submit to my husband always, daily if needed."

I nodded. "Did he examine you?"

"No. He barely looked at me and left as soon as possible, as if I was too ugly to be around for a moment longer than necessary. There are some things even my father's money cannot buy."

"You're not ugly, Alice."

The cynicism laced in her words came out as a laugh. "You are a poor liar, Dr. Elliston."

When I thought of the lies I told since I left New York it was my turn to laugh. "I'm glad you think so." I realized when I uttered it that the comment was inappropriate and offensive to Alice. I rubbed my aching shoulder. "How often do you have relations?"

She *was* much prettier when she blushed. "Whenever Wallace requests. Which isn't as often as it was before."

"I'm sure it's difficult with your husband on patrol so often."

"Yes, but..."

"He's less interested?"

She nodded.

"I am sure his duties..."

"Please don't make excuses for him. I know why he is not turning to me. So do you."

I stopped rubbing my shoulder. I remembered Alice's tortured expression in the hospital, which I assumed was from the death of Private Howerton. "How much of my conversation with Ruth did you hear?"

"I went to tell you of Private Howerton." She looked up from the floor. "He despises being called Wally."

"There is no guarantee the child is your husband's."

"She said herself she is not a whore. Wallace would never do that."

I held my tongue. Alice didn't hear much or she would have known Ruth was, indeed, a whore, only an unpaid whore for Wallace Strong.

Alice continued. "Wallace liked my sister better than me. She was too young to marry, only fifteen. My parents told him I had to be married before Constance. He wanted his commission enough he agreed." Her smile was bitter, knowing. "So you see, I know Wallace prefers young, pretty girls. Constance is much prettier than I. Stupid, but pretty."

"Alice, I wish you would stop inferring you are not attractive."

"I didn't come here to be pandered to, Dr. Elliston. I want to know what I can do to please my husband, to provide him with a legitimate heir."

"What makes you think my advice will be different from the other doctor's?"

"Because you are a woman, a doctor, and a widow."

Damn you, Harriet Mackenzie, I thought. This girl came to me based on a lie. I had no advice to give her on how to interest her husband. She could not compete with her rival in appearance. Though Ruth was ignorant and poor, she had a natural beauty and energy Alice lacked. If outward appearance was the primary attraction for men, however, whorehouses would not be brimming over with successful ugly women. Most men didn't care how a woman looked as long as she was willing, or pretended to be.

"I hope I don't shock you with this question but I will remind you, you brought the subject up."

"Go on."

"Do you enjoy lying with your husband?"

"Enjoy it?" she asked, almost laughing. "How could anyone enjoy it? Did you?"

I almost told Alice the truth, about my brief affair with James, one born of curiosity, affection, and familiarity rather than love. But, suddenly, I cared what this woman thought of me. Instead, I sprinkled a bit of my truth in with a healthy dose of lies. "I only lay with my husband the one night, my wedding night. He left for the war the next day and didn't return."

"I'm sorry."

"Don't be. He was sweet but a bit methodical, as if he was following an instruction manual in his head. There was little passion and it hurt."

Alice nodded. "It stops hurting after a while, but it has never been comfortable."

"I tell you about my experience so you know the advice I am about to give you doesn't come from me, rather it comes from patients I have had over the years."

She was wary, but I suspect she knew the answer before she asked. "What type of patients?"

"Prostitutes."

She hid her horror and disgust well, proving she was truly desperate, as well as deeply in love with her husband. "Go on."

"While I am sure there are women who enjoy relations—I refuse to believe God would create such an act purely for the

pleasure of one sex—all prostitutes make their partners believe
they do. Men are vain and I suspect your husband is vainer
than most. If he thinks being with him is what you want, not
something you endure, he might be more ardent."

I worried she would take my jab at Lieutenant Strong
as an insult, but she did not. "Pretend to enjoy it," she said,
thoughtfully.

I shrugged. "It is the best advice I have to get him back in
your bed, regularly. Who knows, if you act like you enjoy it
enough, maybe you will."

Alice looked skeptical. "There is one other option."

"Yes?"

I narrowed my eyes and wondered how she would react to
this piece of advice.

"Please, Dr. Elliston."

I sighed. "When it becomes too painful, the women use oil."

Alice looked more perplexed and I felt my face flush with
embarrassment.

"To lubricate."

"Oh."

"Vegetable oil," I said. "Not much, of course."

Alice wrinkled her nose. "Vegetable oil?"

"They said the men enjoyed it, too."

She stood from the bed and retrieved her reticule. "Thank
you, Dr. Elliston."

"I don't know how much help I have been."

There was a knock on the door followed by the voice of the
hotel clerk telling me there was a man in the lobby dripping
blood from a knife wound.

"I wouldn't put it past Edna Carter to have cut the man herself. I'm flattered by her determination to have me stay."

"I wish you would. Even if your advice does not help, it was enough to have someone to talk to." She reached into her reticule and removed a silver piece to give me.

"No, keep it," I said. "I fear it is worth much more than my advice."

⌒∞⌒

The man entered the room, holding a dirty scrap of cloth over his left forearm. As with every male patient, Sergeant Washington made a point of keeping the door open and being visible through it.

"Doc," the man said. His hair was flattened with oil and his forehead was white from wearing a hat and his cheeks pale from being recently protected by a beard.

"A bar fight?" I asked, examining the short, deep gash.

"Of a kind."

I held his arm closer to the lamp. "You'll need stitches, I am afraid. This may hurt," I said. I pulled the open skin apart to see if the cut went to the bone. The man never flinched nor caught his breath like many would have. Curious about this stoic character, I looked him full in the face for the first time and was startled to catch him staring at me with narrowed, penetrating eyes. In a blink, his expression was clear and friendly. He might have once been handsome but years of exposure and hard living were lined on his face.

"Would you like some laudanum to help with the pain?"

"No."

I poured whisky into a basin and dropped my instruments in it.

"What a waste of good whisky."

"Ah, but this is not good whisky. I save that for drinking."

"You like whisky?"

I threaded a needle. "I have had it before. I can't say I like it. Would you like some?"

"Depends on if you're serving the good stuff."

"If you're paying I'll serve you whatever you want."

He reached into his waistcoat pocket and removed two gold dollars.

I pulled a bottle of whisky a patient had given me earlier in the day and gave him a glass. He drank it in one gulp.

I sewed his arm. "Are you a farmer near here?"

"Not a very successful one." The man took a deep, steadying breath.

"Am I hurting you?"

"No. How long have you been in town? I don't remember hearing about you last time I was here."

"Two weeks, though it seems much longer."

"Don't like it here?"

I thought of Kindle. "It has a few good qualities. Nothing to keep me here, though."

"It's a harsh life for a woman, and that's a fact."

"I've found unless you're wealthy, life is harsh for women no matter where you are."

The man chuckled and nodded. "I suppose so."

"Mostly, I want to leave because I miss trees," I said, laughing.

"Well, there aren't many of those out here. It's too bad for Jacksboro you don't want to stay. You're doin' a right nice job on my arm."

"Thank you."

"I bet I don't even have a scar later."

"If you follow my instructions, you might not. Or only a small one."

"I thought women liked scars on men."

"I suppose some do." I tied off the last stitch and applied carbolic acid plaster on the wound and bound it with a clean bandage.

"Do you?" he asked.

"In about a week, remove the stitches. Be sure to use a clean knife or scissors."

He stood to leave. "Won't you do it for me?"

"No. I leave town tomorrow." I washed and dried my hands.

"Do you? Well, be careful out there on the trail. Watch out for Injuns."

I ignored the comment. "Try your best to keep it clean and change the bandages regularly." I turned to give him a clean bandage to take with him, but he was gone.

⚬⚭⚬

The differences between my conversation with Alice and Ruth could not have been starker. It beggared belief Wallace Strong would prefer an ignorant dreamer like Ruth to a strong, intelligent woman like Alice. My dawning appreciation of Alice made my patience with Ruth during our parting conversation very thin.

With Ruth's diet, occupation, and an unsympathetic mother, I feared for the future of Ruth and her unborn child.

"You must promise me to see Dr. Kline. He will help you any way he can."

"I don't need no doctor to birth my baby."

"I'm not talking of the birth. If you need assistance before your term, go to Dr. Kline."

Ruth's eyes were wide with excitement. "I don't think Mama will notice. I ain't big and if I do get a little big she'll think I'm getting fat. She always says I'm too skinny. She'll be glad."

"What of your job? You cannot be entertaining men while

310

pregnant. It is not good for the baby and surely they will notice."

"Some men pay extra for it."

"That is disgusting, Ruth. Let us go to your mother together, before I leave."

Ruth was emphatic. "No. She'll either sell me more because of the baby or she'll kill it."

Maybe I should stay, I thought. I could be the buffer between mother and daughter when Mary found out, which she was bound to do. She was not stupid, nor were the other women. Someone would notice Ruth's condition.

She stood before me as straight and unmovable as a marble column. If she did not inherit her mother's coloring, she did her determination. Maybe she could stand up to her mother without my help.

"I want you to swear to me, on the Bible, if anything goes wrong you'll go see Dr. Kline."

"I can't swear on the Bible!"

I sighed in exasperation. She would lie with multiple men out of wedlock but she would not swear on the Bible. It always amazed me where people drew their moral line in the sand.

"Promise me."

She knew she had won. She grinned. "I promise."

I didn't believe her. Nor did Ezra when I relayed the story to him. "You cannot save everyone, Catherine."

"Should saving everyone not be our goal?"

"Yes, but you cannot dwell on the ones you cannot. Move on to the ones you can."

He watched as I replenished my medicine case with the stores from the dispensary. "Are you sure Foster approved this?"

"Yes," Ezra said.

"I don't believe you." I continued to stock my case.

"Have you become so adept at lying you can spot a liar as well?"

"I'm not as adept as you think. Kindle and Alice Strong can see right through me. Has Foster said anything about the letter?" I asked.

"No."

"Hmm. I hope Foster isn't giving me this medicine in lieu of Sherman's recommendation," I said. I looked at Ezra. "I may be self-centered and an accomplished liar but I am not, nor have I ever been, a hypocrite." I held up a bottle of carbolic acid. "I wish you had more. I cannot take your last bottle. I'll get more at Sill, or in Denver." I put it back on the shelf. "You forget I have been forced to be dishonest."

"I haven't forgotten."

"I have lied about two things, my name and being a war widow. The latter was Harriet Mackenzie's lie I went along with to keep the peace."

"Surprising when you consider confrontation rather than peacekeeping is your nature."

I ignored the insult. I wrinkled my nose. "I lied to Pope, as well. I forgot about him. Besides those fibs, I have told portions of my real history where I can and done my best to avoid revealing too much or creating more elaborate lies." Finished restocking, I closed my trunk and turned to Ezra. "What would you have me do? Return to New York?"

"Tell Captain Kindle."

"Why? What good would it do?"

"He could help you."

"No, he couldn't. Besides, he knows."

"All of it?"

"Only that I'm running from something."

"Why did you tell him that if not all?"

I sighed. "It is a long story, Ezra. Tomorrow we will say good-bye and never see each other again. What if Beatrice Langton has Pinkertons following me? I don't want to take the chance my real story might get out. The frontier is not as large as I hoped."

Ezra followed me out of the dispensary and into the office. The trunk containing my personal belongings was open in the corner. He sat in his desk chair and folded his hands over his stomach. "I sense you and the captain are searching for something to keep you here."

"There is nothing to keep me here."

"Even me?"

I pretended to rearrange items in my trunk and closed it. "I was hoping you wouldn't ask." I sat on the trunk and faced Ezra. "You are the only person I would stay for."

"That's a lie."

I shook my head and looked down. "He would ask me to give up medicine. I cannot love a man who would ask that of me."

"From what I have observed, you already do."

I scoffed. "It's ridiculous. I haven't known him a month."

"I fell in love with Dorothy before I said a word to her."

"That's different. Can we please talk of something else?"

"Closing yourself off from people who care about you and whom you care about will not keep you from getting hurt."

No, but it will keep me from hurting them, I thought. Maureen's mutilated face floated in front of my eyes.

I leaned forward and grasped his hands. "Let us say good-bye tonight. I don't want to cry in front of the fort in the morning."

He cradled my cheek in his hand. "Little Katie Bennett. Pretty as the day you were born."

My laughter was choked with a sob. "You always said I was an ugly baby."

"Someone had to make sure you were not the vainest woman alive. Your father was not up to the task. Nor were Dorothy and James."

I clutched the hand on my cheek and kissed it. "I always knew you loved me best." I gave his hands one last squeeze and stood. "Do not forget your promise about Ruth."

He nodded. "Good night, Katie."

I leaned forward, kissed his bald forehead, and whispered, "Good-bye."

CHAPTER
25

It was hours before dawn and I could not sleep. The hospital was quiet except for the occasional cough of a patient downstairs and the whistling of wind through my open window. Despite this, the smell of death permeated my room. The memory of my last night in New York drove me out of bed. I rose, wrapped my shawl around my shoulders, and picked up *The Tenant of Wildfell Hall*. I decided spending the night sitting alone in the reading room, finishing the novel was preferable to being sleepless in a recently abandoned death room.

The wind was heavy with the smell of rain. Lightning flashed in the distance, followed by the low rumble of thunder. I hurried across the darkened, deserted parade ground. I closed the door to the reading room as the skies opened.

I leaned against the door and caught my breath. It was a small, square room, though two windows on each wall gave the space an unexpectedly airy impression. All available wall space was taken up by floor-to-ceiling shelves overflowing with books. Large and small desks were lined up in the middle of the room and faced a rolling chalkboard. A small desk for a teacher sat in one corner. A large paddle with holes drilled in the blade hung on a nail next to the desk.

When my eyes adjusted to the dark I crept to the teacher's desk in the corner. I fumbled for matches and lit the oil lamp on the desk. I replaced the glass, increased the wick, and sat. I was settling into the novel's denouement when I heard a step on the porch. I instinctively turned the lamp down and held my breath. I dared not imagine who might be on the other side of the door. A whisky-soaked enlisted man most like. Or possibly Harriet come to make sure I wasn't enjoying myself too much. I thought of my gun, packed away in my trunk.

Kindle poked his head through the door. "Laura?"

I sighed in relief and turned up the lamp. "I'm here."

He closed the door behind him. "What are you doing here?"

"I am reading in the reading room. Whatever will I do next?"

He sat on the corner of the desk. He looked to have gotten dressed hastily. His shirt was open at the collar, his waistcoat was unbuttoned, and he had forgotten his hat. He was dripping wet. "Is it still raining outside?"

He ran his hands through his hair and smirked. "No more rhetorical questions. What are you reading?"

"*The Tenant of Wildfell Hall.*" I held the book up for him to see.

"What is it about?"

"A woman who escapes from her old life."

"Why did she need to escape?"

"She was married to a depraved man who was beginning to negatively influence her child."

"How Gothic. Where does she go?"

"She moves to the country."

"Does it make her happy?"

"No. She becomes even more miserable."

"Why?"

"She falls in love."

"I would think that would make her happy."

"She cannot be with the man she loves. She isn't free to give herself to him."

"Does he know why?"

I shook my head.

"Doesn't she trust him?"

"Yes. But, she is afraid if her story gets out she will be found. She desperately doesn't want to be found."

"If she trusts him with her heart, shouldn't she trust him with everything?"

"She doesn't trust anybody."

"She should."

I stared at the pages of the book we had long since stopped talking about, but which story eerily mirrored my own. "Why did you come, William?"

"I saw you walk across the parade ground."

"How did you know it was me?"

"I would know you anywhere."

Leave. Leave now.

I closed the book and stood. "I should get back." I shoved the book into the first gap I found. Kindle stood next to the desk, holding my shawl open. "Thank you." I let him drape it over my shoulders. It was a mistake.

He turned me around to face him. I could not bring myself to look up. I stared at the hollow of his throat as he traced his fingers across my jaw.

"We mustn't. It will only make our parting more difficult." He turned my head and kissed my neck just below my jaw.

"Then we mustn't part." I shuddered as Kindle's lips traveled their well-known path to my collarbone.

"I must go." I closed my eyes and tried to remember my objections. "It isn't...I cannot ask...my..."

317

He pulled me close and whispered the one word I never expected. The one word I longed to hear.

"Catherine. Stop talking."

⋘⋙

"I didn't intend for this to happen."

Kindle's head was buried in my shoulder, his voice muffled and hoarse.

"Let us catch our breath before we apologize to each other, William."

He lifted his head and was readying his denial when he saw my smile. "I wasn't apologizing." He replaced his head on my shoulder. "Nor will you."

I ran my hand over the crown of his damp head, my racing heart returning to normal. "When I think back over my life this will not be one of the regrets."

"Do you have many?"

"A few."

As my breathing returned so did my logic, despite Kindle's efforts to distract me, and my desire to be distracted. His lips traveled from my neck to my exposed breast, where they lingered. I wanted to press him against me, to let him devour me again and again, but I knew I could not. "It'll be dawn soon." I gently pushed him away.

He stepped back and helped me stand from my precarious position on the edge of the desk. We rearranged our clothes, which we had neglected to completely shed. His eyes were hooded, his lips wet and plump, inviting. I stood on my tiptoes and kissed him softly, wanting to funnel every new, raw emotion swirling within me to him.

I dropped my forehead to his chest. "What have you done to me?" The memories of our lovemaking were too fresh, the

318

sounds still echoed through the room. I was abashed at my eagerness, my willingness to give and receive. The things I said. It was so unlike my experience with James—awkward, formal, and silent—I wondered if James and I had made love at all. My reaction to Kindle couldn't have been normal. What would he think of me when we parted? I would reside in his memory maybe a step above an energetic whore, and only there because no money exchanged hands. I looked away, smoothed my hair, and tried to push away the self-consciousness creeping into my soul. Kindle put his arms around my waist.

"You don't have to look so embarrassed."

"You don't have to look so smug."

I pulled away and picked up the books that had fallen from the desk. The lamp was overturned, the glass cover shattered on the floor, the wick extinguished. The room was in almost total darkness, for which I was thankful. I didn't want Kindle to see how close to tears I was. I picked up my bloomers and turned my back to Kindle while I put them on.

"Catherine, what's wrong?"

I turned to him but kept the desk between the two of us. I thought of saying a quick good-bye and keeping my fears to myself but I could not. "I hope, in years to come when you think of tonight, you will not think ill of me."

"What?"

"This is unlike me."

"Which part? The part where you made love to me? Or that you enjoyed it?"

"Both." I took a breath. "I have been with one other man but it was not like this."

"Did you love him?" His voice was sharp, abrupt.

I lifted one shoulder. "He was a childhood friend. He comforted me after my father died. I'm not sure how it happened."

"He took advantage of you."

"No. It was nothing like that. It was natural in the moment. I immediately regretted it. He was surprised when I refused to marry him." I thought of the shock and anger in James's face when I said no. I shook my head to erase the memory. "I don't know why I am telling you this."

"Catherine..."

"Let's not make our parting any more difficult than it has to be. It will be difficult enough tomorrow to pretend you're nothing to me."

Kindle walked around the desk and took my hands in his. "Stop." I focused on his hands and tried to ignore his closeness, the smell of sex that lingered in the air around us. "Don't you want to know why I came here tonight?"

"Was it not to find a book to read on patrol?" My forced levity sounded flat, even to me.

"I came here to tell you I am mustering out of the Army. I gave my papers to Foster this evening."

"What? Why?"

He laughed. "You have to ask?"

"Well, yes. You have studiously avoided me since Foster's dinner."

"As you have avoided me."

"I thought it would be easier."

"So did I. The farther away you pulled, the more I wanted you. When I considered your demand I leave the Army..."

"My *demand*? I did not demand..."

He placed his fingers over my mouth.

"The more I liked the idea. I stayed in the Army after the war because there was nothing for me to return to. My family was dead. I didn't have the energy or desire to rebuild my father's farm. Choosing to stay in the Army was the easiest route, so I took it."

"It's your career. I wouldn't want you to give it up for me. You will resent me for it, later."

"It isn't only for you, Catherine. I am tired of being alone. Of following orders I object to. Of being unhappy."

I thought of Harriet's comment the night before. "The Army needs good men like you."

"The Army can survive without me."

"I can be difficult. Dramatic. Self-centered. Arrogant."

"You are also intelligent, witty, compassionate, and tender."

"William, I don't know…"

He pulled me closer. "As well as passionate, and the most beautiful woman I've ever met." He lifted my chin. "The way you responded to me proved I made the right decision." I tried to look away but he wouldn't let me. "You want to be with me as much as I want to be with you. Don't deny it."

I shook my head. "I won't." He kissed my hands. Happiness bubbled within me. I laughed. "What do we do now?"

"You leave tomorrow, like planned. I want you safe and away from here. When you get to Fort Sill, go east to Saint Louis. You wait for me there. I'll follow when my patrol is done. I will be a week behind you. Two at the most. Once the paperwork is complete, we start our life."

"Where?"

He shrugged. "Wherever you want to have your practice."

"You don't want me to give up my profession?"

"Would you?"

Would I? Now that being with Kindle was a reality and not a dream, I couldn't imagine losing him by refusing to give up my profession. I also couldn't imagine my life without medicine.

"It doesn't matter," Kindle said. "I am not asking you to. The Army doesn't mean as much to me as medicine means to you."

"What will you do?"

"We can return to my family's farm in Maryland."

"Maryland? But, I can't return to the East."

"Why not?"

"Didn't Harriet..." The confusion on his face answered the question before I asked. "How did you know my name?"

He smiled. "I finally remembered what the doctor told me when I searched for you. After Antietam."

I let go of his hands and paced. "I should have told you this before we..." I stopped and took a deep breath. "I cannot return to the East because I am wanted for murder."

His face froze. He laughed. "Of all the things you could have said, that is the last I would have guessed."

"It's ridiculous. Completely unfounded."

"Was it a patient?"

"No, her husband. The widow accused me of bludgeoning him with a fireplace poker."

Kindle laughed again. "You? Why?"

"I honestly do not know. She says it is because he ended our affair."

Kindle's mirth died instantly.

"I was not having an affair with him. I am sure I don't need to clarify the point since you know me so well."

"Of course," he replied, though he was not as vociferous in my defense as I hoped.

"The press has crucified me. According to them, I have had an affair with every doctor in New York."

"Why didn't you stay and defend yourself?"

"The family is connected, legally, socially, and very rich. I knew I wouldn't stand a chance."

"But, surely..."

"I couldn't tell them who I was with to defend myself, though it mattered little in the end. The information came out."

"Who were you with?"

I rubbed my temples. Better to tell him. "I was performing a dissection."

"That is not so very..."

"On a body procured from a resurrection man."

Kindle turned away and paced the room.

"I matriculated from Syracuse Medical College. The New York City colleges didn't accept women students and, as such, wouldn't allow me to perform dissections to keep my skills sharp. The only way to do so was through unsavory channels." Kindle stared at the floor as he paced. I couldn't see his face in the darkness. "It was thanks to these dissections I was able to help you, on the plains. For that alone I cannot regret my actions. Nor will I apologize for them."

Kindle stopped and looked at me with astonishment. "I don't care about the resurrection man."

"There's more."

He crossed his arms and waited.

"The body of a woman was found in the river a few days after I left. She was identified as me."

"By whom?"

"I think by the friend who helped me escape, but I don't know for sure."

"They think you are dead."

I rubbed my temples. "I saw a woman in Galveston who recognized me. She had been traveling so didn't know the sordid tale. She has surely returned to New York by now. For all I know, Beatrice Langton sent Pinkertons after me on the next boat. There is a five-hundred-dollar reward for my capture."

"Five hundred dollars?"

"I told you they were rich."

"I cannot believe you've evaded capture for as long as you have. You probably won't for much longer." He walked around the room, thinking.

"Pope knows. He showed me my Wanted poster. I told Harriet last night."

He stopped. "What did she say?"

"Nothing about New York. She asked me if I was in love with you."

"What did you tell her?"

"Nothing. I asked her the same question."

"Are you?"

"With the charm offensive I've been under since the moment we met, how can I not be?"

He grinned, took me in his arms, and kissed me so hungrily I knew we would soon be on the desk again if I didn't slow him down. I pulled away and said, rather breathlessly, "I take that to mean the feeling is mutual."

"Yes." He tried to kiss me again but I turned my head away.

"It will be dawn soon."

"Which is why you need to let me kiss you again."

"No. We need a plan for later."

"Once on the train to Saint Louis, you will travel as Mrs. William Kindle. No one will ever associate that name with Catherine Bennett, especially since no one here knows of our relationship. When you're on the train, and while you are in Saint Louis, whatever you do, do not practice medicine. I will give you enough money to last you until I arrive."

"William..."

"Don't argue with me, Catherine. When I arrive in Saint Louis, we'll get married immediately, then decide where we go

324

from there. Listen carefully to me. I want you to think long and hard while you are traveling about giving up medicine. Shh." He placed his fingers on my lips. "Don't interrupt until I've finished. I only say it because as long as you are a practicing doctor you're in danger. You know I'm right, Catherine. I will always be there to protect you but I don't want to live our lives always moving. Promise me you will think of it."

"You still want to marry me?"

"Why wouldn't I?"

"Are you absolutely sure you are aware of what you're taking on by marrying me?"

"I have a fairly good idea."

I walked back toward the desk, pulling him with me.

"Does this mean we're done planning?"

"I feel guilty for using Harriet's desk. We broke her lamp."

"I'll bring a lamp from my quarters."

"Good idea. But—"

"The longer you talk, the less time we have."

"Excellent point."

We came together urgently, knowing it might be weeks until we were alone again, and lost ourselves in each other until the sun peeked over the horizon.

CHAPTER
26

Before dawn, as Kindle and I were rearranging our clothes for the second time, the downpour from the night before finally exhausted itself. The morning met us with a light drizzle that dusted shoulders, hats, horses, and saddles with tiny droplets of water.

I followed Murphy and Sullivan, who carried my trunks, out of the hospital and was astonished to see a group of people waiting on the front porch to bid me good-bye. Caro stood by herself, off to the side. I walked to her first.

"Good-bye, Caro. Thank you for everything."

She took my hand and squeezed. "I hope we meet again, someday."

"So do I."

Murphy and Sullivan, hats in hand, each bade me good-bye with warmth and a tinge of embarrassment. Corporal Martin thanked me again for the shelves and gave me another bottle of syrup, and Waterman said it had been a pleasure to work with me.

"Good luck, Dr. Elliston," Ezra said, without meeting my eyes.

"Thank you, Dr. Kline."

Alice stood with her husband next to his horse. Wallace Strong kissed Alice on the cheek, whispered something in her ear, which brought out her blush, and mounted his bay. She caught my eye, and with a pleased smile, nodded her thanks to me.

Harriet moved forward and held out an envelope. "With Lieutenant Colonel Foster's compliments."

Holding the envelope, I was struck by its lightness, how inconsequential it was in my hand, though I knew inside held a recommendation with the power to silence all suspicions of my identity. "From General Sherman?"

"Yes."

I suppose I shouldn't have been offended at Foster's absence, but still I bristled at the snub. As if reading my mind, Harriet said, "Lieutenant Colonel Foster is under the weather this morning." She leaned forward conspiratorially. "His gout is acting up. Too much wine the other night."

"Thank him for me."

"I will."

Standing awkwardly with Harriet, I realized how little I knew about her. Almost from the moment I'd met her, our relationship had been antagonistic. I had dismissed her as a bitter woman and hadn't taken the time to get to know her. Our conversation after the dinner party made me wonder if I hadn't judged Harriet too harshly; if I had been in a different frame of mind could we have, if not been friends, at least found a level of mutual respect? When I held out my hand to her, she surprised me by pulling me into a strong embrace.

"Good-bye, Catherine. Your secret is safe with me."

She released me as quickly as she embraced me, and without meeting my eyes, walked away through the drizzle.

I glanced around in a panic. *Did anyone else hear what she said?* Everyone smiled in ignorance, though Ezra furrowed his brow in question.

"Dr. Elliston?" Kindle motioned to the wagon holding my trunks. In a daze, I walked down the hospital steps and climbed up next to the teamster. The regimental band struck up "The Girl I Left Behind Me" and two companies of cavalry and my supply wagon left Fort Richardson.

It was miserable and slow going. The muddy roads and swollen creeks meant the cavalry spent most of their time walking their horses and pushing and pulling the supply wagon out of the mud. When we reached the Red River—which I'll admit to doubting more than once—Kindle's company would head west to patrol for Indians. The remainder would cross the Red into Indian Territory and complete the short journey to Fort Sill.

During those three days together on the trail Kindle and I were civil but distant. The two companies were small enough that any partiality between us would be noticed. There is nothing more observant than a bored soldier on patrol. We used my gun as an excuse to be alone. Each night Kindle worked with me on shooting and caring for my gun. As ruses to be alone went, it was rather inspired, I thought. Kindle could justify standing behind me, touching me, bending his head to speak in my ear. We worked until darkness made seeing impossible, cherishing these fleeting moments more with the knowledge we were going to be separated for weeks.

I pulled the hammer back and fired. The bottle I aimed at shattered.

"Nice shot," Kindle said. He picked up more empty bottles and walked to the tree stump. "Reload."

I opened the cylinder and removed five bullets from my

holster. When he returned he said, "Remember, only keep four bullets in your gun. Carry it on an empty chamber."

"Yes, but this is target practice and I plan on teaching those five bottles a lesson they won't soon forget."

Kindle stood behind me, pulled me back against him. The memory of our night together made me lose a bit of my bravado and playfulness.

He lifted my arm holding the gun. "Aim and fire."

I did, shattering another bottle. "You might be a better shot than I," he said.

I looked up at him over my shoulder and smiled. "Stationary bottles have no chance. Let's hope I never have to shoot a moving target." I stared down the barrel of the gun again. I dropped my arm. I couldn't get Harriet's strange behavior out of my mind. "If Harriet knew who I was, why did she let me leave?"

"Harriet is not the shrew you think she is."

"I don't think she's a shrew. But, she didn't like me in the least when we met."

"I think she admired you very much."

I raised my arm and aimed. "*Admired* is a strong word. She at least didn't think the worst of me in the end, I suppose," I said, and another bottle exploded. I dropped my hand, but Kindle didn't move from behind me. "I've been meaning to ask: Did you find the man from the hotel?"

"By the time I returned to town, he was gone. It isn't the first time I've thought I've seen my brother. It takes a certain personality to survive in the West, a degree of insanity that makes many men resemble my brother at his worst. He's dead. I buried him in Maryland seven years ago."

"You see your brother everywhere you go, just as I see bounty hunters around every corner. We are safe now and can stop looking over our shoulders."

We arrived at the swollen Red River the afternoon of the third day, the first day of clear skies on our march. With no clouds on the horizon, Kindle decided to camp on the southern bank for the night to give the river time to recede before half of our group crossed the next day.

With speed and precision, Kindle's regiment created camp from what appeared to be the shirts off their backs. Once the horses were watered, fed, unsaddled, and picketed the men turned to their own comfort, which didn't amount to much on a short patrol such as this. The goal was to travel light and fast. The men slept out of doors and ate rations of hardtack and salt pork and drank their daily allotment of whisky. A few fires were made to ward off the chill of the late-spring evening.

Kindle, Beau, Strong, and I shared a fire. The officers, typically, socialized little with their men. Enlisted men were required to ask the NCOs for permission to speak to the officers. Some officers, like Strong, took this separation to an extreme, talking to their soldiers only when giving orders. Kindle, on the other hand, went around to his men nightly and spoke to them, usually of inconsequential things. His demeanor was not familiar, he still held himself apart, but it was obvious his men held him in high esteem for the efforts he made.

He and Beau had returned from their circuit of the camp when I accosted him about his health.

"Now that you have spoken with every man in your company you must take a moment to speak to me."

"It will be a much more pleasant conversation, I'm sure."

"Don't count on it. I mean to give you strict instructions on your future rehabilitation."

"In that case, I must sit down."

"On the contrary." I stood. "As part of your rehabilitation, you must walk."

Kindle shot an exasperated look at Strong and Beau. "We'll watch the fire," Strong said.

I reviewed his treatment plan in a much louder voice than necessary. When we were out of earshot, I dropped the act. "I saw your expression."

"Playing a part, my dear. As are you."

We stood on the bank of the Red River, a normally wide and shallow river running deep and fast after the abundance of spring rains.

Kindle glanced back at the camp. Beau and Strong were sitting where we had left them, having an animated conversation about their baseball exploits at West Point, a common theme for the young men and one I had grown heartily tired of hearing.

"Are you sending Beau to Saint Louis?"

"Yes. After this patrol," Kindle said. "He doesn't need to be in the field. He is too much like his mother. Soft-hearted. Easily led by stronger personalities."

"Such as Lieutenant Strong?"

"I don't want to spend our time alone talking of junior officers."

"What would you like to speak of?"

"How sorely my willpower has been tested the last days."

"In what way?"

"You know very well. There are times when I wonder if our night together was a dream. Your expression never betrays our secret."

"Doesn't it? I fear my happiness shines from every pore of my body."

"Are you truly happy?"

"As long as I don't think of our separation, yes. I don't want you to go tomorrow."

"Nor do I."

"How long do you think I will be camped here with Strong's company?"

He studied the river. "It is hard to tell. A day. Maybe two."

"Send Strong's company in your stead. Escort me to Sill."

"I cannot disobey orders, Catherine. As much as I would like to."

"I have this horrible suspicion I'll never see you again. You see? I would make a horrible officer's wife."

"Yes, you would."

"I should have stayed in Jacksboro and left for Saint Louis with you."

"Catherine," he said. "We agreed this is the best way. You can disappear and never have to worry about that Langton woman finding you. She will be looking for Catherine Bennett or Laura Elliston, if you're unlucky. Catherine Kindle will only mean nothing to her if everyone who knows us thinks we mean nothing to each other."

I sighed. He was right. "I hate feeling this way."

"I feel the same."

I was not referring to the prospect of being separated from him, though the thought of it nauseated me. I hated feeling so weak, as if I would never be happy again unless he was near me.

"I have something for you." He reached into his coat and removed a book. I knew what it was before he placed it in my hands. *The Tenant of Wildfell Hall.*

"I read the end," he said.

"What did you think?"

"She got her happy ending. Like we will."

I thought of the long miserable separation the two fictional characters endured before being granted their happiness. "Come to me tonight," I said, my voice husky with emotion.

He did not hesitate. "Yes."

I woke to find a man in my tent, undressing.

I propped onto my elbow. "You'll have to hurry," I whispered. "I'm expecting my fiancé any minute."

Kindle hung his holster on the center pole, draped his coat over it, and hung his hat on top. Using his cane, he sat on the ground awkwardly and with a grunt. He lay down and exhaled. "He's in for a shock, then. I'm not sure I can get up."

I placed my hand on his chest, over his heart. "Are you in much pain?"

"It's always worse when I ride." He took my hand and kissed it. "I will be fine."

"Do you want some laudanum?"

"Can't command men high on opium, though some have tried."

"Who?"

He looked at me in the darkness. "I'm not risking my life to talk about the Army. Did you say your fiancé is a strapping man with a jealous streak?"

"No, but he hides a knife in his boot."

Kindle turned on his side. "Enough talking."

"Whatever else is there to do?"

Kindle's hand resting on my hip pulled my skirt up, bit by bit. I worked on the buttons on his waistcoat. "I've never considered it before, but there is almost as much clothing to get through on a man as a woman," I whispered, working at the buttons of his breeches.

"I'm glad you've never had the occasion to consider it."

"How do you not melt in all this heat?" The cool weather, which the rain gifted us, had changed to a suffocating humidity.

"This is balmy compared to July and August." Kindle stopped and looked down at his hand resting on my bare hip. "You seem to be missing your bloomers, Dr. Elliston."

I shrugged. "I thought I would make it easier on you. I see you didn't have the same consideration."

"I took off my holster."

"How very kind."

Kindle inhaled sharply. "Heavens."

"Are you going to say that every time we are intimate?"

"If it's warranted." He stilled my hand. "I cannot get undressed," Kindle said. "In case of attack."

I covered Kindle's mouth with my own to quiet him. "Do not talk of attacks," I whispered.

Kindle's hand brushed lightly up and down my bare leg. "Then let's talk of our life together."

"Running from the Pinkertons?" I traced a finger down his scar to the cleft in his chin.

"Being Mrs. William Kindle."

"You mean Doctor Mrs. Catherine Kindle?"

"That would mean I am the doctor and you are my wife."

Goose bumps popped up on my legs and I flinched. "That tickles. I cannot think when you do that."

"Hmm." Kindle kissed me and pulled my leg over his. "I like you when you cannot think."

"I thought you liked my mind."

One side of Kindle's mouth curved into a smile. "The more I get to know you, the further down the list it goes." His hand really did have a mind of its own.

"You are incorrigible."

"Yes, we've established that," he said. I gasped and clutched his shoulders. "Many times."

"Have we? I don't remember."

"Don't worry; I'll continue to remind you."

"Heavens." My breaths came in small gasps. "If this is how you intend to, I will pretend to forget more often." We were silent for a while, our tent a dark cocoon of small gasps and murmured endearments until Kindle covered my mouth with his.

After, I lay next to him, my head on his chest, and listened to his heartbeat. He held me firmly against him, sliding his hand up and down my arm periodically. I played with a button on his shirt, as the passion he awakened in me dissipated, leaving my body bathed with a warm glow of contentment. "I never imagined it would be like this," I said in a low voice.

"We will have a feather bed in Saint Louis." Kindle's voice was slightly slurred, on the brink of sleep. "And, a lock on the door, so I can explore every inch of you without interruption."

"Heavens."

Kindle chuckled. "Yes. It will be exactly that." He kissed the top of my head and pulled me closer, as if trying to absorb me into his very being. "Ten minutes, and I must return to my tent."

"Rest. I'll wake you."

"I won't fall asleep." His words were more muddled than before.

"Of course you won't."

His breathing evened out, and within a minute, he snored softly. I propped my head on my arm and watched him sleep, memorizing every line on his face. An hour later, I woke him with a kiss.

When Kindle's company left the next morning, we parted as a doctor and patient should, though I hardly knew what I said. My mind was filled with images from the night before and dreams of the future. My heart overflowed with love and threatened to burst with despair.

To keep my ever-changing emotions from showing I tried to talk with Wallace Strong like never before. He was surprised since I had done little to engage him in the entirety of our acquaintance, but eventually my persistence banished suspicions he may have harbored about my sudden interest in his favorite sport, baseball. When it appeared he exhausted even his interest in this subject, I asked of Alice.

"Alice? She's fine, I'm sure. She's a meek little thing but she is an excellent soldier's wife. Never complains. There is no weeping and hand-wringing when I leave on patrol. I couldn't stand a woman to do that."

"I don't find Alice meek in the least," I said. "Don't mistake a naturally quiet demeanor for weakness. What you have described, her stoicism when you leave, shows great strength. I assure you, she's worried about your safety. She knows to show it would only anger you."

"Has she told you this?"

"I have talked to her very little. It is only my impression of her personality through our interaction and her reputation with the soldiers."

"Reputation?"

"She is well-respected by all of the soldiers, enlisted men and officers alike. She sat by Private Howerton's bedside while you were away and was holding his hand when he died. Didn't you know?"

336

"I did not."

"Of course she would not tell you. I thought one of the other officers might have."

Strong was discomposed. "Someone might have mentioned something about it."

"How did you meet your wife?" I asked.

"Through a family friend."

I did not reply immediately, only nodded my head. I was not surprised when he did not continue. "Alice was one of the few people at Fort Richardson I was sorry to say good-bye to."

"Maybe one day you will meet again."

"Maybe. Though I doubt it. I wish you two a long and happy marriage, blessed with many children."

"Thank you," he said. "Where will you go from Fort Sill?"

I didn't have the opportunity to answer. A warning cry from the soldier on sentry duty rang through the camp. Every soldier reached for his gun, which was always close by, and stood. I grasped my gun as Strong pushed me behind him.

⚬≪⚬≫⚬

The Indians ran their horses straight for the camp. Their bloodcurdling war cries mixed with the thundering of their horses' hooves and the crack of rifle fire.

"No. No, no, no."

It was happening again. This time I knew I would not survive.

"NO!"

Tears streamed down my face. Strong pushed me backward. Fear and anger clear on his face, he moved forward to fight with his men. "Under the wagon. Quick!"

I turned and ran.

Two Indians went after the horses, driving them away amid

the soldiers' gunfire. A second wave of Indians ran through the middle of the camp and out the other side. Strong yelled orders but I couldn't understand what he said. All I could see was the wagon; all I could think was to crawl under it. For a few seconds, my entire world consisted of the space between the wagon and me. I stumbled on the hem of my skirt but caught myself with my hand before falling completely. I ran on, hearing only the sound of my breath and the beating of my heart, until a gunshot turned sound back on. I turned to see an Indian riding directly for me.

I pulled my gun from its holster, across my body, and fired in one smooth, quick movement. The horse didn't slow, but the Indian screamed and grasped his shin. Before I could pull back the hammer and fire again, he scooped me from the ground and laid me facedown across his lap. The horse never slowed down and we never looked back.

◦∞◦

We rode through the night without stopping. I rode in the middle of the group, my hands tied and my feet bound under the horse's belly. Being bound, without a saddle on a rough horse, made it impossible to focus on anything but staying upright and the pain between my legs.

Eventually I grew accustomed to the pain, and thoughts of what would soon happen to me took over. I fought back a sob. *Rape* and *torture*. Two horrible, unutterable words that in my other life elicited feelings of humiliation, despair, horror, and pain but conjured no images. Now I saw entrails spilling from the stomach of a half-dead mother and a baby's crushed skull. I heard the screams of a man being burned alive. Maureen's cries silenced with the blow of a tomahawk. I retched down the neck of my horse and received a crushing blow to the side of my head in response.

How I managed to stay on my horse I don't know. If I did fall I would have remained on the horse, my feet tied across its back while my head was trampled beneath. I witnessed enough pedestrians run over by carriages in the city to know it would be certain death, though not certainly quick. My throbbing head jerked forward and backward with the uneven gait of my horse. I struggled to swallow the bile rising in my throat. Another blow to the head would kill me.

Was dying by my own hand a better alternative? I had no doubt the Indians would kill me after raping me. Was I willing to pay the price of eternal damnation to avoid the purgatory on Earth I was riding toward? Surely a fair God would forgive me for such an act.

I thought of Kindle. He would come for me, I was sure, but it would be too late. I didn't think I could face him after. Death would be preferable to seeing the disgust on his face or, even worse, pity.

The idea grew and a plan formed. It would be a simple task—kick my nag into a run and throw myself to the side. I would likely be unconscious within seconds, dead within minutes. The Indians would cut me from the horse, scalp me, and leave my body for the vultures and animals. There would be no Christian burial, no mourning friends.

My death would matter only to Kindle, Ezra, and James. The others—Alice, Ruth and Mary, the Carters, Harriet, and Foster—would move on until I was a footnote in the history of the plains. Over time, my footnote would become smaller and smaller until finally eradicated from the written word, replaced by more important people, more important events.

Was God so cruel to let me taste happiness, to love for the first time only to take it away? Were my sins so great I deserved this punishment?

The Indians never said a word, nor did they pay attention to me. We rode at a consistent trot through darkness so complete I couldn't see my horse's ears. I became accustomed to my mount's gait and closed my eyes. I imagined the darkness surrounding me into ever smaller cocoons until I dissolved into nothingness, my being snuffed from existence, releasing the burden of life with a contented sigh.

I woke up when I hit the ground. I rolled over onto my back, choking on mud, unaware of where I was or what was going on. Men were laughing and whooping in the distance. I lay on the muddy bank of a rushing river. Everything on my body ached. My injured shoulder screamed in pain matched by the pain between my legs. The right side of my head was warm and tight. I touched dried blood on my temple. Too late I realized I was untied, free. I never saw the hand that grabbed my hair and dragged me away from the river, nor did I hear the scream that tore from my mouth.

⚬⚭⚬

I dipped my shaking hands into the cool water and lifted them to drink. Water splashed out, ran between my fingers. When I looked into them, all that was left was dirt and blood. I tried again with the same result. And again. Anything to block out the heat, the mud, the sun, and the blood.

The pain.

The memory.

They beat me while the Indian whose leg I shattered sat on the creek bank and watched. Blows came from all around me, legs kicking me, fists pounding me. When I tried to curl into a ball, I was kicked in the face. Blood filled my mouth. I coughed and sprayed blood over the legs of the largest Indian. He yelled and the other two stopped. They panted from the exertion of the beating; their eyes gleamed with excitement. I turned my head away when one fumbled with his loincloth.

I knew what was coming. There was no escape. No way to save myself. Even if I had the strength to provoke them into killing me, I knew they would wait until they had sated themselves. I represented every man, woman, and child who had ever crossed their land, every broken treaty, every dead buffalo left on the plains to rot while its skin traveled east to lie on the floor of a Manhattan mansion. They could not make everyone pay for the wrongs done to them, but they could make me suffer.

I wish I could say I met it with pride, that I was able to master my emotions and deny them the satisfaction of my misery. I couldn't. I could hardly move, though I tried. My punches were ineffectual, a nuisance instead of a deterrent. They held my arms and feet down until I stopped fighting. I sobbed and screamed because I could not fight. After the third Indian mounted me I lost the energy to resist, or cry. I stared at the river and listened to the sound of rushing water. The blanket of darkness from the night before returned. I pulled it around me, and I remembered no more.

PART THREE

PALO DURO

CHAPTER
27

"Laura? Laura?"

Diffused light filtered through the tent, throwing the face of the woman standing over me into shadow.

"You must get up."

The voice sounded familiar, as if part of a long-forgotten past.

"They're breaking camp. If you can't walk you'll be killed." She pulled on my arm and I screamed in pain.

"I'm sorry," the stranger said. "At least you're awake. You must get up now. Yahne Muea will be back soon."

Sounds of activity accompanied her as she moved around the tent. I could not focus my eyes to see or my mind to understand. "Who?"

"Yahne Muea. The cruelest woman I have ever known. Get up, Laura. I didn't nurse you for five days to watch her kill you like a dog. Believe me, she wants to."

I was puzzling out why I would need to be nursed when the flap of the tent was thrown back and light flooded in.

First I realized I was not in a tent at all. It was a tepee. An Indian woman stood glowering at me with hard, black eyes, willing the fog of forgetfulness to lift from my addled brain. As the weight of despair and humiliation descended on me the

Indian's mouth softened into a triumphant smile, but her eyes remained hard.

She yelled at the woman in the tent and gestured at me before leaving. Though I didn't understand her I knew what she wanted. I stood through the excruciating pain. Two arms wrapped around me and lifted. "I know it hurts," the girl whispered. "The pain will pass."

I saw her face for the first time. "Anna?"

"Yes. There's no time. Stand here and if she comes back, pretend to do something."

In wonder, I watched Anna continue her work. She was dressed like an Indian in a leather tunic and soft moccasins. Her blond hair was flattened on her head and contained so much grease it looked brown. The skin beneath her left eye was a mottled yellow, the telltale sign of a healing bruise. Her face held none of the youthful bloom it had before and her eyes were wary, constantly darting to the open door. I moved whenever she passed to allow her room and to avoid the smell that followed her around. Despite these changes, it was undoubtedly Anna. She was alive and strong. It was a miracle.

"Beau will be so glad you are alive."

She stopped. "Who?"

"Beau Kindle." There was no recognition in her eyes. "The young lieutenant you met...before."

She stared blankly at me and returned to her task of wrapping the cooking implements, a mixture of crude wooden and stone bowls, Army-issued tin cups, and fine silver forks, knives, and spoons. Anna folded the animal skin around the pile and tied it with a leather string. She lifted it, grimaced as it settled on her shoulder, and walked outside.

Camp activity ceased when I walked out of the tepee. The men stared at me with expressions ranging from resentment

to lust to disgust. Curious children edged toward me until
Yahne Muea scared them away while screaming and brandish-
ing a large stick. She turned to me with hatred burning from
every pore of her round, flat face, lifted the stick, and struck me
across the cheek before I thought to defend myself. She did not
stop there, hitting me with the stick until her arm tired. Anna
stood to the side, watching, her eyes dead. Yahne Muea threw
the stick at me, spat on me, and walked off.

I fell to my hands and knees, sobbing. Blood ran down
my cheek and dropped from my chin onto the flattened grass
below. A grasshopper landed in the pooling blood and was
doused with a drop of my blood before jumping away.

"Come on," Anna said. She lifted me roughly from the ground.

"You're hurting me," I sobbed. "What's going on? Why
didn't you help me?"

"And be beaten for my efforts? No, thank you." She turned
my chin and inspected my face. "We don't have time to clean
it. We have to take this down and get ready for travel." I followed her gaze to the other tepees that had been miraculously
disassembled during my beating.

Inspecting her in the morning light, it was evident Anna's
soul was wounded but that physically she was in much better
shape than I. "Did they beat you like this?"

"There will be time to talk on the trail. Help me and don't
complain. It won't change anything."

⌘

We traveled across a landscape as desolate as the moon. There
were no natural features to act as signposts, no creeks to water
stock. No wonder the soldiers laughed at my naiveté.

I struggled to keep pace with the tribe lest I be beaten and
left for dead. I passed the time wondering how I got there and

internally catalogued and diagnosed my injuries: three broken ribs, making it difficult to breathe; a broken orbital bone above my right eye, making it difficult to see; a gash across my left cheek that would disfigure me, though I would not know the extent until I saw a mirror; three broken fingers on my right hand that would end my career as a surgeon if I didn't see to them soon. The pain between my legs made walking difficult. I didn't know how I received it and avoided probing too deeply to remember. To do so might awaken memories that had retreated into deep folds of my brain, content to masquerade as a nightmare that vanishes upon waking.

Anna walked on the other side of the travois. She stared straight ahead and made no effort to talk to me. Was she afraid showing interest in the new captive would anger the Indians? That they would think together we would try to escape? I looked around me. The Indians ignored us, confident in the security born of three hundred guards and a desolate landscape offering nowhere to hide. Besides the children whose curiosity could not be beaten out of them, though Yahne Muea tried, the only Indians who acknowledged our existence were Yahne Muea, who would turn and glare at me, and a young warrior on a gray horse who walked beside Anna for extended periods of time. When he trotted off to the other men, who rode while the women and children walked, I spoke to Anna for the first time.

"Are we the only two captives?"

"The only women."

"I didn't think Indians took male captives."

"Men, they don't. Boys, they do. There is one who's a brave." She jerked her head toward the front of the line. "Two children—a boy and a girl—who have been adopted as well. They've been captive since they were young. They don't realize they are white, nor do they remember their Christian names."

I looked around the tribe for the children she spoke of.

"You won't recognize them," she said. "They're Mexican. They blend in."

She said everything in a voice devoid of emotion while staring straight ahead. Only physically did she resemble the girl I knew. Her demeanor toward me was puzzling. She seemed not to care fate had brought us together, nor did she care for my well-being. I, on the other hand, saw in her hope I might survive.

I moved around the back of the travois to walk beside her. "I've thought of you so often during these past weeks," I said. "I was sure you were dead or being horribly abused. I'm glad to see you looking so well."

She turned to me with such anger in her expression it took my breath away. "Am I looking well? I'm happy to hear it."

Her reaction nettled me and sparked my natural combativeness. I was not dead yet. "You don't look like you have been beaten to within an inch of your life, at any rate. Tell me, how have you survived?"

"I haven't survived. I've endured." She looked toward the young warrior on the gray horse who was riding back to her side again. Realization dawned.

"He took you as his wife."

The smile was bitter. "Yes. After the Kiowa sold me to his tribe, he claimed me immediately. It spared me the humiliation of being raped by the Comanche, though not the Kiowa. Nor did it save me from Yahne Muea and the other women. They didn't beat me for long. When I fought back I earned their respect. They do everything possible to make my life difficult, but not openly. He wouldn't stand for it."

He was a large man, with a broad face and chiseled features, with an aura of leadership about him. I could understand why he might be considered handsome among his people, but all I saw was a savage who abducted and raped innocent women.

"Why haven't they killed me?" I asked. I knew I was too old to be taken as a bride.

"I don't know. I don't understand enough of the language, but there was a reason they abducted you."

"Me? Specifically me?"

Yahne Muea ran toward me, shaking her fist and yelling. Not wanting to meet the end of another stick, I returned to the opposite side of the travois. Anna's Indian interceded, yelling at the woman and gesturing for her to move away, up the line. She did, but not without unleashing a string of words so harsh their meaning was clear, despite the language barrier. The Indian kicked his horse into a canter to the front of the line.

"He's protecting you."

I laughed despite the pain shooting through my jaw and pointed at my beaten face. "This is his idea of protection?"

"If it wasn't for him, you would be dead. We have moved three times since you were brought to us. Any other white woman in your condition would have been killed."

Three times? I thought. "How long was I unconscious?"

"Five days."

I looked down at my swollen and deformed fingers. Five days? I didn't think I would ever be able to set them well enough for them to heal. My career was over.

"I tried to straighten them but was afraid I would make them worse," Anna said. She sounded for the first time as if she cared about me. It did little to soothe my shock.

Medicine, which defined my choices, my life, and myself since I was twelve years old, was gone. I walked on in a daze, wondering what I would do with my life now that it had been taken away.

Now that Kindle was lost to me forever.

We walked for hours in silence. My mind was numb, vacant. Thinking of the past was painful, the future offered me no consolation in hope, and the present was as desolate as the landscape around me. It was easy to erase thought from my mind, to ignore my physical pain and focus on putting one foot in front of the other.

I blurted the one thought that managed to cut through the fog without thinking of what I said or how I said it. "You never asked about your father."

"He's dead."

"I wasn't sure if you knew."

Anna didn't reply for a while. "I saw everything."

"I'm sorry."

"I saw the Indians first, you know. No. How would you? I was walking alongside our wagon when I saw them. They were already upon us before I could yell a warning. Father was one of the first to die. Then Maureen. I have never heard anyone scream like that. She was silenced with one blow, but he kept doing it, over and over and—"

I interrupted her. I could not bear it. "I hear her screaming my name every night in my dreams."

Anna's cold, hard eyes settled on me. "Maureen wasn't the one screaming to you for help. I was."

I didn't know what to say. What could I say? These weeks, my guilt was centered on failing Maureen. Knowing I had failed Anna brought even more embarrassment and shame. I knew, deep down, that if I would not leave the protection of the buffalo wallow for Maureen, a person near and dear to my heart, I would not have left for Anna.

"When I saw the Indians the first person I thought of was you," Anna said. "I was thinking of you quite a bit. I admired you, what you have accomplished despite society telling you it wasn't appropriate. I was so looking forward to getting to know you better, working with you, hearing about your London scandal." Her face softened with the memory, but was still closed from emotion. "Do you remember?"

"Yes."

She focused on the horizon. "I knew you wandered off, like you always did, and I was afraid they had already killed you. I saw you, standing in the long grass, staring at us. I was so relieved you were safe I almost cried. I saw the horror written on your face before you vanished."

My face burned with humiliation under Anna's fixed regard.

"The first time I screamed for you because I thought you were dead. The second time was for help. I was captured by then. You lifted your head above the grass. Like that." She pointed to a small animal whose head was stuck partially out of a hole, its big eyes warily watching us pass. Anna flinched toward the animal and it shot back into its hole.

"I couldn't have done anything," I said, ashamed at the plaintive note in my voice.

"I know," Anna said with surprise. "You would have been surely killed, like the other women. You survived, though. That's what matters."

❧

The plains dropped off suddenly into the largest canyon I had ever seen. Sheer walls of brightly colored red rock protected the verdant trees and grasses covering the valley. A fast-flowing muddy river, the progenitor of this wonder, snaked along the canyon floor. Compared to the landscape we had left, it was a paradise.

I helped Anna make our camp, despite my broken fingers. I

refused to complain, determined to do what was asked of me, and try to stay alive.

I walked to the river to get water. I knelt by the riverbank and stared at my hands. The broken fingers were swollen with fluid, tender and bruised. If I lived, I would have to rebreak them once the swelling went down if I wanted to ever have use of them again. I dunked them in the water. At the touch of the cool water, memories threatened to wake. I jerked my hands from the river and stood.

Children played while the women made repeated trips for water. A group of naked young men—too old to be children but too young to be warriors—jumped off a large rock into the water. Girls watched from the other side of the bank and laughed at the boys, devoid of embarrassment at their nakedness.

I lifted my skirt and removed my petticoat. It was a pointless garment, even more so when living with a band of Indians clothed in animal skins. Besides, I needed the cloth to bind my injured fingers.

I was searching for the easiest place to start a tear when I saw the bloodstain. *Bloodstain* is too simple a word. It looked like an artist's paint board, blots of blood smeared around and together. Some areas were lighter than others, the material stiff and unyielding. I stood next to the river, puzzling it over. My mind refused to comprehend what I saw. A young Indian whooped and splashed into the river, unleashing a torrent of memories I would spend the rest of my life trying to banish.

A muddy riverbank.

Cool water lapping rhythmically against my side.

The grunts of the Indians as they raped me.

Darkness, stars overhead, a few moments' peace.

Until they returned.

I dropped to my knees on the bank of the river and cried, silently, clutching the petticoat. The children around me stopped playing.

That's how Anna found me. I held out the petticoat to her. "Can you help me? I can't tear it."

She knelt down beside me, took the petticoat and tore it into strips. When she saw the dried blood and semen she paused briefly, before moving on to a cleaner part. When the strips were torn she asked, "What do I do?"

Gently, under my disjointed directions, she wrapped my broken fingers together and placed my hands in my lap. She dipped a larger piece of the petticoat in the river and cleaned my face. Tears flowed down my cheeks.

"Please forgive me," I sobbed.

Anna shook her head. "Shhh. You're going to be fine," she whispered. She rubbed the cool cloth on my wrists. "My mother used to do that. Isn't it refreshing?"

Your cool hand, it's comforting.

I wept harder at the memory of Kindle. If I survived and somehow escaped or was ransomed, there would be no future with Kindle. Any chance of happiness had vanished on the bank of the river.

"Come on." She helped me stand. "You have to carry a bucket in case Yahne Muea sees you."

I held a bucket in the crook of my right arm and followed. Yahne Muea did see us and was not happy. We were placing the buckets down by the tepee when she stalked up, screaming. Anna gently pushed me inside. "Lie down," she said, and closed the flap.

I moved far away from the door, lay down facing the wall, and curled into a ball. Through the walls of the tepee I could hear the muffled sound of Anna and Yahne Muea arguing, one in English, the other in Comanche. Soon, a deep voice joined in. I wondered at the fact the male voice spoke English, though broken, and Comanche when the tepee flap opened, amplifying Yahne Muea's diatribe, before falling closed and muffling it again.

I didn't turn.

"What is wrong with her?" the man said. I tensed, wondering what was in store for me. Was I to be punished for not hauling enough water?

"Keep Yahne Muea away from her."

"Why?"

"She delights in beating her. She can't defend herself."

"What is 'delights'?"

"Likes. It makes her happy."

"She is my first wife. It is enough she does not beat you."

Anna's voice dropped so I could not hear the rest of their conversation. A rustling sound was followed by the unmistakable sounds of Anna buying my safety.

I squeezed my eyes shut and curled tighter into myself, trying to block out the sound of pure selflessness. I stayed that way after the man left, after Anna checked on me. I didn't move nor was I disturbed for the rest of the night. I didn't sleep or think. I stared at the wall of the tent in front of me as silent tears flowed without pause from my eyes.

That's how the bounty hunter found me the next day.

CHAPTER
28

How's your arm?"

The bounty hunter smiled and stared at the knife wound I had bound almost two weeks before. "Excellent. Think you can take my stitches out?"

"Hand me a knife."

"I don't think so."

He sat across the fire from me, eating strips of cooked buffalo meat and drinking whisky. Outside, the Indians were celebrating his arrival by drinking the whisky and firing the rifles he'd brought in payment for me. It sounded not dissimilar to the frontier celebrations I'd heard before, proving drunk men behaved the same regardless of their language or enlightenment.

The bounty hunter ate his meal and stared at me with calculating eyes. His hair was flattened with sweat from his hat to right above his ears, where it fell in soft waves onto his shoulders. A line of white skin showed around the edge of his new beard. His clothes, though dusty from the trail, were in much better condition than one would expect from a bounty hunter. He was not a fop, but he cared about how he looked.

"You ride a gray horse, don't you?"

"Used to. I gave it to Quanah to entice him to kidnap you."
He smiled. "You remember. What gave me away?"

"Your eyes." They stared at me across the fire as they had
across Lost Creek. "I can't believe I didn't recognize you when
you came to get treated."

"Being a chameleon comes with the territory. Eat."

"No."

"It won't do you any good to defy me."

"My jaw is sore from being kicked in the face."

He finished his meal, wiped his mouth with his hand, and
rubbed it over his beard to make sure he hadn't missed anything.
He smacked his lips. "Yeah, sorry about that. I didn't want
them to beat you. But, you did shoot Blue Bear."

His casual acceptance of my abuse should have shocked me
but it didn't. Every human emotion—anger, love, fear, and
surprise—had leaked out of me the night before. There was
only one thing I wanted and the bounty hunter was the only
person who could give it to me.

"Was raping me part of the plan?"

"Goes with the territory."

"I refuse to believe men do the things they do for no reason
other than they can."

"After all you've been through, you have such faith in
humanity?"

"Humanity is irredeemable. We will always make bad decisions and do awful things to each other. We'll never change.
However, there is always a reason behind the things we do.
I'm not going to spar with you. Turn me in for the reward or
kill me."

He looked genuinely perplexed. "Turn you in for the
reward?"

"Aren't you a bounty hunter?"

He laughed. "I've been known to collect a bounty or two, but no, I'm not here to turn you in. Or kill you. If things go right I'll take you to Timberline, Colorado, myself."

"How did you know about Timberline?"

"Like everything else, information has a price."

"Meaning, what? You paid for the information or I'll have to pay to know?"

"Either. Both." He stood. The walls of the tepee closed around us. "Enough talk. We need to go."

"Where are we going?"

"You do ask a lot of questions for a captive. Thought they'd rape the fight out of you."

"Apparently not, though they tried."

He opened the flap of the tepee. The sun blared through the opening onto my face. I raised my hand to block it. A knife glittered in my hand. He paused. "Where'd you get that?"

I nodded to the corner where Anna had unpacked the cooking implements the night before. It had been easy to sneak a knife away when I was left alone in the tent. I did it without thinking, without a plan. I lay, curled, cradling the knife to my chest with my bandaged hand. As the cold metal warmed on my skin I came back to myself. My mind cleared, my resolve hardened.

The man smirked. "You do look like hell, Catherine. What do you think you're gonna do? Kill me?"

"No." I placed the knife on my neck, under my ear. "Myself."

He paused. "Why?"

"Why would I want to live?" He didn't answer and I continued. "I will be hanged if I return to New York. My profession is lost to me. Everyone I love is dead."

"Everyone?"

I struggled to maintain my composure as I thought of Kindle. Would he want me now that I'd been violated by Indians? Did his honor extend that far? I pushed Kindle from my mind. If this man thought I had something or someone to lose he would not take my threat seriously.

"I have nothing to go back to and nothing to go toward."

"Is that so? Billy will be so disappointed."

A knot of dread formed in my stomach. "Billy?"

"A childhood name. You know him as Captain William Kindle." The man straightened and saluted.

The knife at my throat dropped a little.

Anna ducked into the tepee. "Laura—" The bounty hunter had her in his arms with a knife to her throat before I could warn her. He kicked the tepee wall, dislodging the buffalo hide door and throwing us into a firelit darkness.

The orange flames danced on his face and I finally saw the resemblance. The nose. The tall forehead. The beard was a better disguise than I would have ever thought. The shape and color of the eyes were the same but where Kindle's were full of compassion, humor, and sadness, this man's were glittering with hatred and retribution.

"You're Cotter Black."

"Throw the knife into the fire or I kill her."

Anna's eyes were wide with confusion and fear. I threw the knife down.

Black looked disappointed. "That was easy." He stood behind Anna, his arm around her waist, and the knife still at her throat. Black turned and buried his face in her neck. "That fucking grease they put in your hair stinks. But, I can look past it." His hand moved to her breast, squeezed it roughly. Anna's face went blank.

359

"Stop it," I said.

"You don't want to watch?"

"Go ahead," Anna said. "Quanah will be here soon. I would love to see him kill you for raping me."

Black laughed and kept squeezing her breast. "Quanah wouldn't kill me. He needs my guns more than he needs a white whore. He would probably give you to me if I asked."

"Ask," I said.

"What?" Anna and Black asked it at the same time.

"Bring Anna with us."

"I don't need her."

"That's my price."

Black was incredulous. "*Your* price? Since when does a captive get to make demands?"

"You've gone through a lot of trouble to kidnap me, which means my life is more important to you than it is to me."

"You have no weapon."

"What are burned fingers to a dead woman?"

I glanced at Anna and saw a glimmer of hope on her face at the prospect of freedom. I reached for the knife.

"Don't," Black said. "I can't stand the smell of burning flesh. I'll get you a fresh knife if you're so desperate to kill yourself."

"I will do anything you want if you bring Anna. Take her to safety."

"Anything?"

I did not hesitate. "Anything. Or I kill myself and your plan goes up in smoke."

"What plan?"

My mind was working, putting together bits of information and theorizing what the purpose of this all was. Too much was still blank, but I was determined to know everything before it was over.

360

"Don't you know your own plan? Not much of a bandit without a plan, are you?"

He pushed Anna away and sheathed his knife. "I've never met a more infuriating woman."

I smiled for the first time in days. "That's exactly what your brother said."

CHAPTER

29

I thought of taking you to a cave," Black said. "Caves are too dark and depressing. Besides, you're going to love this view."

Our horses walked in a straight line down a narrow trail. With the Comanche's help, Black had tied us to our mounts, with our legs across the horses' shoulders and knotted in front of their chests to keep us from kicking them in the flanks. Black rode in front, leading our horses.

Quanah Parker had not been happy with giving up Anna and drove a much harder bargain than Black expected. By the end of the negotiation, Quanah was satisfied, Yahue Muae was thrilled, and Black's mood was as dark as his chosen name. When he turned from Quanah and saw me, the darkness on his face turned to malicious glee. My stomach turned to water. I knew I would pay a high price later.

Evidently, the thoughts of my impending humiliation and pain put him in a talkative mood. He kept a running commentary of inconsequential subjects for our entire ride.

"Hard to believe this canyon is here, don't you think? Imagine the conquistadors wandering around the Llano Estacado—they named it; did you know that?—when all of a sudden the bottom drops out of the plains and into this beautiful canyon. It isn't as magnificent as the Grand Canyon but it is impressive in its own way."

He turned in his saddle to see us. "Have either of you seen the Grand Canyon?" Our silence didn't deter him. "I suppose not. Well, maybe I'll take you there when this is over, Laura." He winked at me and turned around.

"This is beautiful country. Nothing to the mountains, of course. But these colors take your breath away, especially at sunrise or sunset. Don't you agree, Anna?"

"I haven't given it much thought."

"Haven't you spent time here since your capture? Or are you too busy servicing Quanah to have time for anything else?"

"I didn't know of this canyon's existence until two days ago when we rode into it."

"Ah, spending your time on the plains hunting buffalo? Tell me, did you learn to skin?"

"Yes."

"Excellent! There are plenty of buffalo hunters who will be happy to buy your services."

"That wasn't our deal," I said.

"It was a joke, Catherine."

"More likely a lie."

"I've been called a lot of things but I've never been called a liar. When I say I'm going to do something, I do it."

"Forgive me if I'm slow to trust a conniving, murdering bandit."

Black laughed. "At least you didn't call me a horse thief. That's where I draw the line. I'd kill him first, so taking his horse'd be lootin'. You know all about lootin', don't you Laura?"

"Yes. Your friend Franklin made a fair amount of money off the wreckage of my wagon train."

"But not off you."

"No."

Black turned in his saddle. "You are a bright woman, Catherine. You figured Franklin out, huh?"

"I overheard a conversation between him and Welch. I mistakenly thought the 'he' they were referring to was Foster."

"Foster!" Black attended to his horse as it jumped a deep, narrow, rushing creek. Anna and I grasped our horses' manes and prayed they were as sure-footed as Black's. Anna's stumbled slightly, but she held her seat.

"Foster doesn't graft so much as turn a blind eye," Black continued.

"I see little difference."

Black shook his head. I could hear the humor in his voice when he replied. "It is uncanny how much like Victoria you are."

"Who's Victoria?" Anna asked.

"Billy's wife."

Anna glanced over her shoulder at me.

"Dead wife," Black clarified. "God rest her pious, moralizing, judgmental soul."

"Dr. Elliston is far from pious or judgmental," Anna said.

"Oh, I don't think Catherine has a bit of piety in her. She proved that her last night at Richardson." Black turned in his saddle and sneered. "You two tried to sneak around, to keep it secret. But, I was watching too closely. You want to tell Anna or should I?"

"What Laura did or didn't do doesn't matter to me."

"Her name's Catherine."

"Was Franklin spying on me?" I asked.

"Among others. That night, though, I was watching."

A blush spread over my face and my skin crawled. "I don't believe you. The sentries would've seen you."

"It was a stormy night, or have all the pleasurable remembrances shunted the weather from your mind?" He didn't wait for my answer. "Sentry duty is deplorable in the best weather. In bad weather, they're less than vigilant. But, I would hate for you to think I left the success of my plan to rely on a disinterested sentry. I wore a uniform."

"The same one you wore when I saw you by the stables," I said.

"You noticed me."

"I thought you were a bounty hunter."

"I'm almost insulted," Black laughed.

"Did you kill a soldier to get the uniform?"

"I believe it even still has the bullet hole."

Anna made a disgusted sound.

"Why do you care, Anna? The Army has done nothing to protect you or to find you. They left you to be raped and killed by the Comanche and Kiowa," Black said.

"That's a lie. A patrol searched for you," I said.

"They gave up pretty easy," Black said. "Know where the patrol sent to find you is? Fort Sill." Black turned in his saddle. "They're sure a long way from here, Anna. Sherman will get his pound of flesh from them in the end, but he couldn't care less what happened to you. He cares about saving face. He rode right through the group of Kiowas that took you. Imagine; if he had been paying attention, you might be in Colorado now. With your father."

Black reined his horse around to face us and stopped next to Anna. She looked at him without flinching.

"Catherine's trying to change the subject," Black said. He turned to me. "Or should I call you Laura?"

"I prefer you don't call me anything."

"She loves it when Billy calls her Catherine. She wrapped her legs around him and held on to the edge of the desk for dear life while Billy fucked her. She loved every minute of it."

He kicked his horse forward and stopped next to me. Through my mortification, I met his gaze squarely. He raised his voice in a mocking imitation of mine. "Oh, William! I love you! Ah, ah!" He laughed as my face burned with shame. "I gotta tell you, Catherine, watching you made me hard as a rock. I fucked that little laundress—what's her name? Ruth?—to death after. Of course, no one will ever want to fuck you again after what those Indians did to you on the banks of the Canadian. I bet your snatch is as wide as this canyon."

I closed my eyes and turned my face away. Visions of what had been done to me next to that muddy river invaded my mind. Bile rose in my throat at the thought of being touched again, by any man. I clenched my jaw to keep from screaming against the realization it mattered little if Kindle wanted me, I would never want him.

I opened my eyes and glared at Kindle's brother. "I'm going to kill you."

Black smiled. "I'd be disappointed if you didn't try."

"Who's buried next to your father?"

Black raised his eyebrows. "Billy's told you about our family history?"

"A little."

"I doubt it resembled the truth." Black folded his hands on his saddle horn as if settling in for a long tale. "Being a Confederate officer, I was at Johnson's Island, a rather nice camp, compared to some. The poor fellow buried next to my father was a soldier who had the bad fortune to look a bit like me. He died, an unfortunate accident, and I dressed him in my clothes. I had to pretend to be an enlisted man for the remainder of the time. The rations weren't as good but I was saved having to perform in the officer's production of *The Taming of the Shrew.* Small price to pay."

"Why would you want to be dead?" Anna said.

"There was nothing left for me in Maryland."

"What about your children?" I asked.

"Too young to be of use."

The urge to strike out at the smug, arrogant bastard in the only way I could was too great. "Who's to say they're your children? Beau's resemblance to William is striking."

The self-assured arrogance melted from Black's face. The flare of satisfaction in my breast was short-lived. His hand was around my throat, squeezing. "Did I hit a nerve?" I croaked. I tried to smile in hopes of infuriating him even more.

"If Franklin has done his job, Billy is well on his way here. Your dead body will do as well as your live one. As long as Billy knows you died by my hand, I get the same result. I have a witness now, thanks to your cleverness."

He continued to squeeze my throat, cutting off the possibility of breath as well as speech. The edges of my vision darkened and my face burned. I grasped at his hands, forgetting mine were tied, useless. When I thought I was going to lose consciousness, his grip relaxed, but didn't release. He looked at me as if I was a fascinating science experiment. "You know I can shut you up forever, don't you?"

I tried to nod but couldn't.

"Please, don't hurt her," Anna pleaded.

"How sweet," Black replied. His eyes stayed on me. "It would be perfect. If I know Billy, he loves you as much for your mind as for your body. He's a big talker, our Billy. Did you two have deep, meaningful conversations?"

I shook my head no, still struggling for air.

"You didn't? How disappointing. I'm sure it wasn't for his lack of trying."

"I...woch..." Black loosened his grip enough so I could talk. "Please. I won't say another word. I promise."

He grabbed the back of my neck with his free hand and released my throat. I gasped for air. "If you hadn't begged me, I would have left you alone." His lip curled into a cruel smile, and he punched me in the throat.

I doubled over in pain and gagged. Panic rushed through me as I struggled to breathe. The seconds I couldn't catch my breath seemed like hours. Black watched my agony through narrowed eyes. Finally, air filled my lungs.

"Laura?" Anna said, crying.

"She won't answer you," Black said. "Keep your mouth shut unless you want the same thing to happen to you."

⤬

We crossed a shallow creek and stopped at a stand of trees that went up a hill. Black untied me from my horse first, rightly assuming I would be as docile as a baby. He left our hands bound, looped the remaining ropes around our waists, and then tied me to Anna.

The narrow trail rose sharply between scrubby trees. Lizards, snakes, and field mice scuttled away as we picked our way up the rocky trail and around flowering cacti. The floor of the canyon was the same brilliant red of the walls and soon the dust was floating around us, getting in our eyes and choking our throats. My cough came out as a gag.

Without warning we were out of the undergrowth and at the base of a large rock formation. Two columns topped by boulders nearly ready to topple flanked a flat table of red rock. It looked like crumbling battlements of an abandoned castle.

The final climb was the most difficult, diagonally up the steep side of the rock. Anna slipped and fell face-first. Black continued on, dragging her, as Anna struggled up without use of her hands. I tried to help her, but she fell again. Black didn't stop. I tried to yell at him but only a raspy croak came out.

"Oh! Did you say something?" He stopped and smirked while Anna got to her feet. We continued on the final few yards.

The view was spectacular. The canyon spread out before us, a green carpet of trees in the river valley topped with the vibrant reds and golds of the rock against the canvas of a bright blue sky. I took no pleasure in the beauty around me. I knew it was God's way of masking the darkness underneath. Nothing so beautiful could ever be trusted.

Black untied Anna from me and sat her against a small jut of rock about halfway between the two looming columns. He retied her hands and feet and stayed squatted beside her. "I'm not going to have to gag you, am I?"

She shook her head no.

Black pushed a piece of Anna's hair behind her ear. She didn't move or flinch. "You're the same age as my daughter, or thereabouts," Black said, voice tender. "I haven't seen her since she was a child, but I bet she looks like you. Blond hair, blue eyes. It's a damn shame what they did to you." He sighed.

"You're lucky, you know. I knew a girl like you, not as pretty, who had her nose cut off. One look at her and you know what she went through. In time, you'll look like any other young woman." With a fatherly pat on Anna's knee, Black stood. "You look like a smart girl. Behave and don't get in the way and I will take you to Jacksboro, give you some money to start a new life. Would you like that?"

Anna nodded. "Yes." Her voice cracked. "Thank you."

Black faced me. It was the most difficult act I ever performed, but I steadily returned his gaze. He could do whatever he wanted to me, make me do whatever he wanted, but I refused to let him think I was cowed by him. I had no voice, and no strength, but I still had my mind and my pride.

One side of his mouth crooked up the same way Kindle's did. A wave of sadness, regret, and love almost overwhelmed my resolve. My face remained passive, though, while my heart broke beneath the weight of lost possibilities.

"I can see why Billy loves you," Black said. He laughed at my reaction. "I can see all the questions colliding in your head, struggling to break free. Thank God I'll be spared that."

He scanned the horizon with a shiny brass spyglass. "You look nothing like Victoria but in demeanor you're cut from the same cloth." He paused. I followed the direction of his gaze and saw nothing but trees and scrub. "My guess is she wasn't nearly as good a fuck as you are. She was too godly to be good in the bedroom. Hell, maybe Billy's fucked enough whores in the last few years he's gotten better at it. Who knows?" Black collapsed the spyglass and put it back in his saddlebag.

"Victoria, though, she was too busy saving the niggers from slavery to give Billy much attention. Oh, I'm sure he played the grieving husband to the hilt, but I doubt the loss of Victoria was too profound. I'm sure Billy told you all about Victoria."

I stood with my hands tied in front of me and stared straight ahead. Black's physical resemblance to Kindle was too keen. Black moved forward, his face inches from mine.

"You mean to tell me Billy was able to seduce you without telling you anything about himself?"

I shrugged my shoulders.

"Did he tell you how he got his scar? A pack of lies, no doubt. Billy always was good at making himself look like the good guy, like he's completely blameless."

Black removed a gun from his holster and checked his ammunition. "I've been leaving little clues for Billy for a while."

"Such as?" Anna asked. Her voice was animated, almost giddy, most like at the idea of freedom Black planted in her head. Or possibly she was merely adapting to the situation to survive, much as she had done with the Comanche.

Black loaded his gun. "Cotter Black was the name of a slave on our plantation. This was back in about forty-seven. Billy was twelve. Cotter Black escaped with Billy's help. I let Cotter get far enough away to make the chase fun and told my father. My father tracked Cotter down and brought him back. He beat him with his cane in front of everyone, slave and family alike. He made Billy deliver the final blows."

"You brother sounds like a brave and stupid child," Anna said.

I stared at buzzards circling the canyon floor a half mile away and nodded in appreciation. Anna would be fine.

"More stupid than brave." Black snapped the cylinder into the gun and holstered it.

"Cotter got what he deserved. So did Billy. He never helped another slave, that's for goddamn sure. I knew when Billy heard the name he would wonder if it was me, come to seek my revenge."

"Revenge for what?" Anna asked. "The war?"

Black removed the other gun and checked it, ignoring her question.

"Who's Franklin?" Anna tried.

"The sutler at Fort Richardson. That's not his real name.

Loyal as a dog. I spared his life when I attacked his Army supply train. Nabbed a nice supply of Winchesters. They paid your ransom, Catherine.

"Franklin ran our malingering scam with Welch, among other things. Not a great moneymaker, but for a man like Welch it was enough. We needed Welch to get information Franklin couldn't. When you came along, Catherine, he wasn't useful anymore. Beating him with a cane was for Billy's benefit."

Which is why Kindle had Sergeant Washington guarding me.

He holstered his other gun. "The day you saw me across the creek, Catherine, I was looking for you. It's true. Welch told me about the sawbones who saved Billy's life and I had to see you for myself. A woman doctor. You don't get to see one of those every day."

He circled me, slowly, coming closer and closer with each turn. "You were a revelation, Catherine. Much too handsome to be a doctor." He ran his hand down my arm. I shivered in disgust.

"A woman like you, alone on the frontier. It was plain from a hundred yards away you were raised to be a lady, marry some fat businessman, and have a houseful of kids before you're thirty." He stopped behind me and put an arm around my waist. His breath was sour, rancid, as if he was rotting from the inside. He pulled me back against him. I closed my eyes to block out the sensation of his body against mine.

"I wondered if my luck would change," Black murmured in my ear. "If Billy would finally reveal a little weakness. I've followed Billy across the West, waiting for a sign. Waiting for you." I heard the scrape of metal on leather and felt the cold steel of a knife on my cheek. I inhaled a shaky breath. Urine trickled down the inside of my leg.

"When I heard you accused Foster of grafting..." Black

nuzzled my ear. "I knew you would be my brother's type. And I was right."

My jaws ached from grinding my teeth together against crying or screaming. Every breath was jagged with the effort to control my emotions. If I'd kept my distance from Kindle as I had intended, none of us would be here. Black wouldn't be able to use me as bait for whatever revenge he had planned for his brother.

I looked at Anna. But she would still be a captive. I took a steadying breath and thought of Anna's future, the one thing worth salvaging. She could move past this, have a normal, long, happy life. If I did what Black asked, he would take her to Jacksboro. Despite everything, I believed him.

"I've been on enough Wanted posters to ascertain what Pope showed you that day. You don't have as good a poker face as you think you do, darlin'. I had a pang of conscience about putting Pope out of commission like I did. He's only guilty of being a bad gambler and borderline drunk. Anyone in his position would have turned you in. It was harder than I thought, but worth it when I saw you and Billy on the road to Jacksboro." Black's hand found my breast. I squeezed my eyes shut as he fondled me.

He traced the edge of my jaw with his knife. "I have a surprise for you. Do you like surprises?"

I didn't know what answer he wanted so I remained silent and didn't move.

"I watched the Comanche raid your patrol. When they rode away, I finished the lingering soldiers off." Black pressed the metal against my bottom lip and pulled it down. "I also saved a couple of things for you. Things you will need to start your new life." Black stepped in front of me. "Sherman's letter and a beautiful necklace."

I inhaled sharply and tried to keep my expression passive. Black grinned, knowing he had stunned me.

"When I found my father alone," Black said, "lying in his own shit before Antietam, he made me promise to make Billy pay for betraying and destroying our family. I'm sorry I didn't kill Billy then. If I would've, you wouldn't be here now. The Canadian would have never happened. I can't change that, but I will keep my word to you, and Anna, as I've kept my word to my father." Black's eyes searched my face and lingered on my lips. "Will you keep your word?"

Fear gripped my stomach and twisted, but I nodded once.

Black stepped closer and put a hand behind my neck. His other hand held the knife. "Kiss me."

I tried to pull away, but he held my head firm. The sun sat above his right shoulder, shining in my eyes and turning him into a looming shadow. Though I couldn't see her, I knew Anna watched and waited, wondering what I would do. I thought of her giving herself to Quanah to ensure my protection, and swallowing my disgust, lifted my mouth to Black. I pressed my lips to his and pulled back. He twisted my hair in his hand. "You have to do better than that." The tip of his knife bit into my throat. I pressed my throat against the blade. I would rather die than kiss Cotter Black like a lover. He pulled the knife away, and I spit in his face.

He wiped away the spit and flicked it on the ground.

"You've got spirit, I'll give you that," he said, with a chuckle. He flipped the knife around, and for a split second, I thought he was going to stab me. Instead, he hit me with his closed fist.

I grunted but did not scream or cry. Blood trickled down my cheek. I wiped it off with my hand and stared at it there before smearing it down the front of Black's shirt. He hit me

SAWBONES

again. My legs wobbled, but Black held me up by my neck, like a puppet.

"Do you think I'm going to rape you?"

I nodded.

"No," he said, his voice full of pity. With light fingers, Black brushed my hair from my face. "You're tainted now, Catherine. I wish it wasn't so, but it is." Black pulled my head to the side, exposing my neck, and kissed me softly behind my ear in the exact place his brother favored. I squeezed my eyes closed as memories of Kindle flashed through my hazy mind. "I'm sorry for what happened on the Canadian," Black said, and I heard the timbre of Kindle's low, intimate voice. Black trailed kisses down my neck and back up to my cheek before resting his soft, bearded cheek against mine. "You didn't deserve it. It's a damn shame, a passionate woman like you being ruined like that."

Black released my hair. "Look at me, Catherine." I opened my eyes. Black looked on me with Kindle's eyes. He squeezed the back of my neck gently, as if massaging a kink from sore muscles. "You'll never kiss another man. My brother's nobility? It's an act. He may stay by you, but he'll never touch you again."

I shuddered with the effort to keep from crying aloud. My tears flowed too freely and quickly for the gusting wind to dry them. The sense of numb hopelessness that overcame me after the massacre returned. I thought back to the image of Death riding toward me and wished, again, he had succeeded.

"Shh, don't cry." Black kissed my cheek and the corner of my mouth. "I'm giving you a gift," he whispered, his lips against mine, his hand stroking my hair. "A chance to forget everything you've been through. To let you be loved one last time." When I didn't respond, his voice turned hard. "And, you made a deal. If you break it, I will sell you and Anna to the worst batch of buffalo hunters I can find."

Black lifted my chin with the blade of his knife. "Think of my brother, if it makes it easier."

Sobbing, I kissed him. His lips were soft, pliant, gentle, like his brother's. I turned my head away, my shoulders shaking from weeping. The cold metal of the knife pressed against my cheek as Black turned my face back to him.

"Catherine," he said, his voice low and seductive. He pressed his lips against mine, opened his mouth, and waited for me to deepen the kiss. Swallowing my helpless shame, I let him have his fill, participating enough to hopefully satisfy whatever desire he had, and longed for Kindle. After a time, Black pulled away. I kept my eyes closed, wanting to keep it inside, buried deep, hidden from the realization of what I'd done, and tried to focus on subduing my shaking body, and stifling my sobs. When I had control of myself, I opened my eyes. The wind hit my tear-filled eyes, blurring my vision further. I blinked the tears away and saw Black staring at me in smug triumph. "A goddamn shame."

I lifted my hands and tried to scrub the lingering feel of Black's lips from my mouth. "It'll take more than that to forget me, Catherine." I turned my head away and spit.

His stare shifted over my shoulder, and his face relaxed in relief. "Don't worry." He winked, keeping his eyes on the trailhead behind me. "I won't tell Billy how much you liked it."

He grabbed my shoulder and turned me around. His hand was in my hair and his knife was at my neck again before I registered what I saw.

Kindle stood at the top of the trail, his rifle nocked in his shoulder, his eye trained down the barrel at us. I trembled with relief and humiliation at the sight of him. I could still feel Black's lips on mine, his tongue in my mouth.

"John, let her go!" Kindle yelled over the wind.

"Soon, little brother," Black called.

Kindle took two quick steps forward, his limp noticeable. I reached toward Kindle, but Black held me fast by my hair.

"You just have one more thing to do," Black said in my ear. Black readjusted the knife, pressing the tip hard against my neck. I could hear the smile in his voice.

"You have to kill my brother."

CHAPTER

30

I screamed and shook my head and the sobs returned.

Kindle limped slowly forward, still sighting down the barrel of his rifle at us. "Let her go, John, or I'll put a bullet in your head."

Black pressed his cheek against mine. My body shielded everything but Black's head from Kindle's shot. I felt my hair rip from its roots as Black twisted his fist harder, holding me in place. "You and I both know you aren't that good a shot," Cotter Black laughed.

"You sure about that?"

"Take the shot."

Shoot him and end this, please.

I tried to twist away from Black but couldn't. He chuckled in my ear. "He won't shoot. He loves you too much."

Kindle gripped his rifle and moved another step closer but didn't shoot.

"Drop the rifle over the edge of the cliff," Black called out.

"So you can kill us all? I don't think so."

"I don't want to hurt Catherine, but I will." Black jerked the hand holding the knife. The blade sliced through my neck, followed by the sharp pain of the cut. I gasped and raised my bound hands to my neck. They came away bloody. "It's merely a scratch," Black said, voice low. My reaction and the blood had the desired effect on Kindle.

"Goddamn you, John," Kindle said. He threw his rifle over the edge and held his hands up. "Now, stop hiding behind a woman and fight me like a man."

No, I thought, the second before Black pushed me away toward Anna. I stumbled and fell onto the hard rock ground. With Kindle's leg and shoulder wounds, he wouldn't have a chance against Black. On my bound hands and knees, I looked up in time to see Black sheathe his knife and the brothers run at each other. Just before Kindle was in arm's reach, Black dropped to one knee and punched Kindle in his wounded thigh. Kindle screamed and fell. Black rose and drove his fist up under Kindle's descending jaw. Kindle flew backward and landed on his back.

Black turned away from Kindle and walked a couple of steps toward me and Anna, an amused expression on his face. "I'm sorry he isn't much of a knight in shining armor, Catherine. You deserve better." I kept my gaze squarely on Black and watched Kindle rise behind him in my peripheral vision. Kindle's hair was tousled, his clenched jaw was dusted with the stubble of days-old beard, and his eyes were full of murderous rage. I couldn't help myself; I grinned. Black stopped and turned, and met Kindle's fist squarely. Black stumbled backward, regained his feet, and went for his brother.

Anna was beside me. With fumbling hands, she worked at loosening the ropes that bound my hands together. I did the same for her to the sound of grunts and thuds of hits, the crunch of bone and the scrape of boots on rock. My hands free, I looked up. Kindle had Black around the neck with one arm and punched him in the face with the other, repeatedly. Black's boots scrabbled at the ground, but eventually went limp, as did his entire body. Kindle dropped his brother to the ground in a heap. Kindle kicked Black in the stomach five, six times, and finished the beating with a kick to Black's face. Kindle stood over him, chest heaving, his knuckles bloody and bruised, his clothes covered in red dust. Kindle nudged his brother with his boot. Black didn't respond. I stood on shaky legs and helped Anna stand.

Mechanically, Kindle removed his gun from his holster and pointed it at his brother's head. His white shirt was covered with red dust and droplets of blood, his and his brother's. With a loud screech a buzzard flew a few feet above Kindle, startling him. When he noticed us huddling together, the viciousness in his eyes evaporated. He holstered his gun and limped to me.

"Catherine!"

He held out his arms as if he wanted to hold me but was too terrified to try. "My God, Catherine. What did he do to you?"

How I wanted to talk, to tell him how sorry I was and how much I loved him. When I tried, all that came out was a hoarse, painful "Ahh."

Anna said, "He punched her in the throat."

Kindle found my damaged hands, paused as he realized what it meant for my future as a doctor, and lifted them to his lips. "I love you."

I smiled and nodded through my tears—tears of shame and fear, relief and joy—and hoped Kindle understood. I knew Kindle would get us out of here, would keep me from having to choose.

"Can you walk?"

"Yes," Anna replied. Tears had created streaks of pale skin amid the red dust covering our faces.

With great care, Kindle put his arm around my waist and half-carried me across the table of the rock formation. We were almost to the trail leading down the side of the cliff when Black called out. He stood crookedly, gun aimed at the three of us.

"You should have killed me when you had the chance, Billy." Kindle tensed. "Go. Someone is waiting halfway down."

He turned to Cotter Black. "I should have killed you at Antietam. I'm gonna kill you here and leave your bones to bleach in the sun." He walked toward his brother. Anna tried to lead me away. I wrenched my arm from her grasp. I pointed down the trail and mouthed, "Go," before pushing her away. I turned and followed Kindle at a distance.

"You gonna shoot me with my gun?" Black said. He nodded to Kindle's holster. "Can't believe you're still carrying it. Does that mean you've missed me?"

Kindle glanced down at his holstered gun. "I always liked your gun better than I liked you."

"Take it off and drop it on the ground."

"No." They walked around each other, prey ready to strike, waiting on the perfect time.

"He couldn't kill me back at Antietam, Catherine. Probably thought I would die in prison, save him the guilt of killing me himself." I couldn't see Kindle's reaction, but the grin on Black's face told me he'd hit a nerve. Black flinched forward, as if pouncing, before pulling back. Kindle balked, but regained his composure.

"I got the better end of that fight. Your scar looks good, Billy. Gives you an edge of danger you never had before. I bet the whores *love* the scar." Black did his best courtly bow. "You're welcome."

Black had succeeded in walking Kindle around so he stood between us and Kindle. Kindle stood on the edge of the plateau, alone and vulnerable, halfway between the two columns of balanced rock.

"Catherine, come here or I will kill him right now."

The wind whipped around us, almost deafening in its intensity. I didn't move. Black turned his head toward me but kept his eyes, and gun, on Kindle. "Catherine." His voice held a note of warning. "Remember what I said to you; I keep my promises. It's time for you to keep yours."

I started forward. "Not you, Anna. You stay right there." I looked over my shoulder and saw Anna standing a few feet behind me. *Stupid girl. Save yourself and us. Go down and get help.*

"You've been a good girl so far, Anna," Black said. "None of this is your fight. Remember that and you'll make it to Jacksboro alive. Lie down on your stomach."

Anna looked at me while she obeyed, her expression a pained combination of hope at being taken to safety and regret she hadn't left like Kindle and I ordered. I gave her an encouraging smile at odds with the fear in my breast and turned toward Black.

"On your knees, William," Black said.

Black held his gun on Kindle as he knelt, and motioned for me to come closer. Black's eyes glittered in anticipation as I made my way slowly toward the two brothers. When I was ten feet away, Black stepped forward and kicked Kindle in his wounded thigh. When Kindle doubled over in pain, Black hit him in his wounded shoulder. Kindle screamed and fell to the ground. I rushed forward and grabbed Black's arm as he hit Kindle across the face with the butt of his gun, taking some of the force from the blow, but not enough to keep Kindle's scar from opening.

With a growl of anger, Black punched me on the wounded side of my head. I fell to my hands and knees. The ground pitched and rolled beneath me. Kindle reached his hand out to me and I crawled to him.

"How touching." Black grabbed me by the hair and yanked me to my feet before my hand could reach Kindle. I screamed and grabbed at Black's hands to stop the pain. Black pressed the gun to the top of my head and I stilled. Through my blurred vision I saw Kindle push himself to a kneeling position. He sat back on his heels to steady himself and glared at his brother with a deep and abiding hatred. He spat blood onto the ground, the red of the blood blending with the red of the dust and rocks around us.

In that instant, Black's plan became clear; the last thing Kindle would see was the woman he loved betraying him, as Emma had betrayed John Kindle. I would win Anna's freedom, and have to somehow live with what I'd done.

No.

The bastard was going to have to earn his revenge. I struggled to get away from Black, and punched him as hard as I could in the ribs while stomping on his foot.

"Goddammit, woman." He pushed my head down and lifted his leg. My nose met his knee with a sickening crunch and he threw me back onto the ground. Pinpricks of light danced at the edge of my darkening vision. "You're making this much harder than it needs to be."

Kindle lunged forward weakly, holding the knife from his boot. Black grabbed Kindle's wrist and bent it back. Kindle screamed as the knife fell uselessly from his grip. Black punched Kindle repeatedly in the side of the head, and Kindle crumpled to the ground.

Black picked the knife up and threw it over the edge of the cliff. "Jesus Christ, you two are determined. Don't even think about it." Black pointed the gun in Anna's direction. Anna had pushed herself halfway up. She lay back down.

Lying on my side I watched through half-open eyes as Black

grabbed Kindle's leg and dragged him on his back toward the discarded saddlebags. He pulled out a strip of leather, jerked Kindle to his knees, and tied his hands behind his back.

Kindle mumbled something. Black removed Kindle's gun from its holster and tossed it aside. "What?" Black said.

"Incorrigible," Kindle said. His eyes found mine, and despite his pain, he managed to grin at me. "We're incorrigible."

Black pressed his gun to the middle of Kindle's forehead. "Take a long, last look at your lover, Billy. I knew you'd come to rescue her. Just like you tried to rescue Cotter Black. And my wife, who didn't need rescuing."

"She begged me to help her get away from you, from our father." Kindle was slumped forward and spoke in a resigned voice, as if he'd had this conversation before.

"Lies. Enough about Emma. She's dead because of you." Black jerked his head in my direction. "Go on. Look what you've done to her." Kindle's gaze settled on me. Black continued. "The Comanche, they weren't supposed to fuck her. But, she got a shot off during the attack, hit one of them in the leg. There's nothing worse than an angry Indian. They spent a day on the banks of the Canadian, taking turns with her." Kindle looked away, disgust clear on his face. I closed my eyes, hoping to evaporate, to disappear.

"Father?"

Beau Kindle stood at the trailhead behind us. I pushed myself into a kneeling position and slowly rose.

Black squinted. "Beau? You were supposed to come alone, William."

"Blame Franklin. He wasn't as sneaky as he should have been. Beau overheard our conversation and insisted on coming." Though I was directly in front of him, Kindle looked everywhere but me.

"I thought you were dead," Beau said, in a voice that sounded achingly young.

I turned away from the family reunion. Beneath me, the blood-splattered ground of Palo Duro Canyon swayed like the deck of a ship on a stormy ocean. I held my hand out toward the horizon, a beautiful, cloudless blue against the red canyon, and walked toward the edge of the cliff. The wind pushed against me, blew dust into my face and eyes, replacing the nature's beauty with the memory of Kindle's expression of disgust.

"Catherine, come here." I looked over my shoulder. Black motioned to me with the gun.

Beau stepped forward, and with nervous resolve said, "Father, this is wrong. Let them go."

Black sighed. "I should have known you'd be weak like your mother." In a quick, fluid motion, Black turned the gun from Kindle's head, aimed at Anna, and shot. The ground next to Anna's head exploded and she screamed. Kindle flinched, but Black held the gun to his head before he could move.

"Take off your holster and throw it over the edge, Beau." When Beau didn't move Black said, "Next time, I won't miss."

Beau did as ordered.

"Now, lay down on your stomach." Beau complied.

I faced the brothers. Kindle stared at the ground, unwilling or unable to meet my gaze. Not taking his eyes from Beau, Black said, "Catherine, come here." I walked to Black, who removed his extra gun and handed it to me. It was heavy in my hand.

Black moved behind me and whispered, "You know what you have to do. You and Anna will get your lives back." Black stood close behind me and pointed his gun at Anna. She would be dead before I would be able to turn around and shoot him.

Kindle's head rose slowly, and he finally met my gaze. Kindle's beautiful face was a mask of blood, bruises. Shame. Guilt.

Pity. Regret. I lifted the gun and pointed it at him. His eyes widened.

"Dr. Elliston, don't!" Beau said.

"Shut up, Beau," Black yelled.

The wind flowed around me, silencing everything. Black screamed in my ear to pull the trigger. Anna was sobbing, her eyes closed, her face bathed in tears. Kindle knelt before me in utter defeat. Blood dripped from a cut above his eye. Lips that had gently kissed my breast were split, swollen, and bloody.

I dropped my arm and closed my eyes and thought of our last night together. I heard Kindle whispering how much he loved me, promises of a happy life and home, a soft bed to share and make love on until we were old and gray. A dream lost to us. I tried to look forward and see a future. All I saw was pity and shame, guilt and misery. I focused on the love I'd discovered with Kindle, an emotion I never expected to be blessed with, and was grateful. I opened my eyes.

I only saw Kindle. He spoke but the wind carried his voice far away. I watched his lips move, telling me he loved me as his head moved slightly from side to side. I lifted the gun with my uninjured hand and looked down the barrel at Kindle's eyes. Tears flooded my own, blurring his face.

It is easier this way. I can't see him.

"I love you," I mouthed.

I closed my eyes, put the gun to my head, and pulled the trigger.

⚬◯⚬

The sound of the gun's hammer hitting an empty chamber echoed in my head.

I opened my eyes. Kindle's face was red, his mouth open in a dying scream. When he saw I was alive, relief and shock flooded through him and he sat back on his heels, shoulders slumped. I stared at the gun in my hands, wondering what I had done wrong.

The sound of Black's laughter cut through the wind like a saber. "That was even better than I planned. You'd rather die than kill the man you love! God almighty, Billy, this woman here is a keeper!"

Black's laughter died down, but his happiness did not. He grinned like a proud father. "Did you think I would give you a loaded gun after what I've done to you? By the way, Billy, I did fuck her. Most satisfying one I've had in years. The little laundress is a close second but I was thinking of Catherine the whole time so it doesn't count. I know Catherine's much older than my usual type, but maybe I should branch out to dried-up old spinsters."

Kindle stared blankly at the ground. I shook my head, slowly at first, then more furiously. "Nach, nach."

Black holstered his gun, picked up his saddlebag, and slung it over his shoulder. He sauntered back to where Kindle and I were rooted to the ground in defeat.

"I'll take that." He pulled the gun from my hand.

"In case the idea is running through your head you two might still have a life together..." Black leaned down and whispered in Kindle's ear. With the wind whipping around and the distance, I couldn't hear what he said. Black smirked and kept his eyes on mine as he poisoned Kindle against me. Black winked at me, kissed his brother on the temple, and hit him on the back of the head with the empty gun. Kindle crumpled to the ground, unconscious.

My gaze dropped to the ground. The handle of Kindle's forgotten gun peeked out from beneath the hem of my skirt. I shifted so it was completely hidden.

Black stopped next to me. He studied me. "Wonder if Billy's gonna see what you did as an act of love—and faith he'd save Anna and Beau—or as a selfish act by a selfish woman? It's a good question. One y'all can spend the next thirty years pondering. It wasn't exactly the betrayal I wanted, but it'll do. It'll do." He patted my shoulder. "Good luck. You're gonna need it." He walked on.

"Come on, Anna."

"No! You said if Laura did what you asked, you'd let me go."

"But she didn't do what I asked, did she? I know the perfect band of buffalo hunters to sell you to."

I picked up Kindle's gun and turned. Black was walking away, dragging Anna with him. She screamed my name.

Beau stood. "Let her go."

"Laura!"

"Come with me, Beau. Army life isn't for you."

"Let her go," Beau said, his voice trembling. He stepped forward, fists balled.

"Or what, you're going to fight me?" Black said. He shook his head and laughed. "Have a nice life, son."

I walked up behind Black and placed the barrel of Kindle's gun behind his ear. He froze, moved his head slightly to see over his shoulder, and grinned. "Catherine, well, I'll be damned. Billy's a lucky man, and that's a goddamn fact."

I cocked the gun and pressed it harder against Black's head.

"You want me to let her go? Here." He released Anna. She stumbled away toward Beau. Black lifted his hands. "Take her. Her life will be as miserable as yours, regardless." I pushed his head forward in warning.

My arm trembled. I stared at the spot where the gun met Black's head and thought of what was hidden beneath. Of how Black's sadistic mind had planned and plotted revenge against

Kindle for years. How Black had used me to get to his brother, had paid Indians to rape me and abuse me. I squeezed my eyes shut at the memory of what had happened on the Canadian, of Black's kiss. When I opened my eyes my vision was blurry with tears, but where the gun met Black's head was crystal clear.

"If you're gonna do it, do it. But, I don't think you have it—"

I pulled the trigger. Black lunged forward and fell to the ground, face-first.

"No!" Beau yelled.

Arm quivering, I lowered the gun. Blood flowed from Cotter Black's head and soaked into the red dirt. Beau ran to his father and dropped to his knees.

Anna came to me and put her arms around me, squeezing me. "Thank you," she said, her voice cracking. I stared in disbelief at Cotter Black's dead body, my arms too heavy to lift.

Beau looked up at me in shock, revulsion, and anger. "How could you do that?"

Anna released me, but kept an arm around my waist. "Bastard deserved to die," she said.

I turned away and went to Kindle. I placed his head in my lap and felt for injuries. A knot was forming at the base of his skull, the same spot where his brother had hit him at Antietam nine years earlier. I brushed his hair away from his face and waited for him to wake.

Anna came to me, carrying Black's canteen. She tore a strip of cloth from my skirt and soaked it in water. I bathed Kindle's face with it. He slowly came around. A buzzard screeched overhead, eager to start his next meal. Kindle's eyes roamed around in confusion until finally settling on me.

I couldn't bring myself to look at him. The humiliation of what I had been through, the choices I'd made, was too great. I blotted the blood from his face. Gently, Kindle stayed my hand.

"Catherine." His voice was hoarse and raw with emotion. He reached up and turned my face toward his, forcing me to look in his eyes. There I discovered the same kindness as when he had comforted me in the middle of a thunderstorm a lifetime ago. With my broken, bandaged fingers I traced his scar and smiled.

CHAPTER

31

We rode hard for four days, pushing our horses and ourselves to the limit, to reach the safety of Jacksboro.

Little was said. Questions flooded my brain but I couldn't speak to ask them. Neither Kindle nor Beau had paper or pencil and my gestures were more confusing than illuminating.

Kindle tended to my injuries as best he could with no medicine and I did the same with his. His shoulder and thigh wounds were inflamed, his ribs broken, and I suspected his head ached chronically, as did mine. Waves of nausea and dizziness overtook me without warning, making it difficult to keep my seat on my horse. When I vomited nothing came up but bile. I couldn't remember the last meal I had, though the thought of eating made me ill.

Sleep, during our brief nighttime camps, was impossible. One night, when I closed my eyes, I saw Indians standing on the bank of a river, watching, and eagerly waiting their turn, felt their weight pressing me into the hard ground. Smelled their rancid breath, heard their rhythmic grunts, and their cries of release. Strong hands gripped my shoulders, shook me. I screamed and thrashed against them. I opened my eyes and saw Cotter Black looming over me, hands outstretched.

"Please, no! Not again!" I scuttled away, my heart gripped in a vise of fear, sobbing.

"Catherine. It's me." Kindle's confusion turned to despair. He looked at his outstretched hands in wonder, balled them into fists, straightened, and walked away. Anna moved to sit next to me, pulled me to her, and let me cry quietly on her shoulder.

I didn't see Kindle again that night. He didn't try to touch me again. The brief moment of happiness we had shared in the canyon, where forgiveness reigned and a happy future was possible, vanished.

Beau was despondent and distracted, no doubt thinking of the wreck his father had become. Anna was composed, her eyes firmly fixed on the horizon. She was attentive to me, speaking occasionally about nature around us, but she spoke to the men only if they spoke to her first. Kindle stayed within himself, speaking rarely and only about our journey. He, too, kept his eyes on the horizon. When Kindle caught me watching him he would smile, but it never reached his eyes. I longed to recapture the connection we shared in the canyon, to apologize for mistaking him for his brother upon waking. From the safety of my horse, I held my uninjured hand out to him. He took it, squeezed it gently, and held on. I stared at our joined hands and felt hollowness where happiness should have been. I wondered how long it would take for me to experience more than this, wondered how long he would wait.

❦

We arrived in Jacksboro under the bright glow of a Comanche moon. Rows of canvas tents ringed the outer edge of town. Despite the late hour, men roamed the streets. Piano music, laughter, and the occasional angry shout could be heard in the saloons. Kindle guided us to a back street.

"There's so many people," Anna said.

"Mackenzie is bringing Satanta and Big Tree here for a civil trial," Beau said.

"The crowd will only grow," Kindle said.

We dismounted behind a dark house. I took one step and collapsed from sleeplessness, hunger, and exhaustion. Kindle scooped me into his arms. My head settled comfortably in the crook between his shoulder and neck. Beneath the smell of dirt, blood, and horse sweat was the faint musk that was uniquely Kindle. I wrapped my arms around his neck, closed my eyes, and quietly sobbed. He carried me up the steps and kicked the door four times to knock.

"Shhh," he said. "You're safe now."

I nodded. The pull of sleep beckoned me for the first time in weeks. The door opened. Stephen and Edna Carter stood in the doorway in their nightclothes. Stephen held a double-barreled shotgun. Edna held a lamp.

"Captain Kindle! What on earth…"

"Shut up, Stephen." Edna moved in front of her dumbfounded husband and pulled us in the house. "Quick," she said. Anna and Beau followed and the Carters closed the door.

"Through here," Edna said.

Kindle laid me on a feather bed still warm from the Carters' bodies. I tried to get up, to refuse taking their bed. Edna would have none of it.

"Captain," Edna ordered.

Kindle gently pushed me back down. "Lie down."

"Why isn't she talking?" Stephen Carter asked.

Anna motioned to her throat. "Her throat was injured. She hasn't been able to speak in days."

Stephen was horrified. Edna paused what she was doing before pulling herself together and getting on with it.

"Stephen, boil some water and bring some towels. And put that gun away before you shoot somebody."

Stephen looked at the gun, and seemed surprised to find it in his hand. He broke the barrel and walked across the hall to boil the water.

"I'm going to send for Dr. Kline," Kindle said. I grasped his hand. He was not going to leave me again. I mouthed, "Don't leave."

Edna sat on the other side of the bed, and with only a slight hesitation, took my injured hand. "Dr. Elliston," she said in a gentle voice. "Let us help you."

That everyone thought I needed help rankled. *I* was the one who took care of people. If someone would get my medical bag, I could evaluate and treat myself.

I sank back against the pillow when I realized I had no medical instruments. Black hadn't taken my medical bag from the wreckage, nor the letter from Sherman. We found only the purple velvet bag holding my mother's necklace in Black's saddlebags, proof his promises of a new life were lies.

Edna patted my hand. "I know you don't want help but you're going to get it. No arguments. Now, the men need to leave the room soon so I can get you cleaned up." She looked at Anna. "You can get cleaned up as well. What is your name?"

"Anna Warren."

"Are you? Well, two miracles in one night. You look fitter than Dr. Elliston. Are you injured?"

"No."

"Good. You can help me." Anna glanced at me and followed Edna out of the room. She passed Beau at the door. Beau entered the room, dropped our saddlebags on the floor, and stood in the corner, looking uncomfortable. Edna called him from the other room. Beau left.

We were alone. Kindle sat on the edge of the bed and stroked my hand. I closed my eyes and tried to imagine I was lying in our bed, waiting for him to take me in his arms. Instead, I saw us standing on opposite sides of Palo Duro Canyon, neither making a move to cross for the other.

"Catherine," he said.

I opened my eyes. I wanted to leave every vestige of my ordeal behind. I struggled but managed to speak for the first time. "Call me Laura."

Kindle nodded and smiled. "Catherine is a beautiful name, but I fell in love with Laura Elliston."

I rubbed my throat and wished for laudanum. "Shh. Don't talk," Kindle said. He looked at our joined hands. "Laura, when I return to the fort, I'll be arrested."

I sat up.

"When Franklin told me my brother had you and wanted me to come alone, I didn't hesitate. We left immediately. I'm considered a deserter. As is Beau. I tried to get him to go back but he would not."

"Why did we come back?"

"You need medical attention."

"Let's leave. Now."

"No."

It was physically impossible for me to argue with him. There was too much to say. Goddammit, I thought.

"Why?"

"I have to face the consequences of my actions."

It sounded so noble, so gentlemanlike on the surface. It was a sentiment I would have admired in another life, in other circumstances. His integrity, his inherent goodness when dealing with his Negro soldiers, was one of the qualities I most admired. Now, though, I saw his eagerness to be away from me, to not hear my pitiful attempts at speaking, to banish from his sight my battered body, the constant reminder of the Indians' and his brother's abuse of me and his complicity. I also saw the same determination that pulled him through his injuries and got him back in the saddle in a week. The same determination that won my heart. I knew it was useless to argue with him and, frankly, I didn't have the energy. Part of me wanted to be away from him, to have time to heal and think without the weight of his guilt pressing against me.

"What will happen to you?"

"A court-martial and dishonorable discharge."

I covered my face with my hands. Black's revenge was almost complete. How could Kindle's regard for me survive each of these blows?

"It doesn't matter. I was retiring anyway." He removed my hands from my face and looked me in the eyes for the first time in days. "I would do it again. Without hesitation."

His eyes didn't deliver the same message. They were empty, devoid of tenderness, love, or hate. Weary resignation and disappointment covered him like a shroud.

Edna, Anna, and Beau returned, the former carrying a tub, a washcloth, and soap, the latter two pails full of water. Edna placed the tub in the corner. Anna poured the water in the tub and left for more.

"Captain, time to leave. Stephen has gone to fetch Kline."

Kindle stood, still holding my hands. He leaned forward and kissed my forehead. His lips lingered. His hand cupped my face and he moved his lips to my ear.

"We'll get our happy ending, Laura. I need you to believe that." There it was, the spark of emotion that had been missing for days. "Do you trust me?" he asked.

I nodded.

A ghost of a smile touched his lips. "Good." He kissed my damaged fingers, folded my hands over my stomach, and left.

⚬⚭⚬

I slept. When I woke, Ezra sat in a chair by my bed, his chin resting on his chest, snoring. I tapped his knee and he woke with a jerk.

He smiled. "Good morning," he said. "Or is it afternoon. I am not entirely sure."

I shrugged.

"Can you try to say something for me?"

Yes, but I didn't want to speak with anyone or, indeed, have anyone speak to me. I enjoyed the silence. "Och," I said. I covered my throat protectively and shook my head.

He nodded and took my hand. "Do you remember much about the first night here?"

I shook my head no.

"I didn't think you would. I gave you a large dose of laudanum. You've been asleep for two days. While you were asleep, I rebroke and set your fingers. I am not sure what kind of mobility you will have with them, but it will be better than it would have been. I've stitched up your head and wrapped your chest to support your broken ribs. You will be sore for a long while but you'll heal."

I nodded.

"I've done what I could for you elsewhere. You will bleed for a few more days. However, I'm not sure you will ever bleed again." He cleared his throat and focused on my eyes. "Do you understand what I'm saying?"

I nodded. I sat up and motioned for the chamber pot. Ezra held it while I vomited. I collapsed back onto the pillow. Ezra placed the bedpan beside his chair and grasped my hand.

"Did you tell Kindle?" I croaked.

"No."

"Don't."

He cleared his throat again. "Now, for the bad news. After you were abducted, Henry Pope miraculously recovered and wrote an article about who you are. How you manipulated him into keeping quiet, how Cotter Black beat him to do the same. Edna and Stephen tried to keep it quiet you were here, but when Kindle turned himself in..." Ezra paused. "There is a guard posted outside your door. A New York detective is on his way to escort you back for trial."

I shrugged.

"Don't worry. I've telegraphed James. We'll get you the best lawyer money can buy."

I smiled, patted his hand, and turned my head away. I closed my eyes and feigned sleep. Minutes passed. Finally, Ezra left.

⁗◈⁖

Thankfully, Ezra kept me stocked with laudanum, which, based on my expertise as a doctor, I deemed it necessary to continually flow through my veins. I stayed in an opiate haze for the next few days, making the stream of welcome and unwelcome visitors much easier to meet.

Alice Strong, in full mourning, was the first. I was abashed at not having thought of Lieutenant Strong's fate. Alice told me succinctly: the entire company had been massacred.

"Twelve men murdered for one man's revenge. The guard outside isn't to protect you from the bounty hunters. It is to protect you from the grieving wives and friends of the dead. They blame you, you see."

In a hand shaking from opium and bandaged with broken fingers, I wrote in a notebook provided by Edna, *Do you?*

"If it wasn't for Beau, I would. He's told me the full story."

And Beau?

"He will return to the family farm in Maryland. Captain Kindle swore he'd ordered Beau to go with him so Beau was able to resign his commission. He is as anxious to leave Texas as I am."

I nodded.

"The girl, the laundress?" Alice said.

I nodded.

"She's dead."

My breath caught.

"She died a day or two after you were taken. A customer abused her horribly and left her for dead. The women swear it was Cotter Black, but since no one knew precisely who he was or what he looked like, we will never know for sure."

When I fucked her, I thought of Catherine.

One more person whose life I ruined, whose death I was responsible for.

I motioned frantically for the chamber pot. Alice handed it to me and looked away while I was sick.

I lay back on the pillow with my eyes closed, taking deep breaths.

"I apologize," Alice said. She was red with embarrassment. "It was a thoughtless thing to mention."

I waved my hand in dismissal and dropped it heavily on the bed. I wished she would leave.

"I'm leaving Texas soon. I will go on a stage after the trial. I want to travel with as many people as possible. Maybe we will be safer that way."

She stood. "What you asked before, if I blamed you. I did, until the day I realized I was pregnant. I can return to the East a widow with the child of an Army hero and live independently.

I never wanted to marry. I did it for my family, and for Wallace. If he had lived, he would have made me miserable."

She walked to the door. "Good luck, Miss Bennett." She left and softly closed the door behind her.

⁓❦⁓

The house was unnaturally quiet. Stephen and Edna had taken Anna to dinner at the hotel, leaving me alone. My guard was a taciturn, teetotaling sheriff's deputy who sat in a straight-back wooden chair in the hall next to my door and threw playing cards into his upturned hat. Occasionally, he spat; otherwise he was quiet as a field mouse.

I drifted in and out of a drug-induced sleep, thinking of Kindle, wondering where he was. No one had mentioned him since he walked out the door days ago, nor had he sent word or a note about the progress of his court-martial. Besides Alice and Ezra, none of the people who lined up to bid me a fond farewell visited me now, broken and bruised. I was surprised at how deep it cut that Harriet hadn't visited. I reached for the bottle of laudanum. My bedside table was empty. I wondered who had taken it, and when.

The deputy walked across the hall. I imagined him picking up his cards from his hat and the floor, with the majority being on the floor. His spurs jingled as he walked up and down the hall to stretch his legs. I heard the faint rustle of cards being shuffled between his hands.

I hovered between sleep and consciousness. The events of the past months ranged in front of me like a gallery of paintings come alive. Blood seeping from Black's head; Kindle and Black fighting in Palo Duro; men hunched over a makeshift latrine in driving rain; drinking corn mash and laughing with the laundresses around a nighttime fire; the sound of a razor scraping against stubble; Maureen walking toward me, face glowing with happiness; gazing out over a beautiful landscape; talking to Molly Ebling in Galveston; walking down a snowy street in New York City.

A thump against the outside wall woke me.

I took a deep breath to still my galloping heart. Jacksboro was full of men in for the trial. The sounds of the revelers could be heard through the thin walls of the house at all hours of the night. Most like, a drunk was stumbling around the alleyways, whistling his way back to whichever tent he was paying an exorbitant amount to pass out in. My guard walked down the dog-run in the middle of the house and out the back door to check on the noise.

I leaned over to turn the lamp down when I heard a female voice.

"Hey, Ralph."

"Adella. What are you doin' out here?"

"Come to see you."

"I'm on duty."

"Guarding a killer. She ain't got no gun in there, does she? Might decide to put a bullet in your head. Or hit you with a fireplace poker. She's a manhater, and that's for sure."

Ralph laughed. "She ain't got no weapon. Besides, she's so doped up she couldn't aim and shoot the side of a barn. I'm protecting her from bounty hunters."

The latch on my door clicked and rose. My heart leapt into my throat and I searched the room frantically for a weapon, and settled on a fireplace poker across the room. I almost laughed out loud at the irony.

The door opened slowly. Though my lamp was low, Harriet Mackenzie's silhouette was plain. Relieved, I sat up. Harriet put her finger to her lips to silence me, and crept into the room.

"Share a cigar with me, Ralph?" Adella said.

Harriet placed a bundle of men's clothes on the bed, reached for my hands. She took me in, from my bruised face, broken nose, bandaged hands, the wounds she couldn't see, her distress and concern clear. "Quickly."

I stood for the first time in days and swooned, my legs hardly strong enough to hold me. Harriet caught me and held me in her strong embrace for a long moment. She whispered, "When I heard of the massacre, I hoped you were dead. I knew what you would endure and couldn't bear the thought." She squeezed me tighter, as if she didn't want to let go. Finally, she released me and held me at arm's length. "I'll be damned if you're going back East to hang for something you didn't do."

"I killed Cotter Black." My voice was a hoarse whisper.

Harriet pulled the shift I'd worn for days over my head. Her eyes lingered on the bandage around my chest, the gash on my breast, before returning to my face. "No one will chase you for that."

Harriet put a corset around my torso. "Upside down, and backward," I said, motioning to my breasts. I inhaled sharply through my teeth as she tightened it to flatten my breasts. The cups, which would normally cover my breasts, rested in the small of my back and would be covered by my coat. Harriet handed me a man's shirt. While I buttoned it, she held open a pair of pants for me to step into. She pulled my hair back, tied it with a ribbon, and piled it on top of my head before crushing a hat on top.

"Where are we going?"

"To William. Hurry."

I tucked my shirt in and cinched the belt. I slipped my feet into the boots Harriet provided and donned the coat. We walked out of the bedroom and closed the door. We paused at the open back door. Harriet placed her finger against her lips.

"Wanna poke, Ralph?"

402

"I should probably get back to—"

"Aw, come on. It's the least I could do after smoking your cigar. Or, would you rather me smoke *this* cigar."

Ralph laughed. "All right. Be quick about it."

"Come on, then. Don't want to give the murderer a show."

Harriet peeked around the door and motioned for me to follow. A little ways down the alley, Ralph stood with his back to us, his hands pumping Adella's head against his crotch. Harriet grabbed my good hand and pulled me to the end of the alley and around the corner, heading to the tent city.

A few drunkards stumbled among the canvas tents. One urinated outside a front flap, shook his dick, and returned to the card game inside, buttoning up as he went. I glanced at Harriet, who was wholly unperturbed by the scene. We walked through the tents and out into the darkness of the open plains. A stab of fear stopped me. Harriet turned. "What is it?"

My eyes roamed the darkness in front of us. I knew the openness, the savagery beyond the thin line of light we were leaving. The idea of New York City, with its teeming people and constant light, pulled me backward a step.

"Laura, we have to go."

"Why are you doing this for me?"

Harriet's shoulders slumped as she sighed and stepped forward. She cradled my face in her hands. "The world needs more women like you, not less."

I studied the woman I'd so harshly estimated when we first met. I now saw intelligence, benevolence, and determination.

I covered her hands with mine. "I misjudged you terribly, Harriet. Can you ever forgive me?"

When Harriet smiled, it lit up her entire face. "Everyone underestimates me. That's my biggest strength. Come. William will think we've been caught."

I let her pull me along by the hand.

The darkness was so complete I heard the horses before I saw them. Kindle had his back to us, cinching the saddle of a palomino. Harriet released my hand and stopped. I continued forward, hesitantly.

Kindle jerked the leather strap down, patted the saddle, and turned. Out of uniform he looked diminished, somehow. A close-cut beard shot through with gray mostly covered the scar on his cheek. He looked at my clothes and the hat on my head and grinned. "You look like the orderly who sewed up my face."

The tightness that had been in my chest since Kindle had left me, loosened. "He did a fine job, from what I can see."

Kindle rubbed his beard. "This itches like the devil. When we get farther west, I'll shave it. Can you abide it until then?"

I nodded, pleased he understood how his appearance might remind me of his brother. "What about your court-martial?"

Kindle pulled a letter from his inside pocket. "Colonel Mackenzie has given me a pardon."

"I didn't know he had returned."

"He hasn't," Harriet said. "Stop asking questions and go."

"Harriet, you'll catch hell for this."

"I doubt it. When the trial starts, everyone will forget about the deserter and the murderess. Now, go. Get some distance between you and Jacksboro before dawn."

"Anna!" I clutched Kindle's arm. "I can't leave Anna."

"I will take care of her," Harriet said. "I promise."

I sighed in relief. There was no one I would trust more to care for Anna than Harriet Mackenzie. I embraced her. "In different circumstances, I think we would have been great friends."

"We are." She pulled away. "I would ask you where you're going but it's best I don't know."

"I hope we meet again one day."

"As do I." Still holding my arms she said, "If you ever need to get in touch with me, for anything, send the letter to New Brighton, New York. It will find me."

Kindle stepped forward and kissed Harriet on the cheek. "You're a remarkable woman, Harriet Mackenzie."

She waved him away, but I could see the flush of pleasure his compliment had given her. "Go. Travel fast. Be safe."

Kindle handed me the reins to the palomino and mounted his brother's gray. I mounted my horse and saluted Harriet. She shook her head, laughed, and returned the salute.

Kindle and I kicked our horses into a canter and rode off into the darkness—and to our uncertain future.

AUTHOR'S NOTE

My dad loved watching Westerns. He was partial to John Wayne, but he would watch any Western, any time of day. His favorite, by far, was *Lonesome Dove*. You knew Henry Whitley liked you if he asked you to "watch a little *Lonesome Dove*" with him. When he died in 2008, it was the most natural thing in the world for me to honor him by watching his favorite show. That, of course, led to me reading Larry McMurtry's classic for the first time and spending the entire summer watching any and every Western shown on TCM and AMC, which led to me writing a Western.

Catherine/Laura's story is framed around historical events in 1871—Sherman's tour of Texas forts, the Warren Wagon Train Massacre and the resulting shift in the Army's Indian Policy, Fort Richardson, and the trial of Satanta and Big Tree. I have tried to stay true to the tone, atmosphere, and attitudes of the frontier at the time, but took creative license with some events, specifically the Warren Wagon Train Massacre, to enhance the fictional story I wanted to tell.

The list of the sources I used while researching *Sawbones* can be found at melissalenhardt.com.

ACKNOWLEDGMENTS

Thank you to my agent, Alice Speilburg, for your excellent editorial eye and your all-around awesomeness.

Thank you to Susan Barnes for helping me find the emotional depth to the story and not shying away from the grit and gore and for your patience, enthusiasm, and hard work. Thank you also to Lindsey Hall, Gleni Bartels, Crystal Ben, and the entire Redhook team, whose excitement for *Sawbones* came through every interaction and e-mail.

Thanks to my DFW Writers' Workshop peeps for listening to numerous versions of the first three chapters until I got it right.

Thanks to Kenneth Mark Hoover for brainstorming, beta reading, and telling me, "It's time you learned to finish." It might be the best advice you've ever given me.

Thank you to my in-laws, Jean and Will Lenhardt, for road-tripping to Palo Duro Canyon with me and braving the one-hundred-plus-degree heat to hike to the Lighthouse rock formation.

Thanks to Ledawn Webb, Camey Dill, Linda Whitley, and Stephen Whitley for reading early drafts and giving valuable feedback.

Thank you to Ray Monroe, park ranger at Fort Richardson State Park, for answering historical questions on my many research trips. Any historical inaccuracies not in service to the story are unintentional, and my own.

And, as always, thank you to the three men in my life, Jay, Ryan, and Jack, for your unwavering love, encouragement, and support. Life with the three of you would be perfect if you'd stop asking me what's for dinner.

MEET THE AUTHOR

Photo credit: Stephanie Southard

MELISSA LENHARDT is the president of the North Dallas chapter of Sisters in Crime, as well as a member of the DFW Writers Workshop. She lives in Texas with her husband and two sons.

READING GROUP GUIDE

1. When Laura tells Amos Pike she couldn't kill another man he says:

   "Laura, most everyone comes out here's got it in them. Only they ain't been pushed to the point yet."

   Do you believe that? What situation would drive you to kill another person?

2. When Laura first meets Harriet Mackenzie she believes she knows precisely the type of woman Harriet is:

   "I watched Harriet walk away with pity, which I suspected she would loathe. She was a woman with no place, save by her brother's side. Unmarried and without a profession, she most likely relied on the charity of her brother or surviving parents. Reliance meant subordination. She could not be her own person and, of course, resented a woman like me who could."

   Were Laura's first impressions correct, or incorrect? How did your opinion of Harriet, and Laura, change over the course of the book? Do you think your own first impressions are influenced more by your own experiences and opinions or the behaviors of who you're meeting?

3. Laura's reputation is ruined as much by the implications she was having an affair with a married man as the accusation that she killed him. How would the public's reaction to a similar story be different today? How would it be similar?

4. In Palo Duro Canyon, Laura is confronted with the situation Amos Pike alluded to. Were you surprised with her choice? Why or why not? Do you think she was justified? If not, why?

5. Though Kindle goes after Cotter Black to save Laura and settle things with his brother, he fails rather spectacularly. Did you expect Kindle to be victorious? Were you disappointed or pleased when Laura ended up being the white knight?

6. With Harriet's assistance, Laura and Kindle escape Jacksboro and are last seen riding off into the moonlight into an uncertain future. What would you like to see happen in the sequel, *Blood Oath*?

7. Who was your favorite character and why?

8. Which character would you like to know more about and why?

INTRODUCING

**If you enjoyed
SAWBONES,
look out for**

BLOOD OATH

Book 2 of the Sawbones Series
by Melissa Lenhardt

We smelled him first.

"Hail the camp!"

His appearance was no more or less disheveled and dirty
than the other men who happened upon us, but his stench was
astonishing, stronger than the smoke from the fire which lit
his grimy features. His was not a countenance to inspire confidence in innocent travelers, let alone us. The left side of his face
seemed to be sliding down, away from a jutting cheekbone and
a brown leather eye patch. When he spoke, only the right side
of his mouth moved. Though brief, I saw recognition in his
right eye before he assumed the mien of a lonely traveler beg-
ging for frontier hospitality always given, often regretted.

"Saw your fire 'n hoped to share it with you, if I might."

"Of course, and welcome," Kindle said.

"Enloe's the name. Oscar Enloe."

"Picket your horse, and join us."

"Already done. Picketed him back there with yours. Nice gray you got there. Don't suppose he's for sale."

"Not today."

Enloe glanced around the camp, a dry, wide creek bed with steep banks, which offered a modicum of protection from the southern wind gusting across the plains. Our fire flickered and guttered as Enloe sat on the hard, cracked ground with exaggerated difficulty and a great sigh. He placed his rifle across his lap and nestled his saddlebags between his bowed legs.

"Well, it figures. Every time I see a good piece of horseflesh he's either not for sale or I don't have the money. Turns out it's both in this case." Enloe's laugh went up and down the scale before dying away in a little hum. His crooked smile revealed a small set of rotten teeth, which ended at the incisor on the left side. He removed his hat and bent his head to rustle in his saddlebag, giving us a clear view of his scarred, hairless scalp. I cut my eyes to Kindle, and saw the barest of acknowledgments in the dip of his chin. His gaze never left our guest.

Enloe lifted his head, expecting a reaction, and was disappointed he did not receive one. I imagine he enjoyed telling the story of how he survived a scalping, since so few men did so. I was curious, but held my tongue, as I had every time we met a stranger. Tonight silence was a tax on my willpower, the strongest indication yet that I was slowly coming out of the fog I'd been in for weeks.

Enloe pulled a jar out of his bag. "Boiled eggs. Bought 'em in Sherman two days ago. Like one?" He motioned to me with the jar. I shook my head no.

"Doncha speak?"

"No, he doesn't," Kindle said.

"Why not?"

"He's deaf."

Enloe's head jerked back. "Looked like he understood me well enough."

"He reads lips."

"You don't say?" Enloe shrugged, as if it wasn't any business of his. "Want one?"

"Thank you."

Enloe opened the jar, fished out a pickled egg with his dirty hands, and handed it to Kindle, along with the tangy scent of vinegar. Kindle thanked him and ate half in one bite. "What's the news in Sherman?"

"Where'd you come from?" Enloe shoved an entire egg in his mouth. I watched in fascination as he ate on one side and somehow managed to keep the egg from falling out of the gaping, unmovable left side.

"Arkansas. Heading to Fort Worth."

"Fort Worth?" He spewed bits of egg out of his mouth; some hung in his beard. "Ain't nothing worth doing or seeing in Fort Worth. Montana's where the action is."

"I'm not much for prospecting. Looking to get a plot of land and make a go of it."

"This here your son?" Enloe's eye narrowed at me.

"Brother."

"Well, bringing an idiot to the frontier ain't the smartest thing I ever heard. He won't be able to hear when the Kioway come raiding, now will he?"

"I've heard tell the Army protects the settlers."

Enloe laughed derisively. "Fucking Army ain't worth a tinker's damn. Except those niggers. Now, there's the perfect soldier. Those white officers order them to charge and they do 'cause they're too stupid to do anything but follow orders blindly. Can't think for themselves. Redskins mistake it for bravery and won't go up against them." The corner of Kindle's eye twitched and I knew it took all of his willpower to not contradict Enloe.

Enloe brought out a bottle of whisky, pulled the cork and drank deeply from the corner of his mouth. "If you're expectin' the Army to protect you, better turn right around and go back to Arkansas." He narrowed his eyes. "You're awfully well-spoken for an Arkansan."

"Our mother was a teacher."

He nodded slowly. "Suppose you've heard about the excitement in Fort Richardson."

"No."

"Surely you heard about the Warren Wagon Train Massacre. You do got papers in Arkansas, dontchee? Suppose not many a' you hillbillies can read it." I doubted Oscar Enloe knew a *G* from a *C*.

"We heard about it," Kindle said. "Did they catch the Indians?"

"They did. Sherman himself, though it was pure luck. The redskins were at Sill, bragging about it. Well, Sherman didn't give a damn about the Indian Peace Policy and arrested 'em. Shocked he didn't put 'em on trial right there and tighten the noose himself. They sent them to Jacksboro to stand trial. One of 'em tried to get away and was shot in the back. One less redskin to worry about, I say. Other two were convicted, 'course." Enloe held out his whisky. "Want some?"

Kindle refused. I held out my hand. Enloe ignored my crooked, knobby fingers, foreign to me even now, weeks later, and turned his attention to Kindle. I drank from the bottle and held the rotgut in my mouth, barely resisting the urge to spit it into the fire. It was whisky in name only. The liquid scorched my throat as I swallowed, burned a hole in my stomach. I held the back of my hand to my mouth and saw Enloe watching me with a knowing smirk. Keeping my eyes on him, I drank another swallow, did not wince as it made its way down, and kept the bottle. I only hoped it would numb the pain before Enloe tried to kill us.

Kindle didn't move, flinch or take his eyes from Enloe. His rifle lay on the ground next to him, barely out of reach. Neither moved. "You'd think the massacre and hanging Injuns would be enough to be going on with, but that ain't even the most interesting story outta Jacksboro," Enloe said.

"No?"

"Jacksboro was overflowin' with people there celebrating, wanting to see those two redskins hang. Gov'nor killed their fun, staying their execution. I imagine they've turned their attention now to the fugitives."

"Fugitives?"

"The Murderess and the Major, that's what the newspaper's calling 'em. Catchy name, at that."

"Never heard of 'em."

"Woman who survived the massacre, turns out she's out here on the run. Course, she ain't alone in that, is she? Heh-heh. Supposed to have saved the Major right after the massacre, but we have it from his nigger soldiers so it's probably a lie."

I bristled and drank more of Enloe's whisky to avoid speaking.

"Just like a woman, lured the Major into fallin' in love with her. He threw his career away to go off an save her from the Comanche and then sprung her before the Pinkerton could come take her back to New York."

Enloe put a finger against one nostril and shot a stream of snot onto the ground. "Some think they headed north to the railroad, or maybe south to Mexico. The Pinkerton thought they stayed in the tent city sprung up outside a Jacksboro for the trial. Tore it to pieces one night, searching. Torched a few nigger tents for the hell of it. He's mad cause he was in town that night."

"What night?"

"The night they escaped. I heard tell he decided to go whoring instead of taking the Murderess into custody, as he shoulda. He tore through the tent city like the devil. 'Course, nothing came of it. The Major ain't stupid."

"You know him?" Kindle said.

"Nah, but I heard of him. Has a scar down the side of his face, said to be given to him by his brother in the war."

"The Pinkerton go back East?"

"Can't very well without his prisoner, now can he?"

I glanced at Kindle, whose expression was closed. Enloe pulled a plug of tobacco from his vest pocket. He tore off a chunk and chewed on it a bit, his gaze never wavering from us. He spit a brown stream into the fire. The spittle sizzled and a log fell. "Wouldya lookit?" He laughed up and down the scale again. "Kinda hot out for a fire."

"Thought I'd make it easy for you to find us."

"Didja now?"

"You've been shadowing us for three days. You aren't as good as you think you are."

"Well, I found you, didn't I?"

"Oh, you weren't the first," Kindle said. Enloe's smile slipped. "And, you won't be the last."

In a smooth, easy motion, Enloe leveled his gun at Kindle. "I seem to have caught you without your gun handy."

"True. What made you come into Indian Territory? Alone."

"Who said I'm alone?"

"My scout."

"What scout?"

"The one who's been shadowing you for three days. Where's the Pinkerton?"

"I—"

I heard the tomahawk cut through the air the second before it cleaved Enloe's skull cleanly down the middle. Blood ran crookedly down his scarred head, like a river cutting through a winding canyon. He tipped over onto his side.

I drank his whisky, and watched him die.